D0245125

Praise for Nei...

'Explosive'
Daily Express

'A deft, spooky psychological drama based on a true story'
Daily Mail

'Surprising, serpentine and clever'
Sunday Times

'Close the curtains, pull up a chair, open a book –
and prepare to be pleasantly scared'
Metro

'There's nothing like a good ghost story . . . Neil Spring
is Agatha Christie meets James Herbert'
Stephen Volk

'A triumph of creativity . . . the conclusion
will shock and amaze you'
Vada Magazine

'Irresistible . . . Spring has a wicked turn of phrase'
SFX

'Spring weaves a dark web of romance,
deceit and a lingering curse'
Metro

'Genuinely spine-chilling'
Light Magazine

'A glor...   nights'

Neil Spring is represented by Curtis Brown, one of the world's leading literary and talent agencies. In 2013, he published *The Ghost Hunters*, a paranormal thriller based on the life of Harry Price. *The Ghost Hunters* received outstanding reviews and has been adapted into a critically acclaimed television drama for ITV. His second novel, *The Watchers*, is also in development for television. *The Lost Village* is his third novel. Neil was educated at the University of Oxford. He is Welsh and lives in London.

Also by Neil Spring

The Ghost Hunters
The Watchers

NEIL SPRING

THE
LOST
VILLAGE

Quercus

First published in Great Britain in 2017 by

Quercus Publishing Ltd
Carmelite House
50 Victoria Embankment
London EC4Y 0DZ

An Hachette UK company

A CIP catalogue record for this book is available
from the British Library

ISBN 978 1 78429 861 6
EBOOK ISBN 978 1 78429 862 3

10 9 8 7 6 5 4 3 2 1

Typeset by CC Book Production

Printed and bound in Great Britain by Clays Ltd, St Ives plc

For Owen Meredith

Note

This is a work of fiction, although the village of Imber on Salisbury Plain is very real – a ghost town out of bounds, abandoned at the outbreak of the Second World War. For the novel to work, it was necessary to change the date of this abandonment to 1914, and although some characters are indeed based on historical figures, I have taken liberties with place names and historical events to transport readers to a place my characters were able to explore. But Imber truly is a creepy location: remote, dangerous and eerily deserted ... who knows, perhaps there really are ghosts in that mysterious village. It's likely that in the story that follows, you will meet more than a few of them.

PROLOGUE

I first saw the village when I was ten years old. Before the Keep Out and Danger signs went up. Before the high fences with their coiled crowns of barbed wire.

It was a Saturday afternoon in the appalling winter of 1914, and my father hadn't yet been called away to the battlefields – to his doom. He squeezed my hand as we stood in the drifting snow next to a low wall of mud and rubble that skirted the hilly churchyard.

'I'd like you to remember this place, Sarah,' he said solemnly. 'You remember its name?'

Imber. A scatter of lonely dwellings nestled in a valley on Salisbury Plain.

I suppose at some point on our journey from London we must have glimpsed an ancient mound or stone circle, but if we did, I can't remember. Mostly what I recall from that day is a pub, a manor house and a jumble of whitewashed thatched cottages. And the funeral bells, of course.

'Why did we come here, Father?'

I'm sure he wanted to tell me, but a war had begun and secrets were secrets. He turned towards the church, destined to outlive everything else in this place, and sadness clouded his eyes.

'Sarah, my angel, if ever we are parted, if you should find yourself alone, then close your eyes and remember this place. I'll always be here.'

'But what's special about this village?'

He hadn't brought me to attend a funeral, but it was the sudden approach of a funeral car that stole my father's attention. A few villagers, most of them women, stopped and watched as the hearse pulled up quietly outside the churchyard gate, where a circle of mourners had assembled. The snow, falling more heavily now, obscured our view of them a little, but two figures stood out: a thin, stony-faced man of middle age with a crow-black hat that rose like a column; and, beside him, a woman in full mourning attire, her shoulders shuddering as she wept.

It would be eighteen long years before I truly understood that woman's grief. Before I learned all too well the relentless suffering of a parent who has lost a child.

As the undertaker lifted a tiny lead and bronze casket from its bed of flowers, my father removed his hat, and a couple of elderly women passing us in the street crossed themselves. It occurred to me then how sad and peculiar it was that more of the villagers weren't displaying similar gestures of respect for one of their own, especially one so young. On the contrary, most of the villagers were drawing away, their faces grim. Heads down, shoulders up, casting their gaze in any direction but the church gate and the mourners huddled there.

Did I see something more than detachment on those faces? Guilt, perhaps? Fear?

Certainly, there was no glimmer of prescience for what was to come. For how could any in this thriving farming community know that all of them, every man, woman and child, would soon be forced to leave their homes, and that their village would vanish from every map.

Some forgot about that nowhere place at the foot of the valley. Even me. Until, of course, I was made to remember. Not by anyone living.

But by a dead man.

PART ONE

HOW THE MATTER AROSE

A house is never still in darkness to those who listen intently; there is a whispering in distant chambers, an unearthly hand presses the snib of the window, the latch rises. Ghosts were created when the first man woke in the night.

J. M. BARRIE, *The Little Minister*

– 1 –

THE REVENANT

October 1978

I am haunted by a man who told stories for a living. This cantankerous, ill-tempered and selfish man – the unlikely father of my lost child – is the reason I believe in the supernatural. I know now that death is not the end of life, and I know spirits walk the earth, because of Harry Price.

I saw him tonight.

Not in the flesh – that couldn't have been. My old companion's tombstone is already leaning and choked by ivy. All that remains of that notorious magician, scientist and showman is a date and a name.

And yet, I *saw* him.

A woman in her mid-seventies should be able to tell what is real and what is fantasy, but as I sit here at my desk, my fingers stiff and painful and swollen from arthritis, an icy coldness creeping up my legs, I have reached a conclusion: some stories are never finished. Some voices insist on being heard, even after death. Harry Price's voice is one of them.

Here's what happened. Shortly after nine o'clock, I was in the kitchen at the back of our clifftop cottage, preparing to wash the dinner dishes. Vernon, my husband, was next door in the living room, listening to music on the radio. Karen Carpenter was singing, her floating voice reminding me that we had only just begun. The song raised a smile, which quickly contorted into a grimace, for as I plunged my hands into a cloud of soapsuds in the sink, I caught sight of a flickering light through the window – and my stomach became painfully tight.

The flickering light was moving, bobbing out of the thick darkness, towards me.

I stood in rapt stillness at the sink, looking at the light with an escalating sense of dread. I wanted to leave the room but felt strangely compelled to stay. It didn't occur to me that there might be some mundane explanation for this light – perhaps someone with a torch roaming the fields; I just instinctively knew there was something unnatural about it. But it wasn't the light that made me gasp for breath. What did that was the naked light bulb overhead, buzzing and flickering as if from a surge of power.

I looked up at it – and it exploded.

Instinctively, I flung my hands upwards, to protect my face from the shower of glass. A second passed, two, while I blinked away the dazzling flash, and then I removed my sodden hands from my hair and looked around the kitchen. Back to the window.

And saw that I was no longer alone.

A dark form was in the windowpane, brooding just over the

reflection of my right shoulder. Immediately, I recognised the broad shoulders, the black fedora tipped over his eyes. And I knew, right away, that this spectral form was not an illusion, but the image of a departed soul.

Harry.

I might have turned around then, to confront him, but I was transfixed by his menacing reflection – so clear against the pressing dark.

He looked ancient. Haggard. His skin the colour of old wax. Shiny, stretched over the bone. But it was unmistakably him: the domed, balding head, the pointed ears, the bushy eyebrows and pronounced nose. And those steely eyes locked on mine.

The first time I peered into those cold blue eyes, aged twenty-two, it wasn't just suspicion I saw there, but an intense passion that had made me tingle with excitement.

What did I see now? A look of aching sadness. And something else: desperation.

'Harry,' I whispered. 'What do you want?'

His mouth was moving, but there was no voice.

'I don't understand,' I said. 'Why have you come?'

This time, when he spoke I heard it. No more than a whisper – in the air, perhaps, or in my mind, drawn from my memory.

'Swear to me, Sarah, never to tell . . .'

Then, when I said nothing, only stared, full of bewilderment, at his melancholy reflection, he mouthed one more word: a name. A name that I hadn't heard in such a long time, and that I had hoped never to hear again.

I spun around to confront him – why *that* name, after all these years? – and saw . . . nothing. Just an empty kitchen.

A fire crackling in the grate.

And my own breath, frosting in the crisp air that should have been warm.

'What kept you?' Vernon said, when I finally wandered into the sitting room, trembling and pale. His hearing isn't so good these days. Perhaps, because of the radio, he hadn't heard the light bulb pop, but I was a little relieved. I had no wish to tell him of the dreaded apparition that had vanished from my sight.

'Sarah?' Vernon watched me with puzzled interest from his lumpy armchair next to the radio, a newspaper spread over his lap. 'Something the matter?'

I paused. The memories were there, cautiously shut away, and they would come if bidden. But that would mean inviting them in, and I didn't know if I wanted to remember. These were ugly memories. Dangerous. As jagged as shrapnel.

No, a voice somewhere in my head whispered. *Remember, Sarah – when you consider the abyss, the abyss considers you.*

Better to say nothing. *Trick of the light*, that's what Vernon would say. Trick. Of. The. Light. As if four short, ordinary words could so effectively explain an experience so *extraordinary*.

But then again, perhaps there was something in that. Perhaps I *had* experienced some sort of a waking dream. A vision. Would it be so surprising? Only days earlier I had read a review about a new biography on the man. No wonder Harry Price had walked back into my mind!

That man.

That impossible man.

People have asked me, 'Who was he really, Sarah?' and, even now, the answer remains elusive, but I suppose the simplest answer is this:

Harry Price was a ghost hunter. Loathed and distrusted by many, he was also a showman, whose charisma and energy was second only to his inscrutable persona. It was his lifelong interest in magic that led him into the study of psychical research – driven by a noble need, as he saw it, to debunk the fraudulent claims of spiritualist mediums in a country where the shadow of grief fell long, after the Great War. Detecting fraud became his passion. His obsession. And in time, it became mine – although less so when I realised he was himself capable of the very crimes he sought to expose. Blatant fraud. Trickery. Lies.

Until the moment his body was found in 1948 – slumped over his writing desk, a pen in one hand, a cursed watch chain in the other – he was a wretched victim of his own making. Haunted. By the memory of the son he never knew, the son I eventually misled him into believing I had aborted, and by his elaborate deceptions.

Now, once again, those deceptions were creeping into my life.

'Sarah?'

The questions were brewing in Vernon's eyes. He had taken off his reading glasses and was watching me with uncomfortable scrutiny. I turned away from him, feeling the eerie stirrings of déjà vu. The last time he saw me like this I had paced the house for days before barricading myself in the study, where I finally took up my pen and scratched out a manuscript: the account of how a young woman accepted the dubiously privileged position of confidential secretary to the most fascinating, infamous figure in psychical research, only to fall hopelessly into his orbit.

When I finished writing, I took that manuscript to London and locked it safely away on the eighth floor of Senate House

Library – along with the rest of Price's great library, his equipment and possessions. What would I do now? Write about this
night's visitation? Speak of it?

Yes. I decided Vernon had a right to know: this concerned
him as much as me. And my husband was hardly a stranger
to manifestations some would call 'supernatural'.

'I've seen something.' I heard my voice, thin and quavering.
'*Him*.'

A fearful glint in Vernon's eyes. After a long moment: 'We're
not going to do this again. We agreed never—'

'I *saw* him, Vernon!'

He didn't need to ask me who.

'Sarah, he's dead.'

I shook my head. 'It was Harry. He was trying to tell me
something. He whispered a name to me, Vernon. *Her* name.
Why?'

Vernon's eyes found mine, only for a second but long enough
for me to see they were full of sudden pale fear at the dreadful
secret we shared. Then they shifted away.

We had agreed: we would move on, forget about the ghosts
of our past, live out our days in peace. Only now did it occur
to me that perhaps words couldn't banish old ghosts. Perhaps
words even brought them back.

Vernon sat in silence for a few moments longer, then
reached to turn up the radio. A static, high-pitched whine,
then the newsreader's voice came through. His words put ice
in my veins:

'Skeletal human remains believed to be those of a child have
been unearthed by soldiers training in an uninhabited village
in part of the British Army's training grounds on Salisbury
Plain.'

My hand reached out and found the doorframe. I clung on as the newsreader went on.

'Frozen in time, abandoned hastily long ago, Imber is a ghost village, and has been the army's battle school since early in the Great War, when its residents were evacuated. There is currently no information available regarding the person's identity or cause of death, but police are treating the discovery as suspicious and are appealing for anyone with information to come forward.'

Vernon's mouth had fallen open. He snapped it shut, and glared at the radio. My heart was pounding so hard I could feel my pulse behind my eyes.

'The name, this discovery. The village. What if they're connected? Oh, God –'

'Sarah,' he said heavily, 'I am not doing this again.'

'You can't just distance yourself from this. You were as guilty as anyone else!'

That did it. With a flash of anger, he threw down his newspaper, stood up and strode out of the room.

Swear to me, Sarah, never to tell . . .

I had given my promise, a long time ago.

But it was a promise I could no longer keep.

On too many occasions I have been asked to talk about the most sensational, most disturbing incident in Price's lifetime of inquiry into the unknown – but how to choose? His investigations took him to hundreds of alleged haunted houses, thousands of séances. And I was the one who assisted him, out in the field and at his laboratory on the top floor of 16 Queensberry Place, South Kensington, where we attempted to peer beyond the curtain that separates this world from the next.

And what a time we had. Together, we saw objects hurled around empty rooms – objects that couldn't possibly have been thrown by human hands. Together, we watched astounding mediums join hands with misty human forms. And together, huddled in the abandoned rooms of the remotest houses, we shivered as the mercury mysteriously plummeted.

But only *once* did Price see what he was convinced really was a ghost.

In private letters to his contemporaries – letters leaked to the newspapers but which were never supposed to be published – he describes a séance where something cold and soft touched his hand. He wrote of a spirit that materialised before him and sat on his knee.

Plenty of his critics demanded hard evidence, but Price never provided it. Not the location of the house, not even the names of everyone else present. Later, Price admitted he should never have written about it. The whole affair came at a cost to his reputation: most concluded the story wasn't true, that Price had simply made it up. They called him a liar.

They were only half right.

What Price described in his letters didn't happen as he portrayed it, but it wasn't made up either. More accurate to say he created a story only half true, drawing on earlier events. Events so traumatising he felt the only way he could write about them was to wrap them up in something false. But Price and I shared the knowledge of what was true, what we saw deep in the winter of 1932, at the bottom of a remote valley in Salisbury Plain, in the abandoned ghost town of Imber.

That dreadful village, as quiet as death. Full of cold dismays and bitter despairs. From the start, Price resisted making the trip to that stark and lonely place. I am doomed to remember the state of him afterwards, in his long black coat and flannel suit, eyes wide and pleading. Behind him, the boarded-up mansion raging with flames. His face smeared with blood as he reached out to me with a deathly pale hand, shaking. '*Swear to me, Sarah, never to tell,*' he had pleaded. '*Promise me.*'

I was twenty-eight then. For forty-six years, I kept my promise. But reality has a way of intruding.

When Vernon left the room, I stood for a long moment and stared at the radio, trying to decide what to do. Skeletal remains unearthed?

I could try ignoring this, but for how long? I had been ignoring it my whole life, but now memories, long buried, were surfacing. Shapeless terrors. They could not be interred again; they needed to be faced. Confronted.

With a sinking dread, I went into my study and sat down at the desk – this desk, my hand trembling as I took up my pen.

I will do the one thing I promised Price I wouldn't do. I will disentangle the relics of my guilt. I will write the story of what happened in the lost village of Imber in 1932.

The matter did not begin in Wiltshire, but in London. In a deserted picture house after dark. As I uncap my fountain pen, I can see it clearly: my gaze roams through the darkened auditorium across to the black pit of the orchestra, up to the gilded boxes, up to the domed ceiling and down to the balcony rails.

I should never have gone. Just as I should never have made the trip afterwards, to the dismal village that I had first glimpsed at my father's side on that snowy Saturday in 1914.

But then came the spirit child.

And the soldiers' nightmares, and the tragic church service. The horror and sorrow. And the black, cold, evil.

My name is Sarah Grey. And I need someone to know that the lost village remembers.

The lost village has a secret that must be told.

− 2 −

GHOST LIGHT

London, October 1932

'Who's there?'

The man's voice – urgent, commanding – seemed to reach me distantly, as if I were underwater. I was not, though; I was in a vast field of swaying grass with the sun on my neck, watching a mill wheel turn as I waited.

'Who's there, I say!'

Dazed, I opened my eyes, and grimaced as pain throbbed at the back of my head.

Where the hell am I?

Not in a field, but on the floor, at the foot of a stage. Before me lay a scatter of discarded ticket stubs, and I caught the acrid scent of cigarette smoke. An old converted theatre . . .

The Brixton Picture Palace.

'Show yourself now. I'm warning you!'

I held my breath, listening.

The gruff voice was coming from the back of the auditorium, where a door was ajar, letting through a shaft of light from the lobby. Who was this man? Some of it was coming back to me . . . According to my research, the cleaning ladies didn't arrive until nine in the morning. I had chosen this time for a reason: there was supposed to be no one here after midnight.

My stomach tightened as more alarming possibilities ran through my mind. The picture house owner? Private security? Or worse, a policeman!

What a pitiful figure I must have looked: a young woman in her Sunday best, crumpled at the foot of the stage.

No time for self-pity. Think!

I tried to sit up, but a sharp pain in my left ankle stopped me. So did the pain in my head.

What happened? Think. Try to remember.

Forcing myself to breathe deeply, I sifted through jumbled fragments of memories.

Torch failed. You heard something . . . a voice calling out. Got lost in the dark, went looking around . . . in the auditorium . . . No. You were walking across the stage. Then you . . .

Fell. I had stumbled. Something had made me turn round too quickly. A figure . . .

'I know you can hear me,' called the man, 'because I heard you.'

I *could* hear, perfectly well, but I was struggling to focus on anything. Well, except my ankle. The pain seemed to be getting hotter with each second. It was almost certainly sprained.

That meant trouble on Monday. And what's more, if I were caught, Mr Addison would have questions – quite legitimate questions – about what I was doing trespassing in a picture house after closing time. That was assuming on Monday I would be sitting in my office, and not in a police cell.

'All right,' the man yelled, 'I'll find you myself!'

Perhaps luck was on my side. If my pursuer worked for the picture house, as seemed likely, he might think I was locked in by accident. He might sympathise when he saw a young woman on her own, injured. But – and here was the chief problem – the moment he found my pocket electric torch and the plans of the building I had dug up at the Lambeth public library, any concerns about my well-being would rapidly give way to suspicion. He would probably think I'd broken in to commit a robbery.

Footsteps crept nearer.

I chanced a peek out from behind the row of dark mahogany seats. I couldn't see my pursuer clearly, just a vague outline, a thin dark figure taking apprehensive steps. The circular spotlight from his torch bounced off the barrel vault ceiling and bobbed over the seats, before playing on an enormous pipe organ of silver and gold a few metres away.

Concealed in the shadows at the foot of the stage, my face pressed against the floor, I pulled in a shaky breath.

Held it.

How – *how* – had I come to this?

The evening had begun innocently enough, despite my mother's asking that I stay at home, it being a damp and cold night. Maybe that was a genuine reason in her mind, but what was certainly true was that Mother's eyesight wasn't good and she appreciated me reading to her.

'I'm sorry, I can't disappoint Amy,' I lied. 'Not at this short notice – she'll wonder what's happened to me. You see that, Mother?'

A thin smile. A nod.

When I arrived at the picture house at eight thirty, the lobby was packed with men in suits, neckties and fedoras, and women in fur coats. Gliding behind them, I passed into the auditorium and quickly dropped into a seat at the front. After the lights dimmed there was a brief animation, then a newsreel. Unemployment soaring, the Depression and a man called Oswald Mosley had founded the British Union of Fascists.

Then for the main attraction: *London After Midnight*, a silent mystery picture. Just the sort of film my former boss would have loved – grimy bats swooping about, a house haunted by its memories. Actually, one of the characters rather reminded me of Price: a detective from Scotland Yard who hypnotised his suspects to investigate a murder, cajoling them into confessing. Or something like that. In truth, the finer aspects of the plot were lost on me, but I had been somewhat preoccupied during the show by the thought of what lay ahead.

I hadn't come to watch the film. I had come to remember. To relive what I missed. The thrill of the chase.

Six months previously, I had quit my old job. Turned my back on Harry Price and his magical 'ghost factory' at 16 Queensberry Place, and not just because his gusto, his immense energy and magpie mind had ceased to be charming. As one who was intimately acquainted with his investigations, it had proven impossible not to be frustrated by his pretensions, his secretiveness and his frequent disappearances, his thirst for publicity. There was, however, a greater problem of abject betrayal, after he wilfully embarrassed Velma Crawshaw, a medium under his scrutiny, before a public audience. Exposing fraudulent mediums was the reason Price was famous, the reason I could pay Mother's debts, but this had been a step too far, even for him. Velma had cancer. She would have terrible days to come. And Price knew; yet he had humiliated her. After that, I didn't care about ghosts so much as people. People mattered. Especially the child I had concealed, two and a half years ago, then been forced to give up for adoption.

Price's child.

After walking away from the laboratory, I didn't go looking for similar positions with the Society for Psychical Research. I didn't continue my subscription to *Psychic News*. Instead I accepted a position at a film-publishing house in Soho. The work was mundane, secretarial duties mainly. Now and then there were meetings about promotions, advertising, even cocktail parties – mostly there weren't. Mostly, my thoughts lingered on the job I had left behind. Lately, I had caught myself wondering whether I had been too hard on Price. I had enjoyed that job more than I had been willing to admit.

I had hoped the thrill of the chase would dissipate over time. I had hoped to push down the memories of Harry Price. But, like I said, reality has a way of intruding.

The Picture Palace had fallen silent – and entirely dark.

I lay still, cursing myself for not staying at home with Mother.

You would have been perfectly all right, if only you hadn't fallen. If only the ghost light had been lit.

The ghost light. In those days, every theatre – even the grander picture houses – had one: an exposed bulb standing on a pole at the centre of the stage. Empty theatres are pitch-black places where it's all too easy to stumble off the stage and break one's neck. The ghost light was supposed to be lit by the last person to leave the theatre, and then extinguished by the first person to arrive in the morning.

Why was it extinguished now? At night?

A common belief amongst anyone working in unoccupied theatres was that the ghost light protected against restless or resentful spirits who might play havoc in the auditorium after dark.

Well, no spirits tonight. Just me. Playing havoc.

All was quiet, no sign of my pursuer. But I wasn't near to feeling relief.

Carefully, silently, I lifted myself onto my elbows, keeping my head down, and shuffled forward. A bolt of pain shot up my leg, but I kept moving. If I could just drag myself away from the stage and in between the next row of seats, I might avoid detection, along with all the difficult questions that would entail.

I had barely touched the green velvet trim of a seat when a beam of light dazzled me.

'What do you think you're doing here?'

My breathing stopped. The tall figure of a man loomed over me.

— 3 —

THE PICTURE PALACE
AFTER DARK

I recoiled. 'Don't touch me!'

He was towering over me, but flinched and stepped back when I spoke.

He raised his head. Something not right. His face? It was impossible to see clearly beyond the glaring circle of his hand-held torch.

'Why didn't you answer when I called out?' he asked.

'Do *you* normally answer voices in the dark?'

'I'm asking the questions, miss.'

'And I don't have the first idea who you are!'

'Well, I bloody work here.' He sounded affronted. 'Now, explain yourself.'

I had to squint then, as he brought his torch closer to my face – a blinding white circle of interrogation.

'Sir, please, is that absolutely necessary?'

I was trying to sound confident, but this stranger's imposing stature was not of the sort that normally inspires confidence in a young woman, afraid and alone in the dark. Worse, because of the intense torchlight, I could see very little of him.

At last he said, 'My apologies, miss, I was expecting . . .'

'A man?'

'Actually . . .' He paused, but then shook his head and said, 'Follow me. You shouldn't be in here.'

Because the threatening edge in his voice had now been replaced by a more reasonable tone, fringing on concern, I took his proffered hand and allowed him to help me to stand. The pain in my ankle was still acute, but to my surprise I found I could walk, even if with a limp.

But I wasn't the only one walking oddly. As the stranger led me out of the auditorium, I noticed he did so with short, shuffling movements, almost as if he were uncertain of the route.

A short while later we were in the resplendent art deco foyer, with its sumptuous carpets and the elegant curved staircase. The ceiling was an impressive dome, lit around the edges. Another light was thrown by a solitary lamp at the ticket desk. I saw two signs on the wall nearest me. One indicated the way to the smoking room; the other simply read, 'Ladies, please remove your hats.'

The stranger clicked off his torch, gave me a long measuring look. From the cobweb of lines around his eyes I guessed he was somewhere in his middle age, and he looked very far from healthy. His face was pale and painfully thin, with sunken cheeks so hollow, especially on the left side, it was as if someone had dealt him an almighty blow and left a permanent dent.

And there was something else. Something that twisted my stomach into an uneasy knot.

One eye, his left eye, was unmoving, and seemed to look flatly past my shoulder. His other eye shifted towards me. Strained. Watchful. Wondering.

'So, what were you doing in there?' he asked.

'I fell asleep when the picture ended.'

'Of course you did,' he said, with obvious sarcasm. 'With respect, miss, the ushers check the auditorium at the end of every perform – '

'Yes, and when I woke up there was no one else here.'

He raised an eyebrow.

'And then, you see, I tripped and fell.'

'Off the stage?' he said, measuring me with his good eye. Self-consciously, I smoothed my bobbed hair into place. 'But what were you doing up there in the first place?'

'With respect, sir, that's not the question you should be asking. Is it?'

'It isn't?'

I put more confidence into my voice. 'Why was the ghost light extinguished? I wouldn't have fallen if it had been on. And it's *supposed* to be left on all night.'

The eyebrow climbed higher. 'You work in the business? In theatres?'

'Yes,' I lied, offering a smile, but he only angled his head away from me, gazing at the lobby doors as if half-expecting them to bang open. The side lamp on the curved ticket desk lit the right side of his pallid face, throwing the left into shadow.

Just then, I felt the faintest pull towards him. I hesitate to use the word 'recognition', because I was almost sure we had never met. Even so, the sensation seized me for a second and heightened my interest.

'Forgive me, but do we know each other?'

'No, I don't think so.' He turned back to me. 'You are free to leave.'

'Thank you,' I said, but I didn't move.

I wasn't intimidated any more; I was curious. His voice was even as he spoke, but his gaze darted around in agitation. I had the feeling there was something he wasn't telling me. Something, perhaps, he wanted to tell me. Perhaps, if I was lucky, he might even help with my peculiar mission, for I had come here seeking answers.

I had come to hunt ghosts.

'Your ankle's bleeding,' he said.

I looked down; my stocking was torn and the skin over my ankle bone was grazed.

'There are some bandages in my room. I'll get them if you're happy to wait.'

I should go home, I thought. *But if I leave now this whole trip will have been for nothing.*

'Where is your room?' I asked, and followed his gaze to a nearby staircase, which climbed into shadows. 'Up there?'

'Yeah, that's where the magic happens,' he said flatly. 'Stillness and flicker, light and shadow.'

The penny dropped. 'You're a projectionist.'

He nodded, looking curiously troubled.

I tried picturing the inside of his projection booth, but what came was a melancholy memory: Price in his white lab coat, hunched over his materials for lantern-slide making in our – his – workshop; Price surrounded by batteries and plugs, screws and gadgets; his racks, print-washers, measures, printing frames; his stereoscopic reflex cameras and their many lenses; his projection lanterns.

Seeing all that for the first time, four years earlier, I had thought these had to be the playthings of a vastly intelligent man – a skilled engineer, but also a lonely man, single-mindedly devoted to his interests . . . to his obsessions.

'Actually, I'd very much like to see where you work – if that isn't too much trouble?'

The projectionist looked at me uncertainly.

'Really,' I insisted, 'I take an interest in illusions. Cameras and projection equipment.'

'Uh . . . if you say so.' He sounded dubious.

'Bolex Model C,' I said confidently.

'Pardon me?'

'That's the model of projector you probably use here. Yes? Sturdy construction, grey enamel finish with reel arms strong enough to take, oh, I don't know, four hundred feet of reels? The threading system isn't much good, but the rapid motor rewind is still pretty useful. So is the draught ventilation and cooling system for the lamp. Oh, and the adjustable base – of course!'

He looked impressed.

I gave him a wide and winning smile. 'Like I said, I take an interest.'

As we took the stairs, I became aware of a faint odour. Sulphurous. I sniffed the air.

'Something burning?'

The projectionist paused, nervously, on the step ahead of me and drew his head back. 'I don't smell anything.'

Before I could reply, the main doors into the foyer behind us shook suddenly and violently.

I caught my breath. This narrow stairwell was poorly lit, and as accustomed as I had become to unexpected events and empty dark buildings, the spontaneous movement of objects could still rattle my nerves.

Again, the double doors in the foyer shook – more urgently. Turning, I glimpsed figures silhouetted in the glass, and then came raucous laughter. Teenage boys, I guessed, now running off.

The projectionist sighed heavily, then continued his heavy tread up the stairs, and I followed, passing playbills on the left wall, and on our right, a storage area for the usher's uniforms: white spats and gloves and smart blue tunics.

At the top of the steps the projectionist opened an unassuming steel door, and immediately I was struck by the distinctive aroma of film and a hot smell from the carbon lamps. I hesitated, thinking it might be wiser to wait outside, but he promptly motioned for me to follow him into the cine-chamber.

Almost at once I had the strangest feeling, the strangest impulse to walk right back out again, but I forced myself to stay and look around.

A solitary, dismal place; a tin box, with only just enough room for two people. Most of the space was taken up by two very imposing Ross projectors, fuelled by copper-coated carbon rods, and a record player with a huge notice plastered on the underside of the lid: 'Operator Beware: it is imperative 'pick-up' arm needle is changed after each disc has been played once.'

Fixed to the wall was a humming mercury-arc rectifier contained within a metal cage-like cabinet, and in its eerie, ultraviolet glow I saw that the rest of the walls were covered with switches and buttons; rows of fuse boxes; lens cabinets; input sprockets; fireproof cabinets stocked with reels of film; a fire extinguisher; and, on the bare concrete floor, a pail of sand.

Uneasily, I found myself thinking of Price again.

From behind me, I heard a thud. I knew what it was even before I turned and looked.

The metal door had shut.

My gaze shifted from the door to the projectionist beside me. The alarm must have shown on my face because he quickly said, 'The door self-closes. Fireproof. Regulations . . .'

I nodded, feeling a stab of self-reproach. What the hell was I thinking, coming up here alone – with a stranger? It would be easy for him to do anything he wanted to me . . . I just had to hope he had no ill intentions.

'Can you switch the light on?' I asked, and noticed that he paused for a moment longer than was comfortable.

'Light,' he said, in a voice that was very distant, almost a whisper. 'The light from the projector has the power to entrance, truly. A bright beam cutting through the smoky darkness. A spectacle. Sometimes that beam is all you need.'

'For what?' I asked, feeling nervous now.

'To see the past,' he said slowly, 'present and future.'

He was staring hard at me.

'Anyway,' I said, clearing my throat and nodding at the light switch.

He blinked, then with a sigh he flipped a switch and a stark bulb overhead flickered on, washing us with a cold, bright light.

'Thank you,' I said.

He advanced towards the largest projector and stationed himself beside it, motionless, staring silently through a tiny window down into the deserted auditorium.

Perhaps it was the thickness of his hair, perhaps it was the line of his jaw, but it struck me then that he was younger than

I had assumed. I saw now that his left eye wasn't just unfocused but had a glassy, dead sheen; his voice had the hoarse and cracked quality of an older man; and he moved with the measured gait of someone on whom the years had worked their toll. But all of this, I was sure now, was only an illusion. He *was* young, perhaps no more than thirty-five.

'You actually work in here?' I asked. 'In these horribly cramped conditions? If I were you, I would complain.'

Something in his eyes gave out a warning as he touched the side of his face. 'Men like me, we may as well have no opinions.'

I wondered what he meant by this as I glanced over the canisters of film hanging on the wall and the heavy-looking projectors, all the time conscious of his gaze on me.

It struck me that this poor man's occupation wasn't just depressingly solitary, but extremely unsafe. That narrow staircase we had just climbed had to be a fire hazard. How many times had Price warned me about nitrate film exploding into flame and releasing clouds of noxious smoke? Nitrate film easily caught fire because of the heat from the lamps. That was why projection booths like this one were built to shut down like a prison in the event of a fire – but God help anyone trapped inside.

'It must get unbearably hot.'

'You would think so,' he replied rather gloomily, and just then I felt a chill pass over me. But from where? The metal door was shut flush.

Then my gaze travelled from the door to the projectionist, and I saw the unique device at which he was staring. A projector, much older and smaller than the rest, fashioned from mahogany and brass and adorned with a crucifix and a

winged skull. It was a thing of exquisite quality, eerily beautiful; it looked as if it belonged in a museum of rare Victorian
curiosities.

'It's from Germany,' the projectionist explained. He ran his
hand lovingly along its smooth surface. 'A very early projector,
powered by candlelight, primitive but extremely effective. See
here, the adjustable lens, the moveable carriage system – all
designed for a very specific purpose.'

'What purpose exactly?'

'Wonders,' he whispered, not taking his gaze from the
machine.

It was like watching a young child enraptured with a gift
on Christmas morning.

Next to this projector was a small wooden box, open and
packed with lantern slides painted with indiscernible, colourful images. I reached out to examine one.

'Hands off!'

I flinched back.

'My hobby,' the projectionist added. For a moment, an
oppressive sadness seemed to gather on his face, like a black
cloud. 'The slides . . . I paint them when I'm alone.'

Perhaps if I had asked just a few more questions about
the painted glass slides and the antique projector with its
intricately carved base, crucifix and skull, I would have spared
myself from the sea of abnormality that would soon swallow
me at the lost village of Imber. The first murmurs of those
waters were surging around me then, and I heard them over
the lonely silence. It wasn't just the projectionist's unease, his
defensiveness – after all, he didn't know me, so why should
he trust me?

The truly unnerving observation was the dark hollowness

of his face; there *was* a formidable dent in the side of his head and around his left cheekbone – not quite as though someone had bashed it in with a hammer, but almost. And that single eye with the glassy sheen; it didn't look like an eye at all, I realised now. More like a dusty marble.

'Sir, why are you here, alone, so late? You seem somewhat – forgive me – agitated?'

He breathed out heavily. When he next spoke, something of the old sternness in his tone had returned. 'You seem very interested in me, for someone who was just accidentally locked in, Miss . . .'

'Grey. Sarah Grey. And your name?'

He blinked, and for a moment his eyes were blank. 'Albert.'

I was sure I had never known an Albert. Still, though, a faint familiarity bothered me. Why didn't I ask him his surname? I've asked myself so many times. Perhaps he wouldn't have given me the name, even if I had asked; but if he had told me, so much of what was to follow could have been avoided.

'May I enquire how long you have held your position here?'

'Too long,' was his reply. He glanced out of the window, at the dark auditorium, then back at me. 'Miss Grey, why don't you tell me why you *really* came here tonight?'

There was no need to share the truth – that the history of the picture house had become a consuming passion for me. I replied, simply, 'I'm doing some research on the building. A private history project.'

He looked suddenly afraid. Appalled.

'Which aspect of its history, exactly?'

That was harder to answer. On one level, the reason was simple: three weeks ago, the *Standard* had reported that while the picture house was locked up, deserted, passers-by had heard its organ playing. An interview with Lyndon Clarkson, the picture house manager, was published as well. On the narrow stairwell leading to this very cine-chamber, Clarkson claimed to have seen a blue light hovering in mid-air. Then, when he climbed the stairs and shone a torch on the door of the cine-chamber, he saw the ominous shadow of a man – though nobody else was there.

Of course, I was sceptical. Superstitions run riot: there's barely an old theatre in the country that isn't the setting for stories of spooks in the stalls and goosebumps in the gods, and so it's always been.

But the truth was that over a year earlier, months before I walked out on him, Price had attempted to treat an escalating nervous condition that had been making my life unbearable. Looking back, the reason I was suffering was very clear, even if I hadn't wanted to acknowledge it then. The shadow of guilt at giving my baby up for adoption had lengthened. Rarely would I make it through the night without waking in fitful sobbing gasps. Each morning, the face of a mother, and yet not a mother, looked back at me from the mirror, heartbroken, ashamed and questioning.

I had lied to Price; told him I was in low spirits, that was all. He had attempted to help me with hypnosis, and it seemed that ever since then I had felt drawn to this building, without any clear reason. I still sometimes dreamt of Harry Price – I'd see him sitting in his favourite armchair, speaking to me in a slow, velvety voice. Perhaps it was more than a dream. A memory. Whatever it was, I couldn't access it all. Price was asking me questions, and I was answering, but the detail was lost.

'You're here because of the stories, aren't you? The legends.'

'Actually, yes,' I replied. 'This theatre does have a history, you know.'

He said nothing, but the disturbed look in his one good eye told me he *did* know.

I had read all about the history of the largest and most luxurious cinema in South London. I knew that the first theatre on the site was a conversion of a Baptist chapel, which had become a warehouse; that the subsequent theatre was called the Arcadian and that it was consumed by a fire on a Sunday night in the middle of the last century. Apparently an illusionist from Germany tragically 'miscalculated' his act. That had to be the understatement of the century. Hundreds of children aged between eight and ten were inside when smoke began to billow into the auditorium, and panic erupted.

Eighty-six little bodies were pulled from the building. Charred. Asphyxiated. Many trampled to death.

That didn't necessarily mean the Brixton Picture Palace was haunted, though, did it?

No, but there's an atmosphere, I thought, *a distinctly bad atmosphere*. And now I thought about it, perhaps I did remember why I had fallen from the stage.

Hadn't I glimpsed a small figure, moving in the dark? And heard a child's voice calling for help from somewhere below?

Hard to be certain. I could quite easily have imagined such things. I needed more to go on.

'The reports of strange happenings here,' I said, leaning forward. 'True?'

'One man's truth is another man's undoing,' the projectionist said. 'Gotta be careful what you say. You hear about people being locked up in Bedlam these days for seeing all manner of things.'

'Albert, whatever you tell me will remain entirely between us.'

He looked at me fixedly.

I smiled and said, 'I promise. And if is within my power to help, I will certainly do so.'

Something glimmered in his good eye; I thought perhaps it was hope. His breathing quickened, his fists clenched. 'You asked me earlier about the ghost light on the stage,' he said, 'why it was turned off.'

'I did.'

'You want the truth? The ghost light does not keep spirits away. It attracts them.'

I admit, I was taken aback by this. Not so much the revelation – that would come later – but more that a witness should be so forthcoming. I thought back to Price and our first visit, three years earlier, to the haunted rectory in the hamlet of Borley in Essex. When we met its troubled residents, Mr and Mrs Smith, Price had performed astonishing conjuring tricks over lunch to compel the poor couple to confide in us. He had wanted to test their reactions, smiling as he studied them, as though they were mere experiments to him, playthings. And yet here I was, with none of Price's charisma, winning a complete stranger's trust purely through offering a listening ear.

'Tell me what you have seen, Albert.'

'When you're in here alone late at night after a show, when all the customers have gone home and the only thing left is the ghost light on the stage – I challenge anyone not to be unnerved. Sometimes on the stairs I feel a presence behind me, a woman; I hear the steps creaking and groaning. And I find boxes of flyers and materials moved between rooms.'

'Poltergeist phenomena. That's what it's called. The

spontaneous movement of objects without any apparent physical influence.'

'Call it what you like, it makes no sense to me.' He looked
again out of the little window; the dark auditorium seemed like
a magnet to his eyes. 'Sometimes,' he said, 'after hours, I see
people down there. In their seats. I know how that sounds, but
I *see* them, I do. They don't move, they don't speak, they just
sit there. Outlines in the dark. An audience that isn't there.'

I tried picturing that – shadowy forms of the departed, the
brooding empty seats – and felt the prickle of gooseflesh on
my arms. 'That's why you came down looking for me. You
thought I might be . . .'

He nodded and we fell silent. The silence was a comfortable
one this time, and very quickly it rekindled the vague notion
that I shared a faraway connection with this man. Somehow.
Something in common.

'Well,' I said, to snap him out of his reverie, 'as you can see,
I am no ghost.'

I went to the viewing window and looked down at where
I had fallen from the stage. It was impossible to see the spot
directly from this angle. Which meant the projectionist was
either mistaken or lying, or he had indeed seen something . . .
abnormal.

'I know what you're thinking. You're wondering how I could
see anything with it being so dark in there. But there was a red
light floating and bobbing through the rows of empty seats.
Some sort of . . . orb.'

'I don't recall seeing any light,' I said.

'But it was there,' he countered. 'It was in there *with you*,
Miss Grey.'

That left me cold. But he wasn't finished yet.

'One night,' he said, wringing his hands, 'I was doing my usual checks in the chambers beneath the stage, close to the original eighteenth-century foundations, when I glanced over my shoulder and I saw the figure of a young woman. I called out to her, as I called out to you earlier tonight. I told her she had to leave. Seconds later, she was just . . . gone.'

'Gone?'

'Vanished.'

'And that convinced you?'

His head snapped up. 'I didn't say I believed in ghosts, miss. I'm only telling you what I saw.'

'Thank you, Albert. I appreciate that. And I believe you.'

'You do?' A weary kind of relief came onto his face.

Something beneath the stage. The thought broke in from nowhere, but was too powerful to ignore.

'Take me down there, won't you, please? Beneath the stage. Show me where you saw this woman.'

Albert gave me a strange look.

'I'll go alone if I have to,' I told him, 'but I do want to see. Show me the way down.'

His head was shaking vigorously. 'Working here as long as I have, you get to know a building, every nook and cranny. The chambers below ground are out of bounds.'

'Clearly not to you.'

'Miss, down there, no one can hear you. It's not safe, especially not with your ankle – '

The dusty bare light bulb above us hummed, flickering for a moment. I sprang back, letting out a small cry. Instantly, the projectionist whirled round. His eyes were riveted on the metal door but he made no attempt to open it. His breathing quickened; his shoulders trembled.

Somewhere beneath us, in the foyer maybe, a door slammed.

'We must go –' I started to say, but Albert swung round and cut me off.

'No,' he said. 'No. You don't understand, miss.' He reached for his antique projector. 'I have to leave. I must leave.'

'It's all right,' I said, not knowing if it was or wasn't, but knowing I had to do something. 'Wait here – you have a good view of the auditorium. Keep an eye on me, all right? I'll go and investigate.'

'I really don't think –' be began, sounding close to terrified now, but I cut him off with a reassuring glance.

'Albert, trust me. I've done this before, it'll be all right.'

I sounded confident, but as my hand found the door handle I didn't feel that way. I didn't feel confident at all.

OLD HABITS

Moments later I was alone in the grand theatre foyer, standing before the double doors to the auditorium and peering through the circular viewing window. I saw nothing within but clotted darkness; heard nothing but silence. I put my hand to the doors, pushed them and entered.

The centre aisle sloped downwards beneath an ornate cantilevered balcony towards the stage, and I began to feel my way along carefully, seat by seat. It was pitch black; no sign of the ghostly red 'orb' the projectionist claimed to have seen from his window.

What would Price make of that? Some unknown atmospheric phenomenon?

No, he would go further: he would postulate that Albert was deluded, infected by the superstitions of haunted theatres. Albert saw a light because that was what he *expected* to see, and the loneliness of his position, combined with a fanciful disposition, only made him more likely to see it. Locational bias.

Maybe that was right. Maybe.

I wasn't frightened, but I suppose my nerves were on edge, which was why, rather than venture deeper into that artificial darkness, I stopped and called up to the projectionist in his cine-chamber.

'Albert, please, are you still up there? Switch the ghost light on.'

He made no reply, but he must have heard me, because seconds later the solitary bulb on the stage up ahead buzzed and flickered, before dimming to a steady yellow glow.

His words came back to me then: *The ghost light does not keep spirits away. It attracts them.*

I should go back.

But something was drawing me on. I *wanted* to go on. I wanted, for some reason I did not completely understand, but could not resist, to see beyond the ornate art deco façade of this building, into its heart, beneath the stage; to continue what I had started and to discover why for so many months I had felt drawn to this place and the dank, dingy passageways I knew were waiting below.

And anyway, I told myself, I had been in far worse situations than this. It wasn't as if I were crawling through cobwebs and grime under the eaves of a rambling old house miles from anywhere. That said, the deserted movie palace was certainly eerie. Thickly silent. The ghost light throwing a sickly glint off the acoustic wood and gold wall panelling.

'Albert, you shout out if you see anything from up there, all right?'

No reply.

I focused on the bare bulb up on the stage ahead of me, and crept stealthily towards it.

That was when I caught the scent of burning again, like you do when someone has lit a candle nearby. Except . . .

No sign of any flame, anywhere.

I was standing now exactly where Albert had found me: next to the first row of seats in the theatre. Thankfully, I had tripped close enough to the side of the stage that I had avoided falling into the dark orchestra pit.

I tried hard not to think about those many poor children, who perished here in the fire. A glint caught my eye – something at my feet, throwing back the reflection of the ghost light. Kneeling and straining to see, I could just about make out something small and oblong on the carpet. What was it? Something the projectionist had dropped?

Naturally enough, I picked it up. Holding it between my fingers, I saw that it was fashioned from wood, its angles smooth and regular.

Suddenly – a wracking shudder.

A blinding white flash.

Perhaps it was exhaustion, perhaps I had hit my head harder than I thought. Whatever it was, I felt plunged into a dreamlike obscurity, as though the panelled walls, the carpeted floor, my entire surroundings had fallen away.

I was caught in another place, a warm place where the grass stood waist-high, swaying around me. Everything was still and hazy and silent. Vast and limitless was the view ahead of me, golden fields and little woods ruffled by a late summer wind. In the distance, next to a glistening pond, a mill wheel passed the slow turns of the day. The orange glow of the late afternoon sun showed the rooftops of the nearby village and the white ribbon of a track cutting through a vast forest.

And then, just as abruptly as I had left, I was back in the empty auditorium, where the solitary ghost light cast its sickly glow.

Now the fear came again, spreading through me like a creeping black shadow.

What the hell had just happened? Where had I gone?

The warm place.

I looked down at the object in my hand. Its wooden sides framed a fixed sheet of glass bearing the faintest image. A photographic lantern slide. I felt the strangest sensation. A tingling, crawling in the palm of my hand, but that had to be my imagination. I slipped the slide into my overcoat pocket, and at that instant the giant screen behind me flickered. Burst into light.

I spun round.

My heart almost burst with surprise. The silent picture from earlier was spooling again. In jerky movements, a phantom coach was bearing a young traveller into the land of the dead, white trees like talons clawing their way out of the filthy earth. Some poor soul being stolen away to a monster's castle.

'Albert, can you please turn that off?' I intended it to sound casual, but it came out sounding stern.

On the screen, the hideous form of a creature with fangs approached slowly, emerging from the shadows.

'Albert!' I shouted.

I squinted up towards the cine-chamber.

No sign of Albert.

I began to grow annoyed. Was he trying to frighten me? No. More likely he had abandoned his post; he had said he needed to go. But go where?

Alarm seized me then. Albert hadn't seemed very steady on his feet, not steady at all. What if he had come after me in a hurry and tripped, fallen on the stairs? It didn't explain why he had turned on the projector, but it might explain why he wasn't answering.

I turned and started back up the aisle. I was passing the third row of seats when I noticed that the double doors were open, allowing neon light to seep in from the foyer. A figure was silhouetted in the doorway.

'Oh, Albert, thank heavens. I thought you had –'

I froze.

The shadowy silhouette I was looking at, the figure framed in the doorway, blocking my exit, was *not* Albert.

A thought surfaced and bobbed in my consciousness like a corpse released from the murky depths: a *spirit*.

'Oh dear God,' I whispered, and for an instant it felt as if time had slowed down. Stopped.

'Well, well. Sarah. Here you are. It's funny, but I remember wondering if you were the sort of woman who likes to take risks.'

That voice, those words . . .

The figure took one step forward.

Two steps.

Three.

And I recognised the black frock coat that came down to his knees and the hat in the style of Humphrey Bogart; a black felt fedora, tipped forward.

And I clung to nearest seat and whispered again, 'Oh dear God.'

Just turn and walk away.

But I was too stunned to move.

'Well, Sarah, surely I deserve a "hello"?'

'Harry?'

I felt oddly detached, as if I were witnessing this scene from outside myself.

For the briefest of moments, it was as if the last six months had never happened, that I had never found new employment with Mr Addison at the film company in Soho, or rediscovered my social life at the jazz clubs in Piccadilly. I could still have been the confidential secretary at the National Laboratory for Psychical Research, sharing with Price the thrill of that unpredictable path into the unknown and the exposing of yet another fraudulent spiritualist intent on making a fat living from the bereaved and vulnerable.

His face was shaded but I could tell he was looking at me with focused intensity. I noted the dark pouches under his eyes. He'd been spending too much time in that vast library of his. Alone.

A flash of anger shattered my shock. 'What the *hell* are you doing here?'

'Come now, Sarah,' he said. 'You're a clever woman. It's just a question of cause and effect. What do you think I am doing here?'

'You followed me.'

'I assure you I did nothing of the sort,' he said calmly, removing his hat. 'Oh, don't do this. You know how it is with peculiar old buildings. They have that persistent but frustrating propensity to just . . . reel me in!'

I shook my head defiantly; it was too much of a—

'Coincidence? Lazy assumption. That's just another way of describing something we can't explain. Why not name this encounter for what it is? Synchronicity! *Meaningful* coincidence.' His face lit up with boyish excitement, and he added, 'We are *meant* to be here, right now. You and me, Sarah. We were *drawn* here.'

'I didn't think you believed in all that.' My words came out sounding heavy and sour.

'Well, all right.' He stared at me a moment, then cracked a grin. 'When I saw the newspaper accounts two days ago, the reports of unexplained happenings in a cinema after dark, I'm afraid I couldn't help myself. Honestly, though, I had no idea you'd be here.'

I looked at him doubtfully. It was true, Price rarely lost any time before setting out to investigate. 'Information is like bread,' he used to preach at me. 'It goes stale very quickly – so it's our duty to get it out there as soon as we can, so it can be hungrily devoured.'

'Fascinating old place,' Price continued, glancing around at the empty seats trimmed with green velvet and the flickering silver screen behind me. The helpless traveller in the film had entered the monster's lair now and I was almost expecting the gleaming white and gold pipe organ at the front of the stage to start playing on its own.

Price's gaze floated up to the vaulted ceiling and down to the brass safety rail running around the cantilevered balcony above us.

'Oh yes, most atmospheric. Yes, I'll certainly give it that. But I suspect there's precious little here of any interest to psychical research.'

Something beneath the stage, I thought, with a kind of grim curiosity, and I thought of the projectionist, Albert, and his antique projector, of the intriguing small object tucked away in my pocket, and the warm place to which I had travelled in my mind just moments ago. The experience had the hazy, indefinable quality of a dream, but I could still feel the glow of the sun on my neck and the breeze against my face. It was too eerie.

'Little here of interest,' I repeated. 'You're confident about that, Harry?'

He nodded. 'Heard a door slam, that was all. I had a quick nose about, went up to the projection booth.'

'Did you meet Albert, the projectionist?'

Price looked at me blankly.

'Well, you must have seen him. I was just up there with him. I doubt very much Albert would have just walked out and left me in here,' I said, remembering how he said he wanted to do just that.

'Well, he's gone now, Sarah. We are alone and there's nothing to fear. You can take that assurance to the bank.' Price looked out at the auditorium and shrugged. 'Once you've seen one creaky old theatre, you've seen them all.'

'Then you've had a wasted trip.'

He turned and met my stare. 'Oh, I wouldn't say that.'

The tenderness of his gaze was tinged with an intensity of purpose. He probably thought his expression exuded boyish charm, but all it did was kindle my frustrations.

I threw a look at the vampire on the flickering screen and then glared at my old employer. It was just like him to pull a stunt like this. Creep up to the cine-chamber, set the projector in motion. Thrills and chills were the ghost hunter's speciality.

'Sarah, why do you look at me like that? Such disdain, as if I myself were a trickster.'

I couldn't contain my anger any longer. 'That is exactly what you are! You tricked Velma, one of your closest friends – Harry, she was *dying* – into performing before a live audience when you knew you would expose her as a fraud. Humiliate her.'

'Not this again. I tried to warn her – '

'And didn't you trick me when you arranged to sell the

laboratory from under us, put me out of a job, without ever mentioning your intentions, not *once*?'

'The negotiations were in a delicate phase of—'

'You suppressed knowledge of a hoaxed séance in which I was personally involved. You breezily walked away from the rectory in Borley, leaving the Smiths to deal with the mess you left behind, like some sort of travelling salesman! Then you left me alone in that stinking laboratory of yours for *months*—'

'Sarah, please, I was unwell. I tried—'

'No, you *didn't*! You made me feel worthless!' I brushed his hand aside as he reached out to me. Then, for a moment, a chasm of silence opened between us. He opened his mouth to say something, closed it again. Outside I could hear the winter wind whining around the corners of the old theatre.

The scratch of a match; a cigar went to his delicate lips and glowed. There was the soft crackling of tobacco as he drew in a lungful of smoke.

The scent of burning.

The cigar tip glowing red again.

The floating, bobbing red light.

It was him. He was the one the projectionist had seen. Price all along. No ghostly glowing 'orb', nothing so sinister or otherworldly. Just Price's smouldering cigar. How long had he been skulking around in this auditorium?

'*You* walked out on *me*, Sarah. You had responsibilities.'

'A life going nowhere.'

'Yes,' he said with a hint of mockery. 'I suppose you were going nowhere' – he released a mouthful of smoke – 'until you met me.'

The words skewered me, not just because they were cruel. Because they were true.

Before taking employment with Price, I had been drifting, or, as Mother would put it, 'a wanderer with my head in the clouds'. Taking the job had been a chance to better myself, and to find meaning in Mother's ceaseless grief for my father; to show her, I suppose, that the answers to life's problems weren't to be found with spiritualist mediums communing with the dead, but with honest and open scientific inquiry.

'I'm curious, Sarah; what exactly *is* your new position?'

'That's not your concern.'

'It is well remunerated?' He saw my set expression and added, 'I mean, does the role satisfy you?'

'Very much.'

I could see Price dissecting the lie, reading the concern in my eyes about how we were possibly going to pay the bills at the end of the month.

'And your mother – how is Mrs Grey faring?' he asked pointedly. 'Still squandering every spare household penny on fraudulent mediums?'

I swallowed hard. 'Actually, she has put all that behind her.'

He cocked his head and peered at me through a cloud of cigar smoke.

'She has moved on with her life,' I told him with conviction. 'We have *both* moved on.'

'And yet . . .' Arms spread wide, he cast his gaze around the empty theatre. 'Here you are!' He grinned. 'Old habits – eh, Sarah?'

Fearing the truth was written on my face, I forced myself to look away. Nothing could be more demeaning than to grant him the satisfaction of knowing I missed the laboratory, our work. His dark and exhilarating world. Him.

'Dearest Sarah,' he said softly, 'although you never came close to the eighty words a minute I desired and your dictation was a little woolly, you were – and we both know this – without doubt the most capable, the most reliable investigative companion I could ever hope to find.'

I was startled – he really thought that of me?

His gaze fell to my lips, just for a second, before flicking back up. 'The truth is,' he said, 'I have missed you.'

My mind swirled. His face was open and defenceless. Looking at that face, the hawkish nose, those gimlet eyes and projecting ears, I couldn't help but think of his son. The son he didn't know about. The son I had carried and delivered alone, in secret, and then given up for adoption. April 1930. Concealing the lie had been easier than I'd imagined: Price had been admitted to hospital with heart problems for an extended period, and I'd taken myself away to Yorkshire as my body swelled. Would our son grow up to resemble Price? Would he behave like him?

I hoped not. God, I hoped not.

'Why don't you come back? Come back to the laboratory and work for me.'

My throat closed and my pulse kicked up a gear as I saw not the laboratory but a convent. A nun reaching for the tiny swaddled package in my arms. My hands, my own hands, handing over my beautiful baby – half me, half Harry.

Price kept his eyes on me through the haze of smoke around his head. There was something vulnerable in his expression and for a moment – a very short moment – I felt an aching sorrow for him. He had never even seen his baby boy's face. Never would.

It would be many years before Price learned of his son; and

to my shame, he would go to his grave believing I had aborted the pregnancy.

And whose fault was that?

I swallowed the guilt. Some men do that – they make us liars, even to ourselves.

'Come back?' I shook my head. 'That's not going to happen. That is completely out of the question.'

'Sarah,' he said, 'what if I told you I was in touch with a clairvoyant capable of contacting life forms in distant solar systems? Or that I am due to examine a young girl who can break tables without even touching them and levitate chairs? Then there's a house in Battersea suffering from the most violent poltergeist disturbances. What if I could show –'

I cut him off with a glare.

'You're not even a little curious?'

'No.'

'There's nothing I can do to persuade you?'

'Nothing.'

There was a long, contemplative pause. He looked at me with a glimmer of disappointment, which suggested he didn't approve of my decision but valued his dignity too much to argue.

'Pity,' he said at last, before turning abruptly and striding up the middle aisle, towards the exit. 'Still! Your choice. You're entitled to it.'

Cross, I turned my back on him, and saw, on the screen, a hypnotist putting a woman into a trance. Immediately, I remembered the intense sensation of relaxation when Price had put me under, not so very long ago.

What had I told him when I was in that trance?

My frustration turned to fury. He was impossibly manipulative; I wouldn't stand for it. 'Harry, wait!'

He was at the double doors, one hand grasping a handle, and he half turned back towards me.

I pointed at the movie screen. 'Switching the film on like that. Deliberately trying to frighten me. Why? Why would you do that?'

The way he scowled at me then made me think of the way he had reacted to Mr and Mrs Smith on our very first investigation of the rectory in Borley. Price's impression was that the distraught couple were deeply superstitious, that they *wanted* to believe in spirits. 'It's the bunk they want,' he had told me. 'Not the debunk.' So Price made sure they got it. He never explained to me precisely how he made the pepper pot slide across the surface of the highly polished lunch table, but he did later admit to the trick – and I felt sure that the part of him that had delighted in pulling the strings at Borley, the conjurer within, also delighted in deceiving me this very night.

'I did nothing of the sort,' Price replied stonily.

'Harry, I'm telling you it actually gave me quite a jump. Not at all funny.'

'I did not touch the projector,' he declared indignantly.

I took a moment to process this. 'But you went up to the cine-chamber.'

'Indeed, and it was deserted. Remember, the projectionist *left* – which is precisely what I'm going to do now.' He placed his hat on his head, pulled it low over his brow, and turned to leave. 'Goodnight, Sarah.'

'But . . .' I felt the skin on the back of my neck shiver into bumps. 'If *you* didn't turn the projector on, Harry – who did?'

He looked back one final time and unleashed a cajoling smile.

'As I suspected, Sarah . . . still curious.'

RESIDENTS TO RETURN TO GHOST VILLAGE
Gates to open at hamlet evacuated during Great War
From our special correspondent, Vernon Wall

A village that has been uninhabited for eighteen years is to be opened to its former residents next Sunday.

Isolated in the middle of a low valley, deep in the Wiltshire countryside, stand the crumbling remains of Imber, a so-called 'ghost village' which was evacuated in 1914.

At the outbreak of the Great War, villagers were forced to pack up and leave. Within a month, Imber vanished off the map as it was turned into a military training area.

Surrounded by a ten-foot chain-link fence, a locked gate and Keep Out notices, Imber has since remained permanently out of bounds to the public. But once a year, the guns fall silent, the gates are opened, and civilians are allowed to visit relatives' graves and attend a service in Imber church.

Next Sunday, dozens of locals are expected to make the trip.

David Whitaker Brown, honorary custodian of Imber

church, said, 'A whole community of people sacrificed their homes for the war effort. Of course, when they did so they believed, once the war was over, they would be allowed to come back.'

According to local folklore, some former residents did return to their homes – as ghosts. Visitors have reported hearing music and laughter in empty buildings, and the sound of doors slamming in cottages where there aren't any doors.

Jane Wharton's great-grandfather was the local black-smith. She says the evacuation broke the man's heart, and that he passed away during the move. Jane, who returned to the village to lay flowers on his grave, told this reporter that many other former residents shared her great-grandfather's pain.

'Imber was a lovely little village that has been devas-tated,' she said. 'I don't think my gramps could face it. I believe he killed himself and I wouldn't be at all surprised if the village was haunted by old residents who never wanted to leave.'

The roads through Imber on Salisbury Plain, as well as the church, will be open to former residents. The Friends of Imber Church will be holding a special remembrance service within the building.

For the rest of the year, Imber remains a ghost village, accessible only to the army.

It's difficult to imagine this war zone of shell-damaged, dangerous buildings being returned to civilians any time soon, if ever. But former residents continue to live in hope.

– 5 –

HOME AGAIN

When I arrived home, quietly closing the front door behind me, I didn't notice the ivory envelope that was about to change my life. It was waiting for me on the hall table, under the mirror, but as I hung up my coat, dishevelled and tired, intending to go straight to bed, something made me halt: a dark shape in the parlour, hunched in Father's antique wingback armchair, next to the gramophone.

Mother.

She had a glass of brandy in one hand and a photograph of my father in his army uniform in the other. Her thinning white hair was unwashed and uncombed, her eyes staring ahead, red-rimmed and hollow.

'Sarah, I've been worried to death.'

The antique clock on the wall ticked loudly; I looked and saw it was two thirty. No explanation would be good enough, not at this time in the morning, so I spared her the elaborate excuses.

'I'm quite all right,' I said with a sinking heart, and, taking the tumbler from her hand, I pressed a gentle kiss onto her forehead and whispered, 'Bed now, Mother – for us both.'

A silent nod. Somehow that was worse than a series of questions. Probably she would remain here in her chair until the morning, her head slumped forward, until a rough snore startled her awake. Then I would hear her treading groggily up to bed.

I went out of the room, once again failing to notice the crucial envelope on which my name was scrawled, and stood for a moment in the shadowy hallway. There was so much we didn't tell one another.

Mother knew nothing of the baby I had given up. My little treasure. I remember that time all too vividly, the quiet desperation of an expectant single mother with no one to turn to. The idea of parenting the child alone – an unplanned child, born out of wedlock . . .

No. Shame and fear had put the idea beyond reach for me, obliterating my hopes for a good life. As a single mother, my prospects would have been horribly grim. I'd have been ostracised, brought disrepute upon the family. Scandal. No one would have wanted to marry me.

In my panic, I became convinced adoption was the best solution, partly for myself, but mainly for the child; it was the only way to protect him – to give him the best start in life. I had to do what was best for the boy, however painful, however distressing that would be for me.

It was my duty.

What I remember most about the birth is the nuns at the convent telling me not to feel guilty, that giving up the precious life that had grown inside me was a selfless act. The baby would have a better chance in life with parents who were ready for him, so it was the right thing to do, wasn't it?

That didn't stop me worrying that he would grow up to hate the thought of me, and it did nothing to diminish the heartbreak, or the daily struggle with my guilt.

I had told Price nothing. He was married – to the wealthy daughter of a respected jeweller. If the truth had come out about our child, disgrace would have fallen hard upon his good name.

What I had done – giving up our child, sacrificing that sudden fiery, consuming need to be a mother – I had done for the child, to protect him; but I had also done it for Price.

The thought came to me that evening, as it was always going to; it had just been lying in wait:

When are you going to go back to Queensberry Place? When are you going to go back and work for him?

And quickly after this:

Impossible, infuriating man!

He might have had the decency to offer me a lift home. Though probably my pride would have prevented me accepting anything from him.

Are you sure, Sarah? Sure you're not 'still curious'?

In setting out on my own paranormal investigation, I had willingly unlocked a door. But go back to Price's laboratory? No. It was out of the question. That was what my head told me, and it told me so resolutely. My heart, however, told a different story. My heart whispered softly but certainly that I would, once again, venture with Harry Price into the unknown.

The pain in my ankle had dimmed to a dull ache. Upstairs, I went into my bedroom – a comfortable mess – to inspect the damage, and to wash off my make-up. The face staring back at me from the tarnished mirror was exhausted: dark pits around my eyes, blonde hair hanging shapelessly around a pallid face. I scrubbed it clean, but I couldn't scrub it smooth; the lines that spoke of strain and sadness remained.

When I finally stepped out of my clothes and settled into bed, I lay there, knees drawn up, half listening to an early news bulletin on the wireless: speculation about Hitler's fortunes at the forthcoming federal election in Germany.

Enough. I switched it off.

But I couldn't sleep. My head was whirring. What was beneath the stage at the Brixton Picture Palace? What hadn't the projectionist wanted me to see or know?

Possibly nothing. By anyone's standards, a cine-chamber was an unusual place to work, almost as unusual as Price's laboratory – and unusual places made people do unusual things.

Albert's abrupt disappearance troubled me still, though. Notwithstanding his agitated state, would he really have abandoned the Picture Palace knowing there were two strangers still inside?

That didn't sound much like the man who had hunted me down in the empty auditorium and confronted me. That man would have escorted Price and me from the premises, would have taken care to lock up. Unless . . .

Unless he saw something that absolutely terrified him.

My mind flashed to the antique projector in his lonely chamber, and the box of colourful glass lantern slides.

'The slides,' he said, 'I paint them when I'm alone.'

Of course. That was the object I had found on the floor in the auditorium – one of his lantern slides. Until this moment, I hadn't made the connection. I got out of bed and fished it from my coat pocket.

As I held the lantern slide between my fingers, a compulsion made me raise it to the light. Between the two sheets of glass was pressed a black and white image. It was badly scratched, but it appeared to be of a boy and a girl. She looked about twelve or thirteen, wearing an expensive-looking dress, hair curling around her ears, smiling as she stood before some ash trees. Next to the girl was a younger boy. Handsome. About ten years old. The rest of the detail was difficult to make out but the whole image brought a mystifying lump of sadness to my throat.

Remembering the box of lantern slides in the projection booth, I reasoned Albert must have dropped this, and I decided I would return it to him the next day.

I fell asleep after that, thinking of the Picture Palace after dark. I awoke in the night with the vision of a field of swaying grass, watching the slow turn of the mill wheel. Alone. Waiting for someone. Birds chirped, a church bell tolled distantly, and the sun sank ever lower to the horizon, blazing orange.

Not just a dream, but a memory?

6

OLD FRIEND

Fleet Street. Monday. I had arrived to find myself caught in a frenzy of noise and bustle, journalists hurrying along in crumpled grey suits and trilby hats, scurrying from the pubs to get back to their typewriters. Somewhere behind me, a newspaper seller was shouting a headline from the early edition, fighting to be heard over the clatter of horse-drawn carriages and motor cars.

It was the letter at home that had brought me here. A message from an old friend.

A boy on a delivery bike clattered past me. It had been a hard day at work and an exhausting weekend. I knew what I needed now was to relax, but then I saw what I was looking for – an arched alleyway leading to the Middle Temple; a warren of dark-bricked barristers' chambers and silent gardens.

Glad to escape the stink of hot oil and paper and ink, I passed through the arch into this gothic sanctum, threading my way through passageways and courtyards that were so quiet it was hard to believe I was still in central London. It was almost as if I had wandered into another realm – an oasis of gas-lit passages and wide lawns dotted with dim shapes of trees.

I eventually emerged into a Dickensian courtyard of handsome buildings and stately windows. To my left, a sign attached to the nearest wall informed me that this was Pump Court; above this sign was an ornate sundial bearing the date 1686 and a curious inscription:

'Shadows We Are and Like Shadows Depart.'

I knew from this curious landmark that I had come the right way. All I had to do now was pass through the cloisters up ahead, and I'd find the medieval Temple Church.

I pressed on, passing through another archway, grander than the last, and saw the church, with its rare circular nave – one of the oldest and most beautiful churches in London. Squinting through the sickly yellow fog, I could just about make out the figure of a man nearby. He was sitting on a black iron bench.

With a swirling sensation in my stomach – nerves but also excitement – I approached until I was close enough to be sure it was him. The crumpled brown suit. The trilby hat. The jug ears. I had no idea then what we would later become.

'Mr Wall? Vernon?'

He did not speak, he did not turn round, but beneath his jacket his shoulders tensed.

'I must thank you for your note,' I said. As soon as I had read the letter Mother had left for me on the hall table, I knew I had to accept the invitation therein to meet here today. I was curious – and more – to see the man whose romantic advances I had, not so very long ago, eschewed.

'Miss Grey.' Now he stood and turned to me, and for a moment I was surprised. Unpleasantly surprised. His handsome face was still one of many angles, but I didn't remember him ever being so pale; the skin beneath his eyes was purple and paper-thin. The veneer of pride was in place – he stood tall, levelling his gaze at me – but I wondered what lay beneath. Hurt, I suspected, for the decisions I had made. Decisions that had involved Harry Price and not him.

'Quite honestly,' said Vernon, 'I didn't expect you to come.'

I didn't tell him I had had to leave work early to make our appointment. I didn't tell him that coming here had meant postponing my returning the lantern slide to the Brixton Picture Palace. I simply said, 'In the letter, you said you needed my help.'

'Indeed. A small favour, pertaining to a most delicate matter.' His gaze flicked around the gloomy courtyard and snagged on two passers-by – two bewigged gentlemen in black robes. 'Shall we move over here?' he suggested, nodding towards the side of Temple Church.

We stood like conspirators in an angle of shadows next to the church wall.

'All right,' Vernon began. 'Promise me: complete confidentiality. If anyone should ask, this must be one of those conversations that never happened.'

'Vernon – '

'I'm completely serious, Sarah.' He looked directly at me, jaw tense. 'My job could be on the line.'

'After your many scoops for the *Daily Mirror*, they should be making life easy for – '

'I'm with a new newspaper now. *The Times*,' he cut in. 'Have to earn my stripes if I'm to have any hope of progressing, and my new editor is . . .' He wiped his brow.

'Demanding?

He looked down at his scuffed lace-ups. 'That's putting it mildly.'

I reassured Vernon that he need not worry, and yes, he could trust me. His furtive manner was deepening the curiosity that his hurriedly scrawled letter had awakened in me. 'Muckraking tabloid reporter,' that's what Price had called Vernon when he had first introduced us at Borley Rectory.

'So, what's this about?' I asked.

He hesitated, and behind his chestnut-brown eyes I imagined his mind hastily shifting sentences around. Finally, he said, 'Sarah, have you heard of a village called Imber?'

'Sounds familiar.'

'It's the most isolated of places. Tucked in a valley on Salisbury Plain.'

'Wiltshire?' I nodded. 'I went there once, with my father.'

'But not to Imber?'

'I don't believe so. There are many villages all over Wiltshire. Why?'

'"The village that was murdered", as some call it, or "the village without villagers". A genuine ghost town. Abandoned at the beginning of the Great War. Ever since, it's been used by our government to train soldiers. It has a sad, if fascinating history. With no notice whatsoever, one hundred and ten civilians were summoned to a meeting in the school hall and told they had only a few days to leave. Just like that' – his fingers snapped – 'the road into their village became a road to nowhere. I mean it, Sarah. The place vanished from every map. And after the war, when the civilians asked to return –'

'Let me guess. The War Office refused?'

'It was the Land Committee that said no, but basically yes, you're correct. It was decreed that Imber would remain strictly under military control. Well, you can imagine – the people of the village weren't at all happy.'

'I'm sure they were outraged!' I said, picturing a cluster of low stone cottages reduced to bombed-out shells from battle training, and once quaint streets pitted with craters and tank tracks.

'Their settlement dated back to Saxon times, and here it was being written out of history! Now a campaign's begun: Imber Will Live. They came to me asking me to write an article about their plight. They want the roads reopened and Imber re-established as a farming community and village.'

'And is that likely to happen?'

'Hardly. But as their campaign intensifies, this story could run and run.'

'Which should be useful for *you*,' I said, 'but what's this got to do with me?'

He was looking at me closely now, with the hint of an intriguing smile that made me think of our excursion, during the summer of 1929, to the haunted rectory in Borley.

'Imber may be deserted, Sarah, but its spirit burns bright, and perhaps in more ways than one. Once every winter, on the Sunday just before All Souls' Day, the barriers are taken down, the road into Imber is opened, and former residents and their surviving relatives are permitted to return to their church for a remembrance service. They meet old friends, sing hymns, and light candles on the graves of their loved ones.'

'Sounds a little eerie.'

'Well, it is an eerie place, hidden away down there on the

valley floor, seven miles from the nearest town; surrounded by rusted tanks, all that barbed wire and those Out of Bounds signs. Many of the buildings have been damaged by stray shells. Almost all of them have been left to crumble and rot. I've seen pictures – '

'So you haven't actually been inside the village yourself?'

'No. Only former residents can return – once a year. But,' he added weightily, 'with the date so close now, the army have a peculiar problem in Imber.'

'What sort of peculiar problem?'

He held my gaze. 'One that requires the attention of a peculiar . . . expert. Look at this.' From his jacket pocket, Vernon produced a small black and white photograph of a handsome man in military uniform, no more than thirty years of age. 'This is Sergeant Gregory Edwards. This photograph was taken five years ago, when Sergeant Edwards was first posted to the Imber training facility. Twelve months ago, he suffered a total breakdown – began seeing things after going temporarily missing on an exercise in the woods that border Imber. He's since vanished from the public eye.'

'What happened?'

He gave a shrug. 'The army won't disclose any further details. I've attempted to contact his family and drawn a complete blank.'

His eyes shifted across the gloomy yard to the ancient church crypt behind me. Two more robed barristers passed by, chatting lightly. 'I've had some limited contact with the soldier in charge, Commander Gordon Williams,' said Vernon, leaning a little closer to me and lowering his voice. 'I contacted his office for comment on the Imber Will Live campaign. He consented to a meeting. And in some ways, it was very much a meeting of minds. He confided in me . . . to a point.'

That surprised me. 'Why would the military trust a journalist? I don't wish to sound rude, Vernon, but –'

'After I began digging into what happened to Sergeant Edwards, the army realised that I could be useful to them. You see, as the public campaign gains momentum, the military badly need a friend in the media. A sympathetic ear.'

'You mean someone they can bribe.'

Vernon grinned in a way that gave me an unwelcome tingle. 'I'm not talking about money, Sarah. But access? Well now, that's different. If I help the military now, then perhaps later, when I need insight on a military story, they'll grant me some access. Contacts are everything, and of course there's the small matter of my prospects at *The Times*.'

'You're just going to give up on the Edwards story? Drop it in favour of helping the military?'

A pause. 'Not exactly. I asked one too many questions. Think I dented their trust in me a little. So I promised I'd help them find what they were looking for: an expert.'

'It's still a bit of a gamble, isn't it?'

'So was coming to you,' he said. The grin vanished. 'But I do need your help. The army needs your help. Commander Williams won't allow the public back into the village this Sunday unless he's certain there won't be any problems. His men are spooked out of their wits. They fear the village is . . . troubled.'

I suppressed a smile. 'Phantom monks, headless apparitions, ladies in white – that sort of thing?'

'Not quite.' Vernon hesitated. 'Local folklore says the village is haunted by former residents. Dogs have been heard howling at the old – empty – kennels. In the past year, some of the soldiers have noticed movements in the windows of houses supposed to be empty. Smoke drifting from the chimneys of ruins, the smell of cooking food.

'Ever since Gregory Edwards suffered his breakdown, the other men refuse to enter the woods on training exercises. They think there's something in there that caused it. Some of them say they've seen dark figures moving between the trees, watching them. Some believe the souls of past inhabitants who were forced to surrender their homes still dwell in the village and won't rest until the army are gone.'

That sounded more than a little fanciful to me, but I couldn't pretend I wasn't intrigued. These were hardened military men, hardly the sort who were likely to salute a lone magpie to stave off unhappiness and bad luck. 'What does the base commander think?'

'Commander Williams' chief concern is for the safety of his men. But you see the problem. Imber Service Day is this Sunday – just six days away. Then the roads will open and the civilians will make their pilgrimage into Imber. If the army doesn't open the village, they'll be crucified by the campaigners. But if they do, it's vital he can have confidence that his men are up to the job. They certainly can't risk civilians running riot through the town. It's completely unsafe. Some of the buildings are on the verge of collapse, and there's unexploded debris, shells and what not, in the long grass off the main roads. Watertight security, that's what the commander needs.'

I inched closer to him, feeling the pull of curiosity – and something else. I wondered if that something else was attraction. 'You think there's any possibility these reports of unexplained phenomena could be genuine?'

'Wouldn't it be churlish to assume otherwise?' he replied. I wondered how often the events we had experienced together three years ago in Borley replayed in his mind: the brick that came hurtling through the glass roof; the candlestick thrown by an unseen hand.

Still, I wasn't clear how or why any of this should concern me.

'I need you to attend a meeting with Commander Gordon Williams,' continued Vernon, gazing intently at me. 'If superstitions are indeed infecting the soldiers' morale, marring their judgement, they need the assistance of an expert debunker. Immediately.'

The suggestion surprised me. 'I'm flattered that you think I can assist, Vernon, but do you really think – '

'It's not you they want, Sarah,' he said flatly. Our eyes met. 'You're to attend and assist, but the meeting I need you to facilitate, the meeting that could make all the difference for the army, and even for the former residents of Imber, is with Harry Price.'

I froze, one hand tightly gripping the top of my handbag, my cheeks burning. In the distance, towards Fleet Street, I caught the thin, discordant melody of a busker's violin. A young mother walked into the square, pushing a pram. I quickly glanced away.

Vernon forced a laugh. 'I can see you're not thrilled by the idea.'

'It's a big ask,' I said, my voice sounding pinched.

'Sarah, you know I think Price is an utter scandalmonger. God knows he's a man who puts his own needs before anyone else's. But on this occasion ... Look, I'd contact him myself, but you know the old crook can't stand the sight of me. But you, you're his friend – his secretary.'

'I moved on with my life, Vernon.'

His eyebrows arched.

'I thought you'd be pleased,' I said, feeling a tinge of defensiveness. And didn't a small part of me – perhaps more than a small part – hope this bright and ambitious young man would admit he *was* pleased?

'So, what made you leave?'

I almost said 'you', but only almost. My lips froze. I was being ridiculous. Instead I told him of Price's disgraceful humiliation of his closest friend, Velma; his prolonged absences; the secret business dealings; the deceptions. Throughout my explanation, I forced myself to keep my eyes off the young mother with her pram and the gurgling baby within.

'I *wanted* to move on,' I finished.

'And you *can* move on,' said Vernon encouragingly. He put one hand gently on my arm. 'But I'm in a terribly difficult situation – try to see that. My editor expects me to demonstrate excellent sources within the army. *The Times*, it's a tough gig, and I have a real opportunity here. The army can't risk approaching Price directly – he's likely to have the whole affair up in lights. This must be handled delicately, Sarah. Discreetly. And you know how Price is . . .'

'You mean they want someone to keep him under control.'

'Exactly,' Vernon replied, holding my gaze.

'Well, I'm not doing it.'

Yet at the back of my mind, a shadowy doubt remained: *still curious* . . .

'Sarah, please. You know Price better than anyone.'

Was that true? It was hard to be sure. Harry Price was married to a woman he never mentioned and whom I had never even met. He had a vast array of business interests of which

I had been denied total knowledge. A network of friends he treated more like enemies.

'Harry doesn't have all the answers, Vernon,' I said. 'He just likes to believe he does.'

'Well, the army believes he can help. But we need someone to keep an eye on him, keep him in check.'

'And if he should refuse?'

'He won't. An egotist like Harry would never refuse an opportunity like this. Oh, and Commander Williams doesn't intend to leave Imber any time soon, which means –'

'We have to go to him.'

Vernon nodded hastily. 'Just two days of your time – three at the most. Get Harry to find out what's been troubling the soldiers. Reassure the commander that Imber can open to its old residents. Show the lot of them there's nothing to these rumours.'

Once again, my ears caught the distant whine of the violin on the chill afternoon air.

'Vernon,' I said, 'my ghost-hunting days are over.'

A line of desperation furrowed the skin between his eyebrows. 'Sarah, we saw and experienced incidents at Borley that could not be reconciled with our received wisdom about the world. I asked you then to trust me, remember? I'm asking you again, now. I make my livelihood from facts. I have a healthy respect for them, and it is in the spirit of that claim, in the spirit of truth, that I am asking this of you now. There's too much at stake here to just walk away.'

'You mean your job?'

'Not just that! Good and vulnerable people, soldiers who train hard to defend our country, civilians who have lost their homes – they need help.'

Was he trying to appeal to my better nature? Possibly. Still, I decided to hear him out.

'Do I dislike Mr Price? Fiercely. He's a scoundrel of the first order, just as manipulative and self-centred as the mediums he so piously rips apart. But sooner or later, every supposed paranormal happening reaches his awareness. People write to him every day with their encounters. The newspapers telephone him daily for comment on lurid stories, right?'

It was true. So many ghosts. Price's problem was deciding which to hunt.

'So, I am forced to concede he is best suited to assist in this matter. I need him.'

I weighed this up for a moment. 'But you don't trust him.'

'It's you I trust, Sarah.'

I looked at Vernon for what felt like a long time, thinking of a future that might have been. Recalling the morning after our initial visit to the rectory in Borley, the morning after Price had come quietly to my bedroom. The caress of Harry's touch. The scent of his skin. Going into the washroom to confront myself in the mirror, asking myself, demanding to know, how? How could I have been so careless? But the truth was I knew, deep down, in the murkiest chamber of my soul, I hadn't been careless. I had engaged, I had allowed him into bed. I chose Harry Price. How many people, I wonder, act like that? Purely on secret desires?

'Will you do it, Sarah?' Vernon's dark-rimmed eyes weren't pleading exactly, but they were close enough. I remembered, then, Vernon asking me, as we sat together in the study at Borley Rectory, if I would accompany him on a trip to Bellagio. I remembered his crestfallen expression when I had politely declined. And then I remembered how, despite my decision to stay with Price, Vernon had championed me. Considerate. Respectful. Gallant.

'All right, I'll help. This time. *If* Harry is agreeable.'

'Actually, I need you to do a little more than that.' He hesitated. 'Keep me informed?'

'Spy?'

He tried a smile, but could see it wasn't about to be reciprocated, so he dropped it. 'Given that there's the remotest chance of a story here, and my reputation is on the line, yes, it would be helpful – to know how Price is handling the matter.'

'Oh, perfect.'

'He does tend to let things get out of hand.'

That was true. Like the occasion when Price insisted on spending the night in a haunted bed, and invited reporters from London's newspapers along to watch.

'There's just one more thing.'

I raised an expectant eyebrow.

'Be tremendously careful. I mean that, all right, Sarah? Even if this is just a question of local folklore, why did the army keep what happened to Sergeant Gregory Edwards a secret? What happened to him, and where is he now? I don't want to sound melodramatic but I've heard enough stories about the village now to give me a bad feeling I can't shake.'

'You're right,' I said doubtfully, 'that does sound a trifle melodramatic.'

He smiled. 'I just have a . . . I don't know, a sense that there's something deeper out in that village. Something darker.'

'You want me to find out what's actually going on. Is that what this is really about, Vernon?'

'Yes, if you can. Listen, once you've got Price on board,

let me know. You can expect a direct communication from Commander Gordon Williams to follow.'

Just then, the last church bells of the afternoon began to chime. Vernon looked up, sighing.

'Well, deadlines are looming. Walk with me to Fleet Street?'

I hesitated, looking over his shoulder at the young mother and her baby. She looked happy, smiling proudly down into the pram. She checked her wristwatch and I realised now that she was waiting for someone – a barrister, perhaps? Her husband?

'Actually,' I said, 'if you don't mind, I'll stay here a while and reflect.'

'Oh. Yes, of course. No problem.'

'How will I contact you?'

'Telephone the news desk. That's if you can find a telephone out there.' He began walking away, but then, abruptly, he stopped and turned on his heel. 'Maybe when this business is concluded . . .' He cleared his throat, adjusted his hat. 'That is to say, perhaps we could . . . step out together?'

Pleasure warmed my cheeks; I hadn't even dared to hope. But then Vernon added, 'We could take in a picture?'

A picture. Albert, the projectionist. Troubled eyes, hollow face. *Stillness and flicker, light and shadow.*

'Sounds lovely,' I said, 'but perhaps dinner instead?'

7

TO WESTDOWN CAMP

It was late on Friday afternoon, four days later. The winter sun was sinking beneath the spires of Westminster and casting a pink hue across the London skyline. Tantalising and hopeful – rather reminiscent of my current situation.

While the train snaked out of Waterloo, I settled into my compartment with a copy of *The Times*, pleased to be escaping the city's din and gloom; even more pleased to have caught a direct train to Warminster well before rush hour. All being well, three hours from now I would rendezvous with Commander Gordon Williams in Wiltshire, and, assuming he kept to the plan we had agreed, Harry Price would be there too.

As London rattled by I thought back to the telephone conversation I'd had with the stubborn mule on Tuesday.

'*You* have a worthy case for *me*?'

'Yes, commencing this Friday evening.'

'This Friday!'

'And there's a handsome fee. If you want it.'

'A handsome fee? Well.'

'Look – those are the terms, Harry.'

'A worthy case, commencing this Friday, and for a handsome fee.'

'Do you want it or not?'

His satisfaction when he had answered the phone and realised it was me had turned quickly to suspicion.

'You'll understand, Sarah, I find this a very perplexing proposition.'

'Why?'

'Don't be disingenuous. Only the other evening, you were absolutely insistent that you never wanted to work with me again.'

'I haven't changed my mind about that.'

'No? Yet here you are. Telephoning me. About a worthy case . . .'

'Don't see this for something it's not,' I replied. 'I'll give you the background, all the information you need, if – and this is imperative, Harry – *if* you do one thing for me.'

There was a pause. I pictured him ensconced in his laboratory, standing rigid and alone at the highest window, curiosity glittering in his eyes, his free hand at his side opening and clenching in defiance at the idea that somebody younger and vastly less experienced in this business he called ghost hunting was, for a change, directing *him*.

I took no pleasure in manipulating him; he was still the father of my child, and in my own way I suppose I still loved him, at least a little. Sometimes all I could think about was the magnificence of that passionate moment we had shared together. That one intoxicating, breathless night. Part of me yearned to relive the warmth of his skin against mine, the caress of his touch. Part of me even wondered: what if we had been together? A traditional family? Sometimes I'd allow myself to picture that other life, like you do when you imagine how you might spend an unexpected winning or inheritance. The problem was that imagined life didn't feel real to me. It felt like a story in a book, only one that was doomed never to have a fairy-tale ending. No matter how I rationalised it to myself, the fact remained: Harry Price was married.

Nonetheless, I needed him now. Since my conversation with Vernon I couldn't stop thinking about all that had happened recently – about the village of Imber, and that night at the cinema. And for no reason I could rationalise I felt there must be a connection between them. My mind returned to the hand-painted lantern slide I had found in the dusky gloom of the Brixton Picture Palace, how I flashed into another place, as if transported somewhere else when I touched it. Was that uncanny moment in any way connected to what was to come?

Just as I had promised myself, I had gone back to the Picture Palace to return the lantern slide to the projectionist, only to be met with a further mystery: the doors beneath the shining glass canopy were shut and chained, and attached to them a sign read Closed. It was unsettling, and so, on the telephone to Price, I made the sudden decision to deviate from my planned conversation: to first ask him about the Brixton Picture Palace and what might, or might not, have happened there.

I started with the painted lantern slide I had found on the floor of the auditorium – how picking it up had sparked in me a powerful sensation of dislocation. I finished with my conviction that there was something about this lantern slide that had attracted me to the Brixton Picture Palace in the first place; maybe a connection with the image of whoever appeared on the slide.

There was a very long pause.

'Harry?'

'You realise how this sounds?' he said, with more than a hint of scepticism.

'That's not very helpful.'

Another pause. Then he said, 'The lantern slide. Bring it with you, and I'll examine it.'

'Fine.'

'So, back to your original reason for contacting me, where exactly are we going?'

'Wiltshire. A little place called Imber.'

'Hang on.' The phone clattered down and I heard him rustling some papers in the background, probably retrieving and unfolding an Ordnance Survey map. 'Imber?' Seconds passed. 'No, no, can't see it.'

That's because it's lost, I thought. *A stolen village.*

'Sarah, your source for this assignment – is he, or she, known to you?' Price sounded dubious.

'Oh yes. And I can trust them.'

'But you won't tell me who they are?'

'No. But I will tell you what I know about the case.'

The abandoned village, former residents up in arms, the approaching church service and the soldiers too spooked to do their jobs properly – I covered the basics, knowing that deep down he wouldn't be able to resist. It was just too tantalising.

'Well, it's certainly different,' he muttered, and I surmised from his tone that he had privately resolved the matter: this investigation was about to receive his fullest attention. 'I'll pick you up on Friday at – '

'Thank you, but no. I can find my own way to Imber.'

An awkward silence. I hadn't meant to sound ungrateful, but this was a matter of pride.

And that was how I came to be sitting alone in a train compartment on Friday afternoon, gazing out of the window at the city, and then its outskirts, and then mile upon mile of idyllic countryside, a patchwork of fields and woodland beneath a sky of orange and gold – so serene, with no hint of the strange and dark terrors to come.

The solitude and silence afforded an opportunity to prepare myself for the case. Keen to familiarise myself with some of its finer and more sensitive details, I drew from my small suitcase the letter I had received that week from Commander Gordon Williams and read it over a second time.

Dear Miss Grey,

On behalf of the War Office, I am obliged to you for arranging our meeting this weekend with the Honorary Chairman of the National Laboratory for Psychical Research Mr Price has already sent word to inform us that he will arrive by car on Friday and that your train is expected in Warminster by seven o'clock that evening, at which time a car will be waiting to bring you the remaining distance to Westdown Camp – the base for soldiers training on the Plain and the home of the Defence Infrastructure Organisation.

Before your journey, I should like to impress on you the importance of our meeting and the subjects under discussion being regarded with the utmost sensitivity. I realise that I have initiated this meeting through a newspaper reporter, but I should tell you now that upon your departure, nothing you see or hear in Imber is to be discussed in public.

You have already heard that we need your unique expertise, but you should be aware that I do not lend any credence whatsoever to the more outlandish stories associated with our abandoned village, and I fully expect your investigation to vindicate that view. If we are dealing with a practical joker, I dearly hope Mr Price will identity the perpetrator, so that they may be punished, and so we may continue with the planned opening of Imber to its former residents and their families on Imber Service Day.

Finally, it is my duty to warn you that you will be travelling into an active military training area, which is extremely dangerous to civilians. Imber is located within a desolate parcel of land, a dip on the Plain, and the village is used by full-time professional soldiers and by the Territorial Army, army students and cadets from all over the region. Many people are surprised, even cynical, when they hear that Imber and its the surrounding areas are littered with unexploded debris. Live ammo, unexploded grenades and the like. Why would you endanger your own soldiers, they ask?

The answer is that the village is located within a live firing range on Salisbury Plain. We do our utmost to clear the range at appropriate times, but beyond the public roads, there are always substantial risks, and we should remain mindful of them.

Should you miss your rendezvous in Warminster, you should telephone Westdown Camp and ask for me. You should not, under any circumstances, attempt the journey alone.

On that note, I wish you a safe journey. I look forward to meeting with you.

Yours sincerely,
Commander Gordon Williams

— 8 —

STRANGERS AT DUSK

'Excuse me, miss?'

I opened my eyes gradually. The train manager – tubby, but smartly attired in his fitted green waistcoat – was at my compartment door. Stirring, I reached for my bag to present my ticket.

'Not necessary,' he said primly. 'My apologies, miss.'

'For what?' I asked, and then I realised – the train had stopped.

'There's danger up ahead, along the line. Will be a while before we can set off again.'

I turned to the window, peering past my reflection. The quiet twilight seeped over miles of fields, giving the rugged landscape a stark, sombre look. We certainly weren't in Warminster. We weren't anywhere.

'How long, exactly? I need to reach Warminster by seven o'clock.'

The train manager checked his pocket watch, and shook his head doubtfully.

'It's Warminster where the problem's at. Most likely a fallen branch on the tracks. We'll need to divert to Dilton Marsh. If you're lucky, you can take a carriage on from there.'

'Well, actually I'm headed for the Westdown Camp, and eventually Imber.'

His eyes widened. 'Visiting a soldier friend, are you?'

I thought it better to avoid that question. 'Imber sounds a fascinating place,' I said, hoping he might offer some useful information. 'A whole village out there, so isolated, abandoned and forgotten.'

Apparently, that was a poor choice of words.

'It may be abandoned,' he said, with a trace of hostility, 'but Imber is not forgotten.' He shook his head resentfully. 'Bloody soldiers. What right did they have, eh?'

I nodded, to imply I agreed with his view. Then I tried again: 'Still, I've never actually been to a lost village before.'

He bristled visibly. 'The village is not lost either, miss. You'd do well to remember that. Imber is where it always was, waiting for its people to come home.'

As the train manager had predicted, we were diverted to Dilton Marsh: a poor excuse for a station, looking half-abandoned and consigned to the deepest Wiltshire countryside. I descended from the train there, cursing whatever 'danger' had obstructed the line as I found myself standing alone on the platform. The other passengers must have alighted at the previous stations when I was fast asleep. Ahead of me, a few isolated gas lamps washed the platform in an eerie glow and lit a solitary sign at the exit: 'Time is important to the City Worker. "Dead-on" arrivals, please, passengers.'

I was twenty minutes behind schedule already. Commander

Williams' car would be waiting for me in Warminster, but that was two miles away, and the cold was like an ice pick in my bones. Even if the army did learn about the diverted train and sent a car on for me, I hardly relished the prospect of waiting here alone, in the cold, at this morbidly depressing platform, listening to the wind and the wires in the mere hope that someone would come for me.

I made my way along the platform, determining that the sensible thing to do now was to wait until the next train arrived and perhaps find someone to give me a lift on to Warminster. Or, if I could find the stationmaster, he might be good enough to telephone Westdown Camp on my behalf.

Ahead of me, at the end of the platform and looking down the track, was a figure in a black uniform. This, I soon learned, was indeed the stationmaster, but to my dismay he was less than helpful. Apparently, there would be no more trains diverted here this evening – no trains at all.

'This is an ill-frequented route, miss,' he explained. 'Trains only stop here on request. And this service terminates here.'

'Is there a telephone I could use?'

He shook his head. Apparently, the line was down. 'Only temporarily,' he added.

I gave him a look, conveying my bewildered frustration. What a complete farce! Now what was I to do? That was the question running through my mind as I gathered up my case and bag and emerged from the station into a quiet country lane.

No houses visible. No motor cars. No people.

There was clearly only one direction to take.

Should I try walking? If I was lucky, someone would pass me and offer me a lift, or at least show me the way to the barracks.

The thought passed through my mind that traversing country lanes unaccompanied might not be so wise for a young woman, especially now dusk was falling. How many stories had I read in the newspapers of women mugged – or worse, raped and strangled?

But then I thought, what are the chances, really, of something bad happening to me? In London, during the summer months, Mother was constantly telling me not to walk home from town when darkness fell, but I did, often, and time and time again nothing happened.

Far too often we fear the unknown, but if there was one thing I had learned from working with Harry Price, wasn't it this: that sometimes, the unknown just felt right? Seductive and dangerous, maybe – yet sometimes it still felt right. Exciting.

Besides, what choice did I have? Commander Williams' letter had advised me not to make the journey on foot and alone. Fair enough. But there was no one else around.

Resolutely I set off along the deserted country lane that wound its way through high, spiky hedgerows stripped bare by winter; but as the hedge dropped away on my right side, I was brought to an abrupt halt by a geographical marvel: a vast expanse of utter wilderness which stretched to meet the brooding sky.

Salisbury Plain.

Dusk was creeping over the chalk valleys and the coarse open grasslands, but in the trembling light I could still make out the shapes of the burial mounds and Iron Age hill forts that fringed the distant and craggy slopes. At my feet, the goosegrass gave way to an exposed patch of white chalk, which was gleaming eerily in the fading light.

A breeze carried drifting scents of wild thyme and chalk dust. For a moment, all was utterly silent, but after a few seconds the song of a skylark made itself heard, and then a different, less peaceful sound: the rumble of distant artillery fire.

I flinched. Somewhere out there, hidden in a low valley, were the fragmentary remains of Britain's loneliest village.

I scanned the darkening landscape. A vast expanse of nothingness. Then, in the distance, a single spire soaring out of a gully. Imber church?

Had I seen that spire before? Was it *the* church?

It had been eighteen years since I had last set foot on Salisbury Plain, when my father had brought me here in that hard winter when war broke out. I still remembered we had happened by chance upon a village funeral. But – and this was crucial – I did not remember the name of the village, or why we had come.

Logic told me my father already knew he was to be sent here, to train in one of the camps or secret establishments with the other soldiers who were to be sent into battle. I thought he would be back within the year – that was what Mother had said – but one year turned into two. Three. Four. And before the war was over, the telegram that had haunted my mother's dreams dropped through our letter box and changed our lives forever.

I wondered: had my father entered Imber after the evacuation? Had he trained there? Was I now following his footsteps?

I tried to imagine the thousands of waterlogged trenches that would have been dug out here, then pounded by shellfire; the explosions that rocked the villages hidden within the folds of the downs. What I associated most with our trip here were the uncanny stories I had heard at school: stories of witches in the woods, ghostly hellhounds, spirit highwaymen and the like. The sort of unsettling legends that are smiled at and then promptly dismissed. But there was one girl who delighted in repeating these stories long after the others had lost interest. I can see her now: short, stocky, with more of a boy's physique than a girl's, and a shock of dark ginger hair that never looked clean. 'Hellish Dawn' we used to call her, due to her insistence that an unseen troublesome spirit was scratching blasphemous messages into the surface of her school desk. None of us believed that, not really, but Hellish Dawn had a way of almost convincing you that such an impossible thing really might be true. It was her low voice, her sinister expression and the way she used exact place names and dates to add that extra splash of colour. Now, as I walked the dark lane beside a long row of trees, one of her disquieting tales about Salisbury Plain slid into my mind: a legend she had insisted was authentic. Even now I remember the set, tense look on her face as she warned me of 'the drummer boy's horrible revenge'.

The story went something like this:

Hundreds of years ago, whilst wandering on the slopes of the downs, a sailor recently returned from the sea heard the patter of a drum coming from the woods:

Rat ta rat tat. Rat ta rat tat.

Upon investigating, the sailor encountered a little drummer boy near a lone, crooked signpost. Except it wasn't a boy, not quite. More shadow than flesh, his shape seemed to flicker as he glided near. But this wasn't what made the blood in the man's veins run cold: it was the trickles of blood running from the boy's eyes and the gaping wound across his throat.

Rat ta rat tat, went the little boy's drum.

Stricken with terror, the sailor collapsed. When he recovered, the drummer boy had vanished.

Forever haunted by the soft patter of the drum, the sailor eventually publicly confessed that before his last excursion at sea he had abused his son, then murdered him. The sailor's punishment was just: swift execution by hanging.

And the little drummer boy drifted with him all the way to the gallows.

'It's said that on winter nights, that little drummer boy still roams the windswept plain,' Hellish Dawn had told me, not knowing I had recently visited that very plain.

A rural legend. I hadn't thought of it in years, but as I turned and carried on along the country lane I could not suppress an uneasy shiver. The enormous sky was now less orange and pink, more an inky violet. As daylight faded and I made my way along the deserted gravel track, the image of that boy, throat slit, blood running from his eyes, loomed so fearfully in my imagination, so lucidly, that I kept glancing behind me. Silly, of course.

I arrived at a lonely junction cut by a small, triangular island of rough grass. Alone. Dispirited. I lifted my gaze to a signpost jutting out of the earth like a gnarled sapling. Its three crooked arms pointed the way to destinations that were impossible to make out under clots of moss and flaking paint.

Which way?

For a few minutes, I stood in the freezing twilight, waiting to see if a car or carriage might come along. None did.

Sighing with annoyance, I thought of Harry Price's collection of Ordnance Survey Maps. I had been stupid not to buy my own and bring it – and, for that matter, more sensible clothes, for the wind had become numbingly cold. What's more, the light was fading fast, the trees throwing their jagged shadows over the chalky dust. I hadn't expected to feel so vulnerable, but that was exactly how I did feel: helpless, and increasingly uneasy. I was alone, at night, at risk in the wilderness. In centuries past, solitary travellers like me wandering these tracks would have been easy pickings for the highwaymen.

I had to get to Westdown Camp. Fast.

To my left was thick woodland of green and black. To my right, nothing but bleak and stark countryside.

I looked back at the weather-battered sign, pulled my rough wax coat around me and took the middle road, keeping to its right side along a furrowed bank.

As I walked, quickly now, I tried to summon an image of a waiting bed, with fluffed pillows and a heavy quilt. Then every hair on my body prickled at the sound of twigs snapping loudly behind me.

I spun round, tightening my grip on my case as I scanned the dark spaces between the trees for any sign of life. A deer perhaps? A rabbit?

No.

There, at the edge of the wall of pine trees, about ten feet away, was the shadowy profile of a frail, emaciated figure. A human figure, hunched close to the exposed roots of trees, as if it had just clawed its way out of the pitch-black dirt.

I felt my jaw slacken with shock as the figure slowly, and in complete silence, raised itself up and stood, its head moving left to right, left to right.

It looked like a child. Yes, a little boy.

An icy chill swept up from the ground and into me. *It's the drummer boy. Any moment now I'll hear the* rat-tat-tat *of his drum.*

Unable to rip my gaze away from this astonishing apparition, I took in every detail the shifting twilight would allow. Rags covering his legs, and he seemed to be naked from the waist up. Arms not just thin, but painfully wasted. Belly bloated, as if from starvation. Ribs protruding through stretched skin streaked with dirt. Hair jet black, hanging tangled around a narrow face that was gaunt, sunken, and as white as wax.

But the worst were his eye sockets: I remember thinking with something close to horror that they were like coal-black pits.

He looked . . . hopeless. Disorientated.

My fear was eliminated in an instant, replaced by anger. This was no phantom; it was a young boy, no more than seven or eight. What was he doing out here, and in such a state?

Taking a cautious step towards him, I said, 'Hello? Can I help you?'

Quick as a snake, he shrank back under the cover of the trees and bracken.

'Where are your parents? Do you hear me?'

No words, only the hint of his bleached white face still visible across from me on the opposite side of the lane. I began looking about in the futile hope that some passer-by was in sight. Someone who might help.

At that instant, a nesting crow broke free of the trees, flapping furiously, screeching, and the silence all around was punctuated by a distressing shriek – the child's shriek – so sharp that my heart almost spasmed.

I ran to him then, going against every impulse to run in the opposite direction and escape this dismal place. I dashed *towards* the boy – and into the road.

And that was when I heard the rumble of a motor car bearing down on me as if from out of nowhere.

Startled, I tripped on the hem of my skirt and fell roughly

on my side. Everything stopped. The screech of brakes made
me wince and shut my eyes, steeling myself for the worst.

All that followed, though, was a wave of relief.

The driver had stopped in time.

I felt a sudden cold concern for the boy as I remembered
his piteous shriek, his widening, fearful eyes.

My own eyes snapped open and I saw, in my peripheral
vision, a bobbing storm lantern held high by an approaching
figure, and a handsome black motor car that had drawn up in
the road just a metre or so away from where I lay.

'Miss, miss, are you all right?'

'There's . . . there's a child,' I cried, panic shooting through
me as the stranger helped me to my feet. 'We must go to him!'

The man – tall and attired in a well-tailored dark suit –
looked to where I was pointing wildly, the ink-black place
between the trees where the boy stood. *Had* stood. For he was
gone now, I saw.

Turning back to me, the man removed his driver's cap and
scratched his bald head.

'I'm telling you, he was right there,' I insisted.

A flash of confused alarm in the stranger's eyes.

'Well? Sir, didn't you see him? You *must* have seen him!'

'I saw no one, miss.' He shook his head to reinforce the
point. 'No one.'

– 9 –

IMBER'S PROTECTOR

I gazed out of the side window of my rescuer's Bentley and saw in the distance that the vast darkness was punctuated by bright red flags, presumably marking no-go areas where the army fired live rounds of ammunition. The wind was tugging at the car, but it was a sturdy vehicle and I felt quite safe. It almost seemed that my interrupted journey might never have happened, were it not for the guilt that was steadily staining my conscience as we motored across the desolate downs, heading for Westdown Camp.

We should have searched for the child, I told myself, over and over.

The well-spoken stranger who had found me in the road had been so concerned by the wretched state of my nerves, so worried he had almost driven right into me, that he was far less interested in entertaining the possibility that a child he hadn't seen – a helpless child, lost and starving – was roaming the plain.

'We must telephone at once for the police,' I said to him now, but his eyes refused to meet mine. 'Did you hear what I said?'

'Miss, you've had quite a shock. That's entirely my fault, but I think perhaps you were mistaken about what you saw,' he answered.

I shook my head decisively, struggling to suppress my frustration.

'Even if you're right, I have lived here my whole life, and I assure you, it's not uncommon for locals in these parts to allow their children to wander the downs.'

'But the boy looked desperately unwell,' I insisted, recalling his jutting ribs, his eyes like charcoal. 'And I heard heavy shellfire across the ranges!'

My driver shook his head. 'Doubtful. Artillery fire normally ceases at four o'clock. But even if you did, it's quite safe for civilians to walk in this area, so long as they don't stray past the red flags. Most of the ranges nearby are well secured. If a civilian were at risk – a little boy, for example – one of the wardens would have seen him and raised the alarm. Take my word for it, they are extremely vigilant.'

'Oh,' I said, 'I see . . .'

I straightened up. I had meant to address him formally, but in my agitation, I had quite forgotten the name he had given when he offered to drive me to the camp. Embarrassment warming my cheeks, I slid a sideways glance at him. His eyes were on the road ahead, giving me the opportunity to appraise him. He was bald, with a neat grey beard; his eyes were surrounded by cobwebs of lines. He had to be sixty, at least, and a man of some wealth; his signet ring was almost as impressive as his tailored dark brown tweed suit.

But that suit, although finely cut, looked a little worn. Frayed at the edges. The car, though handsome, also looked old, as if these were the trappings of a man who had known better times.

It was no good – a thorough look at him had not dislodged the memory of his name. So I asked, politely, 'Tell me again, please, who are you?'

In the manner of a polished gentleman, he replied, 'My name is Hartwell. Oscar Hartwell.'

'And I'm Sarah Grey,' I returned; it seemed only proper.

I saw his eyes flick down to my hand, to the naked ring finger. 'Miss Grey,' he said, eyes on the road once more, 'I'm curious. Why is a proper woman like yourself heading out to Westdown Camp on a Friday evening?'

My hands clenched in my lap. 'Official business. I'm helping arrange the Imber Service Day, on Sunday. It's held every year in the –'

'I know where it's held,' he said brusquely, 'and I know what it is. So, I'm assuming you're from the War Office, yes? That's a London accent.'

It was a rather large assumption, but not necessarily an unhelpful one.

Well, I could say, *I've been summoned to investigate – with the greatest psychical researcher in London – a series of unusual happenings right here on Salisbury Plain, in your own little ghost town. As you can appreciate, the army are a little sensitive about opening the village to civilians for a church service until they know exactly what they're dealing with, so they've called in the experts.*

Or maybe I would not say that.

'It's official business,' I said, 'and I'm not at liberty to –'

He cut me off then, but not with words. Without so much

as a warning, Hartwell pulled over to the side of the track and killed the engine.

'Why have we stopped?'

Silence.

Outside, the car headlights washed the chalk track ahead a gleaming white.

'Mr Hartwell?'

Again, he made no reply, his lips pressing tightly together.

With a spike of nerves in my tummy, I asked cautiously, 'What's wrong? Why have we stopped?'

But instead of answering me, he did something alarming: he killed the headlights, plunging the two of us into darkness.

The seconds felt like minutes, but eventually Hartwell spoke:

'Official business, eh? The last time officials came here from London, they stole our homes. Our village was signed over for experimental shelling. Left to crumble and rot.'

I relaxed, but only a little. I had been wondering whether I would have the opportunity to meet a former resident of Imber, and now here it was. I had expected resentment – bitterness, even. I had not expected the stinging hurt I detected in Hartwell's voice, though. This man was evidently still suffering.

'Imber was its own place,' he said to me. 'The loveliest place in the world.' He sighed heavily. 'Little Imber on the Down, seven miles from any town.'

My head jerked. That rhyme. It sounded familiar. Had Vernon mentioned it?

'We used to sing that nursery rhyme to our little ones,' he added.

'What was life like in Imber?' I asked, keeping my voice mild. 'Lonely?'

He took a moment to think about this, staring into

windscreen, as if, within its dark reflection, a picture of the village was blooming in vivid colour.

'My family looked after the villagers for hundreds of years. We drew strength from the land and one another. Seclusion bestows its own rewards, you know. That's true. We weren't hampered by pollution. We didn't suffer strikes or protests or violence. When I think back . . . Oh, how lucky we were. The cricket games on the Barley Ground, the tennis parties at Imber Court . . .'

'Your home?'

'Since I was born, in 1870,' he said wistfully. 'One of the finest manor houses in Wiltshire. Now? It's boarded up, half destroyed by boys playing at being soldiers! We had some grand dances there. My family have farmed Imber for generations. The dances marked the turning of the years for us; by the time they were done, dawn would be breaking over the downs, and my sister and I would do the milking, she in her dress, me in my tails and waistcoat.' He looked at me with utmost seriousness and said, 'Happier times. We were quite separate from the rest of the world, but that didn't mean we were lonely. Only that we depended on one another for everything.'

This man's obvious passion for his old home touched me deeply. Indeed, he struck me now as a man of character. Upright and respectable. Attractive? Yes, and it wasn't just his easy, forthright manner. The grey beard was well groomed, the nose strong. The profile aristocratic.

'I'm not from the government, sir,' I confessed, 'but I have read in the newspapers of Salisbury Plain's ghost village. What happened to the civilians who didn't want to leave?'

'The poor were paid off. Those of us who had money, who could afford legal assistance to challenge them, we were told

we *had* to leave. Those who persisted in saying no were made
to change their minds.'

'You mean through intimidation?'

'No, it went a lot further than that,' he said, with difficulty.
'Old Fred Myers left Imber with a broken arm, said something
about an accident out in the fields. Now, I'm willing to bet at
least half of that statement's true, and I'm sure you can guess
which half.' He peered at me. 'You look surprised. You must
realise the army is capable of such things.'

'I suppose so.'

'Well, they had their day. And we will have our day. You
understand? We lived to die in that village.' He nodded with
quiet purpose, one hand tightening around the steering wheel.
'Our campaign is making excellent progress. We will force an
inquiry into what they did, and reclaim what is rightfully ours.
At the very least, the roads should be reopened, and my own
land returned to me. It is my birthright.'

My curiosity grew. I asked how much of Imber's property
had belonged to him, and was impressed when he reeled off
a considerable list, including the village school and many of
the farms. Even the old mill.

'The military had its sights on Imber years before the war
came.'

'Why?'

'The village lay in the middle of an immense stretch of
land used for practising long-range shooting. And don't you
think it was a huge expense for the government, keeping open
these long, exposed roads on the downs? Just for our use?'
His bottom lip protruded and he shook his head. 'We were in
their way. And when war came, it wasn't just the artillery they
needed to test, but their tanks and guns.'

'But didn't the war effort justify the –'

'Sacrifice?' he cut in. 'We were quite prepared to do our bit. But the military assured us – they *promised* – we could return.' He paused for a few seconds, gazing down at the steering wheel. 'Promises should not be broken. When we die, it is the right of my wife and myself that we should be buried in St Giles' churchyard. Alongside our children.'

I looked questioningly at him.

'My three little girls. Lillian. Beatrice. Rosalie.'

'What happened to them?'

He shook his head. To be sure, Hartwell might be privileged and wealthy, but that had stood for nothing in the face of death; he had lost his precious children and nothing would make up for that.

'We buried Rosalie next to her sisters on the eve of the war,' he said. 'If anyone had said to me then I'd also have a boy, and that he too would perish so young, I'd never have believed it.'

'A boy?'

'Yes. After the evacuation, I had a son.'

An invisible hand clenched my heart and squeezed it: *a son . . .*

'My condolences,' I said, in barely more than a whisper. 'When did he pass?'

'Five years ago.' I heard the quaver in his voice. 'Bless his soul, just five years old.'

'You must wish you could have laid him to rest with his sisters, in Imber.'

Hartwell's head was shaking. 'But Pierre *is* buried in Imber.'

I looked at him quizzically. 'The church is out of bounds.'

'We had to obtain a special grant from the army.' He turned back to stare out of the windscreen. 'My baby girls and my son are there together. Buried in a rotting churchyard behind a barbed-wire fence. Imagine, Miss Grey. If indeed there is such a thing as life after death, my children must wonder why I don't tend their graves more than once a year, why I don't pray in the church where their funerals were held. They must wonder that, don't you think?'

I didn't know how to answer that. It seemed cruel to suggest his children's spirits did wonder at his absence; crueller still, though, to suggest the spirits did not exist.

Hartwell did not seem to require a response; he switched on the engine and our journey to Westdown Camp resumed.

When we reached the rutted track that led to the camp, I took great interest in the surroundings. This was where the soldiers lived; ahead was a guard hut, planted conspicuously next to a bright yellow wooden barrier. Beyond that, lookout towers and various hangars showed austere shapes against the gigantic purple sky. But the spot was so remote it must seldom receive visitors, especially at this hour.

It was eight thirty. Most likely Price and Commander Williams would be wondering what had become of me.

A uniformed soldier in the guard hut nearby looked on as we rolled to a halt just a few metres away from the barrier. I thought how suspicious we must look to him.

Hartwell killed the engine.

'Let me help you out,' he said, opening his side door, but I quickly pre-empted the gesture by getting out of the Bentley and walking around to him. We stood in the cold spitting rain, which had just begun to fall. The wind gusted around me, carrying the distant echoes of soldiers' voices and the rumble of a truck's engine. I was about to say thank you and goodbye, but Hartwell was looking at me earnestly, and I sensed he was about to unburden himself of a question he had been longing to ask. I was right.

'The child you think you saw, tonight on the road. Describe him.'

I did so, shivering as I recalled the wretched boy, the coal-black eye sockets, the distended stomach. It did not escape my attention that as Hartwell listened his face tensed and paled.

He glanced at the soldier, now standing at the door of the guard hut, and then looked at me steadily. 'My advice, my strong advice, is to tell no one what you saw this night. It will be better that way. Do you understand?'

I didn't.

'Do you know the boy?' I asked. 'His family?'

'Please,' he said, 'forget what you saw.' He began to stride back to his car, but then turned and called, loudly enough for the soldier to hear, 'And Miss Grey, be careful not to trust anyone in that camp. For your own sake, don't trust *anything* they tell you.'

INKED PROMISES

Beyond the barrier and the guard hut was the sprawling army camp: a jumble of prefabricated steel huts arcing low from the ground, barracks with green roofs and concrete office buildings around a wide air strip.

I was hungry. My limbs were rigid with cold and ached with exhaustion from the journey, but I was relieved to be here, finally, as a soldier drove me in a Rover past a watchtower and along a well-lit track that led to the largest concrete building, its windows netted with metal mesh.

This must be the camp where they brought Father, when war broke out.

Retracing his footsteps. The only difference was that I had chosen to come here. For him, a stint at Westdown Camp had been decreed, just like the banishment of the people of Imber.

Inside Central Security Control, a narrow, stark corridor strung with lamps led to a doorway with a nameplate on it: 'Commander Gordon Williams'.

'Wait here,' said my guide, before striding away.

Somewhere far off a telephone was ringing. Somewhere else a typewriter was clacking out a memo. I stood alone in the corridor, thinking about Oscar Hartwell. He was a bit peculiar. I couldn't put out of my mind his initial lack of interest in the wandering child; but then, as we had parted company, he had seemed to accept that I had seen the boy and to imply . . . what?

There was no sign of the soldier who had brought me here. I looked back at the office door. *I should knock.* My hand formed a fist and hovered over the door.

'I know you from somewhere, don't I?'

I started and swung round to see a wiry gentleman in a khaki military uniform standing beside me. He wore a pair of small silver wire spectacles, their frames so perfectly round that when they caught the light his eyes looked like a pair of shining coins. His hair was white, his face sunken and thin; his hands were gnarled, the skin raw and cracked and blistered in places. I didn't think this was the commander who had summoned us here, but whoever he was, he exuded an air of stern authority.

'Yes, I *do* know you from somewhere,' he repeated, his eyes searching. 'I never forget a face.'

'I'm Miss Grey. I'm here to see the commander. Perhaps you could let him know I'm here? I've had the most frightful journey and – '

'The commander is speaking to your associate,' he said.

Price? What did he think was doing, seeing the commander without me? What were they discussing?

'You wait here,' the white-haired man instructed.

There seemed little else to do but reply, 'All right. Thank you.'

He turned abruptly and marched away along the corridor. As I watched him go I rubbed at the gooseflesh on my arms – and then flinched when the door next to me suddenly opened inwards. Price's face loomed towards me.

'Sarah! I was here at seven o'clock, as instructed' – he tapped his wristwatch testily – 'seven, on the *dot*. It's almost a quarter to nine now. Where the hell have you – '

I raised a hand to silence him. 'Harry, however inconvenienced you've been tonight, let me assure you I've had it far worse.' I was feeling rather unsettled and unkempt in my blackened skirt, sullied by my fall in the road, and I saw now that the hem had ripped.

I snatched up my case. 'Tell me – is there somewhere appropriate I might change?'

Price winced slightly. He looked back over his shoulder, at the open door behind him, then resumed a more professional tone, lowering his voice and ushering me away from the office.

'Sarah, there's no need to be so short with me. We're a team, remember?'

'For a *few days*, yes, we're a team. After that, we go our separate ways.'

He looked wounded, but I wasn't buying it.

'Look at me, Harry. I'm absolutely filthy! I need to freshen up. Do you know where I'm staying?'

His eyes narrowed.

He opened his mouth to reply, but it wasn't his voice that followed. The voice I heard was deeper, loaded with authority.

'No time.'

I shifted to look over Price's shoulder, into the room. A tall soldier decorated with medals was standing next to a grand desk, regarding me severely. His military bearing was enhanced by his neat moustache and a thin scar running through his left eyebrow.

'*You* are late, Miss Grey, and our problem will not wait.'

Commander Williams' office was spacious but stank of tobacco. The concrete walls were decorated with military plaques, awards and framed photographs of soldiers in uniform. I sat down before the wide desk, with Price beside me. Commander Williams stood across from us, gesturing to a detailed map of Salisbury Plain.

'You'll be heading to Imber at first dawn,' he told us, pointing at a red circle looped around an area I assumed was the village. 'Artillery fire will be suspended, of course, and after that you'll have twenty-four hours to conduct your . . . *investigation*.' The word sounded strained. We were here with the commander's permission, yes, but evidently he had given it with reluctance. 'I won't pretend that your presence here is convenient, Mr Price, but the safety of the Imber civilians must take precedence this weekend. The army has a duty of care, and – '

'So, what's the military up to on Salisbury Plain, hmm?' Price interrupted, gesturing to the wall map. 'There's no war on, no immediate threat to the nation's security. What are you hiding here?'

The commander grimaced. 'You sound almost as paranoid as Mr Churchill, with his incessant war-mongering speeches.'

'Oh,' Price laughed, 'I'm the most paranoid man you'll ever meet, commander, which is why you were supremely wise to call me in. Well, never mind, we'll find out soon enough.' He settled back in his seat, folded his arms and said seriously, 'You're familiar with the finer aspects of my work, I assume?'

'I know you hunt ghosts.'

'Not exactly.'

'It is fairer to say, commander, that Harry here has a half-believing, half-doubting attitude towards spiritualism,' I explained. 'Indeed, he considers the subject worthy of the most serious attention. Isn't that correct, Harry?'

Price nodded. 'Determining the truth about life after death? There could be no greater mission, nothing more important to our understanding of the world.'

'At the same time, Harry thinks we should be on our guard against our desire to believe.'

The commander eyed Price speculatively. 'I'm told, Mr Price, that you can reduce the most convincing accounts of so called supernormal activity to the most mundane explanations. I certainly hope that's true, because we need answers, quickly.' He tilted his chin back, eyeing Price's cashmere overcoat, his black silk necktie. 'Have you consulted with any branch of the armed services before?'

I was almost certain the answer to this question was no. And it would be another nine years before Price became involved again with the military, in November 1941 – the Helen Duncan affair. A spiritualist claimed the ghost of a sailor had informed her that the HMS *Durham* had been sunk, and because she had no conceivable way of possessing that knowledge, the military investigated. Eventually, they charged her with conspiracy to contravene the Witchcraft Act, worried about further leaks. And who was it that so ruthlessly revealed Helen's trickery and helped secure the damning verdict? Helen Duncan had Harry Price to thank for being branded a traitor, for her nine-month stretch in prison. If you believe the reports – and I do – she was dragged down to the cells screaming, 'This is all lies. What are they doing to me?'

'Actually, this is the first occasion I have been called upon to advise the armed forces,' Price told the commander.

Williams nodded, opened his desk drawer and drew out two neatly typed sheets of paper bearing the insignia of the War Office. 'You are to sign these,' he said, handing one paper to Price and the other to me, and plucking two white-gold fountain pens – Pelikan originals – from a pot on his desk. 'The Official Secrets Act.'

Price and I exchanged a glance.

'I will sign this,' said Price, scanning his paper, 'however, I must insist upon complete access to every part of the Imber Range, and complete and total access to relevant witnesses and information.'

Nothing but withering silence from the commander.

'Right then,' said Price awkwardly. He cleared his throat, and scrawled his dramatic, upsweeping signature.

With a twinge of doubt, I followed suit. A promise inked in blue. At the time I fully intended to keep that promise; not for a moment did it occur to me that I would one day break it by writing this account. But how was I to know, then, the extremities of the bizarre and irrefutable world we were about to enter? Of the sinister, harrowing events that would ensue?

Once we had handed the forms back to the commander, he rose and shut them away in a bulky filing cabinet brimming with official documents. Only then did he turn his stern attention back to Price and say firmly, 'Any access you and Miss Grey are granted within this establishment will be strictly on a need-to-know basis. Everything you will see and hear is classified as top secret, and when you leave, you will say nothing.' He glanced down at me and added, 'Not to *anyone* – especially members of the press.'

I understood that he was referring to Vernon, but I was relieved he didn't mention the reporter by name; Price would have been furious. He gave the commander a petulant look and said in a strained tone, 'What I want most, commander, is to understand what has happened to Sergeant Gregory Edwards.'

The commander sat down, drawing a breath.

'I'll come to that. It bothers me immensely to admit it, but bizarre sightings are commonplace round these parts. Indeed, many tales are told amongst the soldiers of happenings in the village.'

'All right then,' Price said, somehow managing to sound both bored and engaged. He leaned back in his chair and stretched his legs out. He glanced sideways at me as if to say, *Take notes, Sarah*, and looked slighted when he saw I already had my pen and pad on my lap.

Keeping one step ahead of him now – that was the only way I was going to get through this.

'I should say, to begin with, that Imber is no stranger to the macabre,' Williams told us. 'You'll see the war memorial on your route to the church. Now, many of the cottages are said to be haunted by former villagers, killed during the last war. Some of my men swear they've seen glowing balls of light, flitting through the village after dark.'

'Hunters carrying lanterns?' Price proposed. 'Reckless individuals straying onto the range when they think you're not watching?'

'No. Our men have pursued these lights on foot, repeatedly. Never once have they encountered hunters. Only these balls of light, the size of tennis balls, they tell me. Lights which display every sign of sentient control.'

I remembered the glowing orb the projectionist at the cinema had told me he had seen floating through the darkened auditorium. Hadn't that light had a rational explanation? Quite possibly, these lights would also be easily explained, but at that moment I was finding it difficult to imagine how. The curiosity must have shown on my face, because just then Williams looked directly at me.

'The real troubles began in and around the Imber church, right in the middle of a training exercise with live ammunition. We had to sound the emergency, call it all off.'

'Why?'

'Because there were intruders in the churchyard. Civilians. Women.'

'What were these women doing?' I asked.

'According to our observers,' the commander said, 'they were tending a grave. Except, as you will soon discover, the churchyard, like the church itself, is permanently locked. Cordoned off by a high fence. And when our men ceased fire and the range warden investigated, he found no one, despite making an extensive search. Then . . .'

Price's climbing eyebrows begged the obvious question.

'The church bells rang. According to Imber folklore, the church bells will only ring when the village is returned to its citizens, or' – he hesitated – 'when a great tragedy is due to befall Imber.'

Superstition. Price was silent, but I could see the familiar glint of scepticism in his eyes.

'Like you, I was doubtful,' Williams said. 'But I myself have heard the long, hollow notes of the church bells, sometimes during the day, mostly after nightfall. They toll seven times, as if for a funeral. Since the women were seen, the churchyard has developed an unfortunate reputation for being haunted, as well as the wooded area behind it. There's a track leading up there – Carrion Pit Lane.'

That name. An unpleasant shiver went through me. I ignored it.

'Some of the more compelling accounts have been reported by soldiers training in precisely that area. They describe an eerie, uncomfortable sensation of being watched. Some even reckon they've seen a ravenous black dog roaming the woods.'

'It's quite possible they have,' I said. 'But roaming strays hardly justify a scientific investigation.'

'What else?' Price asked, but he wasn't looking at the commander. Instead, his gaze was fixed on some framed formal photographs of soldiers on the office wall.

'Soldiers have reported hearing music coming from the church, laughter from the abandoned pub. Phantom gunshots. Distressed cries of men and women being evicted from their homes. Even phantom fires, producing no heat and no smoke.'

Price's full attention was on the commander now. 'Do *you* believe these are genuine hauntings?' he asked.

'I didn't say that,' the commander said, after a pause, 'but shadowy human figures have been seen, roaming the empty lanes.'

Any reports of a wandering child with charcoal eyes? I wondered. I hoped not. God, I hoped not.

'A few soldiers have observed a large, hunched figure lumbering through the village, dragging behind him a long object – a sledgehammer. Some of the more imaginative men believe this figure is the ghost of the last person to leave Imber.'

'And who was that?'

'Silas Wharton. He was Imber's blacksmith. His family left a note on the church door. We kept it there, out of respect.'

Price let those last words hang in the air for a few moments before saying, 'I assume Mr Wharton is dead?'

'According to our records, the blacksmith disappeared during the eviction. There's a story that when Wharton heard he had to leave, he was found by his wife, crying like a baby over his anvil. His family believed he went off to die of a broken heart, that before he vanished he had sworn never to abandon the place. Some of my men have heard his hammer in the village, the distinct sound of metal striking metal.'

A withering look from Price. These were the sorts of urban myths he heard all too frequently, hardly subjects deserving of sober, scientific inquiry. Maybe that was why his attention seemed to be drifting again. He was gazing intently once more at the wall, at a photograph of young men in military uniforms, standing rigid, their faces blank.

The commander's stern tone brought him back: 'Well, are you still adamant you can explain what's happening on the range, Mr Price?'

'It would be more instructive if you would tell us what *you* believe.'

'I sure as hell don't believe in ghosts, Mr Price. The world is sufficiently topsy-turvy without indulging in this sort of thing. No, what scares me most is that my men could be losing their judgement, letting their imaginations run riot. We operate a live firing range in Imber. The physical conditions are designed to test a man's endurance, physically and emotionally. Perhaps' – he looked reluctant to admit the possibility – 'perhaps we've pushed some of the men too far.'

Price considered this for a moment. 'As to the root cause, there is another possibility, commander.'

'And what's that?'

'Deception. Orchestrated by someone *outside* the camp.'

'Civilians? Impossible. Security on the Imber range is fail-safe.'

Price met his eye. Forced a smile. 'The problem with fail-safe security, commander, is that sooner or later it always needs upgrading.'

'You're suggesting my men are the victims of a hoax?'

'Difficult to say, but if it is true, whoever is behind it will have a precise motive.'

'You sound very certain.'

'I am seldom mistaken,' Price replied.

Clearly, the months we had spent apart had done nothing to dent Price's egotism. He was nodding to himself with that trademark resolute confidence. Even so, I couldn't help but admire his uncompromising scepticism.

'The motive could be financial, or more likely emotional,' he went on. 'The mistreatment of the former villagers at the hands of the army, perhaps? Either way, the motive will emerge over time, yes, I feel sure. And when it does, I will take great satisfaction in bringing it to your attention.'

Just then there came a sharp rap at the door.

'Enter.'

From our seats, we looked round. It was the white-haired man from earlier. He had the distinct and unsettling air of an undertaker.

'This is Eric Sidewinder, our senior range warden with responsibility for Imber.'

Sidewinder nodded at Price with a faint contempt. As he

advanced into the room, I found myself wondering if he had been listening at the door, and if so, for how long. He caught my eye, and something flickered behind those coin-like spectacles.

Perhaps he does look familiar . . .

'It's time,' Sidewinder announced to the commander, who stood at once.

'Sickbay are ready for us,' he said, gesturing for us to stand. 'Like yourself, Mr Price, I am prepared to discount most of the stories about Imber. But what happened to Sergeant Edwards leaves even me at loss for answers. He is awake now. I will take you to him.'

He ushered us out of the office and led the way along dimly lit concrete corridors. We passed a dormitory crammed with beds on which soldiers slept. Again, I wondered about Father – had he slept here? Had he walked down this very corridor?

A question occurred to me: was my being here some sort of bizarre cosmic anomaly? An enigmatic attempt by the universe to draw me closer to the man who had meant so much to me? Price had a word for that phenomenon, didn't he – what was it?

'Sarah?'

I gave a small start at Price's inquisitive tone.

'What's the matter?'

I shook my head, feigning ignorance.

'You looked very far off there for a moment,' he said, with a mixture of concern and impatience.

'No, no, I'm quite all right,' I said, attempting a smile, but as I did so, the word I had been reaching for came back to me. *Synchronicity*. Meaningful coincidence.

The idea had a certain mystical appeal, especially the more I pictured my father pacing these stark corridors, but before I could ponder the matter a second longer, the commander

brought me back to the more immediate mystery: the traumatising events that had befallen Sergeant Gregory Edwards.

'Edwards was on a map-reading exercise in the Imber woods
last October when he was involved in an ... accident. Since
then, he has kept almost permanent counsel with the Reverend
Paul Davies, who visits him daily here at the camp. You should
prepare yourselves. Edwards doesn't look or behave as he once
did. He can be unpredictable. I advise you not to get too close.'

That sounded serious to me, but as we hastened along the
corridor, Price merely smiled. 'I wonder what wild stories your
man will tell us, commander. Screams in the woods? Female
shades – grey ladies and the like – waiting in the trees to lure
men to their death perhaps?' He chuckled and said dismissively, 'Superstitions, of course. Just stories.'

Warden Sidewinder, who was walking along with us, had
been silent until now, but he came to an abrupt halt and said
with cold authority, 'Mr Price, you should know better than
anyone that superstitions are *not* just stories.'

'Oh, then what are they?'

Sidewinder's mouth tightened. 'Warnings, Mr Price.
Superstitions are warnings.'

THE HAUNTING OF SERGEANT GREGORY EDWARDS

When the heavy door slammed shut behind us, the hunched, bull-necked man kneeling with his back to us didn't even flinch. I took in our surroundings. We had been told that this cramped and featureless concrete room, with its narrow iron bed, was the sergeant's 'private rehabilitation room', but it looked more like a cell to me, somewhere convenient to hide an embarrassing secret.

'Edwards,' the commander said, 'we have some visitors who wish to speak to you.'

The sergeant kept his back to us, his head lowered as he whispered a private prayer to a miniature figurine of Saint Anthony carrying a cross and the infant Jesus.

'Edwards?' No reply. The commander turned to me then and said quietly, 'Remember, miss, keep your distance.'

My stomach tightened. Why was Sidewinder, standing apart

from us, staring so curiously at me? Was he trying to make me feel unwelcome? Intimidated?

I never forget a face . . .

'Edwards?' the commander said again.

This time the whispered prayer fell silent. Slowly, Edwards stirred; murmuring something, he lifted his head. I flinched, because I saw now that the light brown hair on his scalp was terribly thin, frayed and wispy. Missing in swirling, ragged patches.

'We promise not to take much of your time . . .' Price began, stepping around Edwards and looking down, but then he froze.

What is it? What's wrong?

Price glared at the commander. 'Why the hell didn't you tell us about this?'

And now I was able to see, as Edwards turned and blinked up into the light.

I gasped and said, behind the hand that had flown to my mouth, 'Oh my Lord.' I tried not to stare at the poor man's face, or at least what was left of it. An accident? Edwards had been severely burned. The flames hadn't just taken his ears and his nose, they had swollen his lips to a crust and burned what skin remained a fierce, raw red.

'Who are you?' Edwards asked, in a low, cracked voice. Just speaking those three words seemed a painful effort for him.

'I have been asked to help,' Price said. 'I'm a scientist.'

The sergeant's pitted eyes targeted the commander. 'Ah, finally you do something,' he said accusingly. He made a sound – it may have been a mocking laugh, it may have been a sob. 'No one can help,' he said. 'It's too late for me. Too late for Imber.'

Price had recovered from his shock much faster than I. 'How?' he asked in a level tone.

The sergeant bowed his head into shadow, as if he were too ashamed to explain. Or perhaps too frightened.

'He sustained these injuries roughly one year ago,' said the commander. His tone was matter-of-fact, but not without sympathy. 'During a map-reading training exercise late in the day, Sergeant Edwards here became separated from the rest of the men. We found him the next morning, unconscious. It was a wonder he survived.'

'Where did this happen?' Price asked. 'I mean, where exactly?'

'In the woodlands flanking Imber, at the very edge of the range.'

'Near the old mill,' Sergeant Edwards added, without looking up.

'Talk us through it,' I said gently. 'We can't take away your suffering, sir, but we may be able to prevent what happened to you from happening to anyone else.'

No reply.

I wanted to reassure the sergeant. Foolishly forgetting the commander's warning, I reached down to put a comforting hand on Edwards' shoulder. What happened then occurred so quickly it was a blur. What I remember most is the commander's panicked shout: 'Miss Grey, *no!*'

'Sarah!'

Sergeant Edwards pounced at me, lashing out with clawed fingers. I felt his fingernails – sharp – digging into my neck as the room tilted back. Then my head hit the concrete floor with a crack.

And in a white flash of memory, I glimpsed a house.

An Edwardian mansion with a grand oak staircase.

And then I was back in the concrete room again. The sergeant's weight on top of me, pinning me down, his breath hot on my face, his gleaming eyes so close, and the look in them: fear, the sort of ferocious, overpowering fear that can drive a man to do just about anything. His hands clamped around my throat, and tightened.

'Get OFF her this instant!' came Price's stentorian voice from somewhere above.

The sergeant jerked and cried out at a vicious kick in the ribs, and dropped down beside me. Quickly, the commander and Sidewinder seized him and hauled him to his feet, twisting his arms behind his back.

'What the hell were you thinking, man?' the commander demanded of Sidewinder. 'I bloody told you! We should have sedated him!'

Warily, I turned my head to the side and looked for Edwards. His gaze was still riveted on me, even as the other men dragged him to the far corner of the room, as though I represented some appalling and terrifying threat.

'Sarah?'

Price had dropped to my side. He slid an arm under me and helped me up. That was when I felt the sting in my neck. I reached a hand up and felt the thin scratches of blood the sergeant's fingernails had left around my throat. Price plucked a handkerchief from his pocket and starting to dab at the wounds. I snatched it off him and waved him away.

All at once, the room began to swim before my eyes. I shouldn't have been surprised; I had hit my head, hard. For one awful giddy moment, I thought darkness was about to swallow me totally, but then I steadied myself.

Price stepped forward with parental concern and clutched at my arm.

'Don't fuss. I'm all right. Really, Harry, I'm fine.'

Price hesitated, eyes searching mine, and then his shoulders straightened. He turned to Williams and Sidewinder, who were holding Edwards between them.

'These outbursts have happened before?' he demanded.

Sidewinder nodded, scowling at the commander, who replied defensively, 'Yes, but not since the accident on the range.'

'What happened to me *was not an accident*!' Edwards shouted hoarsely.

I thought to myself, then, that whatever had happened must have burned itself into his memory, into his soul, as well as his face.

'Let him go,' I said to the commander. 'This man is clearly unwell.'

'Unhinged more like!' Price glowered. 'Should be bloody well locked up.'

He is locked up, I thought, looking around the stark and claustrophobic room. Even though he had assaulted me, scared me half to death, at that moment it was impossible not to feel some compassion for this obviously traumatised young man. Perhaps that was foolish, but it was the way I felt. 'I said release him, please.'

Price looked back at me, frowning, but the commander and Sidewinder complied.

Once the sergeant had been released, he shook his head slowly, like a man waking from a drowsy sleep. I confess I was relieved to see he looked appalled with himself, his disfigured features contorting with shame. 'Oh, miss,' he said, staring at the shallow gouges on my throat. 'Forgive me, please. Oh . . .'

Carefully, cautiously, I nodded.

'Why did you attack Miss Grey?' Price demanded, his tone and expression indignant.

But I was remembering the curious way the man had stared at me before and during his attack. Almost as if . . .

'He thought I was someone else,' I said, speaking the thought out loud. 'Is that right, Gregory?'

He muttered something, shaking his head, and then said hoarsely, 'Not someone else, miss. Something else.'

'What do you mean?'

'I suffer . . . visions. Nightmarish visions. Sometimes they take control of me. It's been that way since what happened. In Imber.'

The commander and Price frowned with sceptical disdain, but not Sidewinder, I noticed; he tilted his head and regarded Edwards with a fascination so intense it was almost troubling.

'I'm plagued by what happened to me,' said the sergeant, slumping onto the narrow bed and sinking his head into his hands. 'I'll never be able to put it from my mind.'

'I am afraid this man is delusional,' Price said dismissively.

'Not necessarily, Harry.' There was conviction in my voice. I was thinking of the Edwardian mansion that had flashed into my mind just seconds earlier, when my head hit the floor. Struck by its solitary grandeur, I fancied I could still see that majestic house if I closed my eyes. I felt most strongly that the vision, although brief, was important in a way I could not yet understand. So how could I dismiss Edwards' visions? Why should his possess any less legitimacy than mine?

'Harry,' I said. 'Please let us hear what he has to say.'

I pulled up a chair and sat near Edwards. He looked up at me uncertainly, and I smiled. I think he returned it with the charred slit that had once been his mouth. I tried to see the person in that face, but with so much of it missing, that was hard to do.

'You're safe now, Gregory,' I said, 'so trust me, all right? Tell us what happened to you.'

As if seeking permission to reply, Edwards glanced over at Warden Sidewinder, who duly nodded. Then he looked back at me, and slowly began:

'We were on a night training exercise, in the Imber woods. Those woods are like nowhere else. Bitterly cold, thickly dark. Suddenly, all the other men were gone. I mean, they disappeared. I looked everywhere, but I couldn't find them. It was as if God Himself had stolen everyone in a rapture.'

'How many soldiers were involved in the exercise?' Price asked.

'About fifteen of us.'

'The other men can account for their whereabouts?'

The commander shook his head. 'They all claim to have no memory of that night.'

Price looked curious, then doubtful. 'All right, Edwards. What then?'

'I was deep in the woods when I began to hear noises. Voices. *Women's* voices.'

While Price and I looked at one another, then at Edwards, then at one another again, the commander shook his head and said, 'Impossible. We would have known if civilians had accessed the range.'

'I didn't say they were civilians,' Edwards shot back.

'What were these voices saying?' Price asked.

'The voices – more like whispers, actually – they were telling me to go to Imber Mill. Ramshackle place at the edge of the woods.'

'What's special about the mill?' I asked.

'Nothing,' said Sidewinder. 'It's dilapidated. Boarded up.'

'But there were sounds coming from inside it,' the sergeant said. 'Music, I thought. Singing. Voices and lights, and a strange smell, like something burning.'

'Did you enter the mill?' I asked.

'Yes.' His face contorted and he gave a sudden little shiver. 'I remember there was smoke. And people. No, not people – outlines of people, vague shapes swirling in the darkness. A flickering light. Such a foul odour, toxic. And then' – he closed his eyes – 'there was just him.'

'Him?'

'A little boy.'

I drew in a shaky breath.

Don't leap to conclusions, Sarah. It's not the same child. You're hungry, you're exhausted, and you're on edge. This man's psychological trauma makes him very far from reliable. So don't—

'Anyone who saw the boy would know there was something wrong. He was disfigured and sick.'

'Had you ever seen him before?' I asked, aware that Price was staring at me, intrigued by the earnestness that had crept into my voice.

Edwards was shaking his head, but something about the emotion in his tone when he spoke next told me he might not be telling the truth.

'He was half-naked, not a clue where he was. Terrified. He stood next to me and I touched his hand. It was a dead hand. Cold as a tomb. But I felt a connection with him. A deep, deep bond.'

My chest tightened. I had to ask:

'How old was he? How was he dressed?'

'Young. Five or six. Filthy, in rags. Starving, by the looks of it.'

Oh Lord. It was the same child!

'Sarah, what's the matter?' Price asked, looking at me, his gaze part curious, part accusatory.

I should have admitted that I too had seen a boy like this, a wandering child. But just as I had set my mind to substantiating the sergeant's fantastic tale, I remembered Oscar Hartwell's warning to trust no one in this camp.

'Sarah?'

I waved off Price's question and asked Sergeant Edwards, 'What happened next?'

'When I saw the boy, I was struck with a fear I've never felt before. I ran out of the mill into the woods.'

I tried to imagine this: the burly soldier fleeing through the thicket, tripping over shallow roots and gasping for breath as he bolted from the spirits of the dead.

'I made it as far as the path that leads back to the centre of the village, near the chalk pit, when my legs gave out.'

'We think that's when he found the can,' the commander said in a low voice.

'What can?' Price asked.

'A petrol can. It must have been left behind on a previous exercise.'

Price and I looked at one another with equal expressions of horror. Petrol?

'What did you do?' I whispered to the sergeant, unable to take my eyes off those horrific burns, his missing ears and swollen lips.

When he next spoke, the veins were standing out on his neck. 'I heard them *whispering* to me,' he said. 'I heard them, filling up my head. I could hear the force of their anger and hatred. Blaming me . . . goading me to harm myself.' Then, in a flat voice, he said, 'I used to think ghosts went out when the electric lights came in, but it's not so.'

'You think you heard the voices of *ghosts*?'

He nodded. 'The spirits of old residents who want us out.' His charred face confronted each of us in turn, his glittering eyes imploring us to understand. 'They *made* me do it. They made me pick up that tin can, full of petrol. Made me strike the match!'

His hand shot out and gripped my forearm. 'I think the boy I saw at the mill is some sort of omen. That child brings disaster,' he said desperately. 'For your own sake, miss, go now. Stay the hell away from Imber.'

'That man needs a lobotomy!'

'No, Harry, what he needs is to be heard by people who won't lock him up and casually dismiss what he has to say. I would have thought you of all people would understand that.'

We were outside Edwards' room in the cold concrete corridor. Outside, the wind was really ramping up. Somewhere on the roof a loose piece of corrugated iron was flapping and banging.

'Sarah, he is mentally disturbed.'

'Yes, but did he see that child because he's disturbed? Or is he disturbed because he saw it?'

Price frowned, clearly aggravated at being challenged, just as Warden Sidewinder and the commander exited Edwards' room. They pulled the door shut and stood beside us, both looking as shaken and exhausted as I felt.

'Warden Sidewinder will take you into Imber at dawn,' the commander told us. 'Once on the range, you'll have twenty-four hours to undertake your investigation and provide a full recommendation on our next course of action.'

'I am afraid that one day won't be long enough.'

'It's all the time we have, Mr Price. Tomorrow is Saturday. The Imber Service is on Sunday. Our men normally assist at the event – provide the chairs and tables, clean the church, ensure civilians don't stray from the main paths. I don't want to have to explain to the public and the newspapers why the service can't go ahead this year.'

'I assume you've already inspected the old mill?' Price asked.

The commander nodded. 'Of course. But we found nothing of interest there. The most recent reports of unusual activity have been focused on the churchyard, so that's where I believe you should concentrate your efforts.' He frowned at Price. 'You *will* explain what is happening here, yes?'

Price's jaw became set with determination, but before he could reply I asked another question. 'Commander, what if we should fail? What then?'

Commander Williams cocked his head and, though he was smiling, his jaw muscles tightened.

'Some options are not available to us, Miss Grey. Failure is one of them.'

After a light supper of ham and potatoes, it was time for bed. Outside, as I walked with my case, the silhouette of Hut Three rose to meet me. This was my accommodation for the night, one of the many prefabricated structures I had noticed on my approach to the camp. Its thin, corrugated steel roof arced low from the ground, giving the impression that I was approaching a bunker.

Snap!

I found the switch and suddenly the hut was illuminated by the light of a bare, low-wattage bulb. And oh my, it was a depressing sight indeed. The stark interior walls were constructed from ghastly grey breeze blocks; the floor of bare concrete! Perhaps worst of all were the rows of cast-iron beds that now confronted me, about twenty in all, some of them painted grey, most black.

The sight of so many empty, stripped beds gave the hut an unsettling stillness.

I released a quiet sigh of exasperation.

Closing the door on the freezing night, I saw the jug and grimy bowl on the washstand, selected a rickety brass bedstead somewhere near the middle of a row, and felt my spirits sag.

Still, I had to be thankful. At least I had some privacy!

After slipping off my coat and kicking off my shoes and quickly putting them on again (the floor was freezing), I dumped my suitcase on the shaky bed and began unpacking; toiletries first – make-up, a wooden toothbrush, a bar of carbolic soap.

Then I saw it. The hand-painted lantern slide, lying on my neatly folded clothes.

I had allowed myself to believe that I had been transported, when I touched the slide in the silent auditorium of the Brixton Picture Palace, to another place. I looked more carefully at the image framed in the lantern slide – the young girl in the expensive-looking dress and, next to her, the younger handsome boy in the suit.

I reached out to touch their image, half-expecting to find myself taken once again to that place, standing in the long grass with the sun on my back and a faint wind rising.

Nothing happened. No sense of time passing. No sense of travelling somewhere else. Just a crude lantern slide in my hand.

I slipped it into my coat pocket, feeling a little silly. That crazy sensation of travelling somewhere else was pure fantasy.

It was only after I had washed and was brushing my teeth that the question occurred to me: *Who are they, anyway?*

It sprang up in my mind unbidden, and again as I was changing into my nightdress.

Who are they?

A peculiar question. The image on the slide was clearly old. Very old. Perhaps one way of discovering these children's identities would be to have the image magnified?

I had told Price I would show it to him, and yet now that I had the opportunity I was curiously hesitant to do so. Partly because I was afraid he would mock me; but also because it meant asking once again for his expertise, which would only fill him with the smug satisfaction that could be quite intolerable.

I lay down on the creaky bed. Clear my mind, that was what I needed to do. Forget about Hartwell's warning not to trust the army. Forget about Gregory Edwards' hellish face and the fear he exuded from every pore. Forget about the guilt gnawing away at me for saying nothing to Price of his child . . .

But I could feel my nerves beginning to fray. An unwelcome voice in my ear reminded me of a word Sergeant Edwards had used earlier, a word that did not inspire confidence.

Omen.

That word in my head. It was there, like a swirling black hole, drawing me in.

'It doesn't mean a thing,' I whispered, but only felt more agitated at the sound of my own voice.

Feeling almost devoured with nervous tension, I rolled onto my side, wrapping my arms tightly around myself for warmth. The unavoidable fact was that I too had seen the child – did that mean that I too was now destined to meet with peril?

No. Edwards was just one man, whose mental condition was far from stable. All right, he *thought* the boy was an omen, but that didn't make it true, did it?

Of course not. Focus on the facts.

But one fact I had overlooked, and it came to me now with a dragging uneasiness.

Edwards isn't the only one to express concern about the boy.

Coldly, I remembered the tone in Hartwell's voice when he had said, *'Tell no one what you saw this night. It will be better that way.'*

A chill went through me. *Everything will be fine*, I told myself. *You just wait and see, Sarah.*

But as I closed my eyes, listening to the hut creaking in the wind, hoping for sleep, a distinctly unpleasant and unwelcome question surfaced: What horrors would come to me in my dreams? The wandering child? A ravenous black dog? Or worse, Imber's furious blacksmith, lumbering purposefully towards me. Swinging his hammer.

I shivered; my eyes flew open.

Perhaps, tonight, it would be better not to sleep at all.

PART TWO

A PLACE OF GHOSTS

They say the dead won't harm you; it's only the living who harm you. That's what I tried telling myself, over and over, whenever I went out to that village.

SERGEANT GREGORY EDWARDS, October 1932

The lawn
Is pressed by unseen feet, and ghosts return
Gently at twilight, gently go at dawn,
The sad intangible who grieve and yearn . . .

T. S. ELIOT, *To Walter de la Mare*

– 12 –

ENTER THE VALLEY

Dawn. Grey. Damp. We made our way into Imber beneath low-hanging, swollen clouds in Warden Sidewinder's rattling army truck. A group of soldiers huddled outside a bomb shelter, smoking, and I felt their enquiring eyes on me; I didn't feel intimidated, but I wondered how long it had been since they had seen a young woman in their camp.

Soon we were out on the downs, driving into the drizzly mists which were rolling in and which held now the distant rumble of tanks, the resounding echo of shellfire. We were told that the journey to the lost village would be roughly fifteen minutes, and bundled up in the back seat with Price, I felt every moment of it – every bump, every dip. I kept thinking of Father, of how he must have endured many weeks here of bleaker conditions than this, before being sent to fight, and die, in the trenches. It wasn't just shells and mortars he had contended with here in Wiltshire; it was the rain, the storms and floods for which Salisbury Plain was renowned. The sheer loneliness. How must he have felt, knowing Mother and I were back in London, unaware of where he was?

My belief that I would find my own truths here suddenly seemed hopelessly naive. That belief had led me to leave Mother alone in London, to put my new career on hold. What if Price and I failed in Imber? I knew the answer to that. Outrage from the former residents. Trouble for the military. None of that boded well for rekindling my friendship with Vernon Wall. If we failed, he might as well forget about all those close military connections he needed.

Sidewinder dropped down a gear. The engine sputtered, sending a shudder through the truck, which clattered loudly, as if it too harboured grave misgivings about our mission.

Our driver had been noticeably cold with us both since leaving camp. I glanced at Price and sensed from the glint in his eyes that he was spoiling for a fight.

'I hope this is the right road.'

'Harry, it's the only road,' I told him, keen to avoid any tension between these two.

Sidewinder said nothing.

As we came over the brow of a barren hill, the expanse of the plain opened before us: rugged and rolling, its skyline was stippled with Iron Age hill forts and Bronze Age burial barrows. There was something almost oceanic about this chalk grassland; something both pleasing and terrible, for it was indeed beautifully bleak, wild and raw. Mysterious. But to my amazement Price uttered not a word, even as the morning light, ghostlike, shifted and trembled, turning the miles of chalk from cold grey to tufty brown to glittering silver.

Why so quiet, Harry? What aren't you telling me?

I knew there was something; there always was with him. A memory tugged at me; something I'd been too tired to consider properly until now: Price had been in a private meeting with the commander when I arrived at Westdown Camp. Discussing what?

Although the spectral child who had appeared in the woods at the side of the road was still on my mind, the shock of the previous night's journey had faded, so much so that the experience might have happened long ago. Now I was focused on the task at hand. But as we approached Imber along a deserted track lined with lumps of chalk, I saw, coming up on our left, the crossroads with its rickety sign. Just the sight of it made me straighten up.

'Something wrong?' Sidewinder asked, catching my eye in his rear-view mirror.

I did not mention the wandering child, but I did mention the upright and respectable Oscar Hartwell.

'How do you know *him*?' Sidewinder asked; he sounded almost accusing.

'I don't. We met by chance on my journey here.'

'By chance?'

'He was kind enough to give me a lift.'

'I see. You should know that Mr Hartwell is a tricky individual, Miss Grey.'

'He rather implied the same about you lot. You're familiar with his campaign?'

'Sadly. Hartwell used to be a reasonable man,' he said. 'His was one of the most prominent families in Wiltshire. But since his son passed away, he has lost all direction. His wife even more so. I fear she will end up in a mad house before long. She is Hartwell's second wife.'

'What happened to the first wife?'

'A maternal death. As I understand, she suffered severe blood loss. A stillbirth. It was their first child – a daughter, Lillian. After that, Hartwell met Marie in Paris, on one of his many business trips.'

He told us then that Imber Court had been in the Hartwell family's ownership since the 1500s. That most of the land in the village had at one time belonged to the family; that the Hartwells' coat of arms was believed to be the oldest in the English armorial; and that the Hartwell manuscript of *Richard III* was the earliest surviving manuscript of any play by William Shakespeare. 'They were true and good pillars of the community, but their history is marked by great tragedy.'

'Oh?'

'Hartwell went on to have two daughters with Marie, Beatrice and Rosalie, and they also perished young. Eventually, long years after the evacuation of Imber, they had a son, Pierre. When they also lost him to illness, Marie disappeared from the community altogether. Now Mr Hartwell is consumed with a singular obsession – getting Imber returned to the people. If he had his family, perhaps he'd forget his hopeless campaign.'

'But to lose a wife and four children . . .' I said, trying to wrap my head around the scale of this poor man's loss.

Sidewinder nodded, but his frown only deepened. 'Losing his children doesn't make his arguments sound. Or his judgement. Hartwell is leading a reckless cavalry charge that's certain to end in calamity. Tragedy. Encouraging members of the public to stroll back into Imber is thoroughly irresponsible. There have been too many near accidents. Imber is an immersive training environment for troops to practise urban manoeuvres, to simulate potential scenarios of combat. Even when roads into the village are opened, its buildings and all areas away from the roads remain strictly out of bounds. There's a constant danger of civilians straying from the path and coming across unexploded shell and mortar bombs.'

'You leave *live* explosives scattered on the range?' This sounded incredible to me.

'Our men are highly trained, Miss Grey, but there's always a risk something's been overlooked. It's a sobering reminder of the risks that our soldiers take to prepare themselves for combat. Necessary risks.'

'Was it right to force the residents to leave their homes?' I asked abruptly, and Price made a quick gesture with his eyebrows, as if to instruct silence.

'It was war.'

I could have left it there, but my sympathy for Hartwell was insisting otherwise. 'Yes, I'm sure you needed Imber when you took it. The question is,' I added weightily, 'why do you need it now? In peacetime, with the League of Nations watching over us? Why not return the village to its people?'

Our truck rumbled on to a new track, dustier and bumpier than the last. Every hundred yards or so a sign warned of tank crossings, impact areas and live firing ranges.

'It may have escaped your attention, Miss Grey, that Europe is still not stable. We've got two thousand heavily armoured troops using the plain, training to fight in case of future conflict. The army takes precautions, which is why they have summoned you both here.'

At last, Price spoke up. 'You don't think we can help?'

'No,' Sidewinder replied, and the two men's eyes met in the rear-view mirror. 'And the commander is delusional if he thinks that you can. You, a man who thinks spiritualism can be reduced to a precise and rational science? No, I'm sorry, Mr Price, but your methods will have no currency in Imber.'

Sidewinder's bitter tone surprised me a little. As for Price, he looked thoroughly affronted.

'Warden, all I require are the facts. In this business, they can be frustratingly hard to come by, but facts are all we have. Cold, hard facts. Absolute, inimitable truth. But I see you're not much interested in facts, are you? You've already made up your mind.'

Sidewinder kept his gaze fixed on the bumpy road. 'Like you, Mr Price, I maintain a deep interest in matters of the preternatural; indeed, I have studied the subject intensely.'

That earned a raised eyebrow from Price. If there was anything that annoyed him more than beliefs formed without evidence it was people who claimed comparable or superior expertise on the paranormal. 'You want to know something about the world beyond the veil, Warden? Let me oblige. It's nothing but a bunch of charlatans who delight in deluding hopeful believers. And if, indeed, you are as well read on the subject as you profess, you'll know that most accounts bow eventually to the scrutiny of diligent enquiry.'

'Most. Not all.'

Price frowned and leaned towards the driver's seat. 'That's a native accent, yes? How long have you lived in Wiltshire?'

'All my life,' said Sidewinder.

'Any family?'

'A son.'

'He grew up here too?'

'Yes.'

'Then presumably you told him ghost stories as a boy.

Presumably you told your son something of John Mompesson of Wiltshire? A famous case, Warden. A *local* case.'

'A scoundrel of the first order,' Sidewinder said, sitting upright in the driver's seat and directing his words at me. 'In the summer of 1661, he heard unsettling noises in his home. Drum beatings, scratching and panting noises. Objects moving of their own accord, and sulphurous odours permeating the house. Mompesson claimed that a man he had helped send to jail had, through some form of witchcraft, caused a malevolent spirit to invade his home in order to exact revenge.' He shook his head. 'Of course, the entire affair was a hoax cooked up by Mompesson to profit from those who came to see the spirit.'

Price was looking at Sidewinder with an expression of reluctant respect. He said coolly, 'Well. Always a pleasure to meet someone with a passion for a subject most other scientists have dismissed out of hand.'

Sidewinder grunted and changed down another gear as the truck swung onto a new track, fringed with small whitewashed stones. 'You may be surprised to hear it, but I've read your case reports, Mr Price. Your flagrant disregard for those blessed with the power to see . . . Who are *you* to speak ill of them?'

'I recognise a fraud when I meet one, Mr Sidewinder.'

'As do I, Mr Price.'

'What are you implying?'

'You call yourself a scientist, yet you have no degree, no qualifications.'

'Rubbish!'

'You think I haven't done my research on you? Your books' – he shook his head – 'are hideously repetitive. And your lectures, I'm told, are nothing but an exercise in showmanship.

And you expect me to take you seriously?' He sighed with a slow, contemptuous smile. 'You, a man who takes Fortnum & Mason hampers along on his investigations?'

I'll be the first to admit that I found Price's gusto maddening at times; but even so, I felt I needed to speak up in Price's defence.

'Harry is working, unremittingly, for the recognition by official science of psychic research, Mr Sidewinder.' I thought of Mother and added, 'No one has ever been quite as skilful as Harry in detecting fake mediums and protecting the public from their trickery.'

'You are associating with a sensationalist, Miss Grey,' said Sidewinder, his voice hard and resentful. 'I read his reports on that whole saga in Borley. He destroys most of the evidence, except that which suits his purposes, and then uses that to woo the newspapers. I wonder if Mr Price is even capable of recognising a genuine paranormal event.' Warden Sidewinder shook his head with a look of bitter disdain. 'To speak plainly, sir, I am forced to wonder if there is any evidence capable of convincing you. And if Imber doesn't, nothing will.'

We approached the village from the east, passing a few blackened and skeletal trees.

A murky mist was hanging over the plain like a bad dream. At last a landmark appeared on the far horizon, growing out of the mist.

'That's St Giles',' Sidewinder told us. 'I'll give you a set of keys.'

'You could come with us,' I suggested.

'Out of the question,' Price cut in.

I gave him an incredulous look. 'Harry, we could do with

some guidance, couldn't we? You heard what he said – we don't want to tread on any stray shells. Or worse, any – '

'Land mines?' Price cut in, his eyes glittering.

I gave a small shiver. Something about the way he was staring at me suggested he was quietly thrilled by the risk.

'Yes, exactly, Harry. Land mines!'

'You'll need to keep a sharp eye out,' Sidewinder advised.

'I always do,' Price murmured.

'Most of the main pathways in the village have been cleared of debris, but there's always a chance we've missed some. If you stray from the roads, though, you will be risking your lives. Do not touch or disturb any shells, mortar bombs, missiles or similar objects you might find. Understand? They may explode.'

'Fine,' Price answered, 'but no one comes in with us, Sarah. Until we understand exactly what we're dealing with I can't risk any human incursion jeopardising my investigation.' I opened my mouth to protest but Price added firmly, 'I've already agreed it with the commander: the whole range will be secured the instant we enter, sentries posted at every access point. But we go in alone.'

It seemed I had been right to worry about his private meeting with the commander.

As our truck crested the hill, lumbering downwards into the village, we passed several rusting tanks close to the road and more Keep Out and Danger signs. Hedges of barbed wire. Red flags, whipping on the breeze.

'Can we access the old stately house?' I remembered Oscar Hartwell telling me about his old home, the magnificent dances he had enjoyed there. 'Imber Court?'

Sidewinder shook his head.

'Why not?'

'It's a kill house.' He glanced at me in the mirror and registered my alarm, then answered the obvious question on my face. 'An indoor firing range. The soldiers use it sometimes to train for room clearing, door breaching. Indoor combat situations.'

'The whole house?'

'Most of it. The soldiers say the place gives them the creeps. It's not been used in a while but the land around it is littered with debris that could be lethal.'

'What about the woods?'

'Out of bounds. A recent spot check revealed as many as sixty to eighty high explosives in that area.'

'The old mill?'

A long pause. 'You heard the commander. The Imber Service tomorrow revolves around the church and the centre of the village. Make those locations your priority.'

I was about to ask how we were meant to focus on the centre of the village when most of it seemed to be off limits to us when Sidewinder hit the brakes. I saw a barrier ahead, and beside it a guardhouse from which a young sentry was emerging. The truck stopped and Sidewinder killed the engine.

We had arrived.

The three of us sat there in silence for a few seconds before Sidewinder got out of the vehicle and strode towards the guard, who looked barely old enough to have left school. Price quickly grabbed the tattered briefcase containing his scientific instruments, flung open his door and climbed out; he waited impatiently for me to slide across and exit on his side.

The guard, his face raw from the cold, was exchanging quiet words with Sidewinder. When we reached them, the guard raised the barrier and Price snatched the keys to St Giles' from Sidewinder and marched ahead. 'Come on, Sarah!'

I began to follow, but Sidewinder gripped my arm. 'You're sure you want to enter the village?' he asked me. His face was rigid; in the cold morning light, I thought he resembled one of the stone sarcophagus busts we were likely to find in the churchyard. But for the first time I detected some warmth – or was it sympathy? – from this man. 'I'm telling you: that village is a magnet for unusual phenomena.'

'Apparently so,' I said politely. 'That is why we are here.'

'Imber is dead,' he added, looking towards the village with a searching, baleful glance. 'A dead place. And like every dead thing, it should be left to rest in peace.'

The wind was raw on my face as I looked at Price, standing next to the raised barrier, his overcoat hanging down to his knees, the brim of his black felt hat pulled down over one eye. I gave him a small nod and he flicked his head towards the village. *Hurry*, that signal was saying, *Follow me*.

'I know Harry was reluctant for you to join us,' I said to Sidewinder, 'but if you wanted to, you could.'

Sidewinder shook his head, his gaze travelling past a rusting tank towards the piercing spire of St Giles' Church. 'Miss Grey,' he said, 'the only road worth taking in Imber is the road *out*.'

From the instant we entered Imber and the barrier fell behind us, I felt hemmed in by the valley, and had a distinct feeling of being watched. I told myself it was my imagination, paranoia.

'Try to keep up, Sarah!'

The wind was getting up now, whipping at my hair and making it even harder to keep pace with Price's long strides.

We followed the white dusty track through an avenue of gaunt trees, some of them charred as if from an explosion.

Ahead of us was a mouldering stack of slatted boards, leaning perilously to one side. A barn? Perhaps once it had been.

Soon it was behind us, but my curiosity was only growing about whatever lay ahead. Gradually, the trees on either side of us fell away, and the dusty track levelled out.

'Look, Sarah.'

I followed Price's gaze down to the stony furrows at the side of the road.

'Are those spent cartridges?' I asked.

'Yes. Grenade pins, too.' He stared at me with an earnestness that was distinctly unnerving. 'Keep your eyes on the ground. Be vigilant.'

The track turned right, cutting through a shifting sea of knee-high grass, veering downwards, then becoming steeper still, widening eventually to become a cobbled, cracked road. Price stopped abruptly and shot out an arm to bring me to a halt.

'Well,' he said, scanning, 'here we are. The loneliest place in Britain.'

I heard myself inhale, and then slowly breathed out.

Crumbling grey cottages with broken windows lined the cobbled road. Hawthorn and weeds erupted in tangles from yawning black doorways. Some of the buildings retained their original thatched roofs, but most had no roofs at all, or had been covered with dark green blast-proof sheeting.

Somewhere, a loose shutter was banging, loud and insistent in the wind.

'Oh, Harry,' I whispered, and felt a tremble of awe run through me as my gaze settled on what had once been a quaint cottage, but was now little more than a bombed-out shell. Jagged black spaces yawned where there should have been latticed windows, the rotting frames riotously entangled with ivy. The front door was a dark, splintered space, barricaded with a twist of barbed wire. 'They really did murder this village, didn't they?'

'They had their reasons,' he said flatly.

The wind shifted and died; the banging of the shutter fell away. For a moment, nothing remained but the echo of dismay and despair, floating with us like chalk dust through the abandoned streets as we scanned the pitted ruins, the ivy wildly writhing out of walls that were crumbling and cracked.

I didn't yet know if there were any supernatural presences dwelling here, but something else was clear to me. this village of barren beauty was eternal, a place where the past and present met in uneasy union.

It occurred to me then that these decaying houses weren't just the relics of neglect; they were the causalities of trauma. Time hadn't simply frozen here; time was wounded, permanently in pain. And perhaps . . . waiting? These houses had been homes for families and friends and lovers. A vanished community. Noble people, who had left those homes behind for a greater good; who had gone peacefully, with fortitude and courage.

This village doesn't just belong to the army, I thought, *it belongs to the past*; and every part of me seemed to deflate out of respect for its sacrifice.

I closed my eyes and, for a moment, imagined that I could almost hear the hurried whispers and giggles of children, rushing after Sunday school to play in the fields; I could almost see the wisps of smoke rising from the battered chimneys.

Life, long extinguished, forgotten by most who lived beyond the fences, in the outside world.

'All right, Sarah?'

I opened my eyes and nodded, attempting a smile.

'Then let's find the church.' Price glanced at his watch. 'If we're lucky,' he said, 'we have nine hours before sunset. I want to secure the church completely, every door and window.'

'And then what?'

'Spend some time inside? Perhaps even spend the night.'

'What? We're hardly prepared for that, Harry! No food, no extra clothes, no blankets.'

He gave me a boyish grin and I saw that he was pulling my leg.

'Not funny.'

'You should see your face, though,' he said, chuckling.

Despite myself, I granted him a smile. He touched the rim of his fedora and I felt my heart warm a little towards him. It had always been this way: Price sprinkling just enough charm to keep me interested.

'I'm quite confident we'll come across some answers before sundown,' he added, strolling ahead. 'We'll show Warden Sidewinder a thing or two, now, won't we?'

'Perhaps.'

I wet my lips – something had stolen my attention. Folded into the side of a nearby hill and just above the spire of the village church was a building that drew my gaze and made my throat tighten.

A watermill.

I pointed and Price followed my finger with his eyes.

Imposing and ancient, the mill was also derelict. Yet, even from this distance, it looked grandly impressive: two storeys high, a gritstone building of Gothic design, with iron-framed windows. Once used for grinding corn, probably. I pictured it up there on its lonely hillside, perched next to a large millpond with its own waterfall.

The mental image was clear. Extraordinarily vivid. I almost caught the scent of the place: a building pervaded by a dusty, dirty smell. It was, I felt sure, the sort of building inhabited by narrow staircases, uneven floors and ancient beams. A cold building – I felt that too – full of iron buckets and millstones.

'Sarah?'

I flinched.

Price was standing there, scrutinising me. And all at once I had the strangest feeling, the strangest urge, to tell him a story about that mill. A new story, not about Sergeant Edwards and things he had witnessed there, but about something else.

Someone else.

I blinked, feeling oddly foolish for a second, and then curious.

'Come on,' I said jauntily. 'Let's get going.'

'Yes. We may as well enjoy ourselves,' he agreed, striding ahead. 'Whatever Sidewinder believes, there's nothing here for us to fear.'

I understood from this that he had already arrived at one conclusion: that there was nothing in the way of genuine supernatural phenomena to be discovered in Imber. And there was real conviction in his voice.

But I wasn't so sure. I had the same queasy feeling that had first arisen in me back in London at the Brixton Picture Palace, a sensation of intense strangeness and absorption. Here, as there, I had the prickling suspicion – which I would have struggled to justify in any meaningful, rational way – that everything around me was only a façade, barely concealing something unpleasant underneath.

My gaze became lost in the distance for a moment, then fixed again on the mill, mysterious and somehow awful. I was sure for that instant that a repressed, unnatural presence dwelled here in Imber. Sadness and secrets.

I was sure of something else too.

It would be unwise – reckless, even – to ignore a feeling like that.

– 13 –

POPULATION ZERO

We followed the dusty track towards the centre of the village. On our right, a wall of dead hedges barricaded us from sloping, half-acre allotments, wild and uncultivated. On our left, a shallow stream, thick with algae, wound its way through a thicket of elm trees. Gazing at the dark gaps between those trees, I saw a padlocked gate and a high chain-linked fence topped with razor wire and, beyond, a huge boarded-up mansion.

Imber Court.

I walked right up to the fence, curling my fingers around it, and peered through, thinking to myself that this house must once have been magnificent. The sort of residence that boasted libraries and drawing rooms, replete with wood panelling and plush curtains.

Clearly, this manor had been built for a large family. The many arched windows suggested at least eleven bedrooms. But like everything else in Imber, it had been left to wither and die. Every door was blocked with steel sheets bolted to the masonry. Three storeys had been reduced to two.

I stared at it.

Yes, I felt sure this was the property with a macabre history that had been in Hartwell's family for several generations, now the army's 'kill house'.

Was this also the house I'd seen when Edwards attacked me and I knocked my head?

Hard to tell. Similar, certainly; but that house had been splendid and grand, whereas this house was dilapidated beyond hope. Its appearance summoned images of its cold and neglected rooms, paint flaking off the walls.

'Sarah, are you all right?'

Price was at my side.

'I don't know,' I replied. I had a gnawing feeling that something wasn't right.

I let go of the fence and noticed that Price was studying my face intently, but suddenly he swung round.

'What is it?' I asked, and held my breath as he lifted his hand, instructing silence. I heard nothing. Not even a bird.

After a few moments, he shrugged. 'Doesn't matter,' he said, without concern, and pointed up ahead. At the far end of the valley, the skyline was steepled with an ancient five-pinnacled church. 'This way!'

There wasn't a bird to be heard or any person to be seen. On all sides of us were steep hills, dotted with rusting tanks left out for target practice. One hill was covered with thick woodland; that must be where Sergeant Edwards had suffered his excruciating 'accident'.

Edwards had told us that before the apparition of the boy, before the whisperings that drove him to set himself alight, he had been on a night-time training exercise. His men had vanished, he said, leaving the woods and the rest of Imber completely deserted . . .

'Sarah, you seem most jittery this morning,' Price commented, his voice accusatory.

'No, I'm fine.'

'Quite sure? We don't want old problems resurfacing, do we?'

'Old problems?'

'I mean with your nerves.'

I let that go. We both knew to what he was referring. 'Lead on, Harry.'

As we rounded a corner, a military sign in red and black lettering confronted us:

NOTICE TO THE PUBLIC

DANGER!

IMBER VILLAGE AND THE CHURCH

ARE CLOSED TO THE PUBLIC

YOU WILL BE PROSECUTED

IF YOU ARE FOUND OFF THE

MAIN CARRIAGEWAY

The 'main carriageway' was a long, gloomy road coated in chalk dust and sprouting weeds. Thirty yards or so from the road were the cottages, with roofs of corrugated iron and red-brick walls, blackened in patches from explosions. Their gardens were separated from the pavement by a wall made of mud and rubble and lime.

There was no sign to tell me so, but I knew this was Imber's main street. A road of ruins, barely recognisable.

Except I did recognise it, because I *had* seen it before. Eighteen years ago, on a snowy afternoon. Back then it had been a bustling street lined with market stalls and thriving with life.

I placed my hand against the wall and closed my eyes, picturing Father standing right next to me, his hand in mine. Perhaps Price thought me eccentric, but what did I care? For a moment, I was a child again, right back in 1914, watching some of the villagers bury one of their own.

I heard again my father's voice:

'*Sarah, my angel, if ever we are parted, if you should find yourself alone, then close your eyes and remember this place. I'll always be here.*'

Reaching for the memory was like trying to catch the drifting snowflakes that Saturday afternoon. In a vague and confused way, I saw myself as a young girl, remembered the sadness on Father's face as he took my hand and looked down at me with all the interminable pain a parent feels as they are about to be parted from their child. I'd silently wished for him to tell me why he'd driven me all this way to Wiltshire.

He'd known the village would be taken over by the army. He'd known he was to be posted here for training. And he kept those truths from us. But why had he brought me here before the village was evacuated and his training had begun? Was it to keep a memory of me, his cherished daughter, with him?

Eyes open, I gazed at a settlement transformed. There was the low stone wall that skirted the hilly churchyard. There, the schoolhouse, the ruins of the village pub. And in the far distance, the rotting timbers of the old blacksmith's forge.

'I was here, Harry. Before the war. I stood right here, with Father.'

Price caught my gaze, and looked away quickly, almost as if . . .

'Harry? You *knew* my father trained in this village? How?'

Price nodded, looking shifty. 'I didn't want to upset you. I couldn't be sure it was him, but his name appears in small letters, under the photograph on the wall in the commander's office.' He met my gaze and I felt myself go numb in the wind whipping around us.

I gazed at the track, the pitted stone cottages and the low stone wall, and allowed a perfect stillness to hold me. A silence spanning decades.

'Sarah?'

In that dreamy moment, it seemed to me that a fragment of the precious time I had shared with Father was still right here, amidst these ruins.

Then the deep, rich note of the church bell rang out. Low. Slow. Melancholy.

'Good Lord!' Price sounded thoroughly startled.

He looked towards the high wire fence that barricaded the church, past the Out of Bounds signs and the rows of grey headstones, to the lonely bell tower.

'A funeral bell,' he said, with a mixture of intrigue and wonderment.

That made me think again of the funeral in the snow on this very street, eighteen years ago. Curiosity and a little fear crept into me. 'Harry, we have to get inside the church.'

The bell tolled over the deserted village as Price led the way, the wind tugging at my mud-streaked skirt as we stalked towards the ten-foot-high chain-link fence that shut off the churchyard from the rest of Imber, making it look sinister and dangerous. Just before the fence, nailed to an elm tree, was a battered sign that read, in white letters, 'Consecrated ground'.

Quickly, we passed through a black wrought-iron gate, which surprisingly was not locked, and walked up a steep hill, into the churchyard. On all sides of us, among the shrubbery and straggly trees, there were crooked gravestones, some so ancient they were in danger of being swallowed by the spongy earth.

Before we could get to the church door, more bells began to toll, as if warning of imminent danger, and Prize froze. On his face, quiet caution replaced certainty and arrogance. He rubbed his hand against the side of his head, saying nothing, his eyes flicking distrustfully between the bell tower and the church door.

'Who's in there?' he shouted, starting forward, reaching for the great wooden door.

And just as his hand grabbed the black door handle, the bells ceased.

As their echo fell away, there followed a vast and hollow silence. I shivered. Neither of us spoke. It was an eerie moment.

'Harry, look,' I said, and drew his attention to the faded note pinned to the door. Handwritten. Black ink. I was glad the military had had the presence of mind to protect it from the rain and wind with a clear cover sheet.

'One day, we, the people of Imber, will come back. Until then, time will honour this place, and we hope you do too. Our homes will remain homes. And when men are free and the war is won, Imber will live again.'

The words of the family of the last resident to leave Imber: the blacksmith, Silas Wharton, found by his wife slumped over his anvil, crying like a baby when he heard he had to leave. Silas Wharton, who vanished during the evacuation.

'Now then, let's see,' Price said, fishing in his coat pocket and producing the jagged church key. He wriggled it into the lock. The door shook, but didn't open. He tried again, with no success. 'Blasted man! That warden gave us the wrong key!'

Maybe. Or perhaps something in there doesn't want us to come in.

'I'm sure you're right, Harry,' I said, though I could have sworn I felt the smallest chill brush my neck. 'Let's try the bell tower instead.'

We needn't have bothered; the path to the base of the bell tower was completely obstructed by thick underbrush, and judging from the light masonry forming the shape of an arched doorway, this entrance had been bricked up long ago.

The peal of the bells haunted me as I followed Price back towards the churchyard exit. As I traced that winding, overgrown path, what troubled me most was not the bells themselves, resonating in the cold morning air, or the mystery of who was ringing them, but the childhood memory of the funeral their tolling had awakened for me. The palpable, sinking sense of loss.

I could see them at the corner of the low stone wall – a huddled group of mourners, shadows in my fragile memory. A young woman, sobbing with grief. Her husband, grim-faced, at her side. How old was the child they had laid to rest?

I was struck by a possibility that seemed so feasible, so probable, I was surprised it hadn't come to me earlier: was it Oscar Hartwell and his wife I had seen attending the funeral all those years ago?

And what were the villagers thinking as they had watched the casket being lifted from its bed of flowers? Why had some of them looked so suspicious, so afraid?

I had not thought of these questions since I was a girl, but something about the memory whispered to me that there was more to the story, waiting for me here.

And if that was right, I fully intended to find out what it was.

– 14 –

SEEN AND UNSEEN

I was surprised by how quickly we lost track of time that Saturday morning. Except 'lost track' isn't quite right. As we moved along moss-spotted paths, intruders in this secluded valley, haunting the once bustling streets of thatched, half-timbered buildings, it was more as if time had slowed down.

As bizarre as it sounds, that is what I felt. Time had blurred, as though what was left of the village existed in a reality that was entirely separate from the outside world.

Silence reigned, brooding, biding its time.

I tried pushing the thought away from me as Price took out his camera and snapped a few photographs.

As we made our way amongst the ragged houses, I kept remembering what Commander Williams had told us: of phantom balls of light moving through the ruins; fires dancing around buildings before fading away. In the cold light of day, none of that seemed remotely plausible. But even if there was no truth in those reports, Imber's shell-damaged buildings still looked far too dangerous to enter; the roof over the nearest cottage had almost completely fallen in.

Still, that didn't mean we weren't curious to get a better look.

So we explored a little around the nearby cottages, marvelling at the discarded personal belongings long ago left behind by vanished residents.

On a patch of barren scrubland barricaded with Keep Out signs were two farm wagons, once loaded with coal and corn and pushed by calloused hands but now rotten. Forgotten.

Outside the Bell Inn, we found grimy fragments of broken beer bottles protruding jaggedly from the earth.

The wind stalked us as we approached the old schoolhouse and peered in through a shattered window. What we saw inside was unsettling: a crumbling classroom, with names above the pegs. Tattered, faded workbooks, scrawled pictures on the walls.

I felt sad gazing at those relics, and a powerful sense of disconnectedness. Absence. It was as if we were looking into a parallel reality, another time.

As Price took another couple of photographs of the classroom, I remembered the blacksmith who had worked and lived here and vanished after the evacuation. Silas Wharton.

I turned and looked across the road at the remains of the blacksmith's forge. I pictured him now, hearing the news, his face crestfallen, totally stunned. Then, hunched forward over his anvil, with his head in his hands, sobbing uncontrollably. A broken man.

We were told that after the evacuation of Imber, this poor soul had disappeared, without any word to his family or friends. Why had he left his family behind? And why had no one seen him leave?

A more disturbing possibility was that the blacksmith had ended his own life.

That seemed likely, given that he was reportedly devastated at losing his home. But if he had committed suicide here on the range, where was the body? Hundreds of soldiers had trained in Imber. If there was a body out here, surely someone would have found it by now.

These questions played on my mind as Price looked back at the church tower.

I could tell from his creased brow that he was still troubled by the mystery of the tolling bells. So was I. But it also made me think of his earlier reference to my 'nerves', how he had tried once to help me relax using hypnotism. Maybe what I needed now was to recreate that sense of calm, and the mental focus it would bring.

'Harry, I'm going back to the churchyard. I'd like a few moments alone.'

Price stared at me questioningly. Then, with a curt nod, he muttered, 'Don't wander off.'

Leaving Price to take more photographs, I returned to the crumbling churchyard. From here, standing amongst the swaying grass, I had a totally unimpaired view of the high-sloped valley and a perfect sense of its desolation. Feeling a deep sadness, I looked out over the village, the pitted remains of the many tiny cottages, their only purpose now to help men learn to fight and to die. Monuments to the horror of war.

I tried to imagine Imber as it had been before this desertion. Gardens crossed by lines of clothes hanging out to dry on washing day. On the air, the bleating of sheep, horse hooves clip-clopping through the lanes. The mill wheel on the horizon turning its daily grind as chimneys breathed tendrils of smoke into the Wiltshire sky and smartly attired gentlemen played cricket on the Barley Field.

Nothing now. Not even the distant din of agricultural equipment ploughing the fields.

Just silence. Heavy. Oppressive.

I glimpsed something then, a quick movement at the very edge of my field of vision. There were enough trees in the churchyard; it might easily have been a branch stirring on the wind . . .

I looked to the great elm tree at the far end of the churchyard and saw, in the shadow cast by its overhanging branches, an ornate memorial stone fashioned from smooth white marble in the shape of a lamb. On either side of the lamb were two stone urns.

Something told me there was only one family in Imber who could have afforded such a monument.

With weather-worn angels looming on all sides of me, I crossed the churchyard to examine the impressive monument, and wasn't surprised to find I was right.

IN LOVING MEMORY OF PIERRE HOWISON HARTWELL
APRIL 1925 – OCTOBER 1930
SON OF OSCAR ANDREW HARTWELL
OF IMBER COURT
AND MARIE HARTWELL
OUR LITTLE SOLDIER

There were other graves beside this one, a row of three simple headstones. Each made of concrete, now weathered and spotted with moss.

Stepping nearer the plots, I stumbled on the uneven ground.

It seemed to be collapsing around the graves. Crouching, I carefully noted the names on each:

Lillian. Beatrice. Rosalie.

Remembrances of the funeral, all those years ago, drifted into my thoughts: the upright man in the black hat waiting with his wife at the entrance to the churchyard. Hartwell had lost four children. The deaths stretched back as far as 1895, which, if my estimation of his age had been accurate, meant Hartwell was probably somewhere in his mid-twenties when he first became a father. Lillian had been his first, and according to the headstone, she had been stillborn. Hartwell's first wife had passed away from complications soon after. With Marie he had Beatrice, who had survived until she was two, and Rosalie, who had also died, a little older, and was buried on the eve of the Great War.

My earlier suspicions were correct: it had to be her funeral we had witnessed. The thought came to me then: it wasn't a funeral my father had brought me to see that wintry morning at the outbreak of war, but even so we *had* witnessed a funeral, and not just any funeral, but that of Rosalie Hartwell. That had to be significant, didn't it? Or was it a mere coincidence?

No. If it was a coincidence then it was a colossal one. What about synchronicity, then: *meaningful coincidence?* In a place as timeless and as battle-scarred as Imber, that seemed more likely to me. The universe's peculiar way of binding my father and me together, entwined by events past and present, and those yet to come. Yes. If I had never believed in synchronicity, I think I believed in it now.

But looking at Rosalie's simple headstone, next to her brother's ornate memorial, I was puzzled.

I thought again of my father, once standing at my side, here in this village.

I thought of the dead children in the ground and the child to whom I had given birth.

And I wondered what my father might have said if he had survived the Great War; if I had been brave enough to confide in him the truth about my secret child.

Suddenly a dam, carefully constructed, broke in me and I wept. For Oscar Hartwell's children, taken before their time. For their mother's loss. For *my* loss – my father and my little boy, gone.

I heard a noise behind me – feet crunching on gravel – so I plucked a handkerchief from my sleeve and hastily wiped my eyes. Turning, I expected to see Price on the path.

'Harry?'

No one in sight.

No sign of any gravel path either. If ever there had been a gravel path in this churchyard, it had long since been buried under the deep bed of weeds.

The silence thickened, became deep and absolute. I remained next to the tomb, half-expecting the church bells to sound their mournful toll, and resisted the urge to run away.

But there were no more footsteps. No sign of anyone. And now I had some idea how Sergeant Edwards must have felt when his men disappeared in the woods. I'd been thinking about Edwards and the whispers he claimed to have heard ever since we left Westdown Camp. And now I'd had my own anomalous experience here in Imber: the footsteps, the tolling of the bells . . .

I had sensed there could be some truth in Gregory Edwards' claim to have heard women whispering to him near here, goading him to set himself on fire, and now that possibility seemed ever more likely. And Sergeant Edwards hadn't just heard whisperings; he had witnessed a wandering child, maybe even the same child I had encountered at the side of the road bordering the woods . . . Was it the child I heard behind me just now?

I turned with wonder, and some fear, to the marble memorial next to me. Just five years old when he died, two years ago . . .

'Sarah.'

I flicked my head up to see Price coming through the gate to the churchyard. 'What's been keeping you?' he asked, striding over. 'You look pale. Have you been cry –'

'Harry, you seem intensely interested in how this village is affecting me,' I said, meeting his gaze.

He looked puzzled for a moment, and then a little shifty.

'I know you think Imber holds some profound significance for me, because my father trained here. But my feelings aren't any of your business and your interest makes me uncomfortable. I'm not an experiment to be scrutinised. Clear?'

He nodded.

'Now then . . .' I began, wondering whether I should tell him about the disquieting sounds and the footsteps; but if he knew about the footsteps he would want to stay here, and as far as I was concerned, another minute in this churchyard would be a minute too many. 'Where next? Imber Court?'

His eyebrows rose. 'The old mill, I'd say. Where the sergeant saw that boy. If we set off now, we'll have plenty of time to return to this churchyard before nightfall.'

As if that were an encouraging suggestion! With the bells and the footsteps, returning to this spot wasn't my chief desire.

Neither was venturing to the mill. Price was a fiercely determined person, so I knew it was unlikely I could change his
mind, but I had to try. 'I'm not sure you have thought this
through,' I said. 'To get to the mill, we have to cut through
the woods.'

'Correct.'

I stared at him.

'But what about the unexploded debris? Harry – '

'We'll take very good care. I'll look after you.'

But when had that ever been true? I felt my mouth becoming dry with anxiety. 'The commander said they searched the
mill and found nothing. And he also told us, very clearly, to
stay well away!'

'Which is precisely why we shouldn't.'

He was alight with curiosity, as if he expected to uncover
some great and damaging secret, and I thought, perhaps, I
knew why. His argument with Sidewinder had energised him,
made him ever more determined to prove there was nothing
to fear.

'Sarah, do you want to be the one to explain to the commander – and your mysterious source, whoever that is – that
we've failed abjectly in our mission? Do you want to go back
to Sergeant Edwards' concrete cell and tell him you came all
this way for nothing?'

I looked at him uncertainly; there was such conviction in
his tone.

'I didn't think so. You *need* to know, so don't pretend you
don't. It's the same longing that drew you to investigate the
hauntings at the Brixton Picture Palace.'

I couldn't argue with that.

Price turned; began walking away.

'Harry, just wait!' I said, and he froze. But not because of my instruction, I realised. He was standing next to the lamb carved out of marble – little Pierre Hartwell's memorial.

'Sarah, come and look,' he said. 'Someone has defaced this sculpture.'

I moved to his side and peered at the side of the lamb sculpture. Focused on the official inscription, I had missed this: a series of words, barely legible beneath a skin of moss and bluish-green lichen, had been etched into the marble.

'Look, it's just possible to read it,' Price said, running one finger over each letter. '"May God in His mercy punish those who have wronged us; grant it so that His heavenly wrath stains the souls of those who have stained Imber with the blood of innocents."'

I knew what it sounded like to me: a curse. Crude and embittered, but a curse nonetheless.

Price's eyes met mine. 'Goodness. Someone had a bee in their bonnet, didn't they? Write this down, Sarah.'

Once I had done that, Price recommenced his purposeful stride towards the church gate and the lane that led to the woods.

It took Price a moment to realise he had left me behind, and when he did, he turned and shot me an impatient glare.

'Well, are you coming?'

For a moment, thankfully fleeting, I saw the wandering child's wasted face, his sunken eyes.

'We'll be all right,' Price said. 'We'll be just fine, Sarah. You'll see.'

And God help me, I followed.

15

CREEPING INTO DANGER

The sense of desolation was even more overpowering in the woods. No houses. No sweeping views across the barren valley. And my shoes – low heels suitable for a secretary at a Soho film-publishing house – weren't made to contend with the thick underbrush.

Price was up ahead, fighting through the vines and spindly branches. I'd had to remind him more than once that this was a *live* firing range, impressing upon him the need to go slowly lest we tread on an unexploded shell. I was longing to stop and rest awhile; the morning's events had left me feeling quite drained.

The farther we walked, the more uncomfortable I became. My coat kept snagging on branches, as did my skirt. The rutted foot trail ahead of us was on the verge of vanishing under snarling roots and shrubbery. Without a map, we were walking blind, hemmed in by woods that were thicker than we had envisaged when we left the churchyard and ascended the muddy track known as Carrion Pit Lane. There was no guarantee we would find our way back again before nightfall.

A low tree branch scratched my face, another my hand. Looking about me, I began to feel very anxious, my tiredness bordering on exhaustion.

'Harry, please can we stop for a while?'

'Not far now, Sarah. Keep up!'

Twigs snapped underfoot; branches jabbed at either side of us. Above, through a thick canopy, dusty shafts of light streamed down, but not enough to chase away the shadows, which only seemed to thicken and bulk, as if warning us to stop, go back.

I had never been afraid of the dark before, but these woods were making me short of breath and making my stomach churn.

Price halted. Held up his right hand in a command to stop.

'Danger?' I asked. 'Unexploded shells? What?'

He shook his head. 'Thought I heard something.'

Warily, I looked about, peering between the dark trunks. There was no sign of anything much: just the tangled under-growth and some tall, odd-looking plants with pale stems and white trumpet-shaped flowers that deepened to an inner purple.

'See anything?' Price whispered.

I shook my head.

An unearthly silence. Not even the distant sound of farming equipment above us, on the chalky grasslands of Salisbury Plain.

'Never mind,' Price said. He waved me to follow on.

Suddenly, we heard a scream: piercing, anguished, and unmistakably a woman's.

I gave a small start and grabbed for Price's arm. He whirled round, crying, 'What the devil!'

As his bulging eyes scanned the trees and dark spaces in between, I listened intently, scarcely drawing breath.

Nothing.

I let go of Price. He said, in a low voice, 'Someone else is on the range.'

'But we haven't *seen* anyone,' I replied. Not only had the commander guaranteed our privacy – indeed, Price had insisted upon it – but I still had an all too vivid memory of the barrier lowering behind us as Sidewinder's truck kicked up chalk dust and drove away.

Price didn't appear to be listening any more; he was staring past me, between the trees. 'I wonder,' he whispered, setting his tattered old briefcase squarely on the ground and snapping it open. The lid flipped up, revealing a thermograph, a camera, a bottle of mercury, a sketch pad, pencils and a drawing board. His trademark tools for debunking cases of the paranormal. There was a steel tape measure, plaster, string and tools to seal rooms, doors and windows, and even brushes and powdered graphite for developing fingerprints. And who could forget his trusty bright red Swiss army knife?

'What are you doing?' I asked, as Price plucked out a matchstick.

'Sergeant Edwards said he was compelled to strike a match. As if someone had coerced him to do so. Correct?'

I nodded.

'So let's use this match as a trigger object. See if we can't entice those whispering spirits back to meet us.'

I stared. 'Harry, you can't be serious. That's silly.'

Price looked at me silently and then he slowly smiled.

'Sarah. You told me I ought to open my mind. Let's see if our ghosts are in a sociable mood today, shall we?'

A sensation of pins and needles brushed over my body.

'Harry, I don't think this is a wise —'

He struck the match.

I froze. Around me, the trees seemed to shimmer, as if I were seeing them through a haze. At first, there was absolute silence. The air had become chillingly cold, freezing, and then I thought I heard, faintly . . . low whisperings.

I shuddered. Opened my mouth to ask Price if he heard them too, but before I could get the words out, there was a sudden sound to the side of me. Something moving fast, crashing out of the trees. Sprinting.

I turned. And in that instant I seemed to find myself confronted by the past. I saw a man in uniform. Well built. Broad-shouldered.

Sergeant Edwards.

But this wasn't the horribly burned man we had met at Westdown Camp. This Sergeant Edwards had a smooth and handsome face. And he was holding a can of liquid that smelt very much like petrol.

Before I could shout for Price, I was overcome by a sickening dizziness as I saw Sergeant Edwards lifting the metal can over his head. The pungent petrol inside began glugging out.

I saw the oil glistening on his face, his clothes. Smelt the high, sweet fumes.

'Stop!'

But he was unreachable except to the whispering voices. His eyes had a frozen, bug-eyed look, but they weren't focused on me. They were fixed ahead of him, on something I couldn't see.

He dropped the can and produced a cigarette lighter.

I was so startled I almost tripped over as I turned to Price, my eyes watering.

'Oh my God,' I shouted. 'Harry!'

A flick of the lighter, a blaze of heat and orange light. Then, a sound destined to haunt my nightmares for decades – a howl of ragged agony.

The young man dropped to the ground as the flames licked and twirled around him, his arms flailing to beat the fire from his clothes. But that wasn't the worst of it. The smell of the bubbling fat and skin was vile, like burned liver – a harsh, sickening stench.

'Sarah! Sarah, what on earth is the matter? SARAH!'

Hands gripped my shoulders tightly.

My eyes snapped open. I slumped back against a fallen tree and held on to it, pulling in heavy breaths. 'Didn't . . . didn't you see it?'

'See what?'

'Sergeant Edwards,' I managed. 'Harry, I saw . . . I saw . . . what he did to himself.'

Price looked blankly bewildered. He had expected something to happen to us out here in the woods, but not this. 'Just catch your breath, Sarah,' he said, putting his arm around me. 'Nothing happened. There's nothing to fear.'

I stood that way for a long time, nauseous, faint, trembling, gripping the side of the fallen tree. My head was throbbing, my jaw aching. My mouth was dry and my vision blurred. I struggled to force myself out of the giddy daze, aware that the flesh on my arms was now covered with goosebumps, my hands numbed with an unpleasant tingling sensation. At last Price let me go and stood back.

'You blacked out, Sarah,' he said grimly. Solemnly. 'There was no one here.'

'But I *saw*! Harry, I saw what they made him do.'

'Who?' Price was looking at me as if I had lost my mind. And maybe I had.

I shook my head. I didn't know.

Sometimes there just aren't any words.

'Are you ready to continue, Sarah?'

I blinked at Price, remembering the way the trees had appeared to shimmer around me. The abominable vision had seemed so real; the bitter smell of charred flesh was still in my nostrils.

The thought was a crazy one, but it was as if I had witnessed a replay of a past event. I told Price as much.

'I strongly doubt that, Sarah.'

'May I ask why?'

'The phenomenon you're describing is called retrocognition. Witnessing past events through extra-sensory perception.' He eyed me with a cynically contracted brow. 'Such cases – I mean *convincing* cases – are extremely rare.'

I remembered Sidewinder pouring scorn on Price's objectivity, that he doubted the ghost hunter was ever capable of recognising a genuine paranormal event, and felt myself hardening against his scepticism. 'If you have a theory, Harry, it had better be a good one.'

Price nodded, calculating. He asked me, 'Have you ever read the novel *The Hill of Dreams*?'

I shook my head, wondering where he was going with this, and he smiled, content, apparently, with the opportunity to explain.

'*The Hill of Dreams* tells the tale of a rector's son, Lucian

Taylor, a lad who wanders this world in search of meaning, truth and beauty. One passage stands out in my memory:

'"The form of external things, black depths in woods, pools on lonely places, those still valleys curtained by hills on every side, sounding always with the ripple of their brooks, had become to him an influence like that of a drug, giving a certain peculiar colour and outline to his thoughts . . ."'

I stared at him long enough for him to see I wasn't impressed. 'You think I experienced some sort of – what? Terror-induced hallucination?' I was indignant. His scepticism was maddening!

He raised one bushy eyebrow. 'I have no doubt the experience was real to you. Whether it was real in the *objective* sense is quite another matter.'

Maybe he had a point. I knew just as well as he did the effect that an environment with a traumatic history could have on the sensory capability of someone suffering emotional distress. Parapsychologists like him had a name for such phenomena: 'locational bias'. Locations bleed their peculiar histories, and what we know about them, into our subconscious, causing us to imagine things that don't objectively exist. Making us hallucinate.

And yet the vision was so clear. Either way, I decided, there was danger here in these woods and we should leave. Now.

'I can see a clearing,' Price said, turning. 'It's not much farther. Come along!'

Despite my misgivings, I went with him, feeling ever more certain that we were trespassing now in a bleak and uncertain domain, where the living met the dead; a place of silent loneliness on the borderlands. I was breathing hard as we scrambled through the last thickets into a wide clearing, but then the scene that opened before us quite stole my breath away. a magnificent gully, its rugged walls dropping away from us to a depth of maybe sixty or seventy feet.

'It's a chalk pit,' Price said. 'They're common on Salisbury Plain, but this must be the most impressive I've ever seen. Careful. Stay away from the edge.'

I had no intention of going anywhere near the edge. Instead, I sank down where I stood, sweeping my skirt and coat under me. Sheltering my hands in my pockets, I sat there for a few moments, the wind whistling down from over the plain.

Did I hear something else then, carried on that wind? I could have been wrong, but what I thought I heard was a dog barking.

'So . . . Glad you came?' Price asked eventually.

'Very,' I said tartly, looking up at him.

A smile touched his lips. He crouched down beside me. 'Just like the old days, eh?'

I nodded. 'But that doesn't mean I'm coming back to work for you, Harry.'

The smile vanished. 'You never worked for me, Sarah. You worked *with* me. You and I, we were a team.'

A team? What about when you left me, pregnant and alone to fend for myself, to run your laboratory on my own? Were we a team then?

'Six years was long enough, thank you, Harry.'

'Six *good* years,' he added. And maybe that was true, but only partly.

At times the work had been darkly exhilarating. I thought back to the night we met, a Saturday evening in 1926, two weeks before my twenty-second birthday. It was the gala opening of his laboratory at 16 Queensberry Place, a house that had the distinct air of a gentlemen's club. The newspapers, and every guest in attendance, had been promised 'wonders', and that was exactly what they got from the medium parading before us on a grand stage. What no one was expecting – including Mother, who had cajoled me into going along – was Price's dramatic revelation: '*Ladies and gentlemen, I do not believe in ghosts!*'

You could have heard a pin drop. Price was something no one expected: an exposer of frauds. And I was impressed. I hadn't gone with Mother to keep her company. I'd gone because I was worried she'd squander yet more of the little money we had on dubious spiritualist mediums. She was lost, sick with grief. And as far as I could see, Price and his laboratory offered the closest thing to a remedy.

That night, after his dazzling public performance, my curiosity conquered reason. I'd wandered off to explore Price's laboratory for myself: the dark enchantments of his 'séance room'; the curious trinkets that littered the benches of his workshop, with its bell jars, tool racks, microscopes and cameras; and yes, even the many leather-bound volumes that furnished the handsome bookcases in his private study.

'What are you doing in here?' Price had demanded when he found me. 'Who are you?'

I had felt awkward. Helpless. Guilty. Now, six years later, sitting at the edge of that yawning chalk pit, many miles from London, I wondered how we had come to this; how different things would have been if I hadn't attempted to flatter him that night, remarking how fascinating it must be to work in his laboratory.

'Can you type?' he had asked.

I could. Eighty words a minute.

'Very well, then it's settled!' he had said confidently, and that was when he had stepped towards me, when his hand had brushed mine. I had felt eager to get started. I had wanted excitement, wanted to do good. What could go wrong?

Now I knew the answer to that question. A suppressed scandal, a secret pregnancy. A child I would never know.

'There's something you haven't told me,' Price said suddenly, bringing me back to the moment – to the jagged edge of the quarry. I looked up at him steadily, more steadily than I felt anyway, and he nodded. He didn't know. He *couldn't* know . . . could he? A wave of trepidation broke over me.

Our son.

Heart-stricken, I felt a stab of self-reproach. Price was one of the proudest people I had ever known. What would it do to him if he knew I had given birth to his son and then chosen to give him away? That sort of truth could break a man like Harry, and I cared too much for him to stomach the alarming idea that he had somehow discovered the lie. But when he spoke next, it was clear I had been mistaken. 'You said you had an item you wanted me to examine. An object you brought with you from London, yes?'

The hand-painted projection slide I had found in the Brixton Picture Palace. I still felt unsure about sharing it with him.

'Forget about it.'

'*You* made me agree to examine it, to give my view. Remember? When you telephoned me at the laboratory?'

My gaze dropped to the bottom of the chalk pit.

'You said it was a lantern slide you found at the Brixton Picture Palace.'

My head snapped up and I glared at him. 'I still don't think it was a coincidence we met that night. How could you have known I was there? Unless, well, unless you'd been following me. *Were* you following me? Harry?'

'No. But . . . that's not to say someone else wasn't.'

My breath caught. 'What?'

'I received a letter. Typed. Anonymous. Telling me where I could find you, and when.' He shrugged. 'Clearly, whoever wrote that letter wanted us to meet again.'

'I don't understand. Why would anyone want to follow me?'

'I wish I knew.'

A cold wind sighed. I pulled my coat tightly around me, huddling into the collar. 'Harry, that night I experienced a . . . well, I suppose you'd call it an altered state of consciousness. Extra-sensory perception. Like what happened to me in the woods just now.'

He nodded.

'I feel I have a connection with this village that goes beyond my father's training here,' I went on. 'A psychic connection that also explains the vision I had of Sergeant Edwards. But, tell me honestly – could what I'm telling you even fracture that armour of scepticism you wear so proudly?'

'Fracture?' He made a show of considering this. 'Never. But I suppose such a story might *dent* my armour – just a little.'

'This quest you're on . . . If you *did* ever experience some-thing unexplainable, what would it do to you?'

His eyes flickered with irritation.

'You get your thrill from the chase, Harry. Applying your scientific methods. Proving other people wrong. It's like a drug to you. But what if the witnesses are right? What if these woods and the old mill *are* haunted, and you find yourself with the proof in your hands?'

He went quiet for a moment and his gaze moved past me, down into the plummeting pit. 'A discovery like that? Well, it would change everything. And everyone. Millions of people, their religions, how they live their lives.'

'Then you'd embrace it?'

His eyes locked on mine. 'You know I would. There could be no greater revelation, Sarah, for a scientist. For any human.'

Not since the night we met had I heard him sound so impassioned about his search for truth. His sustained and intense obsession with occult phenomena. His passion.

Once more, I suffered the pull of attraction towards him, except now the feeling was more intense. His gaze was moving slowly, delicately, to my lips. My chest tightened, my heart fluttering. I took a shaky breath.

All at once, Price cocked his head, as though he had heard something, and looked furtively around.

'What is it?' I asked.

The moment was lost.

'Listen. A dog. Barking. You hear it?'

I did.

His eyes shifted excitedly to mine.

'Williams did mention his soldiers had reported a dog, didn't he?'

With a heavy sinking in my stomach, I remembered the commander had indeed mentioned a dog. A ravenous black one. All at once I had a vivid image of a wild and giant mongrel with matted fur leaping out at us, teeth bared and snarling.

'It's probably a stray,' I said quietly.

Price jumped up. 'Come on. We had better keep moving.'

My wristwatch told me it was now two o'clock. The giant mill wheel was immobile, the iron rusted, its lower spokes

submerged in a stinking and vast pond that looked unfath-
omably deep, clogged with weeds and algae. There must have
been a stream somewhere very close by, because I could hear
it gurgling and bubbling, but the mill wheel hadn't turned
for decades.

I halted abruptly, a prickling sensation sweeping over my
skin.

'Sarah, what is it?'

'I know this place,' I told him.

Price frowned. 'You mean you've been here before?'

'I don't think so . . . but somehow I recognise it.'

'Do you indeed?'

He turned a rather unsettling gaze upon me.

My palms were clammy, my heart beating too fast. With
apprehension, I stepped forward, keeping my eyes on the
ancient and imposing mill – a lonely, leering shack of mouldy
boards and gritstone. It was guarded by discarded flour barrels,
clumps of bushes and more of the plants with the trumpet-shaped flowers, white with purple hearts.

The prickling at the base of my neck intensified. I felt a
vein throbbing in my throat. Pain pulsing behind my eyes.
Pain in my chest.

'Sarah?'

The world tilted. I began struggling for breath. An onrush
of something . . .

'Hello?' I called, blinking, clearing my head.

No reply.

Harry stepped right up to me. I sensed he was about to
ask me, eagerly, if I was on the verge of another vision, but I
brushed his arm away.

'Leave me, Harry. If I need your help, I'll ask. Understand?'

He nodded; his eyes held mine for a moment, then they slipped away.

I was glad.

Once again, in his eagerness, he had made me feel like one of his laboratory subjects, something to be studied, when what I really needed was to understand why I was responding to the landscape in such a peculiar way. Why, too, did I still have a nagging doubt that Price was holding back on me?

Was it possible Price *did* understand my visions, and wasn't telling?

It seemed unlikely. It was in his interests as well as mine to ascertain what had happened to Sergeant Edwards, and understanding my vision might help us understand more about how Edwards had succumbed to his fate. No, the idea that Price knew more, and deliberately wasn't saying, made little sense. But then, I pondered, neither did his earlier explanation for my vision.

Harry Price and his secrets. It was impossible to have one without the other.

We walked on slowly, skirting the edge of the fetid pond. Behind us, in the woods, the dog began to bark again, louder than before.

'Wait.' Price snilled the air, his eyes darting around. 'Can you smell that?'

He wasn't referring to the pond's fetid smell. The closer we got to the mill, the more we noticed another scent, a nauseating chemical odour.

'We have to get a look inside,' he said. Still, as we approached the boarded-up mill, I thought I saw the slightest flicker of apprehension on his face.

'Locked!' he said, grasping the handle and rattling the door. I saw that the padlock preventing us from gaining access wasn't just sturdy, but shiny and new. And what need was there for the new iron bars that covered the windows?

As if hearing my thoughts, Price placed his battered brief-case on the ground and from his overcoat pocket produced a small torch, which he shone through the nearest window.

I stepped up to it. Peering between the bars, the first thing I noticed in the white pool of Price's spotlight wasn't the rank, earthy floor, or the leaves, or the dank, stained walls, but what was nailed *into* those walls.

Wooden crucifixes.

'I don't understand,' Price said, but there was a note of vindication in his tone. With almost instinctive certainty he had insisted the army hadn't disclosed to us the full details about this old mill, and now it seemed he had been right.

Some small, some large – there were crucifixes everywhere. A battered oblong table. Candles, too. But these didn't have the appearance of age, like the schoolbooks we had seen in the village, or the grimy bottles. These candles looked new, the wax drippings fresh.

'No wonder the commander didn't want us to come up here,' said Price.

'What does it mean, do you think?'

'Nothing good.'

This time, the dog didn't just bark again. It howled. It could have been my imagination, but it sounded nearer. Much nearer.

'Harry, perhaps we should go now?'

'Yes, yes. First, let me take some photographs of the whole building.'

He went to his briefcase, took out his camera, and began

making a circuit of the mill, leaving me to wait next to the millpond.

I couldn't see the rest of Imber from here, but I glimpsed the spire of the church jutting up into the grey sky. And, deep in the woods from which we had come, an indistinct and dark shape was moving.

Squinting, I tried to work out what it was. An animal? I gave a tiny shudder as I imagined that wild black dog.

'Harry!' I called out, peering harder at the form.

Not an animal. A figure.

It flickered unsteadily and seemed to grow larger.

'Harry, come quickly and see!'

I *needed* him to see. Otherwise, I feared I might really be losing it.

'What in heaven's – '

It was Price, suddenly at my side. And, thank goodness, he *could* see it too.

'Is that a . . .'

Woman. Flesh and blood, dressed in a flowing black dress.

She was standing at the line of trees, maybe one hundred yards away. Her eyes were deeply set, and she regarded us savagely from beneath furrowed brows.

'Hello there, madam!' Price called out to her.

The woman did not move; did not reply.

Cautiously, Price said, 'I think perhaps we should approach and ask – '

She broke into a run. Tearing towards us, hands clutching the skirt of her black dress to prevent her from stumbling. Her face was painfully gaunt, her hair dark and dishevelled, her eyes wild. I knew, the moment I saw those eyes, that I would never forget them.

'Stop! Stop! Get away! Do you hear me? Get AWAY!'

Her French accent was unmistakable; and so was the fiery rage in her voice. What happened next seemed to occur in slow motion, but must have happened in a matter of seconds.

Suddenly, she was upon us, throwing herself towards Price as she shouted, 'Did you see him? Did you scare him away? DID YOU?'

Looking astounded, Price's hands flew up involuntarily, but her hands went to his throat, and with a cry he tripped backwards, his feet just inches away from the edge of the filthy millpond.

'Harry!'

Forgetting my fear, I sprang forward to help, but even before I reached him he had prised the woman off him. Her face was contorted with rage.

'Miss, calm down,' I spoke up, but she kept her gaze locked on Price, and in her ferocious expression I saw that she meant to go for him again.

'This is where he lives,' she said hoarsely. 'He is not to be disturbed!'

'Madam, if you would allow me to explain—'

And with an alarming lunge, she charged at Price again. His fedora went flying as he leapt out of her way. He didn't see the gnarled tree root protruding from the bank of the pond. Perhaps she did, but by then it was too late.

She stumbled, tripped, fell. And splashed into the stagnant pond.

I stared, astonished. Instead of trying to get out of the water, she was wading in deeper. Then she began to splash and flail.

Price gaped. I saw what he was thinking. The pond was

deep. Very deep. There was little chance of her getting out on her own.

'Stay back, Sarah! Under no account follow me.'

Throwing off his coat, he darted to the edge of the pond and took a breath. He looked determined to rescue her as he plunged into the thick water.

In the water, the woman appeared stricken with fear and with panic.

I heard Price gasping as he stroked through the water.

There was a moment when I thought he wouldn't reach her in time – she began to flail more urgently, her dress blooming out around her like a black cloud.

But then, just as the water covered her mouth and nose, he reached out. Grabbed an arm.

Thank heavens!

Except something was wrong. The horrified breath caught in my throat as I realised what it was: now, treading water, Price was struggling.

'Sarah!' he gasped.

He was out of his depth, entangled with weeds, probably. Perhaps they both were.

Think, Sarah, think!

Looking madly around me, I saw what I needed: sprouting from the earth was a long, exposed tree root. It was some ten metres away. I could throw it to them – if I could work it free from the ground in time. But even at this distance it was obvious that the root was tough.

The Swiss army knife!

In the pond, the woman was flailing and splashing and shrieking: 'Leave me! Do you hear? I want to be with him.' It was clear that she had meant to do this. She meant to drown herself. Even if it meant taking Price with her.

'Hang on, Harry!' I shouted, bolting for his briefcase. 'Keep moving, kick your legs!'

On my knees, hands shaking, I flipped the briefcase open, raking frantically through its contents: screw eyes, pocket torch, adhesive tape. No sign of the knife. Where was it?

His coat?

It was ten feet away. Regaining my feet, I pitched forward. Next instant, I was on my knees again, raiding his pockets.

There, suddenly, was the bright red Swiss army knife. Hope surged through me, pulling me to my feet.

'Sarah!'

I darted to the gnarled tree root and dropped down beside it. Then I got to work on the root, sawing at it with panicky strength. It split. Came away in my hand. I leapt to my feet, and hurled it into the water.

'Grab it, Harry!'

He threw out one hand, his fingers groping the air. Just inches away.

Then, with titanic effort, he lunged, reaching . . .

His fingers closed around the root.

Thank God! Oh, thank God.

Slowly, he made it back to the bank of the pond, struggling to keep both their heads above the water. The woman was silent now and her eyes were fluttering, as if she was slipping in and out of consciousness.

As Price reached the bank and staggered up and out, struggling for breath, I saw he was covered in pond scum. He hauled the woman out and I stepped closer to help steady her, but she had already crumpled onto the filthy pond bank, her dress sodden.

'My baby,' the woman gasped between laboured breaths. 'My precious boy. Don't you see? He needs me. He's all I have now.'

Right then I was too shocked to focus on her words. Price and I were kneeling over her. She was shivering violently, her skin grey gooseflesh, her eyelids quivering. Who was this woman? How had she gained access to the range?

She tried to speak again but her chattering teeth defeated her effort.

'Now, now. It's all right, we'll get you dry,' said Price. He was looking for his overcoat.

Suddenly, from behind us, came a furious voice. 'That's quite enough!'

Our heads snapped up. Standing rigidly at the edge of the forest were the commander and Sidewinder. Other uniformed men, three or four of them, were marching towards us. A powerful-looking Rottweiler trotted along beside them.

'Explain the meaning of this intrusion!' Price demanded.

He stood to face them, his face full of confrontation, but the soldiers didn't answer; they went to the stricken woman and hauled her off the ground. One of them slipped off his jacket and wrapped it around her.

Stunned, Price turned to the commander. 'Who is this lady? She needs help.'

'No, she needs to leave,' the commander said. He addressed the soldiers who were helping – restraining – her. 'Get her out of here, now!'

She resisted, struggling against them with impressive strength.

Williams turned and stared at Price and me. 'We told you both to stay away from this location.'

'You also said we'd be alone on the range,' Price retorted angrily. Standing there next to the black pond, drenched, he looked freezing. 'How long have you been trailing us?'

'Since the moment we spotted her,' the commander said, nodding at the woman, who was now being led away towards the woods, 'following you.'

'Murderers,' she shouted back over her shoulder. 'You can't hide what's happening here, especially not from me. I have rights! I'm entitled!'

'Wait! What's she talking about?' I asked. I ran after the soldiers, with Price following quickly behind.

The woman's desperate eyes locked on me. 'Did you go inside the mill?' she asked. 'Did you see him? Tell me you saw him.'

'Saw who?' Price asked.

'My angel,' she said. 'My boy. He left us, he died, two years ago, but I tell you now, he's right here. This is where he comes.'

Now the commander was right beside us. 'She's delusional,' he said. The woman spat in his direction and he rounded on her, his face revealing the full colour of his anger. 'Madam, this is your last warning. If we catch you on this range again, outside of the permitted public opening hours, there will be consequences.'

'Oh, you're right about that, commander,' she said bitterly, raising her head in defiance. 'There *will* be consequences. For all of you.'

16

DECEIVED

'Dammit!' Price said, and slammed his fist down on the commander's desk. 'I have a good mind to make a formal complaint to the War Office. Failing to keep an intruder off the range compromised our entire investigation! Not to mention very nearly costing us our lives.'

A strained silence.

Sitting stiffly behind his desk, Commander Williams raised one eyebrow – the one with the thin scar running through it. I wasn't entirely surprised to see him throw a quick glance at the military plaques and awards that adorned the office walls.

'Mr Price,' he said, finally, 'I had hoped your late lunch might have calmed your spirits.'

Price scowled back at him, practically trembling with anger.

Back at Westdown Camp, four miles from Imber, it had been a good three hours since the distressing incident at the millpond. Our investigation had been cut short. Now the afternoon was ending, and, although still a little in shock, and weary, I was eager to calm Price's temper.

'Harry, the woman who accosted us in the village – '

'She was following us the whole time!' Price cut in, glaring at the commander. 'So, tell us! Who the hell is she?'

Nothing but a stony silence from the commander.

'How did she obtain a set of keys to the church? Clearly, it was her we heard, ringing the bells. Why did she call you murderers?'

The commander's mouth twitched at that. 'Please try to calm down, Mr Price.'

'I'll calm down when you tell me what I want to know!' Price bellowed. Then, with an exasperated sigh, he reached down and grabbed my hand and held it up for the commander to see; scratches striped my fingers from the trees and underbrush. 'Fighting through the woods, for you. All for nothing.'

I yanked my hand away.

'You *were* warned not to enter the woods, Mr Price.'

'That was Marie Hartwell, wasn't it?' I said. The commander shot me a look, surprised, and I added, 'Warden Sidewinder told us Oscar Hartwell met his wife, Marie, in Paris.'

And the woman's accent had been unmistakably French.

Price leapt in: 'Who was she searching for?'

The commander raised his eyes to us self-righteously. 'Mrs Hartwell is gravely unwell, Mr Price. She – '

'We have been misled!' Price shouted. 'Deceived! We came to help your men, yet it's them – *you* – who have failed *us*. Kept crucial information from us. Crucifixes inside the old mill, all over the blasted walls! Were you going to mention those?'

I stood up. 'All right. That's enough for now, Harry.'

He was on the verge of crossing a line, though I understood

why he was angry. He had been made to feel foolish – gullible, even.

'Commander,' I said, adopting a tone I hoped was reasonable, 'given that Sergeant Edwards sustained his injuries so close to that location, and that he witnessed the apparition of a child at that exact spot, it would be very useful to understand the history of the mill, and why its walls are covered with crucifixes. Why did we find candles there, recently burned? Commander, has someone been worshipping there?'

The commander's face arranged itself into an expression of utmost consternation. 'Clearly, the conditions on the range took their toll on your imagination.'

This was insulting and frustratingly evasive, but I kept my temper, even as he instructed us both to forget what we had seen, to say nothing of it to anyone. But at last we had a tangible lead: the crucifixes and candles. We had photographs, too. It was imperative now that we discover to whom the objects belonged. To do that, though, I had to keep Price on side, and judging from his exasperated expression, that seemed unlikely.

'I'm going for a walk,' Price announced.

'What about the investigation?' the commander enquired.

'Excuse me? I very nearly drowned this afternoon. You don't seriously imagine we'd wish to return? You invited me here to detect trickery, and I have done so. You've been hoaxed by Marie Hartwell.' A pause. 'I'm afraid we all have.'

By the time we excused ourselves from the commander's office, Price had at least recovered his temper, but he was still nursing his bruised ego. As we stood in the concrete corridor outside, I saw to my dismay that he had reached a decision.

There were two things Price could never tolerate: being humiliated and being undermined.

'We leave tomorrow at dawn,' he said.

I stared at Price, at the briefcase he was holding.

'I'll be damned if I'm made to look a fool by a –'

'Careful, Harry!' I said curtly, throwing up a hand. Just one derogatory remark from his mouth about that poor woman and I'd strike that stubborn face hard enough to leave a mark. 'No one has made you look foolish. Marie Hartwell was distraught, probably unstable. Unwell. And the fact that she was on the range has only demonstrated that you were right to be sceptical in the first place.'

His chest expanded at that. 'I suppose so,' he said, a touch reluctantly. 'It's just so bloody disappointing. When those bells rang, I thought that maybe we were on to something.'

'I thought that too,' I said. 'But I'm not ready to go.'

He shook his head. 'This investigation has been like the history of spiritualism itself. One long trail of fraud, folly and credulity. Come morning, I'm off.'

'You can do what you damn well like. But I'm not going anywhere.'

He blinked. 'Sarah . . .'

'Clearly, the army is hiding something. The questions we need to answer now are who was Marie Hartwell looking for at the mill, and why were there candles and crucifixes in the building.'

Price folded his arms. 'I'm not spending another day in this blasted place,' he said obstinately.

I couldn't accept that. So far, our investigation had raised more questions than answers. Questions about the military's work here, questions about the village's former residents, and

questions about its alleged ghosts. If anything, I only felt more
determined to stay and see this through.

Convincing him of that wouldn't be easy, but I thought I
knew how.

While Price went out for his walk, strutting briskly away
like an infuriated child, I took a light supper in the officers'
mess, doing my best to ignore the many curious glances from
the soldiers eating there. Dusk fell and I decided on an early
night. My simple bed was waiting for me in Hut Three. After
scraping my plate clean, I went straight there, still pondering
the strange sensation of recognition that had struck me outside
the mill, and the pale little boy in rags I had encountered on
the downs on my arrival. I was so preoccupied with these
mysteries that I failed to sense someone behind me.

'Miss Grey? I have news. Bad news.'

I spun round to see Sidewinder standing on the path, his
deeply set eyes magnified by his circular silver spectacle
frames.

With a shiver, I nodded. Tensed. I didn't trust the warden. He
didn't wear a black suit, but he carried with him the distinctly
unpleasant air of a funeral director, and everything about him
made me uneasy.

'What's happened?' I asked, unable to keep the curiosity
out of my voice.

'I thought you'd want to know – the commander has made
his decision. Imber Service Day will go ahead as planned.
Tomorrow morning, eleven o'clock.'

Just when I had thought our predicament couldn't get any
worse. How wrong I was.

− 17 −

THE HARROWING

In my darker moods, I often wonder how different things might have been at the service if we hadn't so thoroughly exhausted ourselves the day before, if we had only been more alert and noticed the dreadful thing that was happening, right before our eyes, before it was too late.

I did my best, I tell myself. But my best was nowhere near good enough.

That Sunday morning, we woke to discover that snow had fallen overnight and blanketed most of Salisbury Plain. I'd heard people say that the world seems quieter when it snows, but I never truly felt the sentiment until that glistening morning in October 1932, as I emerged from Hut Three with a plan in mind. The snow hadn't just made the desolate plain completely white, it had made it deathly quiet.

Although the snowfall had eased off by eight thirty, the steel-grey clouds suggested there would probably be more to come. Perhaps the Imber Service would be cancelled after all? Not that it made a difference either way to Price.

'I'm leaving now, before this weather worsens,' he told me.

We were outside at Westdown Camp, standing beside Price's handsome Rolls-Royce saloon. I looked at him, remembering his panic-stricken face as he struggled in the pond, and felt real sympathy. How close I had come to losing him. It was an effort, but I had to restrain the urge to just let him drive back to London

'We have a duty to stay, Harry. Can't you speak to the commander? Get him to call off the service?'

But when did Harry Price ever agree to do something that might inconvenience himself?

'If we give the military a reason to close Imber,' he said, 'the civilians will be up in arms. Their little campaign will be all over the newspapers, and I'll be forced to explain why I believe Imber should be off limits. I'm not prepared to put myself on the line like that.'

'So, you're thinking of yourself. Again. We can't just give up –'

'There's no *evidence*,' he interrupted, taking my hand and squeezing it firmly. 'Don't allow your father's memory to bias your interpretation of what we've experienced here. We already know we were hoaxed yesterday by –'

'We *don't* know that! Not for sure. It's what *you've assumed*!' I shook off his hand. 'And besides, Harry, there's something I haven't told you. Something that might persuade you to stay.'

I still hadn't mentioned the wandering child. It wasn't just that I was afraid of being accused of exaggerating ... The memory of my own baby, my torturous guilt, had been in my mind a lot recently. I lived with the fear of Price ever

discovering I had given away our child. A child he knew nothing about. And sometimes the mind was the biggest deceiver
of all, wasn't it? How did I know that the child I had witnessed
at the roadside, his dark eyes boring into me, hadn't been a
projection of my own guilt?

If I had hallucinated, then telling Price about it would be
risky; might betray my guilt, my secret. A revelation like that
would cut him deeply. He had black moods, I knew that, and
I had no wish to discover just how black they could be.

Now, however, we had come to a turning point.

'I've also seen him.'

'Who?'

'The little boy with the pale face and bloated stomach. The
same little boy Sergeant Edwards saw at the old mill. I saw
him too. On the journey here.'

I don't think I'd ever seen him so astonished.

'Sarah, are you asking me to accept that you witnessed an
apparition – a *ghost*?'

'I'm only asking you to take me at my word.'

'Why didn't you tell me this earlier?'

'I had my reasons,' I said quietly. 'But the one thing you
can't do now is dismiss this as a crude case of locational bias,
because I didn't know anything about the reports until after
I saw the child.'

He threw up his arms. 'How do I know? You haven't told me
the first thing about how this case came to you!'

'I made a promise.'

He opened his mouth to reply, closed it.

'Trust, Harry. This is about trust.'

'You really think that boy is the key to this?'

What had Marie Hartwell said? Her 'angel', her boy.

'Well, I can't be certain, but yes. I think it's his grave we found defaced in the Imber churchyard. To learn more, we will have to ask his father, Oscar Hartwell, for a detailed description. Find out how the boy died. And that won't be easy. Though Hartwell's bound to attend the Imber service today. If we attend the service, convince him we support his campaign, perhaps if we offer to help . . .'

'He may tell us all we need to know,' Price finished.

I nodded. Price nodded too, and granted me a half-smile. Perhaps he wasn't sold on this investigation, but he did know I still cared about his mission, that there was a part of me, deep down, that believed I would return to his laboratory and, once again, take his hand and walk with him into the dark.

'Fine. If I can't prevent the Imber Service,' he said, 'we may as well use it to learn something.'

'Harry, do you think someone in the army engineered what happened yesterday?'

He nodded grimly. 'And what better way to lend the whole thing credence in the eyes of the soldiers than by calling in an expert debunker like me?'

'But why would they do something like that in the first place?'

He calculated. 'To conceal a darker, more insidious agenda, perhaps. I sense a weight of secrets hanging over Imber and its history. Remember the commander? His eyes? He doesn't trust us, Sarah. I'd go as far as to say he's afraid of us getting too close to the truth.'

That remark called up Vernon's words: '*I have a bad feeling I can't shake. A sense that there's something deeper out in that village. Something darker.*'

'Sarah,' said Price, 'I'll make you this deal. I'll come with you to the service and learn what we can about this child you saw. But then, if we find nothing, we make our departure. Quickly.'

It wasn't the deal I wanted, but it was better than nothing, so I agreed.

'Mark my words,' Price said, as we went in search of the commander and Sidewinder, 'when today is over, you'll be ready to leave this blasted place and put this whole business behind us.'

Snow was swirling down again when the civilians were finally permitted to enter Imber. Inside the church, soldiers were doing their bit to help, putting out the chairs for the service – a token gesture to many former residents, I felt sure. These were the men they thought had stolen their homes, their lives. No amount of chair-arranging would excuse that. Meanwhile, Price and I stood outside, freezing, in the shadow of the church, and watched a string of motor cars, perhaps thirty or more, creeping along the single track towards the checkpoint, its white barrier raised. As the former residents of Imber drove past the abandoned tanks and warning notices, I couldn't help but feel a warm admiration for every one of them. They weren't going to allow the risk of getting snowed under to deter them from making this pilgrimage. *What must they think,* I wondered, *when they see the ruined roads, the shell-shattered houses, the devastation?*

'Any sign of our man?' Price asked.

He meant Hartwell, but it was difficult to make out any faces through the drift.

'Not yet.' I was trying to sound hopeful, but perhaps I had been wrong to assume that Hartwell would attend. So many of his family were buried here, perhaps the service was just too painful for him to endure.

'There are going to be a lot of embittered people here today,' Price said in a low voice, and I had to agree. A few civilians ambled past us, holding their coats tightly around them, their eyes raking over the ruined cottages, dusted with snow. An elderly couple wandered like frail ghosts through the overgrown graveyard, stooping here and there to clear the weeds from the neglected headstones, their faces etched with anger and grief.

Near them was a woman attired in black, attending to the Hartwell memorial. Did she look familiar? Possibly, but it was hard to be sure; her head was down and seconds later she moved away.

Price saw her, then nodded to the church entrance and said, 'Let's get inside.'

A cool draught brushed my face as we pushed open the heavy oak doors.

Inside the church, down the central aisle, an enormous scaffolding supported part of the roof. The atmosphere was thickly sad as the civilians – I guessed there were forty or more – gazed mournfully at the church's shattered windows and the fresh bullet holes that peppered the walls.

Price's quick gaze made a circuit of the church, taking in the slender candles in every corner, the Union Jacks strung between the pillars, the great metal chandeliers above.

At that moment I heard a well-spoken, familiar voice and turned my head to see a sharp-featured man at the front, surrounded by a huddle of villagers. Tall. Bald. Bearded. Impeccably attired in a black suit. As he took questions, he fidgeted, twisting his signet ring.

'That's him,' I said. 'That's Hartwell.'

We hastened nearer, doing our best to eavesdrop.

'I'll be saying just a few words,' Hartwell was saying, 'much to the army's dissatisfaction, I'm sure. Can you believe they actually asked to see the speech in advance?'

Just then, the reverend entered at the back of the church – a compassionate-looking man with a flushed complexion, in his seventies. As Hartwell turned his head in that direction, he granted me a polite nod of acknowledgement.

He didn't smile though, and I wondered if he still suspected me of working for the War Office.

At that moment, a string quartet – I heard later that they had travelled especially from Salisbury for the service – struck up a sombre melody.

Everyone sat. Even though it was bereft of any of its original pews, St Giles' was full now for the first time in a year, every chair taken. Men and women sat with hands folded in laps. No one spoke. Price and I sat on the right side, a few rows back. The commander was with Sidewinder in the front row, towards the left, his gaze riveted on the reverend as the old man took his place at the pulpit.

For a man who had preached to this congregation for so many years, he looked curiously nervous. All these years later, I suspect that's because the speech he gave was scripted for him by the commander.

'Dear friends, welcome. I know it's cold, and I'm afraid to say that the conditions outside are worsening, which means I am obliged to make today's service shorter than I otherwise would.

'We are here today to worship God, to remember those who served – especially those who made the supreme sacrifice – and to remember those who graciously and willingly sacrificed their homes, this entire village, to the war effort eighteen years ago.'

A pause. His gaze roamed the nodding faces below.

'Sacrifice. That word holds a special meaning for us all, does it not? Christ told us, "Greater love hath no man than this, that a man lay down his life for his friends." Well, no one can argue that the sacrifice we made, as a village, as a community, was distressing and outstanding. We must take solace in knowing that we played our own role in bringing an end to the Great War, for the good of our nation and the Empire.'

Mutterings of support from the congregation; a few nods.

'But' – I noticed the reverend catching the commander's eye – 'we must never forget that members of our armed forces who train hard every day, year in and year out, here on Salisbury Plain are themselves called to a life of sacrifice, and we honour them. May we show our devotion to the heroism of all who fought to preserve a world of peace.'

He looked down at his bible and drew a breath.

'I know that some of you are keen supporters of the noble Imber Will Live campaign. We have with us today a man who most of you know. A man who has worked tirelessly to keep the memory of this special village alive in our hearts Oscar Hartwell, whose family has worked much of Imber for generations, has asked to say a few words, and I would like to welcome him.'

There was muted applause as Hartwell took his place at the pulpit, clutching a sheaf of notes, which he laid on top of the open bible.

The commander was watching him closely, I noticed. It

wasn't surprising that Hartwell had been allowed to speak. Most of the village had once belonged to him.

For a long moment, he gazed down at his notes, saying nothing. When he finally looked up, it was hard not to feel a pang of sympathy for the man. His eyes were glistening.

He cleared his throat and began.

'Friends, it is a testing task for me to stand here in this battered church. You all know why. Most of you either worked directly with my family at Imber Court or knew someone who did. I will never forget the support you offered us that hard winter, when Rosalie was buried next to Lillian and Beatrice. It was snowing that day too.' There was a sad smile across his lips. 'Many of you knew how precious Rosalie was to us, and we will always be eternally grateful to you for your support.'

I couldn't help but feel touched, and I wasn't the only one. At the end of my aisle, a stout middle-aged woman with a downturned mouth and a shock of white hair wiped away a tear.

But not everyone was as moved. In the row behind me, a bald man with a weather-beaten face peered at Hartwell through narrowed eyes.

I recalled once more the funeral I had witnessed outside this very church, and remembered how some of the villagers had watched the proceedings with a mixture of suspicion and trepidation, very like the expression I was seeing on this man's face now.

In the pulpit, Hartwell went on, 'I don't believe many of you ever met Pierre. My son . . .'

I glanced over at the commander and saw him shift uncomfortably in his seat. Price, next to me, was frowning. Why was Hartwell talking about his son – here, now?

'My son,' Hartwell repeated, and I heard the quaver in his voice. 'Pierre was born after the evacuation. If he had lived, he would now be seven years old. But what five-year-old stood a chance against the clutches of the Strangling Angel? I would like to thank Doctor Mitchell for providing the best care available to Pierre. I know you did all you could for him.'

He smiled at a chubby grey-haired man in the congregation, who nodded back and dropped his eyes.

'I've been asked to speak to you about my childhood,' Hartwell continued. 'My memories of the harvest, the endless summers when we picnicked on the downs. What it was like growing up with my sister in the rambling old mansion across the road. But I must tell you, friends, it's not been easy to relive those times. Too much has happened in the intervening years.'

A little puff of frosty air escaped from his mouth; he drew in a breath. Passion, perhaps even obsession, stood out strongly in his voice. He was now glaring defiantly at the commander.

'Around this time of the year – Imber Service Day – I confess that I lose myself in sadness for this wrecked village, which has become a place of ghosts. I ask myself whether perhaps I was wrong to insist that Pierre should be buried here.

'But then I think, *no*. We all love this village; we were born here, some of us have roots going back centuries, and it is right that our families should be buried here.'

I realised that Hartwell was no longer reading from his notes. This part of his speech was coming from somewhere else, from deep within his soul. And that might explain why it suddenly felt so impassioned.

'All we have left is the right to visit this church but once a year. And now even that right is in jeopardy.'

Price looked at me, tense, just as Hartwell got to his point.

'My friends, you have a right to know: the army is considering moving this church, and the graves, permanently.'

A chorus of surprised whisperings rose among the congregation. In the front row, the commander leapt up with an exclamation of protest. 'Enough! This is pure speculation. I demand, sir, that you sit down!'

'But is it true?' The question came from a young man with blonde hair. 'Is this lovely church also to vanish from the map?'

Still standing, Commander Williams tightened his lips.

'Yes, it's true!' Hartwell proclaimed, the veins in his neck standing out. 'They'll tell us not to worry. They'll say the church *must* be moved, for its own preservation. And when we argue – which we will, most strenuously – they'll fight back. They'll tell us it's in the interests of national heritage to "save" this cherished building. In short, my friends, the army will ask us, once again, to make a sacrifice.'

On one side of the church, a few of the soldiers who had been helping earlier stood with their backs to the wall, shaking their heads in disagreement. A few looked embarrassed, discomfited.

'I said *enough!*' the commander threatened.

'This church still belongs to the people, Commander,' Hartwell declared. 'I have a right to be heard, and heard I will be!'

From the back of the church, the young man with blonde hair called out his support. When a few more members of the congregation followed suit, the commander returned to his seat, his face grey and impotent as he glanced nervously at Sidewinder.

Price gave me an apathetic look that suggested he wasn't

impressed with Williams' efforts. In a sense, though, I felt sorry for Williams; as he sat down, I thought I had caught some defiance slip from his face. Perhaps half of him had expected this. The other half hadn't believed for a second it would happen.

From the pulpit, Hartwell scanned the sea of concerned faces looking up at him.

The woman with the white hair now had her downturned mouth wide open. She was shaking her head in strenuous disapproval. 'Who decided the church should go?' she asked. 'On whose authority? When will it happen?'

'Never!' Hartwell said, thumping the bible in front of him. 'This village already made its sacrifice. We were told it wouldn't be forever. A temporary measure. But how quickly the months became years. How quickly promises were forgotten. Well, I say no more broken promises. No more broken hearts!'

He glared down at the commander and the commander glared back at him.

'It wasn't our sacrifice the army wanted, it was our *obedience*. And now the army want us to surrender this church and the people buried here – to surrender our *dead*! Will we tolerate that? Or will we, out of respect for the banished, the lost and the forgotten, and those who lie, along with my own son, in the untended graveyard beyond this church door, *do something about it*?'

A rising rumble of agreement from the congregation emboldened him.

'They tell us we did the right thing for our country. That it was *noble* to help our soldiers. But the soldiers who fight here aren't just learning to defend our nation; they're learning to kill and maim, to shred other men with machine-gun fire.

They're learning to deprive families of their husbands, broth-ers and sons. I ask you, is *that* noble?'

At the side of the church, some of the soldiers looked sourly at Hartwell. The rest kept their eyes on the ground.

In the pulpit, Hartwell shook his head. 'War dehumanises all of us, and it has dehumanised our little Imber.' Again, he thumped the bible in front of him. 'It doesn't have to be that way. We can find what was lost. Because there's a world of difference between a *just* sacrifice, and a sacrifice which is futile and *unjust*. The time has come to return our village to the public.'

The white-haired woman nodded her head vigorously; the young man with the blonde hair at the back shouted his sup-port; even a few of the soldiers lined up against the church wall looked engaged. As for Price, he looked impressed that this audience had been so effectively stirred. His faint smile was that of one showman admiring the skills of another.

Nodding, Hartwell looked around with all the wide-eyed fervour of a fanatic at a revival meeting. 'Fellow residents of Imber, if our country was worth fighting for in 1914, our community is worth fighting for now. One day soon, with your help, Imber *will* live!'

The blonde man at the back repeated the cry. So did a few more. A few seconds later, a chorus of ten, maybe twenty impassioned voices had risen up across the church: *Imber will live! Imber will live! Imber will live!*

But Hartwell hadn't convinced everyone. The bald, mid-dle-aged man I had noticed earlier still had his eyes narrowed in an expression that was hard to read, but I thought it was suspicion I saw there.

At that moment, the door at the back of the church burst open. Snow gusted in.

Every head turned.

'You're as guilty as they are,' shouted a woman, and I imme-diately recognised the French accent. 'Oscar Hartwell, you menace. We both know what you did.'

I angled my head for a clearer view, and saw Marie Hartwell pacing slowly into the nave of the church, her face cold and impassive. By now she had a most extraordinary look. She was attired as before, in an expensive-looking black mourning dress, but her skin was so startlingly pale it looked almost translucent. Her hair, instead of hanging limply around her face, was now pulled up neatly in a bun, and I thought it had developed a streak of grey overnight – if that were possible.

When she reached the centre of the aisle, she stopped. All around, people stared at her – with wariness, it seemed to me – but her eyes were locked on Hartwell, whose face was a mask of tension.

'Why don't you tell them the truth, Oscar?' she said, in a quieter voice that was altogether more unsettling.

For a few long moments, Hartwell stared at her fixedly. Then, with his cheeks reddening, he muttered, 'Please, my love, do not do this now. Not here.'

'My husband seems to have forgotten himself,' Marie cut in. She tilted her head to the side, the rest of her body perfectly still. Like a cat about to pounce, I thought. 'Why not tell them that our son *lives*, Oscar? Not in this world, but the next.'

This comment was met with a few bewildered mutterings. I thought of the grave beyond the church door, the white lamb dusted with snow, standing amidst a tangle of bracken and wild grass.

'Why don't you tell them, Oscar?' she repeated, glaring with hollow eyes. I detected in her voice the same hysterical, desperate tone as before. 'Pierre visits his family,' she went on. 'He still needs us.'

Everyone was staring at Marie as if she was mad.

'Marie, please, sit down,' Hartwell said, looking hastily away from her.

At the front of the church, the commander stood and said firmly, 'Madam, I warned you yesterday to stay away from Imb –'

'And I warned *you*, commander, there would be consequences.'

The situation was making me feel ... not frightened, but on the brink of it. What had the commander told us? That this woman was delusional. Maybe that was true, but the conviction in her voice alarmed me. She was so determined, embittered.

'I have no intention of leaving Imber – not ever,' she said, in a jarringly reasonable voice. 'I have come to join my son.'

Price's eyes met mine. They were shining with a sudden horror.

'Some of you have seen my son up at the old mill. Yet you refuse to speak of him.' I saw that she was staring at Warden Sidewinder, but he only looked away, out of the nearest window, at the snow beyond. 'Some of you have seen him at the crossroads,' she added, and I tensed, but she did not look my way. She fixed her dark-ringed, dangerous eyes on Oscar Hartwell and said flatly, 'My husband has a secret. Blood on his hands. And he knows all too well that our son is here in Imber now – a shadow of his human form.'

'She's mad,' someone said.

'Marie, my darling, you're not well,' I heard Hartwell say, and when I turned in his direction I saw that he was stepping down from the pulpit and hastening towards his wife. His face paling, he looked both wary and furious. 'Come home with me – now.'

'I came to see my son. Don't hate me. I have nothing!'

She turned to face the back of the church and for a moment all was silent.

Then she broke into a desperate run.

'After her!' the commander shouted, and Sidewinder took off down the aisle, Price and I both leaping up from our seats and following quickly behind.

'Marie, stop!' Hartwell shouted. She was almost at the church door, tearing ahead of us, but instead of veering left, out into the drifting snow, she sprinted straight on, towards the back of the church, and slipped through a small door which led to the one place that Price and I hadn't yet explored.

The bell tower.

I don't know who made it to the door first, Price or Sidewinder, only that it banged shut just seconds before they got there. Even as Sidewinder grappled with the handle, a dark intuition told me that somehow Marie had a key, that she had already locked the door from the other side.

The door shook and rattled, but it didn't open.

Price hammered on it furiously.

'Out of the way! Quickly! Let me through!' I heard Hartwell's fraught command behind us, just as Price's eyes met mine. Those eyes were enormous, and full of pale dread. I guessed what he was thinking: she had planned this meticulously, probably yesterday, right under our noses. That knowledge made what happened next all the more harrowing.

'For Christ's sake – get this bloody door OPEN!'

The near panic in Sidewinder's voice propelled Price into

action. He turned and drew back his wide shoulders, then launched his whole weight at the door.

A woman's scream of piercing distress arose from the other side, but it sounded far off. In a bell tower that small, there was only one direction she could have gone, and that was up.

The cry was followed by another rough shoulder barge from Price, and another. Once, twice, three times. Vital moments ticked by, until finally the door splintered in a puff of dust and flew open.

We burst into the bell tower.

I leapt back in surprise as a bird flapped out of a dusty nest in the corner. At first I was only conscious of how gloomy and cramped it was – I guessed just twelve feet by twelve. There was a stale, musty smell that made me think of the Imber mill, and it took me a moment to realise that smell was coming from a rickety old staircase leading up to the bells.

Everyone tilted their head back. Mrs Hartwell had already reached the rickety platform at the top. I glimpsed her scrabbling for something but was forced to look away. Price was changing furiously towards the stairs.

'Harry!' I grabbed at him. 'No, you'll fall right through them!'

He snatched his arm away, defiant. 'She didn't!'

'Harry, no, wait!'

The commander burst into the tower. Waving his hand at his men beyond the door, he ordered them to keep people back.

At that moment, the bells, high above us, started clanging. Hands clamped to our ears against the calamity, we all stared, dumbfounded, at one another – the commander and Sidewinder, Hartwell, Price and myself.

People were congregating behind us, outside the bell

tower door, peering curiously over our shoulders. I moved instinctively to block their view, as if I knew, even then, that something awful was about to happen.

A clatter echoed all around us: an old floorboard had fallen. We looked up. She had set the bells ringing, but was now so high up it was impossible to see exactly what else she was doing.

'What the hell's going on in there?' someone shouted from behind me.

'That woman ought to be committed!'

'What if she falls?'

'Marie, for the love of God, please come down!' Hartwell bellowed, his voice shaking. 'We can try to talk about what's happened with a doctor, or an expert. Someone who understands better than me.'

I turned to look at Hartwell beside me, saw his agonised face as he circled the bell tower, looking up. 'Why don't you go after her?' I asked quickly.

Hartwell shook his head hopelessly. 'I'd only make it worse. God knows what she'd do.' He threw a desperate, pleading look at Price.

'Come on!' Price said to Sidewinder.

The two men flew to the staircase, but it took them less than a second to realise they was never going to reach the top. Bits of rotten floorboards were clattering down all around us now, as if she was purposefully stamping her heels up there to smash the platform they'd have to cross to reach her.

Grabbing Hartwell by the shoulders, I spun him round. 'What's wrong with her?'

'I fear she's gone mad from grief. I've tried my best for her, but she's obsessed with this notion of seeing our son again,' he explained, his face both agonised and wondering, 'in the next world.'

The full impact of those words hit me just as a voice stopped Price in his tracks. Gripping the banister, he peered up into the gloom.

At first, we couldn't hear her, the deep clamour of the bells drowning out her voice. But then the shouts became screams. For a moment, I thought I heard her saying, 'No more, please, no more,' but then I realised that was wrong. She was saying, 'He won't be alone any more.'

We were all exchanging wild looks. With incredible swiftness, Price started up the stairs again, but his right foot plunged through a rotten board. 'For God's sake,' he yelled, 'just get down, before you –'

And that was when Marie Hartwell jumped.

I've had too many years to think about that moment. So it's possible – more than possible, it's likely – that the images and sounds have been blurred. But I'll describe what happened as I remember it.

What I remember most about the instant Marie Hartwell dropped was the sudden snap. I know I can't have heard it, or the crack of her spinal cord, because the bell ringing at that moment was just far too loud, but my first thought was that her neck must have snapped, because it seemed so far to fall.

Price was looking up, eyes bulging, and my gaze was riveted on him, because, quite frankly, I'd never seen such a profound expression of total horror.

Afterwards, he would tell me he had looked up and witnessed the nauseating moment Marie's body had bounced on the end of that rope, the jolt violently jerking her head back and pulling her face into an awful grimace.

'Don't look, Sarah,' Price said fiercely.

Oscar Hartwell was staring madly upwards with an agonised expression, as desperation and denial broke over him in a colossal tidal wave.

'Get her down,' he bellowed. 'QUICKLY!'

There was a horrible jerking and struggling sound above us – probably her legs kicking the air.

And then, finally, I did look.

Something – perhaps the same morbid curiosity that tempts us into peeking at tangled road accidents – made me look, if only to confirm to myself that such an atrocious thing had happened. At first I couldn't comprehend what I was seeing, even as I felt hot tears coursing down my face.

But an instant later I was forced to acknowledge the fact. My legs went weak as I wiped away a tear, looked down at my finger and saw dark red.

Beside me, Sidewinder made a gargling noise of horror. Blood had splashed his face too.

Marie Hartwell was hanging above us, twitching and trembling.

She's not dead, I thought. *Christ, how can she not be dead?*

The rope looked rough and old. She hadn't dropped so far – maybe eight feet. I saw now that the force of the fall had ripped her neck clean open, and blood – more black than red – was haemorrhaging out of her neck, her nose, her mouth.

Oh my God, oh my God . . .

Dimly, I could hear the frightened cries of those in the congregation who had strained to see what was happening, and would now wish forever that they hadn't. Perhaps they thought every death by hanging was swift, or maybe they just didn't know that sometimes, when suicide victims are in a hurry, when they misjudge the height of the drop, death isn't instant; that sometimes hangings can go wrong. Devastatingly.

It's the drop, I thought. *The drop wasn't high enough to snap her neck.*

Her body was thrashing around on the rope; she was gagging and gasping for air. The low gurgling sound coming from her throat made me feel so sick that my hand flew to my mouth. Unless we could get to her, either she was going to die by asphyxiation or she would bleed out.

'CUT HER DOWN!' her husband bellowed.

Sidewinder lurched to his side, but there was nothing for them to stand on. For a moment, I thought they were going to slip on the blackish puddle that was slowly expanding on the floor, immediately beneath the dying woman. One tried to lift the other up, reaching helplessly. She was too high. Her legs kicked, out of control, and with a violent spasm her shoes came off.

'Someone do something!' came a frantic yell from behind me.

That I could move at all was a wonder, but the adrenaline must have kicked in.

Darting for the bell tower door, I pushed back two or three of the onlookers. One of them tried to lunge past me but I gripped his wrist and almost dragged him to the exit with the sharp instruction 'Out, out, out!' Then I slammed the door shut.

When I turned round, I dragged my eyes away from the woman's ruptured neck, her bulging, glazed eyes, to the rope on which she was jittering and twisting. And then I faced Price and said, *'The rope!'*

The rope was frayed – old and rotten and twisting. Price

looked back at me with a sort of stunned understanding. The rope was not going to hold.

Grimly determined, Price and the commander started forward at once. Either they just weren't quick enough, or the rope wasn't strong enough, because just then it *did* snap – and Marie dropped, striking the ground with a wet thud.

There was a sickening splatter of blood.

Reeling back, one hand clapped over my mouth, I glanced at Price on the staircase. He was frozen. Shaking. Staring wildly like a petrified child.

'Oh, Jesus,' he whispered. 'Oh, Jesus . . .'

And for a long, long moment, that was all anyone said.

WARDEN SIDEWINDER'S CONFESSION

For a long, horrible moment, all I could see were dull grey spots, blurring my vision. The shock had made me numb.

When my vision did clear, the first thing I saw was the rope. Dangling above us, twisting emptily on itself.

In stunned silence, we formed a circle around the body.

Maria Hartwell was on her left side, head slumped down into her neck, pupils dilated, blood tricking from the corner of her mouth. The poor woman's tongue was swollen and blue, protruding between her teeth.

I went slowly to Oscar Hartwell, who had crumpled to the ground and was now doubled over, weeping convulsively. Gently, I laid my hand upon his shoulder.

Hartwell let out of a howl of soul-wrenching anguish. That cry seemed to galvanise Price into action, as he whipped off his frock coat and draped it over Marie's body. As he did so, there came from behind us a pounding on the bell tower door.

'Hey!' yelled a man. 'What's happening in there? Let us in!'

'Keep them *out*!' the commander ordered Sidewinder.

More hammering. Fists thudding on the door.

'We have to tell them something,' Sidewinder said. But if soothing words of reassurance were needed, the range warden clearly wasn't the man for the job; he was trembling almost uncontrollably, struggling to get his words out. Without missing a beat, the commander threw open the bell tower door. People were crowding around, soldiers and members of the congregation. With nervous tension on his face, the commander stepped out to confront them. As he closed the door behind him, he glanced back and I thought for a moment he looked more than nervous; he looked riddled with guilt.

Remembering what Marie Hartwell had said in the church, I switched my attention back to Sidewinder. There was a question I needed answering and at this moment, with his defences down, I might finally get a straight answer.

'What did she mean?' I asked Sidewinder. 'About some people seeing her boy? She was looking at *you* when she said that.'

Silence.

'Warden, did you know her son?'

He shook his head, avoiding eye contact, and hurried out to assist the commander.

On the other side of the door, the commander was explaining to the civilians that everything was under control and the emergency army response team were already on their way. I wanted to believe him; but creeping towards my feet was the puddle of dark blood.

I had to swallow my disgust, turning away in revulsion as Price came up to me and said quietly, 'Your mother won't thank me for this. Now it is imperative that we get back to London.'

'Excuse me?' I wet my lips, hearing my voice little more than a dry croak. 'You're suggesting we just *leave*?'

'You've just witnessed an extremely traumatising event, Sarah. You'll need to talk to someone. Or at the very least get some rest, far away from here.'

There was a look of such naked concern on his face that I almost acquiesced. But then I glanced sadly at Hartwell, who was still crouched on the floor, his tear-slicked face dazed and paper-white – it would have been utterly wrong to walk away.

'This isn't about *our* feelings, Harry,' I whispered. 'For God's sake, look at him. That poor man has lost his entire family.'

'*We* don't have to fix this, Sarah. It's not our respons –'

'We're staying. We're helping.'

'But if the newspapers find out, what then? We'll be exposed.'

I matched him with a hard stare. 'That's a risk we'll have to take.'

I could see the gears grinding behind Price's eyes and knew I was still a long way from persuading him to stay. To do that, I thought, I would have to extract from Sidewinder whatever he was holding back, and make Price acknowledge that there was still a mystery to be solved.

The door opened and the commander entered the bell tower. He glanced towards the hunched shape under Price's coat and I saw him swallow hard before he looked up at Price and me. 'My men will secure the bell tower,' he said. 'The rest of you should return to Westdown Camp. Immediately.'

He moved swiftly to Hartwell's side; the broken-hearted man was sobbing into his hands, shoulders heaving.

'Sir, please, come with us now. You're in our care.'

Part of me worried Hartwell was going to lash out at the commander's proffered hand, perhaps even strike him. During the church service, the commander had shown him such contempt that I certainly wouldn't have blamed Hartwell for landing a punch.

Instead, the once-privileged landowner tilted his head up, his jaw set, and gave the commander a poisonous look.

I stepped in. 'Commander, please, allow me,' I said, before crouching down beside Hartwell.

He turned to look at me, tearful, with a bereft and terrible despair on his face. Then he nodded and allowed me to gently help him to his feet.

Allowing Price, Sidewinder and the commander to go ahead, I slowly led Hartwell into the church. It was as silent as death in there now. He staggered slightly and I supported him with my arm.

So nauseating was the coppery smell behind us, it was a relief to step out into the chill October air. A light snow drifted down and the wind was really getting up, whipping at the coats and hats of the civilians who were now heading, shaken, to their cars. Some weren't even moving, just standing around in bewilderment, whispering speculations. Their faces turned to us as we emerged from the church, Hartwell on my arm. He stopped to gaze at his son's memorial stone, the marble carving of the lamb, and out of respect I looked away, beyond the wire fence, to the once cobbled road, now concealed by a fine dusting of snow.

Hartwell began to sob, then squeezed my hand. I took that as a gesture that he was ready to go.

'I am here to help,' I said, in my most soothing voice.

'Thank you,' he said, with honest appreciation, then nodded at the military trucks beyond the churchyard gate; Price was waiting there, with Commander Williams and Sidewinder.

Car doors thudded closed, engines rumbled. In the distance, I could just make out the approaching wail of the ambulance. 'Let's get you somewhere warm,' I said to Hartwell in the same soothing voice. I was gently leading him along the path when the hair on the back of my neck felt suddenly electrified.

I snapped a look back over my shoulder, saw nothing out of the ordinary, and put the experience down to nerves. But as I took another step forward, an unnerving sound that wasn't our feet crunching in the fresh snow rose behind me.

A choking, sobbing.

Crying.

I spun round, feeling a little shiver run down my back.

I looked, and I looked hard, but in vain. There was no one there.

So uncertain was Hartwell on his feet, it took two soldiers to assist him into the military ambulance. After that he was driven to Westdown Camp under the supervision of guards. Price and I travelled separately, with the commander and Sidewinder.

We had barely made it out of the wrecked village when Williams said, 'The newspapers will be calling before the day is out. No one is to speak to them except for me. Understood?'

'A woman dead – the wife of the wealthiest landowner in these parts. You are thoroughly at the mercy of the news-papers,' Price said, and Sidewinder, in the passenger seat, bowed his head in uneasy silence.

He certainly knows something, I thought, *and I'm going to make him tell us.*

The question now, however, was how to do that.

I contemplated the matter as I looked out over the snow-dusted downs, and by the time our jeep rumbled into Westdown Camp, passing a group of anxious-looking young soldiers, I thought I might have come up with a possible solution. But as we climbed down out of the vehicle, I felt a dark cloud descending upon me, an immense sadness, and an urgent need to be alone and calm myself, to gather my thoughts.

'Will you join us in my office?' the commander asked, looking at both Price and me. 'We need to make a plan.'

'*You* need to make a plan,' Price answered. 'We need to rest, and then pack.'

He won't leave, I thought. *He won't just leave me here.*

But I couldn't be sure about that.

Excusing myself, I returned to my hut, feeling agitated. Leaving was definitely not the right thing to do, not now, but I had to admit I was tempted to go.

Having shrugged off my coat, I began pacing; then I caught sight of myself in the mirror over the washbasin and felt a sharp jolt of horror. The sight of the blood – dried flecks of it on my cheeks – made me retch into the sink. I recalled Price's words: 'Now it is imperative that we get back to London ... You've just witnessed an extremely traumatising event.'

I scrubbed my face until it was raw. Then I stared into the mirror, listening to a loose sheet of corrugated iron on the roof clanging in the breeze. I was strong; I *could* cope. I just needed some rest.

But there was little rest for me that afternoon. With waves

of shock and sadness and anger crashing through me, I lay down on my bed, tucked my legs up to my chest and hugged myself like a frightened child. And I cried and prayed and shook.

Afterwards, I would look back on this as the turning point, the moment when our quest for answers began in earnest.

It was approaching four o'clock and I sensed the beginning of a tension headache when I forced myself out of bed, out of my cabin, to go in search of Price. I found him in the first place I looked: at the end of the long, sterile corridor in Central Security Control.

Behind the door, I could hear the commander and Sidewinder talking in muted voices. Something about the newspapers, prying journalists and escalating tensions.

I didn't bother to knock, just grasped the door handle.

The commander, sitting behind his desk, eyed me as I entered the room. He had the telephone pressed against one ear, his free hand covering the mouthpiece. Standing behind his left shoulder was Sidewinder. Behind his coin-like spectacles, his eyes tracked me as I dropped into the nearest chair and locked my gaze on the black and white picture hanging on the wall. There was my father, standing rigidly with some other uniformed men. One of them looked very much like Sidewinder.

'Sarah, you should be resting.'

I ignored Price as he crossed the room to sit next to me.

'Did you hear what I said?'

The fact that Price was in here and not packing to leave made me deeply curious. 'To whom is he talking?' I asked, gesturing to the commander.

'His superior officer.'

Sidewinder was still looking icily at me. He said nothing, but in my mind, I heard his voice: *I never forget a face.*

He followed the line of my gaze to the photograph of my father, then looked back at me. Directly into my eyes. I couldn't be sure, but I thought he was making the connection. It seemed likely he had known my father during his service here at the beginning of the last war, but how well? Discovering more about Father's work here in Wiltshire wasn't the reason I had come here, but I already knew that learning about it had taken on an importance. Perhaps it was partly the reason why I felt unable to leave. But even that wasn't enough to explain the bizarre visions I had experienced in Imber, and the oppressive, almost overwhelming sense of sadness and secrets.

'Yes, sir, I am acutely aware of that ...' As he spoke into the phone, Commander Williams' expression suggested exasperation tempered with begrudging acceptance. 'Indeed. As soon as possible.'

He banged the telephone receiver down, glaring at us. 'Infernal bloody protestors!'

'News has got out, I suppose,' said Price. 'Do you have an official line?'

'Only that a serious incident occurred on the training range today, resulting in the death of a civilian, and that we are investigating,' the commander answered unhappily. 'The War Office want us to open the village again next week, in an acknowledgement of today's tragedy.'

Price pulled a face of disapproval.

'We've heard word from the police that there's already talk of a protest outside Imber – a full public demonstration in support of the Imber Will Live campaign. The War Office want us to welcome the protestors with open arms, if you please.'

'What does Hartwell say?' I wanted to know. As the leader of the campaign, he seemed best suited to advise, and I longed to know how the poor gentleman was faring.

'Mr Hartwell is in the sickbay. Our doctors are doing their best to calm him down.'

That didn't sit well with me. 'Have you sedated him?'

'Mr Hartwell refused medication,' the commander said.

'Yes. Under the circumstances, I think that's wise,' I replied.

The commander squared his shoulders. 'You mustn't think that we have any sort of covert agenda here, Miss Grey. What happened in the bell tower today was indeed a tragedy, and we are acting in the best interests of everyone –'

'As a matter of fact, Commander, you have been less than honest with us all,' I said, sitting upright in my chair. Price looked at me curiously, surprised by my intervention. I fancied I had an opportunity here to make him take a fresh interest in the case. I remembered the crucifixes we had photographed inside the old mill and felt a flush of determination warm my cheeks. 'And now you're fretting because people are going to demand answers about what's been happening in Imber. Personally, I'm with them.'

'Excuse me?'

'With all due respect, Commander, don't the people deserve answers?'

'Sarah.' Price touched my shoulder, but I shrugged his hand off me.

'No, Harry. The military have a duty of care – for the soldiers based here, for Imber itself and for its former residents. The village is in ruins. A soldier has been driven mad and now a villager is dead. I have a good mind to go to the newspapers myself!'

'And violate the Official Secrets Act?' the commander challenged.

'Don't think I wouldn't,' I said, with more conviction than I felt. 'You already know, sir, I am extremely well connected with the newspapers. After all, that was how *we* became acquainted, wasn't it?'

The commander looked uncertainly at me.

Price also cut me an inquisitive glance.

Damn!

'Sarah, to whom are you referring?'

There wasn't just interest in Price's tone, there was suspicion, too.

I could have mentioned Vernon Wall then, explained how we had both been drawn into this situation by a man that Price hated, but Vernon's involvement was a card I still intended to play, so instead I kept silent.

Annoyance had soured Sidewinder's face, but he still sounded carefully reasonable. 'Let's just say we do this your way, Miss Grey.' He glanced at the commander, who wet his lips then nodded at him to continue. 'What precisely would you like to know?'

I switched my attention to Sidewinder, remembering how keen he had been to impress upon Price his encyclopaedic knowledge of paranormal phenomena, how ardently he had objected to our presence here, and how zealous he had seemed in his supernatural beliefs. All of that had to come from somewhere, didn't it? 'Let's go back to the beginning – Sergeant Edwards and the night he doused himself in petrol and set himself alight. Where were you?'

The question echoed in the room.

'Warden?' I asked. 'Edwards stated that his men vanished. Could it be that you were out in the woods yourself?'

'What draws you to *that* conclusion?' said Sidewinder, his tone full of indignant surprise.

'You've already told us it was you who found Sergeant Edwards, the morning after he set himself on fire. I suppose it's possible you just stumbled upon him when you did, but on the other hand –'

'Perhaps you already knew his location?' Price cut in.

I looked at Price, surprised and a little encouraged. Perhaps I had reinvigorated his interest after all. 'We could interview the other soldiers,' I continued. 'They might tell us, even if you won't.'

Sidewinder wasn't looking at me. His gaze had gone to the commander, who gave an acquiescent, if reluctant, nod, permitting him to answer.

'I didn't want it to come to this,' Sidewinder said, glancing at the Imber map on the wall. 'But it seems we have arrived at a reckoning . . .'

I watched the warden as he removed his spectacles, breathed on them and rubbed them on his sleeve. When he placed them back on his face his eyes looked sharper than before, but they weren't focused on us. His gaze was caught on something long ago, something haunting. 'On the night Sergeant Edwards attempted suicide, I was at the Imber mill.'

Price nodded. 'And the other men were with you?'

'Five of us,' Sidewinder said stiffly. 'All except Edwards. He had an inkling about what we were doing, of course, but he didn't approve. He felt our activities were dangerous. But you see, our experiments were showing real promise.'

Price cocked a concerned eyebrow.

Sidewinder cleared his throat. 'Communing with the dead,' he said weightily.

The words were out and hung between us.

For a moment, I half-expected Sidewinder to smirk, to own up to a sick joke. But instead he said, 'Messages were received from the great beyond. *Spirit* messages, warning of grave danger in Imber.'

'You were conducting spiritualist séances at the abandoned mill,' Price said, then he turned to the commander. 'And you, presumably, knew nothing about this.'

Williams shifted a little in his chair. 'The moment I discovered these practices were taking place – when we found Sergeant Edwards injured – I immediately disciplined the men. Warden Sidewinder here told me everything and I hoped that would be the end of it. These séances had been going on for months.'

'That explains the candles at the mill,' I said. 'The crucifixes?'

Williams responded with a sorrowful nodding of the head. 'The séances got quite out of hand. We had to keep a lid on it, you understand? The men were scaring themselves senseless.'

Price looked sharply at Sidewinder. 'What exactly did the "spirits" impart that so petrified the men?'

There was silence, then, as the commander and Sidewinder stared at one another, but the unspoken question passing between them seemed obvious: *Do we tell them?*

'You might as well come clean now,' I snapped. Instead of feeling vindication for having exposed these men's deceptions, I felt the flushes of anger and a gust of determination. An innocent woman was dead, after all, and a soldier horribly disfigured for life.

When the commander nodded his permission, Sidewinder,

white-haired and deathly pale, walked to the wall, gazing once more at the map of the village. He raised one gnarled hand and pressed his palm against it, as if in an act of communion.

'The spirits of Imber seek vengeance for the homes, the lives, that were stolen from them,' he said, in a voice so low it was difficult to hear. 'That night . . . Sergeant Edwards had followed us out there. He overheard. He saw too much. He was so profoundly disturbed by the information revealed to him that it seems to have driven him to suicide. He was a completely broken man. I only wish we had been able to . . .' Sidewinder's voice broke off.

I nodded comprehension of this information and tried working through its implications. Now the blanket of secrecy we had confronted here made a little more sense. If this got out, the consequences for the military on Salisbury Plain would be devastating. Villagers, still incensed at the military's refusal to allow them to return to Imber, especially those whose families had lived there for centuries, would be further antagonised by such news. Outraged.

On the other hand, it was possible Warden Sidewinder was lying to us, but for what motive? More likely he had seen something deeply strange at the old mill, but was mistaken, hoaxed possibly. We had to know more.

'Why didn't you come forward with this information earlier?' I said.

Sidewinder lowered his hand from the map and turned to face me. 'Because it sounds so unbelievable, doesn't it? What would you have done, if you had seen something so phenomenal? Something so controversial?'

Kept it to myself, I thought, remembering the boy I had seen at the roadside. It had taken me long enough to tell Price about that. Was I justified in blaming these men for not being honest with us sooner? Perhaps not.

'I don't blame you for feeling some reticence in coming forward, Warden,' I said, aware that Price was watching me keenly. Hopefully, my bravado was doing something to persuade him to stay. 'Most witnesses to supernatural phenomena fear ridicule. But you might have hinted at the gravity of the situation.'

'I *warned* you,' Sidewinder said harshly. 'I told you, the only road worth taking in Imber is the road out!'

'What was the purpose of the Imber séances?' Price asked. 'Who led them?'

'Oh, just tell them,' the commander ordered. 'Or I will.'

Sidewinder took a breath. 'I myself served as the conduit to the spirit world.'

Price's eyes flicked to me then back to Sidewinder. 'Well, well. I take it you have always held an unhealthy fascination with the occult?'

Sidewinder was silent for a moment or two, then he said, 'Yes. Ever since my son returned from the war. Then he was extremely well acquainted with spiritual and supernatural matters. Eventually, his passion became mine.'

It was the first time Sidewinder had mentioned another member of his family. Sometimes we miss the most obvious clues to the biggest mysteries in our lives, and that was how it was for me right then.

'You're telling us your son was a medium?' Price asked.

'He became one. He grew up in Imber. When he returned to Wiltshire, he was a loner. An outcast.'

'Why?'

'His injuries from war were ... horrific. Severe facial

disfigurement. He found the village wrecked and out of bounds, and he contrived to gain entry. So many of his friends were killed on the battlefields, and he was consumed by a desire to contact them – so consumed that he would wander onto the Imber range, ignoring the Keep Out signs, just to get close to their old homes. Back then, the soldiers who knew what he was up to had a nickname for him. They called him the ghost maker, because he was able to make manifest the apparitions of the dead.'

Price looked dubiously at him. 'Your son coaxed you into spiritualism?'

'He didn't coax me into anything,' Sidewinder replied, affronted. 'I wanted to learn.'

'Why?' Price continued to probe. 'Your son's longing to contact his dead friends I can understand, but the source of your own paranormal enquiries strikes me as rather more curious.'

It took Sidewinder a few seconds to elaborate. 'I caused a death,' he said slowly, looking once more at the map on the wall. 'A long time ago. It was an accident, but I made a mistake, a very grave mistake, and I'll say no more about that. But the mistake led me to spiritualism. And from my son I learned the ways of table tipping, automatic writing, even trance oratory.'

'Mischievous nonsense.'

'You may think so, Mr Price, but my son would frequently fall into trance-like states, speak in verse and experience visions of the dead. Eventually, he was in direct communication with residents of Imber who had passed on. He became a conduit to the afterlife. It was extraordinary, almost magical. They communicated with us, answered our questions, knocking once for yes and remaining silent for no.'

'These séances – where did your son conduct them?'

'At the old Imber mill.'

'And where is your son now?'

'We don't speak any more.'

'That wasn't the question I asked.'

'It is a sad fact, but we are estranged from one another. His séances became wildly out of hand. He was using all sorts of drugs, and he began to hear voices and act irrationally.'

'How so?'

'He created illusions. Began to believe they were real. I think he was losing his mind. He was putting my job in the army in jeopardy, so I told him he had to stop.'

'And when he refused, you made him leave Wiltshire?'

He nodded, barely able to look at us.

'Yet you continued to practise the séances yourself?' Price said, with an exclamation of astonishment.

'Inevitably, I was drawn back to the mill. The power of that place – it was like a drug to me,' Sidewinder said, his voice almost trembling. 'I felt as if I had touched another world, and I needed to do so again. Can you understand that?'

Both Price and I nodded. Of course we understood that.

The commander, sitting behind his desk, looked adrift in a sea of doubt.

'Some of the other soldiers on the base caught on to what I was doing. Followed me. They were curious too. They wanted to witness the wonders of the séance room.'

'And I suppose you were only too happy to provide those wonders,' Price said.

'You speak as though you're accusing me of fakery,' Sidewinder shot back, 'when in fact I have experienced the most remarkable phenomena, both physical and mental, which I have tested meticulously, and which prove the survival of human consciousness beyond bodily death.'

Price crossed his arms. 'That's a bold claim,' he said curtly. 'An audacious claim.'

Sidewinder shrugged. 'You may doubt it, but the spirits of kindred beings *do* visit us. At the mill, our circle was visited by the spirit of a child. A little boy.'

Icy fingers brushed my neck. 'A boy?' I asked.

Sidewinder nodded adamantly.

'A three-dimensional, fully formed spirit materialisation.'

Materialisation. That word called up a memory of a controlled séance I had observed years earlier, at Price's laboratory in Queensberry Place, when a medium had coaxed a ghostly shape to materialise out of a darkened cabinet. At one point, the spirit had even appeared to jangle a tambourine. But all of this had taken place under conditions that were less than ideal, conditions insisted upon by the medium herself – in poor light, for example, using a nickel-plated electric table lamp with a red globe and silk shade! How to tell what was real? It was Price who eventually located the secret compartment in the chair the medium had insisted on bringing. It was jam-packed with masks and wigs and clothes that the medium's assistant would secretly adorn to impersonate the spirits. And if a more ghostly effect was required, stiffened muslin wrapped around the head and draped over the body completed the job. Amazing, now, to think people were fooled by such crude deceptions, but they really were. Thousands of times!

As if reading my thoughts, Price said, 'Spirit materialisations are usually hoaxed with the crudest props. Show me a spirit and I'll show you a broom and a bed sheet!'

'But this was totally different,' Sidewinder insisted earnestly.

'By the proof of my own eyes, we were visited by the spirit of a young boy.'

'Could you identify the child?'

'Yes. It was Pierre Hartwell. Oscar Hartwell's son.'

I felt a sharp stab of shock: the wandering child, his hollow, staring eyes.

'How can you possibly know that?' Price demanded.

'Because his own mother identified him,' said Sidewinder.

'Marie Hartwell? Price looked astonished. 'You involved her in a séance to communicate with her son?'

When Sidewinder nodded in reply to that question, I felt the flush of anger in my face.

'That is why she returned to Imber, over and over again,' said the commander.

'Foolish man,' Price growled at Sidewinder. 'Foolish, foolish man! You're the reason Marie Hartwell is dead. You realise that? Unspeakable charlatan. Dragging a vulnerable, grieving mother to a séance to see her dead son? Filling her head with false notions, false hope! Why, the shock of it must have driven her mad.'

I ached for the Hartwell family. The revelation was unspeakably cruel. At the same time, it was predictable. How many innocent, credulous victims had the supernatural claimed?

My concern quickly turned to Hartwell, in the sickbay. How much did he know about his wife's involvement with the Imber séances? What if he didn't know? That sort of information would be a terrible blow, maybe enough to send him over the edge.

'Remember, the newspapers must learn nothing of this!' the commander interjected sternly, and it was then that the plan that would advance our investigation began to solidify in my mind. A plan involving Vernon Wall . . .

'You mustn't assume that I did something wrong,' Sidewinder said. His eyes were flat and contemptuous. 'Thanks to my efforts, a mother was able to hold her long-dead child in her arms. And it was a beautiful sight to behold.'

'She was grieving,' Price hissed. 'Vulnerable. Probably mentally ill. And you, sir, wilfully neglected a duty of care!'

'You speak with gross and unpardonable ignorance, Mr Price. Does this look like a mental illness to you?'

And with that, Sidewinder fished a curious object from his coat pocket. It looked very much like a dental cast, except its indentations were nothing like teeth.

'This is the impression of the spirit child's hand in putty.'

He placed it gently on the commander's desk.

Price looked quizzical. 'You carry this with you all of the time?'

'I do. Think of it as my rock of faith.'

The four of us glanced down at the unmistakable impression of three small fingers.

'Harry?'

Price looked at me and I looked back at him. The cast before us could quite easily be a hoax; we knew that. We also knew that if it wasn't a hoax, here indeed was crucial evidence of contact between two worlds.

But we did not get the chance to examine the cast. Just then, a sharp rapping made us all turn towards the office door, which opened immediately to reveal the sharp-featured Oscar Hartwell standing there, glowering at us.

– 19 –

LIES BETWEEN FRIENDS

'Mr Hartwell,' the commander said, his jaw flexing – with annoyance, I thought. 'We were told you were resting.'

'I heard from one of the soldiers that there have been enquiries from the newspapers.'

'Indeed, and we are just discussing –'

'How to manipulate the headlines? The news of my dear wife's tragic demise?' he said belligerently, advancing into the office. From the stormy look on his face I worried he was about to throw a punch. 'How bloody *dare* you broach such matters without thinking first to involve me?'

'Actually,' Price said, 'we were discussing your son – Pierre.'

Hartwell looked taken aback. 'And what, pray tell, has my son got to do with you?'

'Gentlemen,' the commander said hastily, 'can I suggest that we all take a seat?'

I offered my chair to Hartwell, thinking the poor man looked impossibly weary. Before he could sit, however, he saw on the commander's desk the queer cast of putty bearing the impressions of three small fingers.

He caught his breath sharply.

Price looked across at me, then stood and angled his head towards Hartwell.

'You recognise this cast, sir?'

'Why, yes. I've seen one just like it, at home. It belonged to Marie –'

He trailed off, his mind making the connections. Then he looked questioningly, accusingly, at Price. 'You said you were discussing my *son*? Now look here, what's all this about?'

Price studied him. 'Do you know whose fingerprints this cast bears, sir?'

'No, why should I? What are you . . .'

He broke off, looking around at us all somewhat self-consciously.

I stood there, numb, anxious, anticipating. Surely to heavens Price wasn't about to disclose to Hartwell the facts of the Imber séances – was he? I didn't believe he would. At least I hoped not.

'You'd better sit down,' Price advised.

Hartwell did sit now, slowly, shaking his head with impatient confusion. And as Price opened his mouth to speak, I barely restrained the impulse to tell Hartwell to clamp his hands over his ears – or better, to get out of the room, for his own sake.

'This will be hard to hear, but the warden here believes . . . Oh dear.' Price took a breath.

I clamped a hand onto his arm. 'Harry, no –'

Almost immediately, the commander rallied to my cause.

'Quite – Mr Hartwell does not need to hear this! Certainly not now!'

'The warden believes he has witnessed the ghost of your son.'

Hartwell jerked his head back. In a terrible silence, his eyes made an uncertain circuit of the room. It was as if Price had pulled the pin on a grenade and lobbed it, and now there was nothing to do but wait for the explosion.

But none came, not at first. Only a quiet, hurt voice. 'Is this some sort of depraved joke?'

'I'm afraid not,' Price answered, picking up and examining the cast of putty.

Then he told Hartwell the rest, about the séances carried out at the Imber mill.

'I can barely believe I'm hearing this,' Hartwell said, his eyes shifting hatefully between Sidewinder and the commander. 'After all that has happened this dreadful day.'

Sidewinder stood up then, and looked down at the land-owner gravely. 'On more than one occasion, I have witnessed the materialised form of your boy,' he insisted. 'Sir, it *was* Pierre. Half dressed, in rags. His breathing low but audible. The power of his voice alone was enough to convert a man to total belief. I believe it is the reason why your wife had the confidence to do what she did today.'

Hartwell's whole body started to shake.

'Sir –'

Hartwell erupted out of his chair, and with a rough yell of rage, he picked up the putty and hurled it across the office.

The commander sprang up. 'Sir, please! Control your –'

'My wife *died* today!' Hartwell yelled, his voice ragged with grief. 'Do you understand the hell I'm going through, all of you? And now you throw this at me?'

The others lowered their gaze respectfully, but not Price. He stood there at the side of the desk, staring at Hartwell with intense fascination.

'Hartwell,' Sidewinder said, 'I tell you, sir, it *was* your son, Pierre.'

Hartwell fixed the warden with his furious gaze. The fire in his eyes dimmed, just a little.

'And believe me, I know how much that child meant to you.'

Hartwell nodded, a little calmer now.

'Your whole life you wanted for nothing else but a son. So many years, waiting. You pinned all your hopes and dreams on Pierre.'

'Yes,' Hartwell mumbled, and his lower lip began to tremble as his gaze went to the map on the wall. 'He was to have everything. Imber Court, the land. It was my dream for him to restore the village.'

'Sir, as God is my witness, your son Pierre returns to Imber,' Sidewinder said resolutely.

Hartwell stared fixedly at Sidewinder, and for the first time his hostility blinked out. It was hard to know whether Hartwell entertained any of this as possible, if he was grasping at this strange new prospect, however unlikely, as any parent hearing such a thing surely would. But I thought I saw the flicker of something else in his eyes then, not just curiosity, but, perhaps, hope.

After a considerably long pause, Hartwell said, 'You actually *saw* my boy?'

'Yes, sir.' Sidewinder nodded. 'Not only that, I touched his hand, felt his fingers close around mine. A dead, cold hand. And I spoke to him.'

Hartwell's mouth was agape, his eyes glistening with emotion.

'He told me he was lonely. He wanted his papa.' Sidewinder clasped his hands together. 'This must be deeply troubling for you to hear, especially now, Mr Hartwell, but your wife also attended the séances.'

'What?' he breathed out harshly.

Hartwell repeated the assurance with solemn sincerity. 'Your son asked for her on his second manifestation. Therefore, I invited her to attend.'

There was a protracted, uncomfortable pause. Then a light of understanding began to glow in Hartwell's eyes. As if he had just remembered something vital and only now was it making sense to him. What was it? Glancing at me, he murmured, almost to himself, 'A woman in the road . . . You! Oh dear Lord . . .'

A curiously cryptic remark, and one, I fancied, that was tinged with guilt; but there was no time to question it just now, for Hartwell turned on Price, and said, 'And I thought I recognised your face. You're that ghost hunter, aren't you? I've seen your photograph in the gutter press. My wife used to collect your books. She'd go on and on about your antics. Debunking hauntings with one hand whilst fanning the flames with the other. Are you encouraging these claims?'

'I am committed to exposing such preposterous delusions,' said Price, holding up his hands, 'and I'm urging you now not to be coaxed through the door of this fantastical man's madhouse!'

'I am not a madman,' Sidewinder protested. 'Pierre was certain to appear at every séance.'

'Certain?' repeated Price. His tone was mocking. 'Certainty

is the enemy of any open-minded inquiry, wouldn't you say?'

Hartwell swallowed, caught his breath. Then he said to Sidewinder, 'Tell me why I shouldn't report you to the War Office right now for gross misconduct.'

Those were threatening words, to be sure, but I thought I detected something else in his tone: an anguished parent's longing for answers. *There's something you're not telling me*, his tone seemed to whisper. *What is it?*

'Your son imparted personal information only he could have known,' said Sidewinder, 'about his illness, about your home. He spoke coherently, rationally. And he warned us' – his eyes flicked to the commander sitting behind his desk, listening carefully, studying our faces – 'if the village is not returned to the community, if the soldiers do not leave, their lives are in grave danger.'

If I hadn't already seen a mysterious childlike figure, I probably would have reacted with more scepticism than I was feeling now; but the image of those charcoal-black eyes, that pale and wasted face, was still imprinted on my memory, so of course I was intrigued.

'Exactly how clear was this manifestation?' I asked Sidewinder.

'I saw him as I see you now. I had no doubts whatever of his objective reality.'

Price frowned darkly. 'And you say the spirit manifested at *every* séance?'

'Every single one. And I would doubt it myself, except . . .' He trailed off.

'Except?'

'Except he comes back. He always comes back.'

'A bold claim,' Price said, not bothering to restrain his doubtful tone. 'But your testimony, however beguiling, cannot take priority over experimental evidence.'

This got the support of the commander, who sniffed and nodded his head.

'Why don't we just go and see?' I suggested. 'Tonight, at the mill.' Immediately, I realised my error, the insensitivity of my suggestion. Hartwell had gone white. 'But my son is *dead*! My wife is dead! And this is unspeakably degrading to their memory. Why would you even think of putting me through this torture? To satisfy the idle purpose of mere curiosity?'

'I apologise, sir,' I said quickly, 'I didn't mean . . .'

There was no point finishing. Hartwell had stalked to the door, thrown it open and marched out of the room. I flinched as the door slammed behind him.

The commander, on his feet now, glared down at me. 'Good grief! Young lady – as if we didn't have enough to contend with today! And you, Mr Price! Why on earth did you bring him in on this? This has gone quite far enough.'

'I quite agree,' said Sidewinder, heading for the door.

Price was silent, gazing distractedly at the plaster cast, which had been hurled into the corner of the room. 'I wonder . . .'

I thought for a moment that he had determined to abandon the whole inquiry, which would really have left us in a pickle. But just as I was about to give up hope, Price said in a low voice, 'No one has ever guaranteed me a ghost before.'

The words were out, and he left them hanging in the air like ripe fruit to be picked.

'The snow is already melting,' I said. 'We could get back to Imber quite easily.'

Sidewinder shook his head vigorously, snatching up the

cast. 'After what happened to Sergeant Edwards, I vowed never to set foot inside that infernal mill again.'

'What are you afraid of?' I asked.

'You saw the crucifixes on the walls?'

'You were afraid you'd accidentally call up vengeful, malevolent forces, is that it? Well,' Price said with disdain, 'I'm sorry to say, warden, that fools are invariably answered by their folly. Still, I suppose I shouldn't be surprised to hear of such nonsense during these long, dark days of winter – the season of the dead.'

'Don't you see?' Sidewinder said, raking his fingers through his shock of white hair. 'Imber is haunted *because* of us. Spirits are coming through into our world precisely because we invited them. And the ghosts of Imber won't rest until their village is returned to its rightful owners.'

'Utter hogwash!' said Price.

'You only have to look at Sergeant Edwards' burns to see how dangerous this is,' Sidewinder shot back.

And perhaps he was right. Perhaps this was getting dangerous. But I found it impossible to suppress my curiosity.

'Take us to the mill,' I said to Sidewinder. 'Lead us in a séance, and let us see this spirit child for ourselves.'

Sidewinder only shook his head with greater vigour. We weren't going to change his mind. Unless . . .

'Harry, be a gem and get me some water, will you?' I said. 'I'm feeling a little light-headed.'

I was surprised by how easily the lie came to me.

As Price trudged out of the room, I turned to the commander and said quickly, 'Listen, I may be able to help you deal with the press. Of course, you already know Vernon Wall, but I have connections, with reporters I trust.'

'You don't think we can handle the press ourselves?' the commander asked.

'I think you'll need help,' I continued, aware of Sidewinder's eyes on me, 'especially if you're expecting more protests. You know, some of these reporters can be tricky to manage, even Mr Wall. Working with them, and with him, I can help you make the case for the military's continued presence here on Salisbury Plain. I'll help you, if you allow us back into Imber. How about it?'

There was a long pause, and I thought the commander was going to laugh at me or flatly refuse. Time was running out. Through the open door, I heard Price's approaching footsteps.

'Commander?' I prompted, a sharp edge in my voice.

Throwing up his head, the commander fixed his stare on Sidewinder and said, 'Do as she asks,' and when Sidewinder opened his mouth to protest he added, 'That's an order!'

'A rather *unconventional* order,' said Sidewinder.

'You created this unholy mess, warden. You can bloody well help clean it up.'

Sidewinder stared at the floor, then acquiesced with a curt nod of his head.

Satisfied, the commander returned his attention to me. 'How soon can it happen?'

'How soon can *what* happen?' said a voice over my shoulder, and I flinched as Price entered the room with my glass of water.

'The commander has agreed we can visit the mill and perform a séance,' I quickly told Price, who pulled an instant face of disapproval. He handed me the glass and, without looking at the warden, said, 'Most mediums are contemptible cheats. We shall see if you are any different, won't we, Mr Sidewinder?'

The warden bristled.

'Very well. Tomorrow night?' I suggested. 'Monday.'

'Halloween,' Sidewinder said, eyes wide.

'Seems ideal,' the commander said sarcastically, and in an eerie way it did.

I took a sip of water, secretly rather pleased with myself for having handled the matter so discreetly. But then the commander said something that set me on edge.

'Your contacts, Miss Grey. Can you arrange for them to be here on camp?'

Price caught my eye and I hastily attempted to change the subject. 'Um, perhaps we can discuss it tomorrow?'

'No, Miss Grey, we'll discuss it now.'

The air seemed to thin. I sipped my water, feeling my sense of achievement drain away as Price voiced the obvious question:

'What did I miss?'

'Your associate here has agreed to lend us the help of her press contacts to deal with our public messages. Who exactly do you propose we call upon, Miss Grey?'

I dropped my eyes. 'I'll have to give it a little thought.'

'For a start, perhaps our mutual journalist friend, Mr Wall?'

Blast!

A deep silence spun out as my whole body tensed. Slowly, Price turned to face me and fixed me with a basilisk stare. No words passed his lips. He could say anything he wanted with those crystalline blue eyes. And right now, they were saying one thing:

Traitor.

– 20 –

DARK EMPLOYMENTS

'You should have *told* me Vernon Wall was involved!' Price thundered.

We were sitting opposite one another, alone, at a long table beneath the barrel-vaulted ceiling of the officers' mess hall, our only company the many portraits of former British monarchs that covered the walls. Unlike many of the buildings we had seen on camp, this one was a permanent structure of red brick, and built to impress with its parquet flooring and panelled oak doors. Tall sash windows overlooked the expanse of Salisbury Plain, upon which dusk was now falling.

Our voices echoed in the vast, empty hall. I had anticipated Price wouldn't be pleased to hear of Vernon's involvement, but the colour of his face suggested outrage.

'I wasn't obliged to say anything,' I repeated. 'You knew the bare facts, Harry. You came here of your own free will.'

'Oh, come on, who are you trying to fool? I had a right to know,' he said through gritted teeth. 'Especially after what happened at Borley. Vernon Wall? Sarah, that bloody man is on a mission to bring me down – as if you didn't know.'

But I hadn't known that. All I knew was that Vernon had been involved with the military in Imber long before us. And right now we needed him – he could help the commander manage the difficult headlines we all knew were looming. I tried to make Price see.

'In exchange for Vernon's help, the warden will take us to the mill and perform a séance.'

'Tomorrow night? Haven't you got a job to go to, Sarah?'

My employment was the last thing on my mind; I would make my excuses.

'Think about what's at stake here, Harry. Sidewinder promised you a ghost. Don't tell me you're not burning to know the truth now.'

He frowned, and I knew that I had spoken to the deep yearning within him that was so much a part of his energy. And, to be honest, I felt more than a little relieved to have finally owned up to the truth.

But I also worried that Price's petulant side, the wild side that too often ruled his judgement, might push him into driving back to London. And then what? Without his peculiar expertise, I'd stand no chance of solving the case. No, I needed Price. And if I was going to keep him onside and regain his trust, I would have to throw him something else.

I remembered Wall's words when he had set me on this mission. 'If Vernon is right, if there is a deeper agenda here, something pernicious or even insidious, then you're the right person to expose it, aren't you?'

His eyes flickered with indecision. By appealing to his sense of moral purpose I thought I might have succeeded in getting through to him, but then he veered in a direction that surprised me. 'Sarah, you seem so willing to trust Vernon. But have you considered that perhaps, just perhaps, it was Vernon who told me I'd find you that night at the Brixton Picture Palace?'

I stared at him. 'How utterly absurd! That would mean Vernon was following me – spying on me. No. Harry, no. What an ugly thing to say!'

'Can Vernon draw?'

'Can he *draw*? What sort of question is that?'

'A serious one.'

'Harry, I don't know. Why on earth is that relevant?' I shook my head, confused. 'Listen, Harry, Vernon came to me directly. And besides, why would he follow me? You're trying to manipulate me, to break my trust in him.'

We sat there in silence, watching long shadows fall across the rolling downs beyond the window. Our conversation had brought a lump to my throat. I was afraid I had tarnished his trust in me so badly that we might never again restore our friendship, and I longed to know what he was thinking.

Price looked sadly at me as he said, 'So many secrets between us, Sarah. Too many secrets.'

He reached out his hand across the table, as though he wanted me to give him something. I knew what it was before he even mentioned it: the projection slide I had found on the floor in the picture house in London.

'You asked me to examine it,' he said. 'In fact, we agreed on the telephone that you would bring it with you. So let me see it.'

'I told you, it's not –'

'Important? I know. So, what's the harm, eh?' He flashed me a smile. 'Go and get it.'

With a sigh of exasperation, I went out of the officers' mess
hall and into the chilly night. I would have to be quick. It
wouldn't be too long before the mess was filled with soldiers
hungry for their Sunday night dinner.

At the bottom of the steps, I turned left onto a concrete
path that led me to Hut Three. As I approached the hut, I saw
someone coming towards me.

Was it Sidewinder? I thought I recognised the shock of
white hair, but it was hard to be sure; the glimpse was fleeting,
and seconds later the figure had hurried away in the other
direction.

Quickening my step, I had the sudden, suspicious idea that
it was indeed Sidewinder, and that he had been nosing around
in my hut – perhaps looking for my notes? That was probably
just my paranoia, but the idea did little to stem the rising
unease I had been feeling since our earlier confrontation with
Hartwell.

A woman in the road . . .

This was still in my mind when I entered Hut Three and
fished the hand-painted lantern slide from my belongings.
When I returned to the officers' mess hall, I found Price standing before one of the tall sash windows, gazing pensively
out over Salisbury Plain, which was now almost completely
obscured by the gathering darkness.

I handed him the lantern slide, and he took it to the long
table at which we had been sitting. Here the light was brighter.
Next, he retrieved a magnifying glass from his battered briefcase and began to examine the slide with assiduous care.

'There are two children depicted on this slide,' he said,
squinting. 'Do you have any idea who they might be?'

'None whatsoever. Do you?'

A moment's silence.

'Not a clue.'

With some haste, he turned the lantern slide over, eyes narrowing as he focused on its rough wooden frame. 'There's a date inscribed here.'

'I'd missed that.'

'Maybe you didn't want to see it.'

'What's that supposed to mean?'

'Never mind.' He shook his head, and carried on as if he'd never uttered the enigmatic remark. 'Well, well. This is a find indeed – a very early example of a magic lantern slide. They were made from paintings or photographs, suspended in crude projectors, then lit from behind by candlelight.'

'For what purpose?'

'Entertainment, mainly. In the hands of a talented showman, accompanied by musical instruments and ingenious sound effects, magic lanterns dazzled hundreds of people with the most spectacular dissolving images. As the lanterns became cheaper to purchase, people began experimenting with them at home.'

'How old is this lantern slide?

His eyes narrowed as he held the slide closer. 'The date inscribed here is 1880.'

'Over fifty years ago.'

'Long before your time, Sarah.' He looked at me thoughtfully. 'And you said originally you felt a connection between this object and the picture house in Brixton, as if this lantern slide drew you there?'

I nodded; that sounded ridiculous now, but it was true.

'When you first touched this lantern slide, you felt . . .'

'Transported somewhere else,' I said, remembering the peculiar sensation of floating away, the glow of the sun on my neck, the breeze against my face. I waited for Price's cynical frown, and when it didn't come I had to wonder why.

'Did you recognise the location?' he asked.

'No, why?'

Price said nothing. He seemed unsettled – agitated.

'Harry?'

'Leave this with me,' he said quickly, slipping the lantern slide into his breast pocket. Just then, a powerful gust of wind rattled the panes of glass in the sash windows.

'Harry, is there anything about Imber, our investigation – anything at all – that you haven't told me?'

Immediately, he shook his head, but I didn't like the look that passed across his face right then. I thought I had come to read Harry Price rather well, and I had the sense now that he was lying.

'Tomorrow night then,' he said, before I could even think of probing further, 'we end this. And return home.'

Back to London. Where we would part company.

'Tomorrow.' I almost gave a sad nod, but dignity made it brusque. 'And the commander wants Vernon to come here. Agree some helpful public messaging for the newspapers.'

Price bristled at that. 'Bring him, then, if you really think it necessary.'

I told him I did think it necessary. Very much so.

After leaving Price to his dinner, I went in search of Hartwell. One of the soldiers milling around in the corridor that led to the sickbay told me Hartwell had gone that way, so that was where I headed. The door to every room here was open, aside from two. One of those doors led into the room reserved for Sergeant Edwards. Inside, I could hear the poor man sobbing.

Looking back, it's easy to say I should have checked in on Edwards, asked what was wrong. Hindsight is a haunting thing.

Instead, I knocked on the other door. There was no reply.

Hartwell is resting, I told myself. *Leave him. You will see him tomorrow.*

And under normal circumstances that would have been the right thing to do. But I kept remembering the bell tower; the awful moment his wife had dropped; the way he had crumbled to the floor at the sight of her body.

Truthfully, I was also still a little curious about his earlier remark: '*A woman in the road . . .*'

I turned the handle slowly, and looked into the darkness.

'Excuse me? Mr Hartwell?'

Nothing. Just a narrow bed against the far wall, bulked with pillows.

Feeling guilty for trespassing, I began closing the door. That was when I heard the creak of the iron bedstead. I peered into the gloom and saw, lying on the bed, cocooned in sheets, a figure curled on its side.

'Mr Hartwell?' I said, this time in barely more than a whisper. 'Are you asleep?'

Again, there was no reply – but this time I felt his eyes on me. No, I *saw* his eyes, gleaming in the cold light that slipped in from the hall.

He's not asleep, I thought. *He's watching you.*

I began to close the door. And that was when he spoke to me, in a voice that was low and menacing.

'You've decided to go through with the séance.'

Turning back towards him, I cleared my throat. 'Yes, sir.'

An expectant silence spun out. There was no need to be afraid – Hartwell was a good man. Indeed, he had my fullest sympathy. Nevertheless, I would be lying if I claimed I didn't feel a shudder tremble through me right then.

'I apologise,' I said. 'This must be inconceivably painful for you. But under the circumstances we feel we need to test Sidewinder's claims.'

'Why? To indulge the fantasies of an egotistical madman, or purely to satisfy your own selfish curiosities?'

There was something about his tone that didn't sit entirely well with me. It lacked conviction, and I was curious to know why.

'Is there something you want to tell me, Mr Hartwell?'

A switch was flicked and light bloomed through the room. The bald and bearded Hartwell had thrown back the sheets and was sitting on the edge of the bed, one hand on the bedside lamp. Amazingly, he was still wearing the black suit he had worn to the Imber church service. I couldn't be sure if he had been crying, but from his flushed face and bloodshot eyes I thought it likely.

'Sir,' I continued, 'your poor wife was obviously drawn to the old mill for a reason. We want to try to work out why, to provide some explanation for what happened to her. And for you, some comfort. Sincerely, sir, my heart reaches out to you for your loss.'

'Come in,' he gestured, his voice softer, 'and please close the door.'

I hesitated briefly; I suppose any woman in my situation would have done. But I did as he asked.

'May I sit?' I asked, indicating the wooden chair next to his bed.

He nodded yes.

'Sir, I can't begin to fathom how you must feel, but may I offer some advice?'

I was remembering how Price had helped me, one year earlier, when my nerves were frayed from grief and guilt. 'Harry is well instructed in the ways of hypnosis – helping patients achieve intensely deep levels of relaxation by inducing altered states of consciousness.'

'Hypnosis?' Hartwell scoffed. 'Party-piece tricks.'

'I wouldn't say that actually. I've undergone it myself.'

'What does it feel like?' Hartwell asked, and for a moment I was back in Price's laboratory, on the chaise longue, listening to his soothing voice, deep and low, taking me back, back.

'Like being asleep and awake at the same time,' I said, remembering slipping into the trance, my hands and feet going cold, my eyelids quivering; feeling distant from my body and hearing myself become uncharacteristically loquacious.

But still, exactly what sort of information – fanatical delusions or buried memories – I had divulged to Price during my trance eluded me. The only constant was the sound of his voice: insisting, probing, urging me to tell him . . . what?

If only I could remember.

And then it struck me – perhaps I didn't need to remember. Perhaps the details of whatever I had uttered would be somewhere in Price's files, at his laboratory . . .

'Miss Grey?'

I snapped back. 'If you wish to try hypnotherapy, sir, it can be arranged.' I smiled and he nodded back. I sensed that a barrier between us had been dismantled a little. 'Now,' I said gently, 'what can you tell me about the Imber mill, its history?'

Silence.

'Sir, the more you tell me, the more likelihood there is that we can help.'

Hartwell sighed. 'The mill was built by my grandfather. It had stood on that parcel of land for more than one hundred and fifty years. It was abandoned well before the rest of the village.'

'And Pierre?' I asked gently. 'What can you tell me about your late son?'

Hartwell's eyes misted over. It was a look I knew well – the same lost and yearning haze I had seen a thousand times in my own mother's eyes.

'My son is dead,' he said dully. 'Never coming back. If you'd seen him at the end of his life, you'd understand that.'

'If you don't mind my asking, sir, exactly how did he die? And when?'

'Two years ago.' He smiled sadly, looking down into his lap. 'Pierre was a brave soldier to the very last. At first, we suspected a simple throat infection, but then the sores came, lesions that wept and wept. When his neck swelled, we worried it was the mumps, but soon –' He broke off, his voice catching. 'Soon his neck was as wide as his head, and a thick grey coating had closed over the back of his throat. I should have noticed the symptoms earlier.'

Feebly I said, 'You weren't to know –'

'I was his father!' Hartwell said bitterly. 'I would do anything, *anything*, to have him back.' His eyelids fluttered closed. 'Even now, all I can hear is that awful hacking cough. Later, when he was nearing the end, it sounded more like a bark. Some nights, even now, I wake up and I can hear it. I ask myself, how – *how in God's name* – could we have allowed that to happen to our little prince? The disease took his vision in the end. The diphtheria, it paralysed –'

'Oscar—'

'Please, don't interrupt me!' he said, so abruptly I flinched. 'It paralysed his eyes, swelling the sockets, turning them black.'

I felt a shudder run through me then, picturing the charcoal-eyed child.

'We nursed him at home.'

'But surely the hospital would have—'

'Diseases like that aren't supposed to afflict families like ours.'

His son became his secret, I thought. *Just like mine.* The only difference was that my son was out there somewhere, alive in the world, and Hartwell's son was dead.

And then I remembered something else from earlier that day.

'I'm sorry to ask this, sir, but today in the church, after your speech, your wife said you had . . . well, she said you had . . .'

'Blood on my hands?' Hartwell nodded. 'Well, it's true in a sense, isn't it? I was telling Pierre I loved him, that he was safe, while telling friends and associates, neighbours, that he was recovering from a touch of flu. Have you ever heard anything so pathetic? I lied to my own son. I told him he would be fine. He was only five, but I think he knew that was a lie. Perhaps he even knew he was going to die.'

His eyes fastened on me. 'You can't possibly understand what that feels like – to keep that sort of secret.'

I swallowed painfully.

Hartwell looked away, shaking his head. 'When Pierre died, I felt empty. So many years of longing, praying for a boy to continue the Hartwell legacy, to run the estate – only to have him taken from me. Then my house, my land, was stolen by the army.' His voice became tear-clogged. 'Now Marie, bless her soul, is gone, and I am truly alone.'

He held his head in his hands and began rocking back and forth. Feeling awkward and hopelessly sorry for him, I placed a soothing hand on his right shoulder.

'Mr Hartwell, earlier, in the commander's office, you said something strange that caught my interest. "A woman in the road." Those were your words. You were referring to me, I think?'

He lifted his head and gave me a thoughtful, appraising look, made even more perturbing by the words that followed.

'The words weren't mine,' he said finally, as if he would rather forget them. 'My wife's.'

'I see,' I said, although I didn't at all. Still, I continued, 'You said in the church that Marie had lost her mind.'

'Very possibly she had,' he said quietly, but the uncertainty in his voice was now unmistakable. He looked at me for a moment, and I recognised his hesitant expression. It was the same look I had seen on the faces of so many other witnesses whose lives had been touched by the paranormal; witnesses who have realised they can live with their experience no longer, and feel the irrepressible need to share it, knowing they can trust you to listen.

And I saw something else on his face: an open honesty. He was ready at last to confide in me.

'My wife sensed things. Believed she was . . . clairvoyant. At first I thought she was merely creative, and I encouraged her to write, to draw. But the drawings she produced were unsettling – no, worse than unsettling. Disturbing.'

He stood up and looked past me now, eyes wide, voice faint.

'Even before this business with the mill, Marie believed

she had contact with the afterlife. She believed that when she drew, the spirits guided her hand.'

I made a mental of note of that. It could be a vital lead.

'By the end, I concluded she had been driven mad from the grief. But now . . .' He looked imploringly at me, an expression of terrible despair across his face. 'Perhaps I have been blind all these years. Perhaps my dear wife was right after all. It certainly seems she was right about *you*.'

'Tell me,' I said gravely. My heart was beginning to thud. Hard.

He hesitated.

'My wife had a . . . I suppose the word you would use is "premonition". She believed she could see events and scenarios yet to be. And there is something else I should have told you before, Miss Grey.'

I nodded at him to continue, even though a part of me didn't want him to.

'After Pierre passed away, Marie told me something that made so little sense at the time that I forgot about it. But now, I see that maybe I was wrong.' He leaned closer and stared directly into my eyes with unsettling intensity.

'She said I would meet a woman in the road. Someone like you.'

I admit, my confidence faltered a little then. But I kept a level tone as I sought clarification. 'What do you think your wife meant? What exactly did she say?'

'A woman in the road. A traveller seeking answers. A wise old soul on her last journey.' He peered at me with a sort of dazed understanding. 'That's *you*, isn't it?'

I realised I had stopped breathing.

'Miss Grey?'

A wise old soul on her last journey . . .

'I've heard those words before,' I said.

And then, with a chill, I remembered precisely where I had heard them: six years earlier, in Price's top-floor laboratory, during an experimental séance with the young spiritualist medium Velma Crawshaw. Poor Velma; with blank panic on her face, the doomed woman's breathing had become short and spasmodic as she stared at me and said in a faint, unnerving whisper, *'Sarah Grey, the woman with two paths and one regret. You must not go!'*

I blinked the memory away, but felt the gooseflesh on my arms.

Must not go . . . A wise old soul . . .

What did it mean? A prophecy? I wasn't sure I wanted to know.

Hartwell was looking at me ponderingly. 'Here you are, Miss Grey, the woman in the road. A wise old soul. Just like my dear Marie said.'

When I said nothing – for what could I say? – he went over to the window.

'I know it sounds like madness,' he said, gazing out onto the night, 'but she insisted and I told her she was wrong. But now . . . now I think that perhaps it was I who was in the wrong! That perhaps I could have saved her if I'd just listened and opened my mind.'

I looked into the window, at the dark reflection of his face, so drawn and anxious, and thought I understood why he had been so reluctant to consider our proposal of a séance at the mill. It wasn't that he disbelieved in such things as ghosts, rather that he was afraid of what believing would mean for him. The very idea had brought him into direct moral conflict with his treatment of his wife.

'What if my wife was right?' he went on. 'What else was she right about?'

He turned round then, and his eyes locked on mine. He looked feverish; but not with grief, I realised – with intent.

'This séance you've arranged for tomorrow – what time will it occur?'

'You want to come? Mr Hartwell, I really don't think that's a –'

'Of course, it was not my first wish,' he said quickly. 'But I see now that a séance might help me come to terms with what has happened, face my own demons. I feel it's what Marie would *want* me to do – to attend and keep an open mind. And if my son should come, perhaps I too will once again feel the touch of his hands.'

He was smiling now, a tear glistening on one cheek.

I reached out to put my hand on his arm and said, 'Mr Hartwell, you've had a tremendous shock today. A séance could be too much of a strain.'

What I didn't want to add, lest it make me sound paranoid and superstitious, was that a séance could be a traumatising ordeal, often riddled with misleading information.

He was looking questioningly at me. 'In what way, too much of a strain?'

'Mr Hartwell, sadly, I know something – much, actually – about grief. It comes unexpectedly, often bringing chaos in its wake. And in that chaos it's only natural to seek some sort of order, some meaning. We use séances and the paranormal as a barrier against that pain, and in so doing we can make unwise decisions.'

'You sound like your colleague.'

I did sound a bit like Harry, but it would be strange if I didn't, given all we had been through. 'Séances can make you doubt yourself, and everyone around you,' I said. 'You mustn't come.'

Hartwell drew his arm away. 'You baffle me, Miss Grey. First, you say my beloved dead son is appearing, on demand, at séances conducted without my knowledge, on land that once belonged to *me*. And then you tell me I shouldn't try to verify that?' I shifted awkwardly. I was no psychiatrist, but I saw that Hartwell blamed himself for Pierre's death, and was probably tormented by guilt. He longed desperately to see his son one last time, if only to apologise.

His presence could be helpful in one sense – with Hartwell in the room, we had a better chance of identifying the spirit child. But if, on the other hand, the affair was a hoax, I knew that the emotional consequences for this grieving man could prove utterly devastating. But, ultimately, whether he attended the séance was not my decision to make.

'I'm coming,' he said with such conviction that I could only nod in agreement.

'All right,' I said. 'Before I go, there is just one more thing.' He blinked at me.

'May I see your wife's spirit drawings?'

'Do you think they might be important?'

A wise old soul . . .

'That depends what they show,' I replied, knowing that the sketches were bound to tell us something about Marie's mental state, but also knowing that was not the entire reason I had asked to see them.

*

At nine o'clock that evening, Commander Williams was just stepping out of his office when I was fortunate to run into him in the corridor.

'Sir, may I use your telephone to call London?'

He was pleased, I think, to see me being so proactive, and it seemed that I had gained his trust, for once I had poured myself some water, he left me alone in his office.

'I'll be back soon,' he added.

On the wall, alongside the other framed pictures, was the formal photograph of my father in uniform, standing with other soldiers. It nagged at my gaze. I wanted that photograph. I wanted it badly.

As I sat and dialled the number for *The Times*, I vaguely wondered how long it would take the commander before he missed it.

'Vernon?' I took a quick sip from my glass tumbler as he answered the phone. 'Thank heavens you're still there. Listen, I've made a deal, one that benefits you. The military will allow you access.'

'To Imber? What's the catch?'

I told him then about the church service, about Marie Hartwell's suicide, and listened to a few seconds of silent shock echo down the line. Somewhere in the background I could hear the steady *clack, clack, clack* of another poor journalist working the late shift.

'Jesus . . . I can't imagine. Sarah, you must feel dreadful.'

I did feel dreadful. The sight of Marie Hartwell's slumped corpse, her blue tongue protruding through her teeth, kept coming back to me. So did the image of her jerking and writhing on the end of the rope as she choked to death. But I also felt galvanised to achieve some justice for the Hartwell family and Sergeant Edwards, and ever more determined to clear up the mysteries plaguing the lost village of Imber.

'The military are worried about protests, and the possibility of a full-scale public rally to champion the return of Imber to the public.'

'You really think that will happen?'

'I'm sure it will happen,' I said, remembering the passion of the congregation during Hartwell's speech. Suddenly, I was picturing the worst: a huge gathering of newspapermen, challenging questions, a confrontation. What if there was bloodshed? What if someone recklessly ventured somewhere they shouldn't on the range and was injured in an explosion? Or, even worse, a soldier acted impulsively and a civilian was shot?

'I promised the army you'd help take control of their problem with the newspapers.'

'You did *what*?' He lowered his voice and I imagined him cupping his hand over the telephone mouthpiece. 'There's always a catch, isn't there?'

'Sorry. It was the only way they would allow us to continue with our investigation. Listen, can you get down here in time for tomorrow night? Trust me, you won't want to miss this.'

'What exactly do you mean, Sarah?'

I pictured Vernon hunched over his desk in the offices of *The Times*, scribbling hurriedly in one of his battered leather notepads.

'This is all off the record, yes?'

'What? Sarah, come on!'

'Vernon, no. Background terms only. Deal?'

He made a reluctant sound of agreement. Only then did I tell him about Pierre Hartwell, whose vandalised grave lay in the overgrown Imber churchyard; a little boy who was aged just five when he was taken from his family by the disease known as the Strangling Angel.

'And you think you saw this child yourself?' Vernon sounded sceptical.

'I saw *something.*'

A pause at the other end.

'Vernon, you know I would never make up something like this.'

'Sorry, I'm not doubting you. It's just, well, a lot to take in.'

'Tell me about it,' I said hastily, glancing around the commander's office. I wanted this conversation to remain strictly between Vernon and me, but I was hyper-aware that the commander could return at any moment. 'Sergeant Edwards saw the boy too, just before he attempted suicide by setting himself on fire.'

'Dear God.'

'And this is going to sound damned silly,' I warned, 'but Sergeant Edwards, and many of the soldiers out here, believe the spirits of former residents who were evicted from Imber, like the blacksmith, have returned now to exact retribution on the military.'

'You're right, that does sound damned silly. But Sarah, it also sounds as though you believe it.'

The preponderance of evidence was becoming hard to deny: Sidewinder's impassioned witness testimony; Marie Hartwell's premonitions; the putty cast bearing the imprint of a child's fingers – all needed further investigation, but considered collectively, in the light of all I knew, the evidence was compelling.

I had a mental image of Imber's churchyard and remembered

the curse we had found scratched into Pierre Hartwell's memorial stone: *May God in His mercy punish those who have wronged us; grant it so that His heavenly wrath stains the souls of those who have stained Imber with the blood of innocents.*

When I pictured the childlike figure at the roadside on Salisbury Plain, when I remembered his lonely grave, and the sound of someone crying close by, when I remembered the traumatising visions that had assaulted me in the woods, I thought that yes, I did believe Imber was haunted.

I believed also that there was an insidious agenda behind the haunting. And if that was so, there was no telling how this would end.

'Are there other witnesses to this ghost child?' Vernon asked. Now he sounded interested, energised, which was what I had been hoping for.

'Actually, yes. The warden.'

'What's his name?'

'Sidewinder. He grew up in Imber. He is adamant the ghost walks.'

'You're sure he's not faking it?'

'I don't think so.'

'Delusional then?'

'No.' I explained about the abandoned mill in the Imber woods, the candles and crucifixes and the surreptitious séances led by Sidewinder. 'He says he learned the art of mediumship from his son, and that the spirit of the Hartwell child returns, without fail, at every séance. A fully formed materialisation. Vernon, he's going to show us, tomorrow night.'

'Then yes, you're right, I do want to be there.'

I pictured the winding, bumpy journey across the downs to Imber. 'Can you make it here by late afternoon?'

In the newsroom at the other end of the line, a telephone rang and a typewriter was still clacking away.

'I can try.'

'Good, and remember – you're not here to sensationalise, only to advise and write sensitively about the forthcoming protests.'

'What does Harry think about all this?'

'What you'd expect,' I replied. 'Except, well, he's being evasive.'

I heard Vernon's sigh. 'You think he's keeping something from you?'

No, Sarah, you're being paranoid, I thought. But I also knew that Harry had lied to me before.

'Sarah, are you there?'

'Yes, sorry.' The picture of the soldiers on the wall was nagging at me again.

With a mixture of dread and determination, I realised I wasn't just going to take that picture and walk out of the room with it; I was going to ask Vernon to do something that went against all my better wisdom.

Something that could cost him his job, or even put him in prison.

'Vernon, there's one more thing. This could be nothing. Call it a hunch, all right? But before you leave London, here's what I need you to do.'

VALLEY OF THE SHADOW

Fallen leaves, damp from the melted snow, squelched beneath our feet. I felt nervous and alert as we wound our way through a tangle of trees, grimacing at the cold. Imber's moribund mill waited for us, abandoned and brooding. With a growing sense of purpose, I was anxious to get there quickly, but as we neared the top of the valley, I paused to look back. From there, I had an unimpaired view of the grim, grey manor house, Imber Court, its windows sheeted with iron. I kept feeling the pull of recognition whenever I saw it, without knowing why.

Ahead, Price glanced back, saw I was still and confidently called, 'Come on, not far now!' A flicker of suspicion flared, but I resisted questioning him yet again on how much he really knew about the history of Imber. I'd get to the root of that mystery soon enough, so long as Vernon succeeded in the task I had set him.

We passed into a clearing strewn with logs and fallen

branches. It was mid-afternoon, but the leaden clouds hanging moodily above made it feel as if the October darkness was already drawing in.

My state of nervousness persisted. Part of it was worry for Vernon; so far there had been no sign of him. After my telephone call the previous night, Commander Williams had assured me that as soon as Vernon arrived at Westdown Camp he would drive him into Imber to join us.

But *would* he arrive? What if he didn't? Earnestly, I prayed he hadn't been caught – otherwise it was curtains for our friendship. And his career.

The rest of my anxiety had more to do with what we had come to do, an act that would be described by many as blasphemous. Thanks to Price, I knew séances could be physically traumatic. We might encounter spectral whispers, phantom figures, drifting lights. Not to mention objects thrown at us from any direction!

Who cared if there were crucifixes nailed into the walls of the old mill? Candles and crucifixes – what good had these talismans done for anyone so far?

We were coming today armed with our own talismans – scientific equipment that would help us scratch the surface and reveal what lurked beneath.

Or so we hoped.

'Sarah, careful!'

I leapt backward, embarrassed. I was so distracted, I had almost run right into Price's back.

'Sorry, Harry.'

'Honestly, you seem away with the fairies.' He blinked and then said, with sympathy in his voice, 'You can always go back to the camp, if you'd prefer – '

'No, no, I'm fine,' I assured him.

He held my gaze for a moment, then trained it on the edge of the clearing. 'We shouldn't linger here,' he said. 'You remember this spot?'

I remembered all right: this was where I had experienced a vision of Sergeant Edwards picking up a petrol can, dousing himself and becoming a human fireball.

'Feel anything now?' he asked, looking intently at me.

I shook my head.

'Let's press on,' Price said, and we set off towards the dark line of trees.

But a low metallic sound made both of us halt. Three heavy, dead notes echoing from behind us in the shadowed woods.

'What the hell?' Price looked around, his mouth slightly open.

The sound came again, low and hollow, but louder now.

Clang . . . clang . . . clang . . .

Was that metal striking metal?

All at once I had an irrational image of a furious blacksmith tracking us through the woods; a blacksmith whose eyes were red from weeping and raw with rage.

A blacksmith carrying a bloodstained hammer.

We listened hard.

No further noises.

'Come on,' Price said, looking uneasily ahead to where the path wound into the shadows. 'Almost there.'

What else could I do? I turned towards Price and the deeper woods, and followed.

In the distance was the dark bulk of the mill, where we had been promised that the dead boy would materialise later. As we grew nearer, I began to experience the same uneasy sense of familiarity that had seized me on our first journey here.

'*A wise old soul,*' Hartwell had said, '*on her last journey.*'

There was only one way to know more: I had to see Marie Hartwell's spirit drawings. But I had no intention of mentioning them to Price – not yet anyway. Not until I knew what they showed. Hopefully, Hartwell wouldn't forget to bring them along. If, that was, he still intended to come.

'Well,' I heard Price say from up ahead, 'here we are.'

Sometimes I think locations speak to us, like our dreams do. We don't always know exactly what they're trying to tell us, but when those messages are imbued with meaning, we sense it acutely. That was how it was for me at that moment, as the abandoned mill rose before us. Sombre. Imposing. Ancient. Its Gothic, iron-framed windows, those intensely black spaces. Queasily, I sensed the ruin speaking to me.

Welcome back, it said. *You've come for my secrets. Well, let's see how well you do.*

I found myself hesitating, staring at the giant mill wheel of rusting iron, its lower spokes submerged in the stinking black pond. The wheel wasn't turning – it hadn't moved in decades – but I allowed myself to imagine that it was turning now. Grinding back the years.

I had a sense then of time engulfing me. My surroundings were changing, receding. Price was saying something, but his voice was a blur; the trees and the ruin lost their outlines, becoming ragged dark shapes. Helplessly, I stared at the wheel as it turned, slowly, slowly.

A sharp pain between my ribs.

I looked down, with a harsh gasp.

Blood. A dark, spreading bloodstain, just below my heart.

An escalating sense of terror.

'Sarah?'

My head snapped up. Price was next to me, looking at me with concern. I could see him clearly now, could see the trees and the tumbledown mill behind him. The hazy, indistinct atmosphere had restored itself, becoming clean and crisp.

'I knew you weren't ready for this,' Price said.

'What, what's happening to me?' I asked between steadying breaths.

His eyes flicked down, past my neckline, and when mine did too I saw there was indeed blood on my blouse. Not the spreading dark stain I had glimpsed in terror just moments before, but a spatter of small scarlet droplets.

Price produced a handkerchief and dabbed it under my nose. 'Pause a moment,' he said, 'hold your head back. The bleeding will stop soon enough.'

Finding a tree to lean against, I did as he advised. Price watched me for a little while, his eyes bright. Not so much with concern, I thought, but with wondering interest, as if I were again a fascinating specimen to be scrutinised.

'What is it?' I snapped. It wasn't pleasant to have him standing over me like that.

He glanced away, towards the mill. There was a moment's calm, and then he stepped forward and pointed at – what?

'Someone's interfered here,' Price said.

Wanting to leave, but strangely fascinated, I followed his pointing finger to the mill and saw what had stolen his atten-tion: the wooden door was hanging open, revealing a rectangle of darkness.

I glimpsed a flitting movement within. Price saw it too, and

I knew exactly what he was going to do, even before he strode forward, his black coat flapping out behind him.

Years later, when Price was dead and I saw his bulking form looming behind me in the kitchen window, I would remember the glittering excitement in his eyes that dank afternoon in the Imber woods, his dedication to exposing the truth, whatever the cost, even if it meant leaving me behind. Harry Price cast himself into a sea he was convinced he would conquer, only to have his every certainty in a safe, knowable world crushed.

'Come out!' he shouted into the windless air.

Two male figures emerged from the low doorway. 'What are you doing in there?' Price fumed, storming up to them.

'We came ahead, to get a sense of the place,' Sidewinder said defensively. He scraped the heavy wooden door closed behind him. 'No need to overreact, Mr Price.' He was talking so loudly I could hear him from twenty yards away. I stepped away from the tree I had been leaning against and crept closer. Price's face was flushed with anger.

'Sarah and I came to secure the damned place – and you've already been inside!'

'Please' – Hartwell held up his hands – 'do check inside, Mr Price. You will find nothing disturbed. It's as we found it.' He shook his head, looking bewildered. Refined in a smart dark suit and tie, he was back to his old, semi-aristocratic appearance, and I noticed he had trimmed his beard for the occasion. 'The crucifixes inside on the walls, the candles – all is as it was. Otherwise, the mill is a ruin.'

That was certainly true. Once it had been a vital building in a village on the downs, but decades of dereliction had reduced it to a tumbledown shack of rotten timber and gritstone.

Quashing the growing unease within me, I tucked the

blood-smeared handkerchief up my sleeve and went to stand at Price's side. Sidewinder looked unsettled already, but when he saw me he grew tense, his eyes hardening behind their perfectly round spectacles.

'It is starting already,' he said. 'You can sense it, can't you?'

I almost asked, 'Sense what?' – but that would have been disingenuous, because I fancied that I *could* sense something then. Apart from the vague familiarity I could not explain, I felt the presence of many dark and implacable secrets somewhere very close to us. And something else: a solemn sadness – a desolation – that had dwelt in this lonely spot for a very long time.

The shadows were deepening and spreading now, like ripples in the filthy millpond. Questions came to me unbidden. Why had this mill been abandoned before the rest of the village was evicted? It didn't appear damaged by fire, or unusable in any way. Had something happened here – something tragic, perhaps – that had caused the villagers to leave it to rot?

'Well, I'm not impressed by your intrusion,' said Price, his face like granite. 'I must insist now that you allow us some privacy whilst Sarah and I secure the site.'

'Perhaps you could accompany me to the churchyard,' Hartwell said to Sidewinder. 'I'd like to visit my little ones.'

'But of course,' said the warden respectfully. He nodded to us both, then led Hartwell towards the woods in the direction of Carrion Pit Lane.

Free to continue with our work, Price stepped up to the mill's battered entrance, and I followed. The slow creak of the door went before us.

A startled bird flapped out of the blackness, causing us both to leap back.

A small smile moved across Price's lips as he looked at me, as if to say, *Well, here we go again.*

And then, side by side, we stepped into the musty darkness.

Down on our hands and knees, we scoured the filthy floor methodically for trapdoors, finding nothing but rubble and moist earth. After that, Price sketched a floor plan in his notebook, carefully ringing every entrance and exit. He fastened gimlet screw eyes to the walls and used them to thread thin strands of cotton across every doorway. Then we took the rotten staircase that climbed into the webbed shadows.

I shivered as the floorboards creaked and strained under our weight. Up here, the air was cool, but thick with the earthy smell of damp leaves that had blown in. I wondered whether there were rats. We hadn't seen any rats; but then again, I thought with a wry smile, we hadn't seen any phantoms, and of course that didn't mean there weren't any.

Occupied in our task, I soon forgot about my worries. As our torch beams bounced off the crumbling walls and the rotten rafters, setting clouds of swirling dust aglow, I found myself thinking only about the brief and magic frisson of those short hours. Price and myself, a team once again, painstakingly working side by side – securing entranceways and exits, sprinkling starch powder to detect any intruder's handprints or footprints, placing thermometers as carefully as one might set a trap. A moment made special because it was so rare. There was something about skulking in the decrepit semi-darkness, trying to master the extraordinary. To govern it. Nothing about ordinary life in London even compared to the uniqueness of this endeavour, the dark pull of adventure that made the heart beat that little bit faster.

Like any other sort of hunt, ghost hunting was all about the thrill of the chase.

It was what came after the chase one had to worry about.

Time seemed to accelerate as we worked. By the time we were done, daylight had fled and a brisk wind had sprung up, wailing around the mill.

Before opening the battered door, Price lit a cigar and stood for a moment, admiring our work, like an artist appraising his masterpiece. In the centre of the floor, a battered oblong table waited for proceedings to begin. Traps littered the mill, inside and out. The finest threads of cotton, barely visible, crossed every glassless window. Flour dusted the floor at every dark entranceway. I felt as I usually felt when preparing a séance room – keyed up. I was also aware that to most people in the outside world the scene must have looked limitlessly eccentric. Some might say silly.

But something was wrong. Something was missing.

'Harry, where are the cameras?' He usually had two or three installed with automatic sensors, mounted on tripods in the corners of the room.

'We're not using them this time,' he said, tapping the ash from his cigar. 'One of the warden's ridiculous stipulations. Reckons they give off negative energy.' These words came out sounding not just sceptical but derisory. 'Well, let's see, shall we?'

'What about this?' I said.

He followed the line of my vision down to the lower portion of the wall.

'The bricks here look uneven, don't you think, Harry? Discoloured.'

'They look burned to me,' he said, apparently unconcerned.

Just then we heard voices outside. I opened the door and stole a look outside.

A figure was approaching.

'It's so good to see you. I thought something had happened to you.'

'Something very nearly did,' Vernon Wall said, and I could tell immediately that my old friend had something vital to tell me. 'I did your bit of business. You were right – the place was mostly deserted. And it was a good job you knew where to find the spare key.'

We stood together in the shadow of the ancient mill as rotted leaves swirled around us on the evening breeze. Vernon breathed out heavily. He looked beaten down, and sallow pouches lay heavily under his eyes. 'That's quite a walk,' he said, looking back at the woods and the way he had come.

About twenty yards away, Hartwell and Sidewinder conversed in low voices with the commander.

'Left my car down in the village. Had to follow the commander from Westdown Camp. Where's Harry?'

Safely out of earshot.

'He's just making some final checks inside. What's in the rucksack?'

'Huh?' He put one hand to the bag's leather shoulder strap, as if he had forgotten he was wearing it. 'Sandwiches,' he said with a grin. 'Want one?'

'No thanks.' I nodded at the mill. 'Step over here.'

The air became pungent as we walked a few paces to the bank of the pond.

'So?' I said.

'Harry cares for you a lot.'

'Why do you say that?'

'Listen,' said Vernon, 'in his office, I found something interesting in his files. About this village – about you. After I got inside – '

'What files?' a hard voice interrupted, and we both whirled round to find ourselves confronted by a glaring Price. 'Well?' Price repeated, stepping up to Vernon. 'Got inside where?'

Vernon gave me a swift look; nervous, I knew. My 'bit of business' for him, of course, had been to break into Price's laboratory:

The top floor will be locked up, but the main building, the library and the smoking room, they'll all be open to members. At least they always were, in my day.

'What am I looking for?'

'Initially? A key to the top floor.'

'Sarah . . .'

'Just listen. In the library, there's a brown leather armchair, to the left of the window. The back chair leg is shorter than the rest. There's a book wedged underneath; it's hollow. The spare key is in there.'

My rationale for sneaking Vernon into Price's sanctum? Education. Reassurance. I wanted to know whether Price really had done extensive research on Imber and its hauntings before coming here with me, whether he was keeping anything from me. Something about my father's time here, perhaps?

'I asked you a question,' Price said, stepping closer to Wall. 'Got inside where?'

'St Giles' Church,' I told Price now. I surprised myself at how easily the lie came. 'I told Vernon he ought to see where the tragedy happened before coming up here. Important, don't you think? If he's to help the army justify to the public their continued presence here.'

Price's eyes narrowed and flicked between us curiously. Might he press the matter? No. Even if he suspected a lie, these proud and independent men needed one another now. Vernon was part of the bargain, the reason we had been allowed to do this.

'So, what now, Harry?' Vernon asked. 'I'm told we're to anticipate wonders.'

Price gave him a searing look. 'I wouldn't hold your breath.'

Just then we were joined by Sidewinder, who sounded more than agitated. 'Ready now, Mr Price?'

'Quite ready, warden. The mill is sealed so thoroughly that not even a mouse could enter undetected. The question is, are *you* ready?'

Instead of answering Price, Sidewinder turned to me and said, 'If the spirit child should visit us this night, Miss Grey, be prepared.' His tone wasn't fanatical now so much as concerned. 'You could fall prey to the same nausea and disorientation that has affected the others.'

What he didn't say was that I was about to fall prey to something far, far worse.

– 22 –

INTIMATIONS OF
IMMORTALITY

'So, Mr Price, where would you like us to –'

Sidewinder froze in the flickering candlelight, and I heard his sharp intake of breath.

Price was standing in the centre of the wrecked mill, next to the battered table and chairs. A length of rope dangled from his right hand. Wearing his black frock coat that fell to his knees, he exuded the sinister presence of a Victorian executioner.

Sidewinder stood in the doorway, eyes pinned on the dangling rope. 'Mr Price? Kindly explain the meaning of this?'

'I did tell you the séance would need to be subjected to my usual checks. And as you can see, those checks are impeccably rigorous. Now please' – Price gestured piously towards a chair at the head of the table – 'be seated, so that I can bind your hands.'

The mood became suddenly ominous.

Sidewinder stepped back uneasily, almost colliding with the imposing figure of Hartwell behind him. Hartwell grabbed hold of Sidewinder's arm and said sternly, 'You're going to go through with this, Sidewinder. Understood? You will follow Mr Price's instructions to the letter. The honour of my family depends upon it. Or so help me God . . .'

'Fine, fine,' Sidewinder muttered, but he didn't sound as though he meant it. He walked stiffly to the rickety chair Price had indicated and sat down.

At that moment, the commander entered the musty gloom, moving to stand next to Hartwell and Vernon. The spectacle and mystery of the occasion was evident in the expressions on the men's faces as they took in the sight of the many glowing candles around them.

'You gentlemen wait there,' Price instructed, then wasted no time in binding Sidewinder's hands. The chair creaked as he drew the warden's hands behind his back and tied them together. I sealed the knots methodically, and Price nodded his approval.

'Really, is this necessary?' Sidewinder said.

Without hesitating, Price's eyes dropped to his tatty brief-case, lying flung open on the ground. 'Sarah, hand me that hammer.'

I did, and watched as Price nailed a copper staple into the floor. He bound Sidewinder again with a long piece of tape drawn through the copper staple and fastened to the table. Finally, he nodded, apparently satisfied.

'Now, if you should attempt to rise from your chair, we'll all see the tug on the rope.'

'I won't rise from my chair,' said Sidewinder in flat voice.

At the entrance to the mill, Vernon, Hartwell and the

commander were watching us in transfixed silence. Striding over to them, Price scrutinised each man in turn, and – reluctantly – they allowed Price to run his hands swiftly over them. He seemed to take longer with Vernon, much to the journalist's badly concealed chagrin.

'What's in the bag?'

'Sandwiches.'

'Empty it.'

Wall shook his head. Price went to grab the shoulder strap. Wall stepped back. He glared challengingly at Price, who was glowering suspiciously back at him.

'I still have some self-respect,' Vernon said cuttingly. Slipping the canvas rucksack off his shoulder, he went swiftly to the door and dropped the bag on the ground outside.

'Satisfied, Harry?'

Price hesitated and then nodded coldly in dismissal. 'Take a seat over there for me.'

Vernon remained where he stood, at the doorway. 'Actually, I'd prefer to observe than participate.'

Price returned a disdainful grin. 'Nerves getting the better of you, Mr Wall?'

'That's right, actually.'

I saw the blank honesty on Vernon's face and felt a flush of admiration. Some people draw their lines and never cross them.

'Fine,' said Price. 'Don't touch anything.'

Sidewinder was sturdily seated at the head of the oblong table, his whole body lashed with rope. Now the rest of us gathered around, with Hartwell and Price wisely taking their places on either side of the warden, ready to catch him should he attempt an act of forgery.

I took my place immediately next to Hartwell, fully aware of the poor man's emotional fragility, and knowing that he would need my support should events become too overwhelming for him.

Standing immediately opposite me, to Price's left side, was the commander, an impassive picture of formality in his military uniform. His stoicism was impressive; no amount of training could have prepared him for this.

'What are those for?' he asked.

He wasn't staring at the waiting Ouija board, or at the heart-shaped planchette supported on castors, which was supposed to slide under our fingers to point at letters on the board and spell out words. What had caught his interest were the three small hand mirrors laid out on the surface of the table, their reflective sides facing up, glinting in the flickering light.

'These provide a little extra light by which to observe ... whatever may occur,' Price explained. 'By catching the candle-light at the right angle, you can better illuminate whatever you wish to see.'

They're like ghost lights, I thought, and I remembered what I had learned from the projectionist at the beginning of this journey: *The ghost light does not keep spirits away. It attracts them.*

With the scratch of a match, a small bluish flame sprang up from the table's central candle. Our faces shimmered strangely in the guttering light.

As Price lowered himself into his chair, Sidewinder said, in a flat voice, 'Everyone now join hands. Bow your heads.'

Price signalled to Vernon, who was still standing at the main door, to bolt it. He did so – but oddly, I noticed, keeping one hand behind his back. A bristling anticipation settled over the group as Sidewinder recited the words that, according to convention, were supposed to protect us from devilish deceptions and demonic illusions:

'Saint Michael the Archangel, defend us in battle. Be our protection against the wickedness and snares of the Devil. May God rebuke him, we humbly pray; and do Thou, O Prince of the Heavenly Host, by the Divine Power of God, cast into hell Satan and all the evil spirits who roam throughout the world seeking the ruin of souls.'

I'm not a religious woman, never have been, but I admit I found something comforting in that prayer as I glanced around the cramped table, my gaze jumping from Sidewinder, to Price opposite me, to the commander and, finally, to Hartwell on my left, whose right hand in mine was warm and clammy. I became aware of how closely we were sitting. The lingering scent of cologne and tobacco served as a reminder that I was the only woman here. *Imagine if my friends back in London could see me now*, I mused.

Hartwell squeezed my left hand tightly. Nerves – most of us were crackling with them. Not Price, though. He gazed hard at Sidewinder, as if challenging him to prove something.

'If there is a spirit present who wishes to communicate, please make yourself known.'

Nothing.

The tawny light thrown up by the small hand mirrors played across our faces.

Outside, it was pitch black. The candles guttered, shadows dancing across the walls as the wind moaned. How could anyone present not be highly suggestible under these conditions? I knew, from the look of hardened concentration on Price's face, that he was acutely alive to this possibility; should anything sinister or untoward occur at this moment, he would be the first to doubt it.

'If there is a spirit present who wishes to communicate, please make yourself known to us,' Sidewinder repeated.

Then he nodded down at the planchette.

Fighting my nerves, I joined everyone else in placing the fingers of my right hand down upon the board.

Still, nothing happened.

The wind died down, and the mill was still and silent. It was as if a thick blanket had settled over the crumbling old building, deadening the outside world. Price noticed it too, I think, and his eyes shifted to me with curious expectation.

That was when the table began shaking and vibrating.

'Jesus!' Hartwell whispered.

The commander's normally firm jaw had become slack.

The table began rocking hard, as if a tremor was ripping through the ground.

'Everyone remain seated!' Price instructed, sounding more annoyed than alarmed.

But it was Sidewinder's reaction I found most intriguing: the man who was supposed to be leading the séance looked quite stunned, white at the gills.

Incredibly, the table began to rise into the air, as if suspended on invisible threads.

'What the –' Sidewinder jerked his chair back.

Hartwell's hand clenched mine painfully hard. 'Who's doing that?'

'Watch the table,' Price said firmly, and we did; we couldn't take our eyes off it. It was floating just a few inches above the floor. Then, in a heartbeat, it wasn't. It dropped with a thud and a puff of dust.

The silence stretched. We stayed that way, too tense for words, for perhaps a full minute, listening, watching the table. Staring into the blackest corners of the mill and wildly wondering what horrors might lurk there, scenting us.

Hartwell spoke first, his voice thin and wavering:

'Was that him? My boy?'

'I don't think so,' Sidewinder whispered. He caught Hartwell's gaze and shook his head, breathless and dumbfounded.

'Then who?' I asked.

Then came a new sound: flat and metallic, from far beyond the mill's walls.

Clang . . . clang . . . clang . . .

Metal striking metal, blow upon blow.

Hartwell's hand was now vicelike around my own. Opposite me, the commander's mouth was twitching, his stoicism beginning to slip. Price, next to him, was stock-still.

Everyone was still holding hands. I threw a quick glance at the door. Vernon was where he had always been. No one was pulling any tricks.

Coolly, Price looked at the commander and then at Sidewinder. They were sharing a private glance, and looked alarmed; remembering, I suspected, the heartbroken blacksmith, who had vanished when Imber's civilians were evicted. But then the commander snapped out of his reverie, releasing my hand and breaking the circle. He stood up.

'Sit down,' Price ordered.

'No,' he said. 'No. I don't accept this. Someone's outside, having a game with us.'

'I don't think so,' Sidewinder whispered. 'Look at the planchette.'

No longer holding hands, we looked and saw that the board was jittering. And yet no one was touching it.

My eyes widened. So did Price's and Sidewinder's. At the door, Vernon was shaking his head – whether in fear or disbelief I did not know.

'Everyone rest a finger on the planchette,' Sidewinder said slowly. He glanced up at the commander. 'Even you, sir.'

Warily, Williams sat down and stretched out a trembling forefinger to the surface of the planchette. The device was set on castors. It would roll and point to letters on the Ouija board under the slightest pressure from our hands.

'Spirit! I beseech you, make your purpose known,' Sidewinder said. 'How did you die?'

Slowly, smoothly, the planchette glided from one letter to another:

M–U–R–D–E–R–E–D

Everyone looked at one another in fear and fascination.

'Where?'

C–H–U–R–C–H

'Rubbish!' the commander exclaimed. He glared at his warden, who was now trembling visibly. 'End this at once.'

'Not yet!' Price interjected. 'Spirit, what is it you want?'

The planchette started sliding again, more quickly now.

V E N G E A N G E

Nervous glances were exchanged all round.

If we were to believe this was indeed a spirit from the great beyond, then its intentions were clear: it had come to torture the soldiers who occupied the village of Imber, and to drive them to madness or death, until they left.

'Tell us who murdered you,' Price demanded.

'I said stop this – now!' the commander thundered.

But the planchette was already moving to the letters.

T–H–E–A–R–M–Y

That seemed to electrify Price. 'Who murdered you?' he said urgently. 'We need a *name*.'

H–A–R . . .

I threw a questioning glance at Hartwell. He shifted uneasily in his seat. Was it spelling his name? Surely not. But, oh God – wait. What about Price's name? That was quite a leap, but possible?

The planchette continued to glide.

O–L–D

'Harold?' Price repeated. 'Somebody called Harold murdered you?'

I held my breath; I think we all did.

'Is that correct, spirit? Harold attacked you?'

Y–E–S

A sensation of agonising dread sliced through me.

H–A–R–O–L–D–G–R–E–Y

And then, outside, we heard it again: the metallic strike of what sounded distinctly like a blacksmith's hammer.

− 23 −

THE UNKNOWN GUEST

I leapt up, breaking the circle and almost toppling my chair.

Bolting from the doorway, Vernon was the first to make it to my side, but I quickly waved him away. 'Sarah,' he said, 'what's wrong?'

'You broke the circle,' Hartwell called, sounding disappointed. 'How am I supposed to see Pierre?'

I said nothing, looking back across the room at my companions. I was willing to bet Price already knew what had shocked me, why I had broken out in a cold sweat.

'We must try again,' said Hartwell, grabbing for my hand.

I stepped back, out of his reach.

'No,' the commander said firmly. 'Everyone is shaken, that's clear. We should get back to the camp. Miss Grey is evidently upset, and the warden looks . . .'

I think the word he was about to use was 'exhausted', but he trailed off as he looked as Sidewinder.

Behind his circular spectacles, Sidewinder's eyes had rolled so far back in his head they looked like white marbles. His breathing was deep, cavernous. He was apparently in a trance.

'Sit down, Sarah,' Price said quietly. 'Now is not the time.' He glanced towards Sidewinder.

With unbearable apprehension, I took my seat. The commander did the same, though with noticeable reluctance, and we locked our eyes on the warden, who was slumped in his chair, head lolling.

There is something distinctly unsettling about seeing someone entranced, even if you suspect them of faking it. It isn't so much the way their personality vanishes, it's the fear of whatever may slide in to replace it.

A cold blast of air rushed through the mill. There seemed to be more smoke in the room too, probably coming from the candles.

Sidewinder's whole body jolted, as if he had been struck with a bolt of electricity.

The commander reached forward. 'Warden?'

'Silence!' Price hissed.

Sidewinder jerked his head back and his chair began to creak as he coughed fitfully, as if he were about to be sick. I *smelt* something. Strange, unpleasant.

I tried to ask, 'What's happening?' but I couldn't open my mouth. The atmosphere was thick. Oppressive. The only sound Sidewinder's tortured breathing. The outlines of everyone around the table were blurred by a thin mist. Even the edges of the table seemed to melt away. I felt weary and light-headed.

For a few seconds, nothing happened. Then Sidewinder took a long, shuddering breath.

Something, some ghastly white substance, was coming from his nose. I thought at first it must be mucous, but seconds later, it seemed also to be streaming from his eyes, his mouth.

Next to me, Hartwell whispered in astonishment, 'Is that *ectoplasm*?'

The substance was gleaming. Glistening. There was so much of it that it began dripping from Sidewinder's chin. I began to feel sick.

Price was staring rapturously at the luminous matter streaming from the warden's face. The glutinous substance was flowing down his chest, pooling in his lap.

Slowly, Price extended a cautious hand, dabbed one finger in it.

He flinched with surprise. 'It's freezing!' he whispered, his eyes flashing with amazement. And just then, I thought I saw, only for the briefest instant, some of his defiant scepticism slip from his features.

At the same moment, the pungent, chemical smell from before grew even stronger.

And then we all heard it.

Emanating from the furthest and darkest corner of the room, far beyond Price's shoulder, came a low sigh, a soft whisper.

At the head of the table, Sidewinder's whole body went rigid. He said, in a curt voice, 'We are now in the company of the dead. Pierre is here. Do not speak.'

I felt the temperature plummet.

Price gave a small shudder, and half-turned his head, as though he had sensed someone behind him. A presence.

The whisper came again, more clearly this time. A child's voice.

'*Papa ...*'

Price's eyes bulged. Again, he cast a look over his shoulder into the gloom. There was an emotional cry from Hartwell next to me, and an exclamation of fearful surprise from the commander. Vernon Wall, at the doorway, didn't flinch.

My first thought was that Price was up to his old tricks. Anticipating that nothing would happen, he had decided not to break Hartwell's heart, and to give him a little hope by rigging the room.

But since when did Price care enough about other people's feelings to betray his passionate and sincere desire to get at the truth?

'Oh my God,' the commander whispered. 'Look!'

All eyes swivelled towards the darkest corner. I could make out the faint outline of a figure, slowly shimmering into visibility. The shock was immediate.

'You see it?' I whispered across the table to Price.

As he looked slowly round at me, I sensed there was a change beginning in Harry Price, a change he had perhaps yet to acknowledge even to himself; a vital change.

'I see it,' he whispered back. 'But I'm not sure I believe it.'

'*Papa . . .*'

Hartwell began sobbing. 'Pierre? Is that really you? I can hear you . . . Oh my Lord. It's not possible. I can *see* you.'

Shortly after this occurrence, when Price wrote about the mill séance in an exchange of private letters (carefully changing the names of the location and everyone involved), he would describe what happened next as 'the most remarkable case of materialisation, or rather alleged materialisation, I have ever witnessed'.

It is with considerable hesitation that I publish this account, as I have had only one sitting and have been unable, as yet, to obtain independent corroboration of the extraordinary 'phenomenon' that I witnessed.

Many times have I been asked for my 'best ghost story', for the most thrilling and sensational incident in a lifetime's inquiry into the unknown and the unseen. I have investigated hundreds of alleged haunted houses, sometimes, as at Borley Rectory, with exciting results. I have attended thousands of séances, many of them in my own laboratory, in an attempt to pierce the veil that separates this world from the next. I have sat in poltergeist-infested homes in which objects have flown about – objects which no human hands could possibly have propelled. I have seen crude limb-like materialisations form before my eyes when experimenting with mediums. I have shivered again and again as I watched the mercury level plunge during a séance.

But only once have I seen what YOU would call a ghost – a solid, three-dimensional spirit from, apparently, the other side of that veil.

Inside the dark and icy mill, no one moved.

A ghostly figure was faintly visible in the farthest and blackest corner. It had the unmistakable shape of someone small . . .

Hartwell's eyes met mine in mute disbelief. I could see that he was only just keeping himself together. The memories and desires of a father were fusing in his eyes.

'Oh my God,' he managed, with a look of painful regret. 'Marie was right.'

'Not so fast,' Price whispered. He had turned in his chair to face the motionless apparition. His face was invisible to me; I could see the back of his head shaking from side to side. He kept his voice low, controlled, as he asked, 'Is this the figure you saw at the roadside, Sarah?'

My hands shook. I found myself quite unable to answer him. I was holding my breath. Fascinated. Scared to death.

The figure, it's almost translucent!

'Sarah?'

'I – I'm not sure.'

The noxious chemical smell from before pervaded the mill with greater intensity. I was becoming light-headed. Wispy tendrils of smoke were slipping around our heads. The whole atmosphere was one of unreality; a dreamlike haze of gloom.

'Now do you see?' Sidewinder said in a low drawl, slumped back, his head lolling. 'It is no lie.'

More of the white substance was flowing from his nose, pooling on the floor. Gleaming. A trail of it led to the figure . . .

'He will approach us now,' Sidewinder said. 'Join with us, spirit.'

A stunned silence spun out. A terrible silence.

I swept the hair from my eyes, straining to see more of the dark figure. *We can't all be hallucinating this, can we?*

And then, as if hearing my thoughts, the figure slowly tilted its head to one side, watching us.

My heart almost burst out of my chest!

I screwed my eyes shut and at the same time heard a gasp from the commander, who was just as shocked as the rest of us.

'It's *moving*,' Price whispered.

My stomach sickly tight, I braced myself to look again, and saw the dark figure lumbering awkwardly towards us, not making a sound. The scene before my eyes began to sway a little. A dreamy, almost euphoric sensation stole over me. Price and the other men looked similarly affected, their faces drowsy and pale in the quivering candlelight.

'Harry, what's happening?'

Glancing anxiously over his shoulder at me, Price looked a little less suspicious than before. He looked almost, well, helpless.

'Pierre?' Hartwell muttered. 'I am here. Pierre, my dear boy!'

Boy? It seemed an odd choice of words. Before us was a cadaverous wraith, its legs concealed by billowing grey rags, its naked torso skeletal and bone white. It glistened with the same horrid substance that exuded from Sidewinder's body.

'Come to me now. Come to your foolish father.'

Price turned in his chair, watching frantically as the ghostly, hollow-eyed figure slowly moved behind Sidewinder, stopping at Hartwell's left side. Silent; as still as ice.

At the doorway, Vernon – like the commander – was staring in rapt fear. The room had become so cold that my breath was frosting before me. And all the time, my vision was blurred with that dreamy, ethereal quality.

'Come to Papa,' said Hartwell, in a thick, tear-clotted voice. 'Oh, I've missed you so. Here, let me feel the touch of your hand . . .'

I swallowed, touched by the father's words and chilled by the physical form of the dead boy I thought I now recognised as Imber's wandering child.

Taking quick inhalations, I plucked up one of the hand-held mirrors from the table in front of me and angled it to catch the light of the centre candle, aiming it directly at the inhuman thing, to discern its features more clearly.

And now I saw with vivid horror the jet-black hair, hanging tangled around a narrow face that was gaunt and sunken in; I saw the charcoal eyes, the painfully protruding ribs. He looked roughly seven or eight years old.

It was him. Hartwell ran a trembling hand over the figure's shoulder.

He told us afterwards that the skin was soft but freezing, and so clear it was almost translucent; that when he pressed his ear against the apparition's breast, he could hear his heart beating and feel his breathing.

'I – I don't understand,' Price was muttering, his head still shaking in confusion.

I believed, then, his iron scepticism had been breached. It was melting before my eyes.

'How? How?' He gave a deep, shuddering sigh and straightened in his chair. 'May I question him?' Price asked Hartwell, and the child's father nodded keenly.

'Where do you live, Pierre?'

No answer.

'What do you do there?'

No answer.

'Do you play with other children?'

No answer.

The figure never looked at Price. It just stared at Hartwell with dead eyes. Then Price asked a final question, leaning forward in the hope of catching an answer.

'Pierre, do you love your papa?'

Under the ghastly candlelight, we saw the figure's expression change, his eyes light up. A faint but fervent whisper: 'Yes, oh yes.'

The figure had barely lisped these words when Hartwell gave a pained sob.

I should say this: for a moment, Price no longer looked the implacable exposer of frauds. Fighting to get his breath, he stared with spellbound, helpless fascination. His entire world was collapsing. After a moment, he found his voice and asked Hartwell, 'Do you think Pierre might come to me?'

Hartwell nodded. For a moment, nothing. We all held our breath.

And then the figure began to move in an almost floating motion, behind Sidewinder, and towards Price. I tried to take in every sound and every movement but it was hard to focus in that room; my vision kept blurring, my mind drifting.

What I remember next is Price, opposite me, angling himself to face the figure. Reaching out his hand to the figure's shoulder. Hesitating . . .

'Harry, are you sure?' I whispered.

Price was staring at his hand, which was just a few inches from the figure's shoulder. His fingers were trembling. It wasn't like him to allow nerves to get at him. Then he steeled himself.

Almost having to force himself, he reached out a little further, and his fingertips connected with the figure's shoulder.

And then, a quiet gasp from Price as the horrible truth impacted.

'Oh, so very cold,' he muttered. 'Dead cold.'

And that scared me; because if this was a real child, I thought, a living child, Price of all people would know – wouldn't he?

He drew back his hand in a sort of dreamy astonishment, scrutinising the white viscous substance that was now sticky between his fingers.

The figure was in my direct line of sight. It had dark, intelligent eyes, which gazed into Price's without blinking. As the commander, Hartwell and I watched – stunned, and in Hartwell's case, emotional – Price took up one of the small mirrors to illuminate the manifestation, and swept it up the length of the figure's wasted arm.

Now, except for the entranced Sidewinder, and Vernon, who was standing rigid with terror at the main door, we all looked at one another in mutual astonishment.

Price whipped round. His grave expression seemed to ask me, *Is this really happening?* To which the only reasonable answer – for it was dictated by our own eyes – had to be yes. It was happening.

The ethereal figure drew yet closer to Price's side.

'I – I have to know,' he muttered, 'how this can be. How . . .' His voice trailed off.

'That's enough,' Sidewinder said drowsily. 'I can no longer maintain the connection.'

The small figure began inching away from us, back into the shadows.

'Pierre, please don't go,' cried Hartwell. His voice was full of pleading agony.

Price sprang from his chair and his arm shot out towards the figure. There was cry, a scuffle in the darkness as candles were knocked over and extinguished.

For the quickest instant I thought I glimpsed Price grabbing the apparition's arm.

Suddenly, a flash!

Everyone jerked at the pop of a bulb.

And then the figure slipped free of Price's grasp as easily as a seal in water.

Sidewinder opened his eyes, as if awakening from a deep slumber, and looked groggily around the darkened room.

'Where is he?' Hartwell cried with impotent anguish. 'Where did my boy go?'

He sprang up and began searching in the intolerable darkness. As he did so, more candles were scattered and went out.

'Wait, careful,' Price shouted in the chaos. He was unsteady on his feet, his voice drowsy. 'We need light. I need to see where he went! I need to search.'

'What was the flash?' Sidewinder muttered thickly. 'Was that a camera flash?'

We all looked in the direction of the flash, towards the door that led outside.

I had expected to see Vernon standing there. What I hadn't expected was his ringmaster's smile, sly and triumphant as he lowered his camera.

'I said no photographs!' Sidewinder exclaimed. Holding onto the table, he rose unsteadily to his feet and made a convulsive gesture to claim the camera. 'Hand it to me this instant!'

Vernon looked at me for a moment, with a trace of self-consciousness, as though he was trying to convey a modicum of private apology.

Then the young journalist turned and ran from the mill.

24

THE CONVERSION
OF HARRY PRICE

'Vernon – please, wait! Come back!'

I stood in the doorway, scanning the atrocious darkness for the man I had trusted. I thought I saw the bobbing of a torch, but within seconds it had vanished.

He would be lucky if he made it safely down the hill in this light, but Vernon was nothing if not daring. I knew he despised Price, but I hadn't expected him to contravene Sidewinder's ban on photographic equipment. An abject betrayal. And who knew what exactly he had managed to capture on film?

'How the hell did he get the camera in without us seeing?' Sidewinder demanded.

I turned to the warden. 'The camera was in his rucksack, of course.'

'But he left that outside.'

'Yes, but he could easily have retrieved it when we weren't

looking,' I said. 'The atmosphere was so disorientating I doubt any one of us would have noticed.'

'Indeed,' the commander said. He shook his head and came to the door. 'Bloody hell, I need some air.'

Hartwell remained sitting at the séance table. 'Where did Pierre go?' he asked. His eyes, bloodshot from crying, targeted Price, who was struggling to light the extinguished candles that lay scattered about the floor. 'My boy, my poor boy. You bloody scoundrel, Price – you frightened him away!'

Then I saw something I'd never seen before: Harry Price, shell-shocked. Stunned into silence. His hands were trembling as he straightened his coat, composing himself. Here, miles from anywhere, gazing uncomprehendingly at the séance table, was a man who had dared to peer beyond the night and for once hadn't liked what he had seen. He couldn't control it and he couldn't explain it. He looked pitiably lost, a man shipwrecked on the shores of his own doubt.

I walked briskly over to him and put my hand on his shoulder. He blinked at me, as if it were he who had been in a trance. He reached for one of the mirrors. The reflected light flickered across his face – for a moment he was almost demonic.

'How do you explain it?' the commander said. 'That can't have just happened.'

'It can and it did,' Hartwell said, already sounding more confident. I looked for distress or terror in his face and failed to find it. There was only seething resentment. 'And now I see that my poor wife was right. The dead – my own son – are reaching out to us to insist we reclaim what is ours. Our village. *And we will take it back!*'

Framed in the doorway, the commander stared. 'Now, don't be so hasty.'

Hartwell rose from his chair and kicked it over.

'Mr Hartwell,' the commander said abruptly, 'everything you've seen and heard in here is classified, and you are not authorised to say anything about it.'

'I don't answer to *you*!' Hartwell said, taking a step forward. 'But I'll make damned sure that you and the War Office and all your men answer to the living, and to the dead, for your crimes, Commander. Every one of you.'

The commander stood there for a moment, his hands balled into fists. Then he stalked towards Hartwell, locking eyes with him. 'You don't know anything!'

'What I know,' Hartwell said darkly, 'is what the dead have told us this night. You heard those noises from outside. You saw the message spelled out – we all did. The army's hands are drenched in blood. You didn't just evict the villagers of Imber, you abused those who refused to leave. The blacksmith? That man didn't die of a broken heart, and he didn't vanish. You *murdered* him.'

The commander's mouth fell open. I saw the doubt in his face, the consideration that Hartwell may have pulled a devious trick, and I also saw fear – fear that the spirit message had been real.

And if it was . . .

I felt a hot tear snake down my cheek.

'Something you want to share with us, Sarah?'

Hartwell's question – delivered in a hard voice – startled me. I shook my head and wiped a hand over my cheek.

'Bloody journalists,' the commander said, glaring at Price, then me. 'The two of you had better retrieve that photograph from him, like your lives depend on it.'

I nodded. But I wasn't just thinking about the photograph,

or the incredible phenomenon we had just witnessed. I was thinking about the allegation of murder that had just been spelled out on the Ouija board – and my own father's name.

Harold Grey.

Before leaving the mill, I forced myself to complete the job at hand, and checked every possible exit. All of Price's seals and controls were unscathed – unlike Price himself, whose hands were ice cold as I led him out of the mill and dragged the wooden door shut behind us.

Sidewinder and Hartwell had a gone on a little further ahead with the commander. Much in need of reassurance, I kept my gaze on the white circles of light thrown by their handheld torches as they halted and waited for us at the belt of trees some twenty yards away.

Price stood at the side of the filthy millpond, looking around uneasily, as if he half-expected the dead child to pounce at him from out of the darkness.

'Harry?'

Distantly, Price said, '"The sight of a spectral arm in an audience of three thousand persons will appeal more to hearts, make a deeper impression, and convert more people to a belief in the hereafter, in ten minutes, than a whole regiment of preachers, no matter how eloquent, could in five years."' He met my gaze. 'Those were the words of P. B. Randall. Conan Doyle quotes him directly. The old dupe.' He shook his head, as if appalled by the truth now evident. 'Who would have thought he was right?'

Standing there with his shoulders sagging, the once swaggering ghost hunter looked impossibly vulnerable. Stricken.

'Then you're convinced it was genuine?' I asked.

'Aren't you?'

'It needs further investigation.'

'You weren't as close to the figure as I was,' he said with the fervour of a man suffering a devastating epiphany. 'I had not bargained for anything so striking as this. I touched him, Sarah; you saw I slowly passed my hand across his shoulder. Hartwell did also. He felt his respiratory movements. He felt his beating heart!'

'Which would imply, surely, that the figure was a living boy. Not a ghost.'

'I didn't say I thought he was a ghost, as such, Sarah.'

'Then you're going to have to explain better, Harry, because at this moment I'm not following your logic.'

He fell into a thoughtful silence, then glanced my way again.

'You remember Velma, Sarah? She told us spiritual entities can interact with the physical world by enveloping themselves in ectoplasm.'

'Harry –'

'I dismissed ectoplasm as artificial matter produced by regurgitation with the help of the diaphragm.'

I raised my voice. 'And your experiments demonstrated you were right to do so!'

He flung his arms wide. 'But what if I was wrong? What if the form that appeared to us this night represents direct evidence of an afterlife and communication with those that have passed on?'

Struck by his words, I reminded him that since the séance had terminated he had collected a sample of the viscous substance that had exuded from Sidewinder. Now he had the opportunity to study it.

'Oh, I will study it, have no doubt.'

'Until that analysis is complete, I think—'

He gripped my wrist. 'Did the figure *look* like a living person to you?'

'Well, no, but—'

'You saw, just now, its fluorescent outline, the way it shimmered. You saw it was induced to appear, as we were promised it would, as if from nowhere. You *saw* the ectoplasm issuing forth from Mr Sidewinder. If it was a living boy, how did he get inside the mill? How did he get out?' He shook his head with self-reproach. 'What if I was too sure of myself, Sarah? What if this boy is the closest thing to proof of the spiritual realm I have ever encountered?'

It was a possibility, granted. But believing it so readily was out of character, especially for a man normally so critical and exacting.

I began to worry if there was something else, something I didn't yet understand, influencing his judgement.

Perhaps sensing my doubt, Price let go of my wrist. Then he shook his head and said something that told me there were changes coming for both of us. Changes and trouble.

'I am, more than ever, convinced that I was wrong to be so doubtful, so dismissive,' he said, looking hopelessly at me with swimming eyes. Price, who was normally so strong, so resolute, now looked anything but. 'All these years, I was mistaken. Sarah, whatever will I do now?'

Two hours had passed and we were back at Westdown Camp. I was in Hut Three, lying on my bed, trying to sleep, when a hurried knocking got me up and padding across to the door.

'Are you awake?' From the other side of the door came Price's voice. 'Pack your things. We're leaving.'

What?

Ten minutes later, I was dressed and outside. The moon was high, a silver disc turning the curved steel huts and barracks into ghostly, shimmering shapes. I arrived outside Central Security Control to see Price emerging from the building. He strode stiffly to his Rolls-Royce.

'Where's your case, Sarah?'

He was already climbing into the driver's seat, and the determination on his face told me what he was planning: get back to the laboratory, analyse the sample of ectoplasm, write to his followers announcing his encounter with the undead to the world.

Of course, he'd have to change names and locations, but the story would be out there. And I could empathise a little with his zealousness. Imber had given him the biggest story of his life; an unexpected and unsettling investigation that had shown him just how wrong he had always been. But to an egotist like Harry Price, being wrong also meant something else: his reputation had to be protected, and at any cost.

'I said to pack! No time to lose.'

'But I'm not ready to leave,' I told him.

He gave me a look of frustration tempered with incredulity, and all my old resentment about his dominating attitude surged up. I was determined not to let him bully me.

'Our work here isn't done,' I said, picturing Father's face. *My work isn't done.*

Vernon's voice came into my head then: *I have a bad feeling I can't shake. A sense that there's something deeper out in that village. Something darker.*

I wanted to ignore Vernon's voice. It was pushing me onto a path I had no wish to walk, towards the mystery of a blacksmith murdered here eighteen years ago.

Murdered by a man with my father's name.

I shook my head and took a step away from Price's saloon.

'But, Sarah – I'm relying on you to get that photograph back!'

'Vernon has his own agenda,' I said, feeling disappointed and worried. 'I've no idea where he's gone or what he's planning.' And then there was Hartwell's agenda. No doubt he would get to work bringing together an assortment of former citizens to fight for the Imber cause. 'You shouldn't rush to put out this story, Harry, not until – '

'What the hell is *wrong* with you?' he exclaimed, banging his hands on the wheel. 'Are you denying what we saw out there? You think it was a hoax?'

I didn't know. I had replayed the mill séance in my mind over and over, both the preparations we had made and the moment when Price had scuffled in the dark with the small figure, and I was at a complete loss to explain how it *could* have been a hoax. The door was locked, every window and door sealed with wires that had remained perfectly intact. What's more, Hartwell had confirmed the child was indeed Pierre. Which meant either he was mistaken – which seemed very hard to believe – or that Pierre was still alive. But I had seen the boy's grave.

However, if we had really seen Pierre Hartwell's spirit, did that mean the other message was also genuine? An allegation of murder and a call for vengeance? I hoped not. God, I hoped not.

I thought about Sidewinder and Hartwell, whom we had

discovered coming out of the old mill before we had gone in ourselves. They had only emerged at Price's inquiring shout. We hadn't detected any evidence of fraud, but that did not necessarily mean no fraud had been committed. Or – to use another well-trodden mantra – did the absence of evidence mean evidence of absence? No. Look at all the cases of spiritual mediumship we had amassed. Not one escaped explanation eventually, and the explanations – like fraudsters regurgitating cheesecloth they passed off as ectoplasm – were often ingeniously simple. Many of the mediums, especially Velma Crawshaw, had fooled us initially.

'This is personal for you now, Sarah,' said Harry, cutting into my thoughts.

'I feel as though it always was.' His head cocked to one side, questioningly, so I told him honestly, 'Sometimes I feel I was meant to be here, as if my whole life is about this place.'

'Do you know why you feel that way?' he asked in a low voice.

I shook my head and said, 'I have to pursue my own answers now. With or without your help.'

He nodded, his face grim, and turned the key in the ignition. Moments later, the only sound was of the wind and his engine fading away over the desolate downs. He had left, but the question he had put to me lingered, coming back to me incessantly for the rest of the night.

Why did I feel I was meant to be here, that my whole life was governed by this place?

25

OLD WOUNDS

I slept a little, but not peacefully. As the first glimmers of that cold and wintry dawn broke, I lay on my narrow bed in Hut Three, staring at the arced ceiling. My emotions were in turmoil; I could hardly believe Price and Vernon had abandoned me here.

I wanted to be furious with them both, but mostly what I felt was sadness, an aching disappointment. I had always assumed I could rely on one of them; but the idea that both men could fail me, so insensitively and at the same time, was just too hurtful. Now I had to face facts: I was alone, not knowing what to believe about the spirit child who haunted Imber or about my own father and the awful accusation, imparted during the séance, that nobody had understood but me.

Fighting the urge to cry, I got out of bed and dressed. Everything depended on me now. The time for thinking was over. I had to act.

Picking up the photograph of my father that I had taken from Commander Williams' office, I went to find the one man I thought might have answers.

Warden Sidewinder's office was in Central Security Control, at the end of a long echoing corridor. Dark, windowless, sinister.

I knocked on his door.

No answer.

Steeling myself, aware that I was very much crossing a line now, I gripped the handle and turned it. The door swung open and I caught a glimpse of his distinctive shock of white hair. He had his back to me and was standing over a desk with its drawers thrown open, papers in disarray.

He swung round and glared at me with sharp consternation. 'I'm busy!'

'This won't take long,' I replied, trying to visualise Price standing beside me, urging me on. 'May I come in?'

'You may not,' he replied coldly.

As I had expected, the warden looked exhausted from the night's séance, but I detected a hint of something else in his demeanour too, something troubling. He looked very defensive.

Guilty?

Marching forward, he closed the office door and joined me in the echoing corridor.

'I'd like to know something.'

'Oh, I'm sure you would, Miss Grey.' He looked me up and down.

'How well did you know my father?'

'I'm not aware that I did.'

'Harold Robert Grey,' I said, producing the photograph. I angled it towards him. 'You're pictured here with him.

Look at the date: October 1914. Just after the army took over Imber.'

Behind his coin-like spectacles, Sidewinder's eyes widened. 'Harold's daughter?' He nodded, satisfied. 'Yes. I told you I never forget a face. You do look so like him.'

You look like someone too, I thought. *But who? Who do you remind me of?*

'I want to know more about the Imber evacuation before the war. How was it handled?'

'History irks me.'

'Why? Because you're ashamed of your part in it, or because you fear Imber's former residents?'

'Is this about what happened during our séance? The blacksmith?'

'His name was Silas Wharton. And yes. What do you know about him?'

'You're presuming we were acquainted.'

Perhaps it was a presumption, but not an unreasonable one.

'You must have met him.'

He shrugged. 'He was supposed to have been the last person to leave the village.'

'Yes, but *did* he leave? I heard that he vanished. What if he's still out there?'

Sidewinder's face tightened. 'I'd be very careful, Miss Grey.'

'Of what?'

'Stepping onto bridges you're not prepared to cross.'

'It's too late for that,' I replied, conscious now of how close he was standing to me in that windowless corridor. I felt almost intimidated, but my mind was still so focused on my father's name coming through on the Ouija board that I did not feel I could let this go. 'You were here when the army commandeered Imber. What happened when residents refused to leave? Was there an argument? A fight?'

'You have no need to know.'

'But I'm going to keep asking. So tell me!'

My voice echoed down the corridor. The warden pondered my demand for a considerable moment, and then I saw the trace of a malicious smile.

'In the days before Christmas of that year, when news of the evacuation was presented to the villagers in the school hall, your father was present. The news hit them hard. Many of them wept. We were to take everything they had, you see. Their land, their agricultural equipment, their sheep. Very little compensation.'

'It's appalling,' I said, not afraid to reveal my full disapproval. 'You left them with practically nothing.'

'I was part of the village. The eviction set us free. Living out there on Salisbury Plain in desolation, trust me . . . we were so isolated we were practically prisoners.'

'And my father participated?'

'Oh, he did rather more than participate.' He snatched the photograph from my hands. 'This was taken just a few days after the eviction, in the churchyard. You saw the note the blacksmith's family left on the church door? His heart broke all right. He chained himself to the church railings. Refused to go.'

I remembered the unnerving and peculiar sounds I had heard in the churchyard, the footsteps on gravel, the sound of sobbing and the dead sound of metal striking against metal.

'We used his hammer to break the chains, cut him loose.'

'Then what?' I asked, feeling pangs of dread. Reminding myself, over and over, *He vanished. The blacksmith vanished.*

Sidewinder's eyes were piercing, and as cool as marbles. 'He was a good soldier, your father. Dependable. Obedient to the last. No task was too great, or too horrific.' He gave me a discomforting smirk. 'Your father always did what was necessary. Always.'

Surrounded by row upon row of young soldiers hungrily eating their breakfast, I sat at the end of a long table in the officers' mess, trying to suppress my awkwardness under so many speculative stares. It was Tuesday morning. By now Price would be back in London. I pictured him hunched over his typewriter in his gloomy study in the townhouse in Queensberry Place, clacking out sensational letters about our experiences here. It occurred to me now, as I forced down another spoonful of watery porridge, that in deserting me Price hadn't just robbed me of his expertise; he had also taken with him the projection slide that I had brought from London. The slide he had pressed me to give him and had promised to analyse.

A handsome soldier planted himself on the bench next to me, his gaze falling to my chest. I was feeling ever more lost and self-conscious. I shifted away from him, only to notice some of the men on the opposite table making jokes, more eyes on me.

If only Vernon hadn't also disappeared. I remembered the pop and flash of his camera. Whatever his plans, I now had little chance of learning whatever he had discovered in the files at Price's laboratory in London. My emotions were in turmoil; I needed help.

There's one man who can still help, I told myself, as I stood up and walked briskly from the mess hall. With the wind at my back, I hurried towards the main building and inside, until

I found myself in the cold concrete corridor leading to the sickbay, and Sergeant Edwards' room.

The black and red burns on his face, neck and hands still made it painful to look directly at Gregory Edwards. The poor wretch was lying in a streak of grey light that fell from the window and onto his bed, reading what looked like a black leather-bound bible. I knocked lightly on the open door and he twisted his head towards me. 'You're still here?' he rasped. 'I heard that colleague of yours upped and left in the night.'

I nodded, and asked if he could spare me some time.

'Come in, shut the door.'

Well, of course I hesitated – the memory of his earlier spontaneous attack was still fresh in my mind – but I needed information. I had to show him I wasn't afraid, so I closed the door and drew up a chair beside his bed.

His eyes were fearfully bloodshot. I wondered if he had been crying.

'The last time we spoke, Sergeant, the warden was here. And the commander. I had the distinct impression then that you don't trust them.'

'I don't,' he said, staring intensely at the small statue of Saint Anthony on the floor.

'I need to tell you what happened at the Imber mill. What – who – I saw.'

He met my gaze then and said, cautiously, hopefully, 'You don't think I'm crazy?'

'No. Sergeant, I saw the boy too. You described undergoing a vision when you were in the woods. You heard whisperings. A very similar thing happened to me.'

Without delay, I recapitulated the fearful events of the

earlier night, describing every moment of the séance and explaining why this mattered to me now so personally.

'I understand,' he said at last. 'You are afraid that your father was involved in something horrendous in Imber?'

'I don't believe that. I don't want to believe it. My father was a good man, one of the best. But it's not just that. Harry Price is absolutely convinced that the phenomena we witnessed out there were completely real. And I need to know.'

A faint expression of sympathy moved over his charred face. It encouraged me. 'If there is anything you haven't told me that could be relevant to my investigation, Gregory, now is the time to share it.'

The bull-necked man swung his legs off the bed, his shoulders heavily hunched, his eyes red, and it occurred to me that he resembled Hartwell – bereaved and in search of solace. Suddenly, I remembered that on the night Marie had died, I had heard Gregory sobbing in this very room. Just as I was trying to fathom why he would have been crying on that particular night, the question came to me: had he ever seen Marie on the Imber range? Had he spoken to her? Known her?

'Sergeant? Gregory? Did you know the Hartwell family?'

He nodded.

'Sir, please. Was Marie a friend?'

He shot me a look that betrayed more than it was meant to, and all at once I understood.

'Oh, goodness, you were –'

He nodded, and I saw tears brimming in his eyes.

'She deserved better than Hartwell,' he said, sobbing. 'I loved her so.'

'Did Hartwell know?'

'I don't know. He would prevent her going out. It wouldn't surprise me if he did know.'

The revelation felt as though it could be significant, and it made me wonder about the Hartwell family and their long history of troubles. I offered my hand. The sergeant took it.

'What do you intend to do now?' he asked.

I thought of the Hartwell gravestones, standing just beyond the barbed-wire fence in the tangled churchyard. The idea arising in my mind was almost too horrific to contemplate.

'Hartwell saw his son at the séance,' I said, thinking out loud. 'Or someone he thought was his son.'

'Yes.'

'Except Pierre is buried in Imber churchyard.'

'Yes.' Gregory nodded solemnly.

'But is he? I mean, do we know that for sure?'

We locked eyes.

'Sergeant, I know what we must do.'

'It's out of the question, Miss Grey!' said the commander, sitting down behind his desk. He looked surprised and displeased to see me. 'I'm not even sure you should still be here. It was Mr Price we needed and – '

'Sir, I want to establish whether we have been deceived. To know if someone is orchestrating an elaborate hoax to cover up a serious crime committed in Imber a long time ago.' I lifted my chin. 'Are you aware of any such crime, commander?'

'Why don't you take a seat, Miss Grey?'

'Why don't you answer my question?'

'I don't care for the bite in your tone!' He paused for a moment, troubled. I saw his mind working through the implications of what I had asked him to sanction. 'Pierre Hartwell is dead. The certificate of death isn't enough for you?'

'Is the coroner who signed it still alive?'

'I don't know. I'll have to check.'

'Do that. If he isn't, we must do as I've suggested, and we must do it quickly.'

'Miss Grey, it is unlawful to disturb any human remains without – '

'First obtaining the necessary legal authority. Yes, I know.'

'And the graveyard is consecrated ground. We'd have to obtain a Bishop's faculty and a licence from the Home Office. Besides, Hartwell will never agree to it. His own son?'

'I don't mean any disrespect, commander. And besides, Hartwell doesn't have to know.'

'What about his supporters? They regard the church, the graveyard, as their own property. If they should hear about this, what then?'

'They'll be outraged. So we must act quickly. Your men are more than capable.'

Behind his desk, Williams rose his feet, torn between duty and curiosity. Like me, he had seen the wandering child. A part of him had to be burning to know the truth. Finally, he nodded in resignation. 'You really think Pierre could still be alive?'

I had no evidence, but I had to believe that he could. For my own sanity, I had to believe that there were no ghosts, no messages from beyond.

'Open the grave and let's find out.'

26

OPEN GRAVES, CLOSED MINDS

There was no crackle of distant artillery fire. No echoing rumbling of tanks. On that crisp winter afternoon, the only sound that broke the silence was the dull thud of the shovel striking earth. It was later that Tuesday afternoon, and I stood in the church porch, watching Sergeant Edwards digging up Pierre Hartwell's grave.

Two soldiers stood by, supervising, and thinly disguising their disapproval.

It had not been easy convincing the commander that Edwards was the best person for this job. A recovering burn victim, possibly insane? No, there were certainly plenty of other men better equipped for the task.

But Edwards had insisted, pleaded, that he should be the one to do it. It helped that the commander himself had witnessed the manifestation of the spirit child. Now, he and Edwards had something in common, which was possibly why he capitulated and permitted Edwards to perform this most gruesome task.

Of course, now, with the benefit of hindsight, I understand why Edwards had wanted to do it; at the time, I thought it was to help me.

The breeze shifted and for the briefest moment I thought I caught the quiet sobbing of a man. And was that the sound of footsteps? No. Imber was deserted this morning. We had seen no one, except the soldier guarding the main gate, since we had arrived.

Well then, I told myself, *it's your imagination.* Everything I had learned – consciously and subconsciously – since my arrival in Imber was quietly subverting my senses and my interpretation of what they were telling me.

The first time I had entered this churchyard, my mind had been considerably more open to extreme possibilities than it was now, and Price's mind had been resolutely closed. We had swapped roles. One of us was wrong – I just prayed it wasn't me.

From the grave, there came the harsh sound of a shovel striking concrete.

'Miss Grey!' Edwards exclaimed. 'I have something here.'

He had dug immediately in front of the marble sculpture of the lamb. I rushed to the graveside and looked down. Edwards, the poor man, looked ragged with exhaustion, but I saw that he had reached what had to be the burial vault.

'Well, that confirms it,' he said, looking pale. 'There's definitely a vault here.' He looked solemnly up at me. 'Satisfied now?'

I wasn't, not at all. For a moment, I felt a pang of guilt, ashamed. But I wasn't going to let him see that. If we didn't look inside the grave, I would never know for sure.

'Open it, please.'

He looked pained. 'That's going to involve removing the burial lid. Another hour, probably.'

'Do it.'

Edwards gave an acquiescent nod and got back to work. The poor man. I helped where I could, and so did the other soldiers, especially with the rope that needed to be attached to the lid of the burial vault and pulled.

Then I waited, and as I waited I felt the hot, quick rush of blood in my veins, faster and faster. The nerves like nettles in my stomach.

Sometimes, knowing the answer to a question is worse than not knowing. That was how it was for me between that macabre Tuesday afternoon and lunchtime the following day.

After our grim expedition to the churchyard and the discovery we made there, the commander was absent. He seemed to be avoiding me. Even Gregory Edwards was unreachable for a time. He was taken off for a debriefing. Then he said he needed time to recuperate, to recover from the shock.

I suppose I needed recuperation time as well, but time was the one thing we didn't have. My mind was storming with questions.

At lunchtime the next day, Wednesday, I found the commander in his office, sitting behind his desk with a thick file of papers before him.

'You've been avoiding me,' I said, closing the door. 'I need to talk to you urgently.'

'We are in the middle of something here.'

Turning, I saw that he wasn't alone in his office. The stone-faced warden was standing behind the door, his eyes riveted suspiciously on me. Whatever they had been discussing before I barged in, the atmosphere was uncomfortably strained.

'What is it?' I asked. 'What's happened?'

The commander hesitated.

'Please, I would like to help, if you would permit me.'

Rubbing the fatigue from his eyes, the commander picked up a letter from his desk and read from it: '"Notice to quit. We the people hereby serve notice on the War Office to vacate and deliver up to the county of Wiltshire the parish of Imber."' He raised his eyes to me glumly. 'It's the Imber Will Live campaign. They're no longer content with meagre protests. They're arranging a mass rally in the village.'

'When?'

'Tomorrow.'

'How many expected?'

'Five hundred, perhaps.'

'Quite a show of unity.'

'It'll never happen,' Sidewinder broke in. 'You think they'd risk open conflict with the military?'

'After what happened to Marie Hartwell?' I said. 'Yes, I think they would. I don't want to sound rude, Commander, but many of them will think you robbed an entire community of their homes, that you had this coming.'

'We need to prepare,' said the commander, stroking his moustache. I could see the need for reassurance in his face, and that worried me. People who needed reassurance were always more easily manipulated, and right then I wouldn't have trusted Warden Sidewinder if my life depended on it.

'We could apply for an injunction to keep them away,' the warden suggested.

The commander shook his head adamantly. 'We're in an

extremely precarious position. We need to foster an atmosphere of good-natured cooperation.'

Sidewinder's eyes rolled. 'Sir, they are serving us with a
formal notice to quit! Threatening to occupy the buildings.'

'Well, that is out of the question,' said the commander. 'Half
those buildings could collapse at any time. But we should allow
them to come to Imber. It'll look heavy handed if we don't.'

'You want to placate these irresponsible people?'

Commander Williams raised his voice. 'Our marshals will
manage the roads and prevent people accessing any of the
buildings. Understood? I want radio controls at every point.
See to it.'

Sidewinder nodded. He stalked to the door and departed.

Once we were alone, I pulled up a chair and sat before the
commander's desk. His eyes narrowed. 'My men have already
told me . . .'

'Pierre Hartwell's grave is empty.'

He nodded grimly.

'How can you explain it?' I asked.

'I can't. I suppose Hartwell may be able to shed some light.'

'Then let's ask him.'

He shook his head strenuously. 'And compromise ourselves?
Out of the question. We exhumed that grave without proper
authority.'

'We must ask Hartwell!' I protested. 'Besides, he has a right
to know. This is his son, for pity's sake! And now we have good
reason to suspect the boy is alive.'

There was a long, long pause. 'Not necessarily.'

'What do you mean?'

The commander looked down again at the file on his desk.
'I'm afraid there were more.'

'More?'

'Disturbed graves.'

'Oh Lord. How do you –'

'When you left the churchyard, I asked my men to check the other graves. Most of the Hartwell family graves showed signs of disturbance, of having been dug up recently.'

'Were they empty?'

'We haven't yet exhumed them,' he said grimly.

It occurred to me very forcibly at that moment that I had missed this clue on my first visit to the churchyard. But the memory was clear: hadn't I almost tripped on the uneven ground that seemed to be collapsing around the graves?

'Who would disturb the graves? Why should they? When?'

'I have no idea,' he muttered, 'but I'm thinking of asking the warden to lead a full investigation.'

'No, sir. I'm not sure that's wise. He's far too closely involved in events.'

The commander's face tightened. 'I'll decide who I do and do not trust, Miss Grey. Right now, you're treading a fine line on that boundary yourself.'

I tried my best to sound reasonable and respectful. 'Commander, we both know Warden Sidewinder has had privileged access to the Imber range; and he has lied before. Don't forget that it was he who led the séances at the mill. Now we know that Pierre Hartwell doesn't lie in his grave, Commander . . . well, I don't think the boy ever died. I think someone's got him and has been using him to deceive your men – perhaps to scare the army away, perhaps for other motives. The warden could be involved.'

'But how – and *why*?' His face showed how ridiculous he thought the suggestion. 'No. Sidewinder lives here on camp.

This job is his life. Why jeopardise his own interests? And besides, there's no conceivable way he could have kept a seven-year-old boy here, not without us noticing.'

'Perhaps he keeps the boy somewhere else.'

'Where?'

'I don't know, but remember, he does control who accesses the range. He could smuggle the boy in any time he wanted to.'

Slowly, the commander nodded, but his tone was still sceptical. 'Let's say you're right, that Pierre Hartwell *is* alive. Whoever's behind this scam would have needed outside assistance.'

'Yes, I would think so.'

'From whom?'

I found my mind turning to the evening after Marie Hartwell's suicide, Sidewinder telling us how he had acquired an interest in the occult and supernatural matters.

'What about Sidewinder's son?' I said. 'Didn't he tell us his son could manifest the apparitions of the dead and the absent? He had a name for him. What was it?'

'The ghost maker,' said the commander, his mouth twisting unpleasantly.

But I was beyond that name now. There was something else. Something to do with Sidewinder's son. I closed my eyes tightly. Concentrated. And the warden's words came back to me: '*His séances became wildly out of hand. He was using all sorts of drugs, and he began to hear voices and act irrationally . . . He created illusions. Began to believe they were real. I think he was losing his mind. He was putting my job in the army in jeopardy, so I told him he had to stop.*'

My eyes snapped open. 'Where did his son go?'

'I'm not sure I remember –'

'Sir, please, do try!'

The commander was out of his depth now, and he needed help. It was in his interests to work with me, and he knew it.

'Wait. Yes, I recall.'

I nodded urgently, leaning closer.

'Sidewinder's son suffered badly with facial disfigurement. A war injury.' This we already knew, but its significance hadn't yet dawned on me. 'He said he found it difficult being with people, that he needed to work alone. In the dark.'

A jolt passed through me, fizzing down every nerve.

Work alone, in the dark?

'Miss Grey? What is it? You've gone terribly pale.'

'The warden's son.' A tremble in my voice. 'What was his name?'

He screwed his face up, thinking.

'Please, try to remember. A child's life could be at stake.'

A light in the commander's eyes. A name on his lips.

'Albert.'

Oh God . . . Oh God.

'That's right,' he said with mounting confidence. 'Albert. He went to London, to work in one of those picture palaces . . . became a projectionist.'

PART THREE

PHANTASMAGORIA

I am only satisfied if my spectators, shivering and shuddering, raise their hands or cover their eyes, out of fear of ghosts and devils dashing towards them.

ÉTIENNE-GASPARD ROBERT

27

BENEATH THE STAGE

In the bleakest moments of my life, I have relived the fateful journey I made then. I was frantic as I demanded the commander drive me to the railway station. Every detail remains unpleasantly vivid for me. The look he gave me, as though I had gone mad. Pacing the platform for the train. Rain pouring down as the train snaked back to London, and then as the taxi ferried me from Waterloo to the picture house in Brixton.

I tried to tell myself I was overreacting, that this was a tenuous connection at best, but I knew better. *You thought Warden Sidewinder looked familiar, of course you did. He reminded you of Albert, his son!*

It was getting on for seven o'clock when I found myself knocking on the double-door entrance of the picture house. The last time I was here, I'd met the night watchman, and the same man looked at me now, warily, with the same wine-soaked eyes, as I insisted on knowing the whereabouts of the projectionist.

'Albert? Now what you be wantin' him for?'

'Is he here?'

'Closed, closed, still closed,' the guard said. 'Something the matter with Albert?'

I recalled the projectionist's troubled eyes, the dent in the left side of his face.

'*One night . . . beneath the stage . . . I saw the figure of a young woman. I called out to her . . . Seconds later, she was just . . . gone.*'

I thought, yes, there was something very much the matter with Albert.

'Sir, can you please let me into the auditorium? I have reason to believe I'll find Albert in there. I want to look beneath the stage.'

The guard shook his head. 'I never go down beneath the stage, miss,' he said gruffly. 'No one does.'

I was sure there was a good chance I would find Albert below the stage, though I no longer believed the ghost stories he had spun for me. Perhaps I *had* believed, before I knew anything of Albert's history, his drug taking, his connection with Imber, his séances, which his unnerving father had told us drove men to madness. Now, what I suspected, very strongly, was that the projectionist was a dangerous man.

I suspected something else too. Just before falling from the stage, a noise had made me turn round. I had wondered whether that noise was the voice of a child, calling for help, and now I worried that I was right.

As I entered the deserted auditorium, the same sense of dread that had overwhelmed me on my first visit here returned, but it was stronger and more oppressive. As I paused to look about, memories caught me: falling from the stage, injuring my ankle, the light of the projectionist's torch bouncing off the gilded banister rails as he hunted me down.

On my journey to London that afternoon, I had carefully gone over in my mind the circumstances that had first drawn me to the picture house – the inexplicable certainty that I was connected to it, personally and deeply. I've never believed in fate, but I felt the same sense of certainty, even stronger now, the troubling inner conviction that everything that had happened in Imber had happened for a reason. I was meant to find something, or someone.

The night watchman – who had sobered up somewhat in the face of my urgency and agreed to let me in – led me to a small wooden door to the left of the stage. It creaked open when he pushed it, revealing thick darkness beyond. 'Leads down to the cellars, miss. You'll need a light.'

I reached into my coat pocket for my handheld torch. I think that was when the watchman realised that I meant to go on with this venture, because he set his suspicion aside then and said, in a tone of doubtful concern, 'Miss, I really should come down with you.'

'I want to go alone.'

'Sure?'

Wait, I thought. *Someone else needs to know you're down here.*

I fished in my pocket for a pen and paper. Scrawled a number and gave it to him. 'Telephone this man, please – ask him to come here immediately.'

'What should –'

'Tell him Sarah worked it out. Tell him the warden and his son were responsible. Tell him I think Hartwell's boy is alive. And tell him, for God's sake, to come quickly.' I saw the night watchman's bewildered expression and added, 'He'll know what it means. Please, just hurry and do it!'

'All right,' he said begrudgingly. 'But shout out if you need me.'

Nodding, I told him I would. Then, with blood thumping in my ears, I clicked on my torch and confronted the darkness below.

'Albert, are you down here?' My question echoed back at me. 'Albert, it's Sarah Grey. Listen, I know about your father, Warden Sidewinder. I know about his deceptions in Imber.'

Silence.

'Albert? Where is Pierre Hartwell?'

No sound came back to me through the shifting, slanting shadows.

Carefully, I edged down the steep stone staircase and emerged in a wide chamber. Sweeping my torchlight over the damp walls and floor, I saw a rusty knife, a goat skull replica, even a Victorian pram. Discarded stage props or the collection of a man gone insane?

There was something else down there, something that looked very much like a blacksmith's hammer. The mere sight of it was enough for me to suffer another shock because I didn't think finding that hammer down here was a coincidence. I didn't think it was a coincidence at all.

My footsteps echoed as I passed into another chamber. This one was smaller, with a low vaulted ceiling, and here a foul smell pervaded the air; not the damp, stale smell one would normally associate with a cellar, but a familiar chemical, toxic odour.

Something on the ground caught the light from my torch.

Crouching, I saw it was an industrial-looking padlock that had been left next to a trapdoor, which was flung back.

'Hello?' I called. 'Anyone there?'

I peered down into the yawning darkness and saw, far below, a soft yellow luminescence, not unlike the glowing light that had materialised during our séance at the Imber mill.

Under the ledge of the hatch was an iron ladder that seemed to be securely fastened to the wall. It plunged about fifteen or twenty feet into the gloom, maybe more. I looked all about, listened, but could detect no signs of activity below.

Carefully, I lowered myself through the trapdoor, gripped tight to the ladder and began to descend.

One, two, three . . .

Each rung was accompanied by the echoing clang of my shoes on iron.

A rustling, scurrying noise came from somewhere below me.

Then –

Dammit!

The torch slipped from my fingers and clattered downwards, and when it hit the stone floor its light was extinguished. As much as I wished otherwise, it wasn't the rustling noise that had jolted me into letting go of the torch. I thought I had felt something in the darkness below, something cold, touching my leg.

No, you imagined it, I told myself, and in a moment of resolve that now seems foolishly naive, I told myself there was too much at stake here to hesitate, that I must carry on down.

With fearful expectation, I allowed my foot once again to come off the ladder, into the black space . . .

And then I froze, as if my whole body had, in that instant, turned to ice.

A hand had seized my ankle.

A stone-cold hand.

I gasped, tried to pull my leg up and away, but the icy grip tightened. Fingernails dug into my flesh, trying to pull me down.

My chest began to burn with ragged, panicky breaths. I tried desperately to clear my head, to think.

What should I do?

If I let go of the ladder, wasn't there a chance, a strong chance, I'd land on whoever had hold of me?

It's a hell of a risk, Sarah.

But I had no choice. I couldn't just remain there, frozen halfway down a ladder, in the clammy grip of God knows what. I was terrified, but I had to do *something*.

With a horrified grimace, I prepared to let go.

28

STILLNESS AND FLICKER

But before I could let go, the bony fingers uncurled and suddenly my ankle was free.

Stay in control.

Now I thought the better thing to do, possibly, was climb back up. If I was quick, I could get back to the upper cellar and call to the night watchman for help.

But I did none of these things, because it occurred to me that whoever was down there in the darkness might not want to hurt me; perhaps what they wanted was my help.

Stranded there on a ladder in a dank cellar, this outcome didn't strike me as particularly likely – but it had to be possible, didn't it?

As if in answer to this question, there came then a small voice from below. Hopeful. Afraid.

'Mummy?'

I looked down, but I could see nothing but musty darkness.

'Is that you, Mummy?'

My heart clenched, for this was unmistakably a child's voice. And although I knew the idea was outrageous and impossible – not least because *my* son would be with a new family, far away from here – the distressing thought came suddenly into my mind that this was my boy. Speaking to me.

Still gripping the iron ladder, I began to tremble as I remembered my baby's beautiful, smooth face. I saw him now, swaddled in blankets, cradled in the arms of the nun as she took him away.

Your son. Your own son.

'Mummy? *Maman*?'

That word, that beautiful word, jerked me out of the past, into cold, terrible reality. *Maman*. French for Mother.

I started down into the implacable blackness.

No sooner were my feet on the ground than one of them collided with the torch. I snatched it up, flicked it on and pivoted. The beam fixed on a pale and tiny hand.

I jumped, startled. Then a waxy face with frightened eyes loomed towards me.

'You're not my *maman*.'

The boy from the crossroads, the same boy from the séance, stood before me.

Pierre!

How my heart ached for this poor child. He was naked from the waist up, his arms like wasted sticks, his ribs painfully protruding. No wonder his eyes looked so hollow, his cheeks so gaunt. He was dangerously underweight and smelt sourly of body odour, his whole demeanour one of ragged exhaustion.

I was struck by a wave of crashing anger as I saw something else on his wasted arms: they were mottled with fresh bruises.

Any fears I had previously harboured of him, or of vengeful

spirits, fell away. Now, peering into that vulnerable face, I felt nothing but the maternal, protective impulse to rescue him, to understand how he had come to be here.

And to punish the monster responsible.

With mounting nerves, I shone my torch around our grim surroundings, remembering Albert's dented face, imagining him looming out of the shadows, grasping for me. What if he was down here now, with us?

There was a miserable mattress on the ground; a plate, a rusty knife and fork.

We were standing in a large domed chamber. The walls were made of bricks so old they had cracked in places and blackened with age. The floor, also of brick, was thickly covered with dust that smelt ancient; and there was another odour pervading the air, a horrible odour. The same noxious whiff from before.

My pulse quickened as I kneeled and put one reassuring hand on Pierre's frail shoulder.

'My name is Sarah, Pierre. I'm here to help you.'

He blinked at me through blurred eyes. 'Where's my mummy?'

I wanted to say his mother was worrying about him, that she was waiting for him at home in Wiltshire. But of course she was not. She had become a tragedy of the lost village, a suicide victim who was destined now to be buried in a cold, dark spot in unsanctified ground, far away from living sight.

'It's all right, Pierre, you'll be safe now.' *Because I'm going to get you out of here,* I almost added, but didn't. Because then I saw the rope knotted around his ankle, and when I followed the rope with the torchlight, I saw it was fastened tightly to an iron rung embedded in the curved wall.

I had to restrain myself from cursing out loud the brute

who had done this as I stole another panicky glance around the darkened cellar. Perhaps I was mistaken, but I thought I had just seen something move in the hopping beam of my torchlight.

I directed the light at the opposite side of the chamber and saw there was an opening, an alcove receding into the blackest darkness.

My heart began thudding even harder.

For pity's sake, hurry. If Albert should find you here now . . .

'Let's get this off you,' I said to Pierre, shakily putting down the torch and reaching for the knot. 'Quickly, tell me, who did this? Was it a man, Pierre? A man called Albert?'

Silence. And then a distinctly disquieting sound: heavy footsteps, dragging towards us.

Groping for my torch, I clicked it off.

Crouched down next to Pierre, I whispered, 'Do you know what's happening?' For although the footsteps had ceased momentarily, I could still sense movement in the darkness, on the opposite side of the chamber. And something else: burning.

The boy uttered just one word: *'Phantasma . . .'*

And before I could ask what that meant, he began coughing and covered his mouth. My eyes began to water and I saw, with a jolt of alarm, an eerie luminescence glowing softly in the dark. The glowing light was emanating from the opposite side of the chamber, and becoming steadily brighter.

A thin smoke – more of a fog, actually – was slipping slowly into the chamber, and the foul chemical smell was suddenly much stronger. Pungent. My head felt light. And then, as I was slipping my hand into Pierre's, a bolt of fear smacked through me.

There were *things* silhouetted in the drifts of smoke. Shapes with wispy edges, translucent, shimmering with light.

And the shapes were moving.

'Pierre,' I whispered, 'what is it? What's happening?'

I was pulling the boy close to me, thinking desperately, when he brought his hands up to cover his eyes.

He can see the shapes too.

What's happening?

I was dizzy, too dizzy to stand, and I couldn't stop staring into that unearthly light. The threads of reality began to untether for me right then. And for a split second, as if I had been wrenched out of my body with a burst of light, I was somewhere else.

I was waiting, watching the turning of a mill wheel. Imber's abandoned mill, but not abandoned. This was the mill in its glory days, when the days were long and children chased rabbits out of the cornfield. How old was I? The sun was warm on my neck. In the distance, sheep were bleating.

I waited, watching the trees sway, watching the shadows lengthen, until suddenly a figure appeared.

Wait! What are you doing?

He grabbed me roughly around my wrist, and I—

I tried to cry out but no words came, only hacking coughs, my vision twisting, distorting. The smoke and the light were opening a shimmering window to another time.

Astounded, I looked into the past, a scene wrapped in a ghostly fog, and I saw a story unfold before me.

A freezing winter morning in a village miles from anywhere. October 1914. I've seen this before. There is the schoolhouse, the manor, the cottages; there, the low wall made of mud and rubble.

Above, on a hill littered with graves, is the church. In the distance, on the downs high above the village, farmers work the land.

It's snowing, and in the church tower the bells are ringing slowly. Mournfully.

The day of the funeral.

I turn to my side and see him. My father. He removes his hat respectfully, watching the approaching funeral car. Two women at the side of the street are nodding, staring. Afraid.

I turn and follow their gaze to the churchyard gate, where the grieving family stands. The mother is sobbing, shoulders shaking. She's much younger now, but with a plunge of my stomach I recognise her as Marie Hartwell.

She's aware of the villagers watching her, but dares not look up. She knows what they are thinking. How can it be? How can yet another Hartwell child be dead? The man next to her – thin, handsome, stony-faced – wears a towering black hat. It is unmistakably Oscar Hartwell.

Marie gives him a look of pure hatred.

He responds with a dark glare, the sort of look that warns, 'Keep your filthy mouth shut.'

I watch as –

I was back, abruptly, in the smoky haze of that underground chamber, crouching down on the ground with the boy. From the billowing smoke came a low hissing sound.

Pierre was trembling, squinting, not at me but into the smoke. At something awful.

'*Phantasma*,' Pierre said again, his hand trembling as he pointed.

I wish I hadn't looked.

Something awful was in the chamber with us. An evil presence. An apparition so abysmal and so shocking that all I could do was shake my head helplessly in a drowsy terror. Never in my life had I expected to see something so monstrous.

Materialising in the smoke, just ten paces away from me, was the ambiguous shape of an animal with matted brown fur. It took me a few long seconds to realise what it was, and when I did, my chest hitched with raw terror.

I was staring at the grotesque, rotting head of a wild boar.

I almost screamed then, as my hands began to shake violently. The boar's black eyes, sentient, baleful, fixed on me. Its razor-sharp tusks were bared, and it seemed – God help me – to be drifting through the wispy smoke, getting nearer with each second. An acute stench of wet, rotten fur was close, so vile that I wanted to vomit.

Pierre and I scrambled backwards until we reached the wall, terrified.

Courage failed me. I began gasping for breath and my eyes popped open in horror as a new apparition infested the chamber: a human skull with a rat crawling from one hollow eye socket.

I drew back, crouched there on the filthy ground, absolutely appalled.

'Enough,' I cried. 'Please, no more!'

But I realised, with a chill of horror, that there were more dark and fantastical forms sliding in around us, a kaleidoscope of hideous and unearthly spectres, writhing in the mist: a swooping winged creature; a ram with giant horns; a jackal. It snarled and Pierre wailed in fright.

Beside myself with fear, I yelled for help, wrapped my arms around Pierre's shuddering body.

What's happening? Why can't I think clearly?

The smoke billowed, the phantoms swirled, malevolent and

irretrievably evil. Now, a new one surged forward, a translucent woman in flowing black garments.

A nun, her face drawn, her fingers and toes blackened. Her eyes blazing, fixed on me.

I shrieked and pulled Pierre closer, trying to shield him from this unearthly creature. The rope around his ankle strained.

The nun reached out for me with wasted arms. There was nowhere to run now, no chance of escape.

No hope.

29

DEVIL'S SNARE

Ripping my gaze away from the terrible spectre in black robes, I saw that Pierre's mouth was agape; I could feel his skinny frame trembling with terror.

Then a man's voice, low, almost threatening: 'Here you are.'

Whirling round, I was horrified to see, between us and the iron ladder, the dark figure of a man so shrouded in the thin smoke he could have been made of it. He was holding something. I strained to see . . .

Oh Jesus, oh God.

A blacksmith's hammer.

I felt a seething black fear then, the utmost despair.

'Please, wait, whoever you are, just –'

The bulking figure came flying towards us and swung the hammer.

I gasped as it whistled past my face. A piercing crack echoed all around. I looked up at the nun in front of me, but she had changed.

What? *What?*

The nun's face was now a spider's web – a crazy pattern of lines. And I realised: I was staring into a cracked mirror.

Suddenly, the mirror exploded outwards, showering the floor with shattered fragments.

I fell back into the legs of the man standing over me, hands curling at his side. Those hands, that hooked nose, the sweep of the forehead ... My whole body sagged with exhausted relief.

Harry!

It was *his* voice I had heard. He who had swung the hammer. He must have retrieved it on his way down here.

'Wait here, Sarah.' His black frock coat flapped out behind him as he strode into the smoke and the glowing light and the few ghastly shapes still flickering around the cellar. He shouted – so loudly, so powerfully – 'Albert Sidewinder, enough. SHOW YOURSELF!'

The flickering light blinked out. Every last lurid spectre melted into the whirling smoke. Groggy, Pierre and I were left crouching in the gloom, surrounded by glittering shards of glass. Shaking off the dizziness, I groped for my torch and drew the boy close, afraid he had been caught by flying glass, but he seemed all right, just frightened and shivering.

Limbs trembling, my breath laboured, I shone my torch around, splashing Price in a sickly light as he re-emerged from an alcove on the opposite side of the chamber.

Wait. Not just Price.

He was dragging a hunched figure with him, hauling him to his feet.

'Is this who you came looking for, Sarah?'

I rubbed my eyes. Recognised the dented face. The left eye

like a dusty marble. I nodded. Yes, this was the projectionist, Albert – Warden Sidewinder's estranged son. When he saw me, his eyes bulged with surprise and fear.

At that moment, Harry Price's face was burning with anger, the scariest thing in the room. With a roar of magnificent fury, he slammed Albert back into chamber wall, one hand clasped around the projectionist's throat.

'A trick! Clever and sophisticated, but a trick nonetheless. Ghosts and gadgets, yes?' Albert was shaking his head, not looking at Price, who called out to me, 'See that, Sarah? In the alcove?'

I shone my torch that way again, the dusty beam illuminating something on the floor: a small, antique-looking projector, fashioned from mahogany and brass and decorated with a crucifix and a skull with wings.

'A magic lantern,' Price declared. 'There's an oil lamp back there too. Grab it!'

I did, fumbling with the small oil lamp until the room flickered with an orange glow. I set it down on the ground near the ladder. All the time, the projectionist was against the wall, unsuccessfully struggling against Price's grip.

'Thought you'd dabble with the phantasmagoria, did you? Projecting lurid images onto smoke and glass? An antiquated conjuring trick. Using drugs to heighten the illusion, to induce visions! Is that what you and your father did to us at the mill, in Imber? I'm willing to bet so. That's why we all felt so drowsy. What did you use, eh?' He tightened his grip around Albert's throat, sniffing the air. 'Nitric acid mixed with sulphuric acid for the smoke, and what else? Something intense and short-lived, I suppose. Something to create altered perceptions of the self. What was it, mescaline?'

Albert struggled some more, straining.

'Tell me!'

Albert's eyes moved quickly from side to side. 'Devil's Snare,' he admitted finally.

Price's eyes widened. '*Datura stramonium?*'

'Harry, will it harm us?' I asked, glancing at Pierre. The boy looked like I felt: distraught and afraid and dazed.

'Nasty side effects,' said Price, moving his full attention back to Albert. 'Anxiety, racing heart, dizziness, headache. Feel any of that, Sarah?'

I nodded.

'You'll feel disorientated for a time, with blurred vision and a dry mouth,' Price replied. 'The plant will be behind the lantern. Lots of it, I should think. Sarah, go and get it.'

Without waiting to ask why, I did as he instructed, filling my pockets with the small paper packets that Albert had stored back there, and then returned, groggily, to the chamber.

He didn't tell me so at the time, but when I later looked up *datura stramonium* I discovered that inhaling it in high doses could prove fatal.

'An extremely potent hallucinogenic,' he added. 'Even smelling the flowers of *datura stramonium* can induce the richest visual hallucinations. Commonly found in Britain in cultivated ground – roadsides, fields, forest edges . . .'

A memory caught: tall plants with pale yellow-green stems and white, trumpet-shaped flowers with flashes of purple within. I had seen them outside the Imber mill. So close to where the séances were conducted. Where I had felt disorientated, overcome with harrowing visions. I told Price immediately and saw his interest heighten.

'I see. Is that why you chose Imber's mill for the séances?' he asked Albert, who, still struggling against the wall, muttered something unintelligible. 'Sorry, what's that? Speak up!'

Albert looked at Price directly, his face contorted with inner torment. 'The drug allows me to channel the dead.'

'Of course it does, silly me. You're the "ghost maker"!' Price shook his head. 'We've met your father, Albert. We know all about your experiments, how you lost control.'

'No, no. The lantern slides, the lantern itself – they enable me to converse with old souls. That's what my father could never understand. The drugs enhance my –'

'No, they do NOT!' Price bellowed, spittle flying from his lips. 'Your drugs induce aural and visual hallucinations. Violent ones. Whatever your father has told you, you're not capable of raising ghosts. No matter how eerily convincing they are, séance tricks and light projections do not bestow upon you nec-romantic abilities. Just as egg white and cheese cloth does not pass for ectoplasm under the eye of a powerful microscope!' Price glanced at me. 'Now, I don't yet know why, but you have colluded with your father to manufacture deceptions that have driven innocent men – including yourself, it seems – to madness. And now you must answer for your crimes.'

His patience extinguished, Price threw Albert forcefully to the floor, where he landed in a heap.

'Question time! Why go to all this trouble for us? All this smoke and mirrors?'

Albert struggled to speak, his voice still dazed from the drugs. 'I'm – I'm protecting myself.'

'From what?' Price's voice echoed around the chamber.

There followed a long pause, Pierre's frightened sobbing the only sound. Then Albert turned his head, cutting me a disconcerting glare.

'Her.'

What the hell have I done? Why does he need to protect himself from me?

As if hearing the question, Albert began shaking his head fearfully, never taking his eyes off me. 'You. Always you,' he said, fitfully. 'Down here with *me*.'

'But I've never been down here before.'

'Liar!' His ragged voice bounced around the chamber.

Beside me, Pierre coughed pitifully. 'Don't you worry, little man,' I whispered to him. 'Everything's going to be – '

'I saw this moment, you know. I made drawings of you! Detailed drawings.'

I looked at the projectionist, divided between confusion and anger. I had no idea what he was talking about. What's more, Price's face showed a small hint of understanding, which baffled me further. As Price looked towards me, we heard an unexpected sound.

The click of a safety catch.

I froze.

Price swivelled around to find himself confronted by the barrel of a service revolver. With a speed and agility I had not expected, Albert had leapt to his feet and pulled the revolver from his inner jacket pocket. He brandished it towards Price, a crazed look in his one functional eye.

'Stand over there!'

Price's feet crunched over shattered glass as he took his place next to me, close to the ladder and the cowering child. Probably, he was wishing he had searched Albert.

I got shakily to my feet, stepping in front of Pierre to shield him from the madman. Shoulder to shoulder with Price.

Albert's demented focus turned on me. 'You remember the night we met, miss?'

With a chill, I tried to ignore his gun, his trembling hand, his twitching finger. I concentrated instead on his dented face. I nodded.

'I told you about the ghostly female figure beneath the stage.'

There was a moment of crackling communication between us.

'It was *you*. Always you. In these cellars. For months and months, the magic lantern presented you to me, in the smoke. A projection of this very moment. You understand? I had a premonition of you. An old soul.'

I stared at him, speechless.

'You are an old soul,' he repeated, 'and we are connected by our time in the village, Miss Grey. That's why you found me. You were drawn here, to me.'

'Nonsense,' I insisted, though my voice trembled.

With his free hand, the projectionist produced from his pocket a wooden and glass lantern slide very like the one I had found upstairs. 'They are like windows for me. They enable me to see the past and the future. They allow me to speak with old s—'

'Rubbish,' Price said abruptly. 'Time doesn't flow backwards. We can't peer into the future like we dip into our memories of the past. Your illusions in the smoke are projections. Nothing more. Fantasies!'

'NO!' Albert yelled, the revolver shaking madly in his hand. 'They are forces independent of the mind. The past, present and future, we can glimpse them all. They are entwined.'

I felt sure he was insane, driven mad by his own illusions and drugs. But those words he had used to describe me . . .

Old soul.

Albert took a step towards me. I felt as though he was looking right through my eye sockets and into my brain, flicking through my memories as though he were turning the pages of a book. 'I see what was,' he said, 'and what is still to come.'

His hand tightened on the gun, keeping me in his sights. 'The visions in the smoke – *you* know what I'm talking about, Miss Grey.'

I do know, I thought. *You're talking about the warm place. Where everything is still and hazy and quiet; where the mill wheel passes the slow turns of the day.*

'You don't believe I foresaw this moment?' he asked with a loaded tone. 'Haven't you wondered how the two of you crossed paths, the same night, in this picture house? Didn't that strike you as peculiar?'

I didn't like where this was going. Not one bit.

'Didn't you think it just a little coincidental?' His voice became condescending, quietly menacing. 'It was me, the ghost maker. I brought you together.'

I expected an instant cry of disbelief from Price, some rebuking dismissal, but for once he was silent, and I felt an immediate, paralysing betrayal. Albert picked up on it instantly. A bemused smile played on his lips as he said, 'He hasn't told you, has he?'

'Harry?'

Albert released an intolerable laugh. A brutal laugh.

'Your friend hasn't been straight with you, miss. Not one bit. I drew a picture of what I saw in the smoke. I drew *your* face, Miss Grey. So, I contacted someone I thought might help me understand.' He looked knowingly at Price. Resentfully. 'Someone I hoped would be willing to listen. His reputation is the talk of the town. I wrote to him, more than once. I sent him letters. I sent my drawings, detailed descriptions, of you, Miss Grey. Because I knew you would be here. I foresaw it.'

A thudding realisation; Price's explanation for that night coming back to me:

I received a letter. Typed. Anonymous. Telling me where I could find you, and when. Clearly, whoever wrote that letter wanted us to meet again.

Price's face was paling, his eyes avoiding mine.

'Harry? You never mentioned any drawings!'

'He didn't?' The projectionist took a step nearer. 'What a shame, that the great Harry Price can't recognise the truth when it's presented to him. Well, I can. When I saw your face in the smoke down here, Miss Grey, do you know what I thought? I believed you were dead, a vision from beyond, warning us to stop our interventions in Imber. I see now that I was wrong, that God was sending you to help, to put an end to this awful thing we have done. Do you understand?'

'No,' I replied quickly.

'I had a vision of this meeting, this moment. I knew you would come. I *made* it happen.'

'For what purpose?' I asked. 'Albert, what do you *want*?'

His answer left me in no doubt that our biggest struggle was yet to come.

'I want help.'

30

THE GHOST MAKER

The domed brick chamber glowed under the flickering rays of the single oil lamp at our feet.

I stood between Pierre and Albert, my body rigid, unwilling to trust Sidewinder's son, no matter how much sincerity was in his voice.

'If you needed our help, why wait, hidden away down here with the boy? Why not just come to us? Why bother with the elaborate light show just now?'

'I wanted you to understand, to see. The Devil's Snare induces physic experiences, letting the rest of the world fade out, opening your mind to realities beyond the reach of normal senses.'

'Albert – '

'Let me speak!' Albert silenced Price, his eyes bulging with a zealot's fanaticism. 'You will hear me. And you, Miss Grey, are going to believe me, even if the great Harry Price does not.'

Price shifted awkwardly. Albert's hand with the gun was

shaking again. I was terrified that if it shook much more, one of us was going to get hurt. Badly.

Trying to put some empathy in my voice, I said, 'I know how lonely you must feel, and I'm willing to listen. I want to believe you. But Albert, why not let Pierre go? He looks like he needs fresh air, doesn't he?' That was an understatement. The cowering child looked deathly pale. Half dead. 'How long has he been down here with you, Albert?'

'Years.'

'Why? Why have you kept him imprisoned in this godforsaken place?'

'My father,' he gulped, his voice straining. 'My father made me. You see? I answer to him.'

'Just let Pierre go,' I said, 'and we'll talk. No one needs to be harmed.'

A moment of indecision flashed across Albert's face, broken by a quick nod.

Price gave Albert a look of harsh contempt, and then stooped and began working to loosen the knot around Pierre's ankle. 'Is it true?' he asked. 'You and Warden Sidewinder – your father – kidnapped this boy, faked his death and faked the hauntings?'

Still training the gun on us, Albert gave Pierre a guilt-filled glance, and nodded. 'Some of them were real . . .'

'Really? Well, what about the ones you *did* fake?'

'It is not my guilt alone. I . . . contributed.'

'By helping your father to orchestrate séances like the wretched one we attended?' said Price. 'Séances intended to drive the soldiers out of Imber?'

Was that the only motive? It sounded grossly simplistic to me. And risky.

'I have made a mistake,' he said, his voice cracking.

'A mistake? You melted a young man's face,' Price hissed. 'Sergeant Edwards spends every day in agony because of what you did. You and your father ripped apart an innocent family.' He gestured to the trembling Pierre, whose ankle he had almost worked loose from the knot. 'At the Imber mill you used drugs to convince me this poor child was a spirit. You even convinced his own mother and father! How? Why?' Albert let out a wretched sob.

'Answer me!' cried Price.

'I'm the one giving orders,' gasped Albert, the gun shaking ever more wildly in his hands.

My breath caught. He was unravelling – and quickly. We needed to get Pierre to safety.

'Albert? I interrupted. 'Let's take this one step at a time. Pierre can climb up and wait in the upper chamber, all right?'

He nodded, and Price and I immediately directed the boy towards the ladder. Pierre looked uncertainly back at us.

'Go on.' I nudged him gently. 'You wait up there for us. Everything will be fine. I promise.'

My heart was in my mouth as Pierre climbed the ladder, Price standing beneath it to catch him in case he should fall.

'Well done,' I said to Albert, swallowing with relief. 'You did the right thing.'

Albert glared at me. He still had the service revolver on us but now his eyes were brimming with tears. 'After the war,' he said, 'I needed to see my friends who were gunned down. Imber was a small village, and we had been a strong team. I missed them so. When my father saw my artistry, the wonders I could create with my projections, a plan was devised. To fake the boy's death. To use him to help get the soldiers out.'

'You provided the way,' I said, 'and your father, Sidewinder, provided the means.'

Standing in the centre of the chamber, Albert nodded again, but now his face was souring as he looked across at the filthy mattress. 'He forced me to keep the boy down here.'

Barely able to control my anger, I took a step towards him, trying to pretend the gun was no longer in his hand. 'Don't you understand the enormity of what you've done? A faked death. A kidnapping. The abject maltreatment of this child! Why would you participate in something so obscene?'

There was a long silence. 'I told you before, I had to work alone in the dark.'

'I don't see what that has to do with –'

'I helped my father for the same reason I hide down here, away from the world.' He raised his free hand to his strangely dented face. For a moment, his hand hovered very close to his left ear. And then the impossible happened.

The left side of his face came away in his hooked fingers.

Cheekbone, jawbone, half of his nose – all were removed to reveal a deep black cavity.

'Oh, good lord . . .'

I heard Price draw a shocked breath.

'Do you have any idea what it's like to go through life disfigured like this – a horror to others, and to yourself?' Albert asked bitterly. The service revolver was shaking again.

That face, I'll never forget it. Blown out of his head. Ruined. Grotesque.

A war injury, I thought. *His father told us so.*

That sort of injury condemned a man to isolation, unless it could be treated, or covered up with a mask. That was what he was holding now in his shuddering hand – most likely a copper prosthetic.

I had read about the treatment in the newspapers. After the Great War, after the horrific injuries suffered by soldiers on the battlefields, talented sculptors would take plaster casts of the intact areas of a maimed veteran's face, then craft a partial mask, which was painted to match the skin and tied to the head with string. Crude by today's standards, but the idea was to help people like Albert fit in. Those who didn't feel able to do that sometimes took jobs out of the public eye, often working in the dark.

I wondered how many other men like Albert were out there, men with severe facial disfigurements, cowering with shame in hot, cramped projection booths?

I dared again to glance at his face, his true face, if that was even the word. It was impossible not to feel some pity. And now another piece of the jigsaw fell into place.

'Your father paid for your prosthetics in return for your help, didn't he? That's how he persuaded you to keep the boy here, embroiled you in his deceptions.'

It was the truth, I could see it in his face.

'What I don't understand is why your father, a man serving in the army himself, would want the army out of Imber?' I asked. It made no sense to me. Unless . . .

'Someone else is involved,' he said heavily. 'We are both being blackmailed.'

'By whom?'

Albert turned to Price. 'Come on, Harry Price. Earn your stripes. You were present at the mill séance. How did we get the boy into the mill without you seeing?'

Lost for an answer, Price shook his head, his face blank.

'We made certain every entranceway was sealed tight,' I said.

'You didn't notice the discoloured bricks in the back wall?' Albert asked.

'A concealed entranceway?' I asked.

Albert nodded.

Price's eyes were full of doubt.

'Oh, Mr Price,' Albert said, with a trace of contempt. 'You didn't notice the lower portion of the back wall was partially constructed from *false* bricks?'

'What?'

A flash of memory:

'*The bricks here look uneven, don't you think, Harry? Discoloured?*'

'False bricks made from foam. Those bricks concealed a gap in the wall just large enough for the boy to crawl through. Just small enough not to be too conspicuous. Painted foam bricks, which were quietly removed during the séance. The magic lantern was positioned at that exact opening.'

'Even if that were true,' said Price, 'how would you get him out again so quickly?'

'The candles were extinguished,' I said, remembering how we were plunged into darkness. 'When Vernon's camera went off, there was a struggle.'

Albert was still nodding. 'In your struggle, there was time for the boy to slip out. Time for me to put the bricks, light as they are, back into place. The opening was only small. Of course, the poor light helped.'

'Tell us now,' I said, 'who else is involved? Who's the accomplice?'

'The same monster who is blackmailing my father.'

He uttered a name, and left me dumbstruck.

31

IMBER WILL LIVE

'Oscar Hartwell? You're saying the boy's *father* is behind this?'

My voice echoed off the damp cellar walls as I took a sidelong glance at Price and saw that he too was stunned. Pierre's father?

Impossible! I remembered Hartwell's display of grief during the séance, his absolute bewilderment when the boy had vanished. I hadn't doubted the man's sincerity then, not even for a moment.

But now I remembered something else: my arrival in Imber and Pierre's ghostly appearance at the roadside. Wasn't it Hartwell who had appeared, just seconds later, almost running me down?

Oh God, how could I have missed it?

What other clues had I missed? They came to me now, flooding my mind: the villagers who had regarded Hartwell with trepidation at his child's funeral, and later, at the church service. Hartwell had attributed all of that to his son's disease, but now another memory made me see this in a different light; when Price and I had arrived at the mill, the warden was already there, alone, with Hartwell. Certainly, we had thought it odd – Price had been the first to demand the two men explain themselves. But never had the possibility entered our minds that the father himself was behind the trickery. To force his son to endure such misery, to imprison him in a London cellar, suggested there was much at stake for him in the orchestration of this devilish deception. He had either much to gain or an unfathomable amount to lose. With the looming public rally in Imber, both possibilities were equally worrying.

'Why would Hartwell do that to Pierre?' I said, looking up at the hatch through which Pierre had escaped. He must have heard me, for just then his little face peeped down at mine. I wanted to hug the wretched child. I smiled reassuringly at him and then turned back to Albert and Price. 'Why would Hartwell do such an abysmal thing to his own *son*?'

Doubt flashed across Albert's ruined face.

'Did Marie know?' I asked.

'I don't know. I don't think so. Hartwell told her Pierre was dead, practically pushed her into madness.'

The idea sickened me. 'Why would Hartwell do something so cruel, so risky, so absurd?' I shook my head.

'Why else? To reclaim his cherished Imber Court. He wanted the soldiers gone.'

I struggled to think, my head still groggy. 'But having a son meant everything to Oscar, and to the Hartwell family. Would he really go to such extreme measures – falsifying his son's death, deceiving his wife?'

I could see Albert struggling, still training the gun on us.

'Please, that's enough, Albert,' said Price.

He glanced down at the gun, looked up at us, and took a step nearer – aiming at Price. 'You have to listen, before it's too late. Hartwell and my father are planning something atrocious for Imber. A reckoning.'

Price's gaze wavered between Albert and me. 'What reckoning?'

'The public rally,' Albert replied. 'Imber Will Live.'

'Tomorrow?' I asked. 'Commander Williams has already taken steps to ensure the paths are made safe . . .'

I trailed off, realising that task – that vital task – had been entrusted to Warden Sidewinder. A sense of dreadful foreboding came upon me as I pictured the hordes of innocent civilians marching onto land that hadn't been secured.

'What exactly are the protestors planning?' I asked Albert.

'They want to make the War Office a laughing stock and reclaim their heritage.'

'By occupying the buildings? The church?'

He nodded. 'And the cottages, Brown's Farm, the Bell Inn, even Imber Court. That's where Hartwell will head, is my bet – his old home. And there'll be too many people for the army to stop it.'

'How many people?'

He shrugged. 'Two thousand, perhaps. Maybe more.'

This is bigger than the commander thinks. They're completely unprepared.

Trying not to sound panicked, I told Price how the commander was planning to placate the protestors by allowing them to use the road into the village, and how Warden Sidewinder was assisting him with that mission. That, despite my warnings,

I suspected the commander still trusted Sidewinder, or was at least protecting him. Why? I had no idea.

When I had finished explaining, Price looked gravely concerned. I was willing to bet that, like me, he was imagining the nightmare scenario: women and children, entire families, trampling over that shell-torn range, exploring decrepit buildings that weren't remotely safe.

'The unexploded debris,' he murmured. 'Would they be so reckless?'

'They would if my father assured them it was safe,' said Albert. 'He is the warden.'

'But the casualties could be unimaginable ...'

'Which is exactly what Hartwell wants.'

'Is he totally insane?' Price exclaimed, overcome with alarm and, I thought, remorse. I couldn't be sure, but I wondered if he now bitterly regretted abandoning the investigation – abandoning me – when he had.

'A public tragedy,' said Albert quietly. 'It would seal the army's fate and guarantee a public inquiry, which would probably lead to the eviction of soldiers from Imber. Forever.'

'If you knew this, if it concerned you so, why didn't you report it someone?'

'Who? The range warden? The commander? Who would listen to the frenzied, preposterous claims of the ghost maker?'

There was only one answer to that.

'Harry!' I grabbed his arm. 'We have to get back down there, warn the army. Make Hartwell and Sidewinder confess.'

'We'll have to prove it first.' Price glared at Albert. 'There's one thing I don't understand. How does Hartwell wield so much power over your father? You mentioned blackmail. Is it money? Or does Sidewinder have a secret he'll do anything to protect – a secret Hartwell knows about? Whatever it is, it must be formidable. Otherwise why would your father – a serving member of the army – agree to help Hartwell in the first place? It can't just be to pay for your prosthetics. There's more to this tangled alliance, isn't there?'

A silence. I shivered. I was desperate to get out of the cellar, to get Pierre up to the fresh air too, but there was no way we could leave now.

'Albert?' urged Price.

Of course, I know now that Price was correct: there was more. Much more. Another secret, the worst secret of all, about Imber and its evacuation. About what the military did, the action they sanctioned. But it wasn't for our ears, not at that moment.

'This is your fault,' Price said threateningly, forgetting the gun trained on him. 'The lives of innocent men and women and children could be at stake. Tell us what we need to know!'

'If there is a secret,' Albert shouted, 'I don't know what it is! Why do you think I brought both of you together? To investigate!'

Price stepped away, his fists clenched in anger and frustration. 'Come, Sarah,' he said, motioning towards the ladder. 'We must go.'

The look on Price's face at that moment, I have never forgotten. His eyes were brimming with sincerity and sorrow and a little shame, and I felt my heart ache for him a little, despite his neglectful and selfish behaviour. Would I have felt that way if I'd known what Price was still hiding from me? I doubt it.

'Go,' Albert said, gesturing to the ladder with his gun. 'Leave me.'

He had a peculiar melancholy air about him.

'Sarah.'

'Just a moment, Harry.'

I went to Albert's side, deeming it unsafe to leave him alone with his service revolver.

'Let me have the gun, Albert.'

He flinched away from me.

'I kept my side of the bargain – I listened to you. Now, please, give me the gun.'

Gently, he passed me the service revolver, and at the touch of the heavy, cold metal, I realised I had never held one before. I had never wanted to either.

Slowly, like a rite of faith, I knelt and placed the weapon gently on the ground behind me. Price wasted no time in snatching it up and slipping it into his pocket.

'Now, let's go,' he said.

No time to lose!

Glass crunched under my feet as I made my way to the ladder. Then a second thought made me pause.

I turned to look back at the man who had created such chaos. An accessory to evil. With his head lowered, perhaps in shame, perhaps remorse, he was standing next to the magic lantern projector, gazing at its intricately carved winged skull.

'I want it,' I said. 'The magic lantern.'

Albert's hands curled at his sides, his mouth fell slightly open.

'It's evidence,' I said in a firmer voice. 'Give me the projector. The slides as well.'

Suddenly, all my fury at the cruelty and ill-treatment suffered by Pierre Hartwell surged up in me, obliterating any fear of the man who had done this. You might think that was brave of me, or even foolish, but honestly? It was easier to show that anger, now, knowing he wasn't armed.

'GIVE IT TO ME!'

Albert raised his gruesome face to me with slow purpose, but I didn't see the acquiescence I'd hoped for. He looked desperate. And if we had learned anything back then from the Wall Street Crash of 1929, it was that desperation could drive the sanest men to madness. If desperation could make well-adjusted city workers throw themselves from buildings and put guns in their mouths, what could it do to a man who already believed he could summon ghosts with an antique projector and see the past, present and future in its lurid light displays?

'You can't have it,' Albert said. 'The phantasmagoria is my world.'

'Your world just collided with another.' My heart was hammering in my chest but I strained to imbue my voice with firm determination. 'That magic lantern could prove useful in Imber, Albert. If you just allow me to – '

He leapt for the lantern, gripping it as if it was an object on which his life depended. *Either the drugs or the lantern shifted your perspective too,* I thought, remembering the warm place, the history of Imber in the mist. Albert was looking silently at me, as if he knew that I too had been influenced by the dark, mysterious machinations of this contraption.

'Sarah?' Price intervened from the bottom of the ladder. I saw from the resolve on his face that he had no intention of leaving me alone again. And I saw something else, and it worried me. His hand was in the pocket in which he had placed the gun.

'Let me handle this,' I said firmly, then turned to the projectionist. I remembered what he had told us about his strange drawings and took a breath. 'Albert, if there's something you know, something connecting me with that village, then you have to tell me what it is.'

A long pause.

'Be very careful,' he said finally. 'There are secrets in Imber that must be told. And very soon, you're going to find out what they are.'

He glanced over my shoulder and I followed his gaze to the hammer with which Price had shattered the mirror. It lay discarded on the ground.

He's going to pick it up, strike me with it.

I took a cautious step back, my hands curled into fists.

From behind me, Price called, 'Sarah, hurry!'

And Albert spoke. 'Why do you fear the village?'

The message accusing my father of murder came back to me . . . But that had been a hoax. I knew that. Yet in my mind's eye, I saw Silas, the Imber blacksmith, chaining himself to the railings outside St Giles' Church, saw him shrinking back, struggling, as rough hands forced him to the ground. Had that man been murdered by my father? How much did Albert know? He said he had experienced a premonition of this night, our confrontation in this cellar. Did that mean he also knew how it would end?

I heard myself saying, 'I fear the village because of what my father may have done there.'

'That's not your fault,' he said, nodding as if he understood the sentiment only too well. Then he looked at the hammer again.

I held my breath.

'Sarah?' Price was at my side.

I let out a long breath as Albert gently, reverently, nodded to the projector and told Price to take it. 'There are secrets worse than any living horror in Imber. Find out what they are, Miss Grey.' He bent, picked up the hammer and handed it to me. 'Bring Hartwell and my father to justice.'

I took a final glance at the projectionist's ruined face.

'How did the planchette move during the séance? How did it spell out those messages? That name.'

He cocked his head in a way that suggested he didn't understand.

'At the mill,' I clarified. 'The spirit messages we received from the blacksmith. That was you, wasn't it?'

No reply.

'It had to be you. Somehow.'

Albert's head remained cocked.

'For God's sake, Sarah,' said Price, his hand now on my arm. 'Hurry!'

I moved towards him, carrying the heavy hammer, then turned and locked eyes with Albert one final time.

Once I had started climbing the ladder, I didn't dare look back.

– 32 –

MESSENGERS OF DECEPTION

With a rumble of the engine we were off, speeding through South London. Part of me wished I was driving; Price was one of those men who was born to be driven, which I suppose is a nice way of saying he should never have learned.

'Harry, can you please slow down?'

'How are you feeling?'

'Hazy,' I replied, as he swerved round a corner. But that was an understatement – my head was pounding. The Devil's Snare was still playing havoc with me: one moment, I could vividly see the passing townhouses and parked cars, then their outlines would smudge and they would lose their colour. 'Pierre?' I turned round. 'How are you feel –'

The boy was sleeping. Apparently peacefully, thank God. But his face was grey, he was shockingly thin, and the clusters of bruises on his arms were all too clear. 'Should we take him to the hospital?'

Price kept his eyes on the road. 'We have to get to Wiltshire, end this madness. We'll stop on the way, get the boy something to eat.' He gave me a sideways glance, curious. 'You saw something down there, didn't you? Something in the smoke?'

I considered telling Price about the peculiar visions: waiting in the sun beside the ancient Imber mill. Hallucinations, or something else? Perhaps it was a psychic emanation made possible by the Devil's Snare. Or a hollow coincidence. But somehow I didn't think so. These experiences felt like marvellous, *meaningful* coincidences. Price had a term for that sort of phenomenon, didn't he? *Synchronicity*. I felt as though fate was poking me in the back, like everything was pointing to a deeper, more profound truth that I might uncover in Imber.

'I did see something,' I admitted. 'And you don't look surprised, Harry.'

'Why should I be surprised when so much of this has happened before?'

'What do you mean?'

He saw my alarmed face and rushed to explain. 'Albert Sidewinder isn't the first person to have pulled a stunt like that. In Revolutionary France, people were packing themselves into crypts to get the living daylights scared out of them by illusionists claiming to raise the dead. As for the phantasmagoria, you both got off lightly, I'd say.'

'Oh?'

'Well . . .' He squinted at me, reconsidering. 'Perhaps that's a tad disingenuous of me, but two centuries ago, the phantasmagoria light shows in Germany were intense enough to drive their creator to a tragic end.'

That sounded melodramatic and implausible, and there was a time when I would have been cynical. I wasn't now.

Not when I remembered Albert below ground, clasping his service revolver with that dangerous, half-crazed expression. Thinking of the gruesome projector with its skull carving on the seat behind me, I asked Price more about this historical necromancer. 'What did he do? What was his name?'

'Johann Georg Schröpfer. Owned a coffee shop in Leipzig. Hosted séances, which he enhanced by using a magic lantern. Painted the ghastliest images – ghosts, corpses, demons – onto glass slides and projected them onto smoke.'

'It sounds so crude.'

'Well, it was. The technology was nothing compared to today's. But Schröpfer accomplished all of this while practising and teaching witchcraft. I know it sounds absurd, but hats off to him – somehow he convinced his customers he really could converse with the dead.'

'A bit like Sidewinder and Hartwell did with us, in Imber.'

Price nodded quickly, the strength in his features crumbling just for a moment.

'People must have realised the images weren't real,' I said.

'Sometimes.' He looked at me briefly. 'Mostly, the drugs threw their senses awry.'

The drugs. I exhaled heavily, remembering the grey smoke slipping into the dank chamber beneath the stage, remembering my visions of gruesome spectres, their movement and colour. Their sheer striking lucidity.

Having met many self-proclaimed psychics, I knew what they would say about my experience and the abject terror it had awakened within me. They would say I had glimpsed something of the clairvoyant's world. But I did not want to consider that possibility, not even for a second.

I was committed now to knowing the truth. As if sensing

my curiosity, Price rather suddenly said, 'You know, Sarah, in ancient times, Native Americans would ingest Devil's Snare to commune with deities through visions, to communicate via means of telepathy.'

'Is that so?'

With a pang of nervousness, I swallowed hard. What if the Devil's Snare *had* awakened some latent psychic ability, allowed my subconscious mind to reach back into the past? To connect with the physical surroundings of Imber.

Past, present and future.

If that was true, had the Devil's Snare truly enabled Albert to see what was going to happen beneath the Brixton Picture House, to predict my involvement?

What if the drug had allowed my subconscious mind to access other possible realms of understanding? I checked that the plant extracts I had taken from the chamber were still safely sealed in the small paper bags in my coat pocket. They were.

'Harry, I know you try to be as scientific as you can, but is there the slightest possibility Schröpfer *was* communing with the dead? Any possibility that the drugs *did* awaken in him some sort of extra-sensory perception?'

Price's expression said it all: cold, hard cynicism.

'And what sort of tragedy befell Schröpfer?'

'What do you think?'

'He became undone?'

Price nodded, turning our car onto Kennington Road. 'All those nights of trying to wake the dead, smoky ghosts floating about the room, inhaling drugs like Devil's Snare – eventually it drove him to suicide.'

'How did he . . .'

'Torched himself. Set himself ablaze, before a live audience.'

'Like Sergeant Edwards!' I said, aghast. 'He was at the mill; he was exposed to the drugs. Do you think it worked a similar effect on him?'

Price nodded, but I sensed he had left something vital unsaid, and I wondered if it was something about Schröpfer. It was, although I wouldn't discover exactly what for many decades, certainly not until after Price was dead, and by then it would all be said and done.

'Don't agonise, Sarah. Your exposure to the Devil's Snare explains your disorientation.'

Perhaps that was right. Did it also account for the paranoia holding me in its grip? As we drove through London on that late evening, the city felt both unfamiliar and threatening, a city of hidden squares and mysterious arches; a city whose gated gardens and ancient cemeteries were never to be entered alone. A city of secrets.

'Harry, why didn't you tell me the projectionist brought us together?'

'Well . . . I couldn't be sure.'

There was that evasive tone again. I noticed that the expression in his eyes had hardened.

'You've had a long, quiet interest in Imber, haven't you?'

He didn't deny it, which worried me.

'Why?'

After a long pause he said, 'I'm afraid, very afraid. I'm afraid something wicked occurred in that village, Sarah. Something tragic. In time, I feel sure the answers will surface, but for now, my instinct says the less you know, the better.'

'You're playing with me.'

'I'm protecting you.'

'Controlling me.' A pause. 'Albert sent you a letter explaining where to find me. Sent you drawings – of me. Didn't you think I'd want to know?'

He sighed deeply. 'I'm not the only one who has been less than honest, am I, Sarah?'

That made me think of our child, of whom I hoped he still knew nothing. And suddenly I felt the cold grasp of fear. I decided not to ask any more questions about what he did or didn't know about this investigation. After all, I knew my own secret wouldn't just break his marriage. Very likely it would break his heart.

As we sped over Vauxhall Bridge I told Price of the developments that had unfurled in Imber after he left. I made sure to mention the disturbed graves we had found at the churchyard – graves of the Hartwell family.

'Do you think the disturbed graves are connected to the Imber hauntings?' I asked. 'It's not clear to me why they should be, or how, but I thought I heard unusual sounds in that churchyard. Footsteps. Someone crying. And remember, according to Commander Williams some of his men thought they saw women there, tending graves.'

'It's certainly possible,' Price said. 'But for now, we must do all we can to help the boy.' He peered into the rear-view mirror at Pierre, huddled up in the back seat.

I felt a sudden urge to hug that child close to me. 'Poor soul. His father wants Imber Court returned to him very badly. It was his home . . .'

'Yes, but I think this goes deeper.'

'You think Hartwell is hiding something at Imber Court?'

'Very possibly. We will search the place from top to bottom.'

Price's face tightened. 'But there's somewhere we must go first.'

Instead of driving us out of London, towards Imber, Price swerved the saloon onto Millbank and began accelerating towards the city. Towards Fleet Street.

'Sir, are you expected? Excuse me, sir, you can't go in there!'

'This is a pressing matter and it will not wait!' Price gave the prim secretary a scathing look as he stormed past her desk and flung open the door to the newsroom.

She leapt up in protest, and I held back, Pierre at my side. I was torn; Price needed me in there, but there was no way I would have left the child in the car alone, and it didn't seem appropriate to march him into an office full of strangers. 'I am so terribly sorry about my friend,' I explained. 'But it is rather urgent, I'm afraid.'

Perhaps sensing my dilemma, my desperation, the prim secretary's attitude softened. She was about my age, perhaps nurturing hopes of becoming a mother herself. The tender smile she was giving Pierre certainly suggested so. It also suggested she had changed her mind about allowing us inside.

'All right. Would you like me to watch him for you for a moment?' Her eyes were wide and sincere. Caring.

'Thank you. I'll be very quick.'

And I was. The clacking of manual typewriters surrounded me as I followed Price into the newsroom. The hour had passed ten o'clock, but there were enough assiduous reporters in here for me to feel self-conscious. Stressed, tense-looking young men hunched over their desks, bashing out stories. Price was scanning the smoky room. His gaze located the man determined to betray him.

'Scoundrel!' he shouted.

With a jolt, Vernon looked up from his typewriter. He noticed me before he saw Price marching up to him, and his eyes almost bulged out of his skull.

'Vernon, I want the photograph you snapped. And the negative!'

'Too late,' Vernon said, rising from his chair. 'The printing presses won't wait, Harry. You're finished.'

Price saw the sheet of paper in the typewriter and rolled it out. For a few seconds, I watched his mouth form silent words as he read the report, then saw beads of glistening sweat break on his brow.

'Let me see,' I said, angling over his shoulder so that I could read the article.

A psychic investigator, notorious for exposing fraudulent mediums who make a living from deceiving the bereaved, has been implicated in an indecent hoax involving an innocent child.

This reporter is aware that Mr Harry Price, who is the honorary chairman of the National Laboratory for Psychical Research and prides himself on his high moral probity, attended a séance in the company of members of the army at a secret location on Salisbury Plain earlier this week.

During the séance, the malnourished figure of a boy who was thought dead 'materialised' in clear view of everyone present, including this reporter.

Mr Price, who reached out and grabbed the boy, who was naked from the waist up, declared himself astonished at the so-called materialisation. But, aside from the deeply worrying physical conditions I have described, there was nothing extraordinary about the figure I witnessed. It was that of a normal child, who arrived in a terrible state, frail, severely underweight and dishevelled.

One would think that a man purportedly as critical and exacting and inventive as Mr Price would recognise a real human boy when he saw one. Apparently not. Unless, of course, he had a vested interest in claiming otherwise.

The child in the photograph has not yet been identified but sources close to our correspondent have suggested that Mr Price was complicit in an exploitative and irresponsible hoax.

Supporters of Mr Price must now ask themselves if he really is the expert he claims to be, or if he is, indeed, a flagrant fraud.

I turned sick at heart. How could Vernon have done such a thing? Price's face was knotted with rage, his hand trembling. There was an anxious moment when I feared he was about to throw a punch at Vernon. Instead, he snarled at the journalist. 'This is worthless, even for you! Does your vindictiveness know no limits? You can't print these despicable insinuations! I'll be ruined!'

But Vernon said nothing to the man he was determined to wrong; he only stared at his white face, triumphant.

'Vernon, I'm not sure this is the right approach,' I said.

For a moment, Vernon looked small and tired and bitter. It broke my heart a little to see him that way. Then, abruptly, his look of vengeful determination returned and he plucked up from his desk what looked to me like a freshly developed black and white photograph.

'You'd ruin a man to further your career?' Price demanded.

'Isn't that what you've been doing your whole life? Deriding spiritualists as the laughing stock of the thinking man.'

'My intentions have only ever been on the side of truth, yet here you are presenting me to the world as –'

'The self-aggrandizing, irresponsible sensationalist we know you are.'

He handed Price the photograph. 'That's a copy. The negative stays with me.'

Price looked down at the image and his lips began to tremble. 'This is an outrage!' he shouted.

Every typewriter in the room fell silent. I glanced out over the rows of desks and saw many curious faces angled our way.

Feeling most uncomfortable, I studied the photograph. It made extremely disturbing viewing. There was the half-naked Pierre, standing at the side of the battered table. There were the rest of us, our eyes like silver discs. And there, with his hand resting on the boy's skeletal shoulder, was Harry Price. 'We thought it was a spirit!'

'Not *we*,' Vernon said quickly. '*You*. Now the world can know the truth.'

These words came out sounding sweetly sour.

'I can see now why they call this the street of shame,' Price said, throwing his glance around the room in disgust, before fixing his eyes on Vernon and hissing, 'Have you bothered to consider how this story will reflect on Sarah?'

'The story doesn't mention Miss Grey.' Vernon looked at me a little doubtfully, struggling to keep the conviction in his voice. 'I wasn't planning to use the part of the picture that shows her, either. And if anyone should ask, the truth is that

Sarah stopped working for you a long time ago, disillusioned by your methods. You've kept so much from her, Harry – which is grossly unfair, you must see, when she is so open with you.'

Guilt stabbed me. I couldn't bring myself to go along with Vernon's plan, and I felt betrayed that he had used me to get the upper hand over Price, but this was not the time to dwell on such grievances.

'Your story is inaccurate,' I told Vernon.

'In what sense?'

'We do know the identity of the boy from the séance.'

Vernon looked at me gravely, his jaw working as if he were struggling with something. Evidently, he still believed the false premise – that Pierre had died two years previously. It fell to me, therefore, to show him the truth.

'Come with me to the outer office. And then outside.'

Price snapped his head towards me and I held up a finger as a gesture for him not to intervene. Perhaps it was the realisation that he was in over his head that prompted him to let me try and defuse the situation.

Reluctantly, Vernon took up his coat and scarf and came with us to the outer office. When he saw Pierre, bone thin, sitting drowsily on a stool next to his secretary's desk, he gasped. 'That's Hartwell's son?'

'Yes, we believe so.'

I smiled at the secretary and thanked her for watching Pierre. Then I lost no time in leading the journalist out into the icy evening and to the car. Price followed on with Pierre.

'Vernon, listen to me. This is vital. Harry is not the story here. He's not the enemy. You have to help us now.'

As we came to the parked black saloon, Vernon trained his gaze on me and I saw the trace of doubt in his eyes, a sign that he might, just might, be prepared to believe me. What a relief that would be.

'You actually think Hartwell faked his son's death? Seriously?'

'Yes,' said Price, joining us. 'And exploited the boy to convince the army they were being haunted by this "wandering child", an invention so perfect even the British army were taken in.'

'Even you,' Vernon added heavily.

'Even me.'

They looked at one another, defeat on both their faces. Then they looked at Pierre.

'But you're very much alive, aren't you, little man?' said Price. 'And thank God for it.'

'Sometimes, a little grounding does you good, Harry,' I said, nodding at him, then at Vernon. 'You two gentlemen have something in common.'

'What's that?' Vernon asked, with some reluctance.

'Energy and hope. Passion. Use that passion now.' I smiled down at the boy, who was clinging tightly to Price's hand. 'Use it for good, to help Pierre, to end this.'

Finally, mercifully, Vernon nodded his agreement. Searching his trouser pocket, he withdrew the negative of the damming photograph and handed it to Price. I helped Pierre into the back seat of the car and then, giddy with relief, told Vernon what we had learned.

'Unfortunately, Warden Sidewinder was a well-placed accomplice. Not only could he hide the child with his son in London, he could use his son's conjuring skills to manipulate the séances. And, crucially, he could smuggle Pierre into Imber without detection. Remember, security on the range is his to direct and control.'

'Which is why we must get down to Wiltshire immediately,' Price added. 'We have vital work to do in Imber.'

This triggered a new reaction from Vernon. There was something about his manner now, resolute and determined, that impressed me.

'I'm coming, I can help.' He peered into the back seat of the car, but not at Pierre. 'What the hell is that?'

'A magic lantern,' said Price. 'Think of it as a Victorian entertainment, the forerunner to the projectors we use today. Remember the luminous glow about Pierre during our séance?' He nodded at the lantern. 'Using this device, that's how Sidewinder worked the deception. It was hidden in the shadows. When the boy made his entry, Albert sneaked it in through the opening in the wall. Now we shall make it work for us.'

'Do you have a plan, Harry?' I asked.

He made eye contact, holding my gaze long enough to spark a little hope. 'I have a plan.'

And so we set off, on what I prayed was our last journey to the lost village.

THE LOST VILLAGE

A freezing, dense fog had descended on the mud-churned road into Imber. In the gloom, the headlights picked out a sign nailed to a dark, wintry tree:

IMBER SHALL LIVE!
KEEP OPEN THE ROADS
SAVE THE CHURCH OF ST GILES
PRESERVE OUR HERITAGE

As our car rumbled to a halt at the military checkpoint, I was alarmed to see the barrier raised. I was even more alarmed by the complete absence of military security.

Seeing my unease, Price said, 'Don't worry, it's not yet dawn.'

But it will be soon.

I was looking for any sign of the approaching protestors, and I saw it then – behind us, far off, beneath the sulphurous sky, was a glowing skein of light: a pre-dawn convoy of vehicles, headlights ablaze.

'Start the engine, Harry. Hurry, we have to find Commander Williams!'

The car jolted as he floored the accelerator and we bumped along towards the centre of the village, past the rusting military tanks discarded like corpses beside the road.

Anxiety was gnawing at me.

I looked back and saw Pierre stirring, and Vernon laying a reassuring hand on the boy's shoulder. A small part of me was insisting that we should turn back now, get away. But what strengthened my resolve to continue was the suspicion – no, the certainty – that today we would find truths in this desolate village.

And God help me, I was right.

The only clue that the Bell Inn had once been a public house was the creaking black and white sign bearing its name, which the army had allowed to remain hanging from the side of the building; that, perhaps, and its imposing size and prominent position in the centre of Imber. Otherwise, the old public house was a nondescript red-brick ruin, being slowly engulfed by shrubs and tangled ivy. Its nearest neighbour was a row of lonely, windowless cottages.

Outside the inn, Price killed the engine. I followed him out of the vehicle to confront a scattering of soldiers who were assembled in the deep blanket of fog that was rolling through the abandoned village. It was a thick fog that seemed to catch in the throat; it set my eyes watering and blurred the light from our car headlights into a sickly yellow glow.

'What's happening?' I asked one solider. 'Why is the road

open so early?' My anxiety ratcheted up a gear as he explained that the men were under strict orders to welcome the approaching rally, not to stand in their way.

'They'll be here as soon as the sun is up. Maybe sooner.'

'But what about the —'

'Relax. The main roads have been cleared of any debris, miss.'

I looked urgently at Price, then at the solider. 'What about the rest of the range?'

A new voice made me whirl round. 'Well, I'm a little surprised to see you two back in Imber so soon.'

Commander Williams' face was tense as he strode towards us. 'Mr Price, Miss Grey, we have a big morning ahead of us, and I don't appreciate —'

'You utter fool!' said Price, stepping up to the commander and pulling him aside, out of the hearing of the other soldiers. 'Close the roads, keep the people away.'

'Why?'

I pointed to the back seat of Price's Rolls-Royce, where Vernon and Pierre were watching us expectantly. It was a relief to see the boy looking so much more alert now, even if the evidence of his cruel neglect remained painfully etched across his gaunt features. 'There is much to explain, but we have been deceived, sir. Hartwell's son is alive and well.'

The commander's pupils dilated with surprise as he looked at Pierre and then at me.

'A most mysterious business,' he said gravely. 'You were quite correct to have your doubts, Miss Grey. Well, clearly we must inform Mr Hartwell at once.'

'You think he doesn't know?' snapped Price. 'Commander, you invited me here to detect trickery and I have found it.

The mill séance was a hoax. The ectoplasm I recovered and analysed was nothing more than egg white and thin strips of muslin. Hallucinatory substances and a dexterous light show completed the illusion. You wanted to know who has been menacing this village and your men, did you not? The culprit is Oscar Hartwell. He needed help, and he acquired that help in a tangled alliance with your warden and his son, Albert.'

The commander looked rather startled by these accusations.

'Sidewinder is, to my knowledge, a good man, Mr Price. I would not entrust the safety of this range to him if I thought otherwise. You say he has conspired with Hartwell. Do you have proof of this?'

Price nodded towards the back seat of his car. 'The boy is the proof. He will verify all I have said.'

The commander was looking more than a little disturbed now. 'If you're asking me to cancel the rally, I'm afraid you're too late. Sidewinder has already given the all clear. We have invited the press to today's rally, agreed to do interviews.'

'Cancel them.'

'The War Office needs us to be sympathetic towards the Imber cause.'

Price's face betrayed his exasperation. 'Good God, man, people's lives are at stake! Put marshals on the main gate. Encourage people to turn back.'

'I don't understand – '

'Hartwell faked his son's death and fabricated your hauntings. He is a dangerous man. Most likely he's insane! He orchestrated this rally in the full hope that a civilian be injured. Killed.'

'Why? To try to reclaim his property?'

I empathised with the commander's doubtful tone. As

motives, these sounded irrational, and not very likely to succeed. 'There must be more to it than that,' I said, remembering that Albert had told us Hartwell would go directly to the manor. That house intrigued me; I had a very strong inclination that we should make it a focus of our efforts. 'Perhaps there's something inside Imber Court that Hartwell wants. Something he left behind. Something he's hiding. Commander, if you can't call off the rally, please give us access to the house.'

My face must have reflected the urgency in my tone, because the commander studied me for what felt like a very long moment.

'Sir, please. We were told Hartwell would head there, so that is where we must go.'

For a moment, a grimace of indecision flickered across his face, then made way to an expression of rather touching admiration. 'The path approaching the house should be clear. However, the land adjacent to Imber Court, and the land immediately behind, is scattered with all sorts of debris. There may even be land mines.'

'We'll approach from the front.'

'It's a kill house, a shell. There's nothing inside it.'

'Have you been inside *yourself*, Commander?'

'No, but –'

'Who confirmed it was empty?' Price cut in.

There was an awkward pause, the commander avoiding eye contact.

'Well, well,' Price said, his eyes narrowing shrewdly. 'Our friend Warden Sidewinder has led you on quite a merry dance, hasn't he? Commander, if Hartwell should approach that house, as we believe he will, don't stop him. We must know his secret. I fully expect Sidewinder to follow.'

The commander was nodding, the heat of anger rising in his chiselled face. He looked a little embarrassed too. After all, some of this was his responsibility. It was clear he had protected Sidewinder's interests, and I wondered why.

'If this is true, there will be a full investigation,' the commander said stonily. 'Be under no illusion, Sidewinder will be held fully to account. But I need hard evidence. Proof.'

Price nodded, although I sensed he was only just managing to conceal his frustrations. He thought the commander was weak, spineless, and I was beginning to think so too. 'I have a little practice in coercing artful deceivers into confessing,' he said. 'Can you get Mr Wall and the boy somewhere safe?'

The commander nodded. 'I'll arrange secure transportation for them back to camp, and I'll grant you access to Imber Court. But remember what I said about the land to the side and the back of that building. Do not venture out there, or you're likely to have your legs blown off!'

Price tipped the rim of his fedora. 'You have my word.'

'Good.'

The commander flicked a curious glance at Price's coat pocket. 'Mr Price, are you carrying a weapon?'

Price gave him a mulish look.

'I can't have a civilian taking live fire arms in there.' He held out a hand. 'Let me have it.'

Price reluctantly drew the service revolver from his pocket and handed it carefully to the commander. Then the ghost hunter turned and marched towards his car.

The commander shouted after him to wait. 'Mr Price! You'll need the keys to Imber Court's gates.' He caught up with Price and drew him aside for a private word. Despite the commander lowering his voice, I overheard his first words: 'There's something vital you must know about Pierre.'

Behind a padlocked gate and a wire fence topped with razor wire, Imber Court awaited us. It was a great hulk of a house, home for over two centuries to the Hartwell family. Here, generations of children had laughed and played. But now it was deserted.

Morning was breaking over Salisbury Plain, throwing a strange purple hue over the terrain when we got out of the car. Unlocking the gate, Price looked back at me and said, 'You're sure you want to do this, Sarah?'

The wind whispered, rustling the dead leaves at our feet and catching at a loose piece of corrugated sheeting, making it clatter. It was enough to make my skin prickle with anticipation. I wasn't backing out now, but there was something I was burning to know.

'The commander told you something, Harry. About Pierre. What was it?'

Price stared silently ahead at the looming, decrepit mansion.

'Harry?'

It began to rain harder. Price fished in his pocket for something and pressed it into my hands: the lantern slide I had found in the Brixton Picture House, the night I tripped and fell from the stage.

He lowered his voice to a tone of utmost gravity. 'Once we're inside that building, keep this on you. At all times.'

I glanced at the slide, then at the mansion, then at Price, confused.

'Just do it, please,' he said, squeezing my fist around the

slide. 'Trust me. And make sure you tell me immediately if you experience any more visions. Understand?'

I blinked. 'I thought you said they were hallucinations, that they didn't matter.'

'Yes, hallucinations . . .' His voice had lost some of its conviction, I thought. And the way he was looking at me – I couldn't read it.

'Now come on,' he said, in that typical Harry Price style. 'Hurry!' And off he marched.

I pocketed the lantern slide. And as Price unlocked the gate leading to Imber Court, a sense of disquiet gnawed at me, and this time I didn't think it was paranoia. Price knew more about the whole investigation, had *always* known more, and he had deliberately kept me in the dark. For reasons known only to himself, he was still keeping me in the dark.

With the gate unlocked, Price went to the car for his equipment. Within moments, he had the blacksmith's hammer in one hand. In the other, he carried the battered briefcase, which contained his equipment, candles and matches. He asked me to hand over the Devil's Snare, and I did so. The magic lantern was my responsibility for the moment, and I tried not to give away how heavy it was as I took it from the back seat.

The faint glimmer of dawn seeped across the bruised sky, illuminating the convoy at the neck of the valley. I could make out many motor cars and tractors, and a stream of protestors – farmers, their employees, former residents of the village. There were men on foot too, and riding horseback. The sight of that convoy only strengthened my resolve to end this nightmare.

Yet when I turned to look again at the manor house, its crumbling pillared entrance festooned with moss and ivy, its many wide and arched windows, that resolve was drowned out by another feeling.

'Harry, I have the strangest sensation of déjà vu. But I know I've never been here.'

He said nothing; he just watched me.

'It's probably just subjective knowledge,' I said. 'Subconscious.'

'Probably,' he echoed, and I caught a quick smile on his lips.

'Harry?'

With a whirl of his coat he turned, quickening his stride through the rain towards the boarded-up mansion.

I took a nervous breath. *Here we go.*

– 34 –

KILL HOUSE

Time seemed to slow down as we unlocked the main gates and approached Imber Court. A strange stillness settled all around us.

There, over the pillared entrance, was the family coat of arms. The instant I saw it I was overwhelmed with an intense feeling that I knew the mansion, inside and out. I could almost picture the creaky warren beyond those crumbling walls – the vast cellars, the soaring attics and the winding staircases. But perhaps, I told myself, my memories were of a different house altogether.

Most of the windows were covered with wooden boards and corrugated iron sheeting, and yet the house seemed to be willing me to enter.

You're imagining it, I told myself, but as Price led us in through the main entrance – an oblong of deep shadow – the sensation became undeniable. *Come to me*, the house seemed to be saying. *Come on in, Sarah. It's perfectly safe.*

We were standing now in a vast hallway, the air fetid with mildew and rot. There was a tremble in my hand as I drew out my pocket torch and clicked it on. Perturbed, I surveyed our surroundings. How to describe them? Bleak. Ruinous. The floor was thick with dust, the walls blackened with scorch marks. Dry leaves had blown into drifts against the skirting boards. And on the far wall, a great mirror was shattered and pocked with shellfire.

'It's quiet,' I said nervously.

Price gave me a dark look that seemed to say, *It's always quiet in the eye of the storm.*

As I looked around the hallway I fancied I could almost – not quite, but almost – discern the bulking, handsome furniture, dark panelling and old portraits that once must have stood here; could very nearly hear the shrieks and shrill laughter of the many Hartwell children whose graves had been so cruelly desecrated.

'So, which way?' asked Price.

I was about to answer 'How should I know?' when I thought that actually, inexplicably, I *might* know the way; that if I trusted my feet, they would lead me to where we needed to be.

Swallowing my trepidation, I led us slowly by torchlight through the musty half-darkness towards a once-grand oak staircase that looked ready to collapse.

'Up there?'

'Yes,' I said, starting up the stairs as fast as I could manage with the magic lantern weighing down my left hand. All my thoughts were now on the projection slide in my coat pocket, and a curious tingling sensation that had begun in the nape of my neck. *You know this house, and this house knows you.*

Once we arrived in the upper hallway, I looked around

quickly, and caught a familiar smell, something very much like baby powder, and immediately I felt a profound sadness, as though someone no longer alive was trying to communicate with me, to whisper secrets to my heart. A lost soul: a mother perhaps, or her baby. Or both.

The feeling quite confounded me, but I felt it as keenly as the sensation that in entering this house I had somehow stepped back in time. An unpleasant sensation, and an impossible one, because I was adamant I had never set foot inside Imber Court.

'Try down there,' I said, nodding towards a dark passageway, and once again my neck tingled. We went slowly, the floorboards groaning beneath us, passing a bathroom of shattered ceramic tiles and a small room that was penetrated by a single shaft of cold, bluish light, slanting in through a hole in the roof.

We rounded a corner and I was struck by an unnerving feeling that somebody connected with this house knew me, and had something they needed to tell me, or show me. Who, and what, I had no idea, but as we approached the wall at the end of the corridor, the feeling only became more powerful.

Something about that wall: dark, rough, uneven.

'No, this isn't right.'

'It's a dead end, Sarah. Let's try downstairs.'

My hand gave an involuntary spasm, as if shocked with a bolt of energy.

'No, there is a room back there! I just know it.'

Price gently, apprehensively, put a hand on my shoulder, but I turned away from him sharply. My instincts were screaming at me not to give up; there *was* something here. So, hardening myself, I put down the magic lantern and pushed against the wall.

'Oh my God. Harry, did you see that?' I stepped closer, examining the wall. The bricks had shifted – ever so slightly, but they *had* shifted.

Price was staring now.

'I *told* you, Harry.'

But how on earth did I know?

He quickly put down his briefcase.

'Sarah, stand back. Let me try.'

With backbreaking force, he shouldered the wall. Impressive. Then struck it with the hammer. Some of the bricks came loose and dropped into the clotted blackness behind. What was back there? A compartment? A secret room?

'How – how did you know?' Price asked.

I felt an urge to confide in him that the lantern slide was guiding me, but hesitated.

'Did your father bring you to this house? Before the evacuation?'

'No.'

He was looking intently at me. Waiting.

'Harry, this house is *alive*. I know how that sounds, but I have the strangest feeling we're meant to be here, just like I had a feeling I was meant to visit the picture house in Brixton. It's all connected.'

'I believe you,' he said, not looking at me now, but at the crumbling wall. 'Do you know what's behind here?'

'No.'

His eyes lit up with curiosity, one eyebrow pulling up. 'Do you think we're in danger if we look?'

I shrugged, and with that Price began working more of the filthy bricks free. Finally, one powerful kick brought what was left of the wall tumbling down in a puff of dust.

An awful smell hit me. It was close and heavy. Filthy and earthy. A smell of too many years, of memories long entombed.

With a curious dread, I edged forward, staring hard into the shadows.

'Harry, what the hell is that?'

Two glistening green eyes were peering out at me. It was a Victorian doll, propped up on a wrought-iron bedstead, and I could make out two others in the gloom behind it.

Their glinting eyes looked out at us from white porcelain faces. The smallest was a baby doll wearing a white bonnet. The largest, in the middle of the three, wore a ruffled white dress and had tumbling black hair, tied up in a green ribbon. Its lips were blood red. But the eyes ... the eyes were the worst. Glassy. Soulless.

Something about this unnerving tableau was nagging at me. My instinct said these dolls did not belong in this dark and dreary house. They were propped up amongst heaps of blankets and other soft toys: monkeys, bears and rabbits.

The strangest thing was, aside from the shattered mirror downstairs, these were the only personal belongings we had seen anywhere in the house.

'Was this a nursery?' I asked, hearing the awe in my voice.

'Whatever it was,' Price said, 'Hartwell went to great lengths to keep it away from the army, probably with Sidewinder's help. I'll wager that, if he does come here, it's this room he'll want, and we will be ready for him.'

Slowly, we advanced. My pocket torch threw a wavering beam around the room, picking out a hulking wardrobe, a rickety desk, a boarded-up window framed by rotting, moth-eaten curtains.

My breath caught. To convey the sudden weirdness of what

happened next is almost impossible for me. I saw a woman, her back to us. She was motionless, facing the desk. Oddly, there were papers there now. Drawings – human sketches made with charcoal on white paper – that had not been there seconds before.

Though I couldn't see her face, I knew instinctively who this was. I made a careful mental note of her attire: the drab tunic, the ankle-length hobble skirt. Garments from an earlier time – twenty years at least.

Slowly, she turned to face me. Marie Hartwell – much, much younger than the woman who had hanged herself in the bell tower.

With deep sadness and an awful dread, I trained my gaze on her, yet she seemed completely oblivious to my presence. Her eyes were red and puffy from crying. And she was cradling something. A child.

The child wasn't moving.

Her mouth opened in an expression of cold horror. For an instant she seemed paralysed by fright.

Then she, and the child in her arms, vanished.

I blinked, shaking my head.

The rickety desk was now as it had first appeared, its surface devoid of any drawings.

'Sarah?'

Feeling a crawling fear in my stomach, I looked over at Price. 'Oh Harry, I think unspeakable events happened here.'

He stopped scanning the room and moved closer to me. 'Sarah,' he said quietly, 'did you see something?'

'Marie Hartwell.' My voice cracked. 'Oh God, Harry, we're on the verge of something.'

My neck was tingling again. I put down the magic lantern

and fished the lantern slide from my pocket. I felt an instant heat. And something else – a visceral revulsion.

I was about to inform Price when a distant horn blasted outside.

Dropping his briefcase and the blacksmith's hammer, Price tore himself away, heading into the corridor, to the nearest window that wasn't boarded over, and looked out.

I followed and saw that beyond the stream and the avenue of elm trees, hordes of demonstrators were assembling on the village's mud-churned main street, climbing out of vehicles, dismounting from horses: men in tweeds, housewives, children in their school uniforms. They had made their way to the very centre of Imber in the sheeting rain, waving banners and green flags. A line of soldiers was keeping them back from the wrecked buildings.

'Not much time,' Price said, troubled, and with haste he strode back into the secret nursery and crouched by the magic lantern on the floor. 'Help me, Sarah.'

My heart squeezed with apprehension as I understood what he intended to do.

A gale was beginning to rage across the downs, almost whipping away the voice booming from the loudspeaker: 'The road along which you have passed has been cleared to ensure your safety. Under no circumstances should you leave the road. The ground has not been cleared and it is not safe!'

Price's head snapped up from the lantern. 'A few small adjustments, and there, it's ready! Just one more vital factor . . .'

He bounded out into the corridor; there was the flick of a cigarette lighter and I became aware of a crackling sound, then a familiar and unpleasant odour.

Burning.

When Price retreated back into the room, which I had decided was indeed a nursery, he had a handkerchief pressed over his mouth and nose. 'Someone's coming. I caught a glimpse of them through the window,' he whispered.

'Hartwell?'

'I couldn't be sure.' Stealthily, he crouched down beside me in our hiding place, behind the desk. 'Keep your head down, Sarah. Cover your mouth. Remember how we felt during the mill séance? How you felt beneath the picture house? Burning these leaves can induce visions, confusion and delirium, and, in large enough quantities, cause a complete inability to differentiate reality from fantasy.'

'This is a colossal risk, Harry.'

His eyes held mine, unblinking. Shining. There was no going back now.

'Whatever happens, I'm pleased we found a way to work together again, Sarah. Thank you.'

He smiled, and so did I. Then his glittering eyes flicked down to my lips . . .

Oh Harry, how different our lives could have been. We could have had a life together. A family together.

Then, from the bowels of the house, came a man's voice. 'Hartwell? It's time! Oscar, where the hell are you?'

I started. This voice I recognised. It was Sidewinder.

An alarming thought struck me. 'Harry, what if he's armed? We're trespassing, and he's well within his rights to use maximum force.'

'So are we,' Price's replied, his eyes glinting mischievously.

I saw then the dark clouds of smoke blooming in the outside corridor. That was the Devil's Snare, burning. If Sidewinder was going to venture upstairs, walk in here and discover us, he would have to inhale the smoke.

Although Price was grinning, I remained dubious about his plan.

'Harry, won't he see it burning?'

'Indeed, he might,' Price whispered, 'but I have concealed the hotplate well within the alcove of the corridor wall.'

'That's all very well,' I replied, 'but he's hardly likely to be fooled by his own illusions.'

Price sounded assured as he said, 'Perhaps Sidewinder, like his son, is no longer capable of discerning reality from fiction. And remember, he *is* afflicted by one chief disadvantage.'

'What's that?'

'Sidewinder is consumed with a fervent passion to believe. And hope is the enemy of truth, Sarah. Hope makes us liars sometimes, even to ourselves.'

Dimly, from beyond the walls of the house, came the noises of the public rally: horns, drumming, chanting. If I closed my eyes, I could almost see the protestors charging furiously through the ruined village that had once been their home, challenging the nervy soldiers who were ordering them not to leave the road. And if they did . . .

I felt my limbs tense with unhappy foreboding, afraid that at any moment we might hear the blast of exploding military debris. I tried to keep my face turned away from the corridor; I was already feeling light-headed and dizzy. I saw then that Price was picking up – what? In the gloom, it was hard to make out.

Just then, a furious voice bellowed from out in the corridor: 'What the HELL?'

'Here we go,' Price whispered.

The scratch of a match, the flare of a tiny blue flame, and Price ignited the candle that powered the magic lantern. An eerie, flickering light spooled out, jerky, throwing distorted shadows all around us.

In my head, suddenly, came the projectionist's voice. *'A bright beam cutting through the smoky darkness. A spectacle. Sometimes that beam is all you need.'*

Floorboards creaked under approaching footfalls. Heavy. Slow.

I held my breath, my expectation building.

'Who is it? Who's in here?' He was coughing against the smoke.

This isn't going to work. He's going to recognise the smell!

Peeking around the desk, I saw, venturing into the room, an angular figure in military uniform, and a shock of white hair. Sidewinder. His breathing was harsh and laboured, as if he feared a grave threat awaiting him here in the darkness. And as he stepped into the beam of ghostly light I saw that his hands were clenched into fists, the whites of his eyes shining with fear.

'What on earth . . .'

When Sidewinder saw Price rising up in front of him, shoulders squared, he cocked his head to the side, as if he couldn't quite believe what he was seeing. Then his whole body jolted. Behind his perfectly round spectacles, his eyes were at once stricken. They bulged at what Price was holding.

The blacksmith's hammer.

Price raising it menacingly.

Sidewinder's composure disintegrated, his face as white as a sheet. 'Stay back, stay away!' he yelled, throwing up his hands to shield himself.

Price stepped forward, his voice deep and ragged. 'Tell the truth, Sidewinder. You know what you did to me. We both know.'

Sidewinder was frozen to the spot. 'But you're *dead*, you're not real!'

'I'll show you how real I am,' Price growled.

I squinted at him through the smoky room. Price appeared . . . different, somehow.

Was it Price?

I wasn't sure. Price had become . . . someone else.

A blacksmith?

It's the Devil's Snare, Sarah. It's only the Devil's Snare!

'I've done nothing wrong!' Sidewinder stammered. 'I did my duty.'

The room began spinning.

'GET AWAY FROM ME!' Sidewinder screamed at Price, waving his arms frantically.

'You know why I'm here, Warden. Confess. Tell the secret.'

'No.'

'We both know what you did. What control does Hartwell wield over you? How has he blackmailed you? Why?'

'Leave me in peace,' Sidewinder pleaded, his voice cracking, and suddenly my perspective shifted, the fringes of my vision exploding in light, as if I were seeing this scene in a moving photograph.

What's happening to me?

'You're dead!' Sidewinder screamed, staggering back. 'Keep away!' At the entrance to the room, where the Devil's Snare fumes were most intoxicating, he stumbled on the fallen bricks, sending him sprawling to the floor.

'You will admit your guilt,' Price instructed, looming over him, furious, dark as hell.

He was going to compel Sidewinder into confessing what happened to the blacksmith eighteen years ago outside the Imber church, and I had no control over what that truth would be. Would he confirm my direst fear? Had my father done something despicable to an innocent man in this village? I felt terror then, seething, black terror that I would hear the truth.

My vision blurred with soft pastel colours. The smoke and the light had become a flickering projection of another time . . .

A remote village, miles from anywhere, where the winters are cruel and the summers stretch forever. An iron sky hangs over the downs, which are hard with the morning frost. No sun, no warmth, just a damp, keening wind.

Outside Mrs Daniel's bakery is an abandoned wagon that will soon turn to rot. There are people about, but not many. In their tough, hard-wearing boots, they lumber towards the wagons. Their tractors line the road behind me, the road out of Imber. Like the homes they are leaving behind, their faces look weathered and bereft of hope.

Rain begins to pour down, turning the terrain to mud. The military have already begun commandeering other parts of Salisbury Plain. I hear the thundering hooves of cavalry horses. I see trudging soldiers. Tented accommodation.

In my military uniform, I take it all in. I observe the desertion of the shell-shocked village.

A superior barks an order at me. 'Private Grey!'

I am taking control, showing the men and women who have lived here which way they must now go. As I carry out my task, I pretend not to see the villagers' tears. I must not disobey orders. There's a war on now, and I must do what I'm told. It is my duty.

One man has chained himself to the church railings. The blacksmith. A desperate attempt to remain. The warden, a man called Sidewinder, orders me to shoot – actually shoot! – this civilian in the head.

I can't! I can't!

'We have to evacuate this village if we're to win this war. Whatever the cost.'

I shake my head, stepping back.

The blacksmith pulls himself to his feet. He speaks with heart-breaking passion. 'This village may be lost, but it will never belong to you. You have treated us appallingly.'

Sidewinder raises his pistol. The blacksmith stares into the barrel of the gun, paralysed with fear. But then Sidewinder stops, lowers his weapon. Presses the infernal thing into my own shaking hands.

'Do it. There's one bullet left.'

A black despair spreading through me, I shake my head in refusal. My family. My dear wife and daughter. My Sarah, what would she think of me?

'That's an order, Grey!'

I raise the gun, my hand trembling. Close my eyes tightly as I squeeze the trigger. The gunshot blasts across the valley. Echoes. Dies.

I open my eyes slowly. The blacksmith's face is pale and drawn, but he is alive.

The bullet has lodged itself in the stone church behind him. There's a long, heartfelt moment of understanding and respect between us. He looks such a kind man, and grateful. I know disobeying the order wasn't wise, but I'm beyond caring. I've kept my humanity.

As if I could ever kill an innocent.

'What's wrong with you?' Sidewinder asks, straining to sound as though he's still in control. He snatches the revolver from me. I give him a look of hardened contempt.

And Sidewinder gives the blacksmith a slow, horrible smile. With his free hand, he reaches down and closes his grip around a long, hefty hammer. He feels its power, the supremacy it gives him.

This blacksmith who has chained himself to the church railings and *means never to leave this village is a problem, but a small problem. An obstacle. And small obstacles can and must be overcome. Sidewinder thinks that it will be easy. And if I won't accept his duty, he will. He must. The hammer rises . . .*

The blacksmith shrinks back, screws his eyes shut.

'You should have left with everyone else,' says Sidewinder. He is already fantasising about how he will dispose of the body. He could burn it. He could throw it in the chalk pit at the top of Carrion Pit Lane, where it will never be found. Or in the deep millpond.

I step forward, intent on stopping him, but it's too late. He dodges me, raises the hammer and swings it.

I yell out! A ragged, high cry, a sound I didn't know I could make.

There's a wet, heavy thwack.

The blacksmith's mouth falls open, as if he's trying to say something, or draw a final gasp, but there's no sound, no scream. A trickle of blood from his ear. A long, slow drip.

His face goes slack. Sidewinder lifts the hammer to land another blow, but I lunge at him, knock him to the ground. There's a struggle, frantic. He's stronger than me, on top of me, raining down blows. One almost knocks me unconscious.

Sidewinder is on his feet again, his eyes full of insane malevolence.

'Stop, stop!' I shout, as I see the hammer come down.

The blacksmith's head implodes with a hideous crack.

Then he's gone. He slumps, face forward, with a sickening thud.

I lie there, frozen, gazing in abject horror at what is now an unrecognisable pulp of hair and blood and brains. 'What have you done?' I hear myself whisper. 'Oh Jesus. What the hell have you done?'

IMBER'S HORROR

I tried shaking these shadows from my head as I drifted back to Imber Court, to the smoky secret nursery, lit with the ghostly flicker from the magic lantern. The first things I saw were the padded bodies and bone-china faces of those unnerving Victorian dolls. Then I turned my head, and saw the hammer raised high. Price was standing over Sidewinder, who was struggling to his knees, swiping wildly at the smoky air.

'No nearer! You hear me? I wasn't responsible. It was Harold Grey!'

But I wouldn't allow that.

'Liar.'

He spun round, dumbstruck, as at last I stood up from behind the desk.

'My father was a good man. An innocent man. *You* murdered Silas Wharton.'

Sidewinder was looking frenziedly at me through the

haze and seemed almost ready to confess. Ghastly pale, he stammered:

'But – but – try to understand.'

'I do understand. Perfectly. You acted alone.'

'I was under orders,' he said, wringing his hands.

Suddenly, a new voice was in the room: 'Shut your mouth, bloody fool! You've been had!'

'Christ's sake – it's not my fault,' said Sidewinder, swaying where he stood, glancing fearfully from Price to me. 'Hartwell *made* me collaborate with him, do you see? He threatened me. Forced me.'

'I said *silence!*'

There was movement in the yellowy smoke, and a figure stepped out of it. It was Hartwell. Coughing against the burning Devil's Snare, he grasped Sidewinder's arm and shook him roughly.

'What ... what happened?' Sidewinder murmured. Disorientated, he rubbed his swollen eyes.

'Harry and Sarah here thought they'd play a trick to induce you to spill your secrets.' The light from the magic lantern flickered on Hartwell's fierce face. His imperious tone suggested he was managing to maintain his composure, but his fluttering eyelids revealed the truth: the drug was already working its strange effect on him. He glared at Price, at the hammer in his grip, and said cuttingly, 'Mr Price, take your companion and leave my property. Now.'

'We know the secret,' Price said tightly, his eyes glittering with abhorrence. 'We know your son is alive, we know you have deceived others into believing he died. We know that you drugged him, kept him tethered below ground. And we know the warden here is guilty of a murder you've known about, sir, for eighteen years! You have used that knowledge to work upon his fears, to blackmail him. Did you see him commit the murder, I wonder? Were you watching? Did you obtain proof?'

'*May God in His mercy punish those who have wronged us*,' Hartwell snarled. '*Grant it so that His heavenly wrath stains the souls of those who have stained Imber with the blood of innocents.*'

Clutching the lantern slide tighter, I took a step towards him. 'Why did you do it?'

Hartwell hesitated. He looked wild-eyed and haggard, the light from the magic lantern turning his face a sickly yellow. 'I won't be trodden on. I won't be deprived of what's rightfully mine – my ancestral heritage.'

My vision swirled, bright white, and I was ripped from the room again.

Marie Hartwell, young. Here in the room, cradling a dead baby. Wracked with grief.

I opened my eyes. 'No, it goes deeper than that,' I insisted. There *was* a secret here, one that had to do with Marie Hartwell. And her children, perhaps. 'What was so important about this room that you had to hide it behind a wall?'

Before he could answer, there came distant cries and horns from the public rally, hundreds of voices calling to the drum-beat in unison for Imber to live. That chorus of voices was much nearer now. The sinister image of the warning signs outside came back to me disturbingly, along with an almost certain premonition of approaching disaster.

'Get outside,' Hartwell said to Sidewinder. 'What we need is a well-timed accident. Order the guards to allow the protestors onto the range. Don't let them near this house, just the rest of the village. Do it!'

Sidewinder hesitated, his gaze unfocused.

'Do it now!' Hartwell barked.

A wave of panic swept through me. Price and I both stepped forward, intending to block Sidewinder's exit, but we stumbled. Price looked unsteady on his feet and my own vision was swimming. We had breathed in too much Devil's Snare.

Hartwell saw his chance.

With a snarl of anger, he charged at Price, sending him stumbling back and crashing onto the ancient desk, which collapsed in a cloud of dust.

'Harry!'

The two men scrambled on the floor, Hartwell on top of Price, pinning him down.

I started forward. I had to help if I could.

'You should have left when I said!' Hartwell raged. Price was writhing beneath him, trying to buck him off, but Hartwell had one murderous hand around his neck, the other reaching back, groping for the hammer still in Price's hand. Then Price dropped it and I darted forward, stumbling in the haze.

An arm roughly grabbed me from behind.

'You bitch, you stinking bitch!' yelled Sidewinder, right in my ear. 'I should have *killed* your father!'

Pain exploded in my back as he landed a punch, sending me staggering into the shadowy corridor. I fell forward, face down, just a few paces away from the shadowy alcove where Price had left the Devil's Snare burning in a metal dish.

So close to my face.

Don't inhale, don't inhale.

But it was impossible not to gulp in the smoke. Just a few short and panicked breaths and my vision disintegrated into a blur.

Hartwell's a murderer.

A sudden wave of certainty washed over me.

He murdered his family, probably in this house.

I saw it clearly.

This nursery, decades ago. The ash light of dawn filtering through the shuttered window. A boy of around ten, with shaggy dark hair and dressed smartly in a suit, a boy who looks very much like a young Hartwell, sits on the edge of the bed, completely still, listening to another man sitting next to him. I can't hear the words, I can only see the dreadful purpose in the older man's eyes. Finally, balefully, the boy nods, understanding what he must do. It will be for the good of the family. For the good of Imber. The boy's eyes are terribly wide and dark. Murderous.

Opening my eyes, coming up from the vision, I found I was lying on the floor in the dark, smoky corridor. Above the noise of the horns and whistles outside, the voice of a demonstrator on the village road was still amplified.

I was expecting to hear Price and Hartwell fighting in the nursery, but the only sound nearby was behind me: Sidewinder agreeing he would do as Hartwell had asked, he would go out and order his men to allow the protestors onto the range. To allow innocent civilians into the buildings that had not been made safe.

Dimly, I envisioned what would happen: protesters swarming into the village, oblivious that they were walking to their doom.

An explosion.

Women or children blown to smithereens.

Quickly, silently, I struggled to my feet. Price lay unconscious on the nursery floor, beside the shattered desk. There was a large gash above his right eye and blood streaming down his face. Hartwell stood over him, going through his pockets;

and in the space created by the fallen brick wall, Sidewinder had his back to me.

Take him by surprise.

My heart had never beaten as hard or as fast as it did in that moment, but I had to act now. And that meant swallowing my fear.

I drew in a breath and charged at him.

Sidewinder spun round just as I threw the punch. An explosion of hot pain burst through me as my fist connected with the right side of his face.

'Argh!' he yelled, snaring my collar. Then, with a furious cry, he elbowed me in the face. *Crack!* As hot blood gushed from my nose, the shock of the blow sent me stumbling back into the room. I closed my eyes, only for a second, but when I opened them again I saw to my horror that Sidewinder was holding the blacksmith's hammer.

'Stay away,' I croaked, tasting blood on my lips, smelling once again the sickly, earthy odour that pervaded this room so heavily.

But Sidewinder raised the hammer and lunged. I dodged it. He went for me with his free hand, grabbing me roughly by the throat. We fell back in a gasping struggle, crashing into the pile of bedclothes and soft toys and strange Victorian dolls.

Hartwell spun round, appalled, as if we had desecrated a family memorial.

'Harry!' I screamed. 'Help me!'

But on the other side of the room, Price lay unmoving on the floor.

'Get off the bed!' Hartwell yelled, but Sidewinder was oblivious, a raging madman. He was on top of me, yelling, his face thrust into mine, so close I could smell his hot, nicotine breath.

'Your father let me down – disobeyed a direct order. I've lived all these years with what he forced me to do. You do see it was your father's fault, don't you? DON'T YOU?'

With a shriek of fury, I clawed at his face. Gouged him. Crying out, he dropped the hammer. Frantically, I reached for it – amid the dolls – but then he was on top of me again, pinning my arms to the bed with both legs.

'Get off me, get OFF –'

A hand clamped over my mouth. Another around my throat. Tightening. Squeezing . . .

Oh God, oh no – please, no.

Now both hands – strong, large hands – were on my neck, struggling to throttle the life from me. My knees came up; I tried to kick him in the back. But I was weakening quickly. My lungs burned. My vision darkened . . .

Then, unexpectedly, Sidewinder released my throat and I sucked in an enormous gulp of air. And a part of me – a naive part – prayed he had changed his mind. But his eyes remained lit with the same manic, murderous intention. He had only decided on a different way to do it.

'Please . . .' I began, but he was already groping on the filthy bed for the hammer.

Get up, I thought. *Run!*

But all my energy was depleted. I felt just as lifeless as one of the discarded china dolls.

Sidewinder had the hammer in his hand, was holding it so tightly his knuckles had turned white. 'Give my regards to your father,' he said in a flat voice, raising the hammer high. And I knew this was the end.

A hot white pain exploded in my hand – the lantern slide. All this time, I had been holding on to it, just like Price said.

As Sidewinder brought the hammer down I *made* myself roll – and the hammer missed my face by a hair's breadth.

I was in such a state of shock, and so disorientated, I barely noticed the shattering sound that came suddenly from my left, the sort of sound a china cup might make if you dropped it on a stone floor.

At the other side of the room, Hartwell's head snapped up. 'What have you done?' he demanded of Sidewinder, staring over at us. He had been keeping a restrained distance from the bed and from us during Sidewinder's attack. 'What the hell have you done?'

Sidewinder wasn't looking at me any more. I should have been relieved he wasn't trying to kill me at that instant, but my overriding emotion was one of confusion. Because now the warden's face was ghostly white, his entire body rigid, as though someone had drawn a steel wire through his spine and tightened it.

'Oscar?' Disbelief in his voice. He dropped the hammer, and it hit the floor with a heavy clunk. 'What is . . . what is *this*?'

No reply from Hartwell. For a few seconds the only sound was of the rally down in the village. The drum beats kept rhythm with my heart as I watched Sidewinder stoop to examine something on the bed behind me.

He leapt back. 'What the FUCK?' he screamed. 'Oh God! Oh God, no!'

A sound like shattering china . . . Only one thing in the room would make a sound like that.

That smell again. An awful smell.

A sharp chemical cocktail.

Steeling myself, I slowly turned my head. The largest doll – the one with the white dress whose black hair had been tied up in a green ribbon – was no longer propped up on the iron bedstead. In the mad scuffle, she had been displaced and lay just inches away. Her glass eyes were gone, her porcelain face nothing but a jagged hole of broken china.

I felt the stab of alarm as I realised what had been nagging at me when I first laid eyes on the dolls: one of them was very large.

A little *too* large.

And the more I studied them, the more they looked like . . .

Rolling from the bed, I leapt to my feet, struggling to breathe.

How long did I stand there, staring? It could have been seconds or minutes. All I knew was that we had finally been confronted with Imber's horror – a secret so horrific it diminished the importance of anything else, made talk of hauntings and ghosts sound positively pathetic.

Not just a china doll, a child *inside* the doll.

A dead child's blackened face.

I doubled over, gagging, closing my eyes – as if that would banish the horrible truth. 'Oh God,' I cried. 'Say it's not so. Please tell me they're not – '

Hartwell's voice was flat and emotionless. 'My three little girls.'

I retched, stole another look at the largest doll. The girl's features, previously hidden beneath the china, were a wasted decay of blackened bone. Once more, my stomach heaved. 'What have you DONE?'

Stepping carefully over Price's unconscious body, Hartwell approached with menacing purpose. I was incapable of thinking clearly, but I clenched the lantern slide ever tighter and a memory flashed through me. I was picturing the empty grave

Sergeant Edwards had uncovered with me in Imber's church-yard; picturing the commander's face as he told me the other Hartwell graves had shown signs of disturbance.

Then, as if seeing the scene on a movie screen, I saw Hartwell outside this room, trespassing under the cover of night in the Imber churchyard.

I saw him taking ragged, frosted breaths as he dug them up.

I don't know how I knew that, but I *did* know it. A voice in my head told me so; it was the voice of someone no longer alive. Someone who had wanted me to find these girls, and who – I now felt sure – had drawn me here.

'You exhumed the bodies of your own children?' I said, hearing the repulsion in my voice. As I spoke, tears came to my eyes.

'It was simple,' said Hartwell, his eyes widening with the memory. But there was something in his self-confident exterior that faltered then, only for a moment, revealing a look of raw, wounded grief. Some small part of this man's rotten mind still possessed a kernel of sanity, and it had just glimpsed the abject horror of his actions. The impression was fleeting, though. Within seconds, the calm, insanely matter-of-fact tone was back in his voice. 'Sidewinder here gave me access to the range whenever I needed it. So, I dug down, cut the holes in the caskets and pulled them out.'

Sidewinder was staring at the madman, dumbstruck.

Wiping my eyes, I dared to glance once more at the pathetic remains. I took in how carefully they had been dressed, even down to their stockings and boots. What I didn't yet know, and what the police would later confirm, was that Hartwell had attempted to embalm these long dead bodies, used lipstick and make-up on their china faces and put music boxes inside their rib cages.

I turned to Sidewinder. 'Did you know?'

He shook his head, mouth agape. 'No, upon my soul, I didn't.'

Then, gazing at the corpses, Hartwell said something that turned my blood to ice.

'Oh, my babies. They were so cold out there in the churchyard and I felt guilty. You see, Miss Grey? I had to bring them home and warm them up.'

Sidewinder's face contorted in revulsion as this revelation sunk in. His expression in that moment has never left me, even after all these years: *How did it come to this?* Then Hartwell said, in a voice so calm it was unnerving, 'My father and his father before him also engaged in the practice, whenever it was necessary.'

'What practice?'

'Strangulation, suffocation.' He nodded at the horrid simplicity of these acts and I wondered whether the cumulative effect of the Devil's Snare burning in the upstairs corridor was making him tell us fantasies or delusions, or if this was the unspeakable truth. I decided it was the latter, the drug forcing the awful confession from his lips. 'It really is as easy as placing your finger in the child's mouth and choking them.'

An image of my own baby, swaddled in blankets, ripped through my mind.

A parent who murdered their children? The idea was abhorrent, incomprehensible. Why would he do it? If there was a path to understanding an act of savagery so terrible, I honestly couldn't see it.

'But why?' I cried, numb from shock. 'Why on earth would you do such a thing?'

Hartwell gave me a look of withering condescension, as if he knew about my own child, my own guilt.

'When I blamed the deaths on disease, most of the villagers believed it,' said Hartwell, his words coming slowly, cautiously. Stepping over Price, who was still lying unconscious on the floor, he went to the boarded-up window and stood very near to it, gazing at the wood with a look of admiration, as though he could see right through it and out over the village. 'Well, why wouldn't they believe it? My family has owned this land for generations.'

His words took me back to my earlier vision. His dead wife, Marie, in this very room, cradling a child – a dead child. Beatrice?

Had Marie known? Surely not. If she had known, she would have run with her children to keep them safe or informed the police. Or, more likely, murdered Hartwell in his sleep.

Had she suspected? Perhaps, but even then, her capacity to act, to protect, would have depended on her mental state. Had the deaths driven her desperate, mad? Or had Hartwell plied her with drugs? Warped her mind too? Anything seemed possible.

In quiet terror, I looked at the three corpses on the bed and a horrible question occurred to me. 'Why murder one child as a baby and allow the others to live for longer?'

I felt a roll of nausea when Hartwell said, 'With every death, Marie longed for another child. I couldn't take them all as newborns – too suspicious. Better to wait a little while. In any case, we kept trying for a son. That was the point. Because it was a *son* I needed, a son to ensure the continuation of the family name. My own father impressed that upon me from my earliest days.'

I looked guardedly at him, then at the bed, remembering the young boy from my vision. Taking dark orders from an old man, decades ago, in this very room.

I thought of the funeral I had witnessed as a child, the fear, suspicion and loathing on some of the villagers' faces. Oscar Hartwell not crying.

I thought of Marie Hartwell's suicide – her screaming at the congregation in Imber church that Hartwell had blood on his hands.

I thought of the graves in the churchyard, the names on the Hartwell gravestones: Lillian, Beatrice, Rosalie.

He killed his daughters until he got a son. Recorded the births and murdered them, merely because they weren't useful to him. An inconvenience.

As if reading my horrified, questioning expression, Hartwell said, 'I don't expect you to understand, Sarah, but a great deal of money and land was at stake. When the community was ripped from us, I used my son, my dear Pierre, to get it back.'

A flash of memory: Rosalie's funeral. The villagers watching Hartwell with suspicion as he laid yet another of his girls to rest. And then Pierre's 'death' ... Had they known Hartwell longed for a son? Suspected? What better way to deceive them, to win their sympathy for his plight, by pretending he had lost the one thing he cherished most?

With mounting revulsion, I looked at Sidewinder, who was frozen at the foot of the bed. His face was blank, his eyes watering.

I felt sick in my stomach and sick in my heart. It was the most depraved, the most sadistic thing I had ever heard.

'You faked your son's death! Kept him prisoner! You murdered your daughters.' My throat was tightening, my neck painful and swollen from being choked. I swallowed my tears, looking aghast at the three bodies. 'Such precious lives – gone.'

'Precious? What good were the girls anyway? A female child couldn't continue the family name, would never have understood business. But a son – '

Get out, Sarah. He's insane. Get out, NOW!

But I was rooted to the spot. I couldn't leave Price. How badly was he injured? Was he even breathing?

In my hand, the lantern slide grew hot – uncomfortably hot. As if needing to be noticed. To be used?

My gaze dropped to the magic lantern on the floor.

Is that what I am supposed to do?

Sidewinder looked electrified with panic. As his gaze targeted the entranceway to the upstairs hallway, the only way out, I thought he was about to flee for help. Hartwell must have thought so too, because with lightning speed he lunged for the blacksmith's hammer.

Sidewinder's face convulsed with fear. Spinning, he made a dash for the exit, but stumbled, falling heavily to his knees.

Behind him, Hartwell dragged the hammer from the floorboards.

I stood back, horror-stricken, as Sidewinder desperately scrabbled forward, hauling himself to his feet. Grabbing the door frame, he pulled himself up, throwing a panicky glance over his shoulder. Hartwell was standing in the centre of the room, insane and murderous, the blacksmith's hammer at his side.

There was a chilling moment of eye contact between the two men.

And then, with a savage roar, Hartwell charged. The white-haired warden barely made it three feet into the corridor before Hartwell seized his shoulders and spun him round.

There was a spray of blood, metal smashing hard into the side of Sidewinder's skull. He dropped, slumped face forward to the floor with a horrible, heavy thud.

'Lying bastard had it coming,' Hartwell spat.

From beyond the house came the growing sound of horns and beating drums.

Hartwell turned to look at me, his eyes shining like white-hot metal.

'Well, Sarah,' he whispered hoarsely. 'Just us now.'

– 36 –

END GAME

With staggering swiftness, he was upon me, his rough hand stifling my scream. A bolt of pain exploded in my ribs as he landed a punch and brought me to my knees. Gasping for breath, I looked up, and there was Hartwell looming over me.

Oh no, oh no, please, oh no.

In one hand, he held the blood-spattered hammer.

Perhaps it was panic, perhaps it was the lingering after-effects of inhaling the Devil's Snare, but I saw what happened next in blurry slow motion.

A dark figure sprang from the shadows.

The hammer hissed past my face.

And the hellish nursery echoed with a grunt of shock as the dark figure crashed into Hartwell and took him down, hard, onto the floor.

I gulped in a breath, scrambled quickly up. 'Harry!'

His face was grey and bloodied, but he was alert – alive. In a flash, he was on his feet, as dark and as tall as a storm, and backing away from Hartwell, who lay stretched out on the floor, blinking groggily.

Without a flicker of hesitation, Price kicked the hammer away from Hartwell's grasp and then rushed to my side, shaking and trembling.

'I thought I'd lost you,' he whispered, putting a tender hand to my face. 'My dear Sarah.'

Gently, carefully, he held me close. I clung to him, pressing my head against his chest, feeling the tremors run through his body. For a moment, my emotions were so strong that I was barely capable of speaking. In that one moment, all I wanted – all I needed – was him. Just Harry.

We separated finally, smiling exhaustedly at one another. A team once more.

Wiping the blood from around his mouth, Price took a moment, quietly staring at the three dead girls with a mixture of sadness and fear. They lay there on the bed, amongst the other soft toys, in miserable disarray. Scattered and crumpled.

The fear dropped out of Price's face. What took its place was another emotion: a limitless, plunging sorrow. Genuine heartache shimmered in his eyes. But as his gaze found Hartwell, who was now stirring, his expression hardened with something else: the ghost hunter's fury.

Innocent children had been murdered. Lives ruined.

A price would be exacted.

'Aren't you forgetting someone, Oscar?'

Hartwell's eyes locked on him from the floor, savage and questioning.

'Who do you think you've forgotten? Think, Oscar. Sidewinder's son – the projectionist who helped you conjure your illusions? Or how about your own precious son?'

Hartwell started at the mention of his boy.

Price's face was now a study in barely contained anger. He took a step towards Hartwell. 'You and Sidewinder convinced the army they were operating in this village at the mercy of ghosts. You used drugs to terrify Sergeant Edwards – so badly that he set himself ablaze! Probably you used drugs on your wife, yes? Addled her mind. You did all this – and more – to preserve the male line in your great and noble family. To restrict inheritance rights to your male heirs. So surely, Oscar, surely you want to know about the boy you used and cheated to accomplish your goal. Surely you want to know *everything* about him.'

'I know everything about my son.'

'Ah – not true.'

'He's in London.'

'Wrong again,' said Price, shaking his head defiantly. 'We found him, Oscar. And guess what? He's safe. Right now, your precious son is in the one place you've always wanted him. He's home. Pierre is right here, in Imber. Under army protection.'

'You're lying,' said Hartwell – but his voice wavered.

Price squinted, considering this. 'Well, I *might* be lying. You'll have to make up your own mind, I can't do it for you.'

Price's voice was cutting, every word a knife against this monster. 'But what I can do, Oscar, is make you a solemn promise. *They're coming for you* – the protesters, the former residents of this village you've whipped into a fury – and when they hear of this chamber of horrors, when they see what you have done to these poor children, I promise you, they will want vengeance.'

Hartwell was shaking his head.

Price advanced on him slowly, anger blazing out of him.

'There are no ghosts in Imber, there never were. You're going to be arrested. You'll be thrown in prison, and then ... then you will be hanged.'

'My son will lie for me. He'll pro – '

'Protect you?' Price's eyebrows shot up. 'I wouldn't be so sure. Because I know something else about your son. Something that will haunt you for the rest of your miserable days.'

'I know everything about him,' Hartwell retorted furiously – desperately. 'He is my son!'

Price had white fire in his eyes. 'Is he?'

Hartwell froze. Stared at Price. 'Of course he's mine.'

'Wrong.'

'You don't know what you're talking about!'

'Don't I?' Price was vengeance personified, shoulders squared, his face thrust close to Hartwell's. 'Then why do you look as though the Devil has reached into your chest and tightened his dirty claws around your heart? Pierre's true father is someone whose life you ruined – the man you left for dead in the woods. And if you're not afraid, you should be, because when he learns the truth ...' He clamped a hand on Hartwell's shoulder and smiled coldly. 'Sergeant Gregory Edwards is a man trained to fire on the enemy.'

I had felt for a time the commander was concealing a secret, hadn't I? This surely was it. Edwards' affair with Marie had produced a child.

'It's not true,' said Hartwell, breaking free of Price's grip. 'How *can* it be true?' He staggered back against the wall. His face crumpled.

'Tell us where she's buried,' Price demanded.

I stared at him, confused.

'Harry?'

'There's one more, Sarah. One more little girl, who should have lived.'

What was this? Hartwell only had three girls, didn't he? *Didn't he?*

Hartwell's silence said it all: there was a final horror here, waiting to be unearthed.

Price rounded on him. 'WHERE IS SHE?'

'Stop, stop, stop,' Hartwell said, wary and furious.

'Well, perhaps I can help you remember,' Price replied, undeterred. Urgently, he rounded on me, snapping his fingers. 'Sarah, the lantern slide.'

I was looking at him, mystified.

'Give it to me!'

I did, and he stooped to slot it into the magic lantern. The image that flickered out onto the wall was almost life-size. A projected image of two children: a dark-haired boy in a suit standing primly next to a girl with crystalline blue eyes, hair curling around her ears.

Hartwell gave a strangled cry, jumping back in surprise, and as he did so a bolt of what I can only describe as psychic power smacked through me, so powerfully that for a moment I struggled to breathe.

It's Hartwell, a voice in my head said. *The boy on the lantern slide, the boy in the suit, is a young Oscar Hartwell.*

And the girl standing next to him?

'Confess!' Price raged. 'Tell us where to find her!'

Hartwell was in motion, backing towards the bed, towards the soft toys scattered there, reaching for something in his jacket pocket. As he tore it out, it glinted silver.

A nickel-plated silver cigarette lighter.

'We lived to die in this village, my wife and I,' he said calmly, words I recognised. He looked crafty, ready to end this, one way or another. 'To be buried here, with our children.'

'You don't need to do this,' Price implored, holding out one hand.

Hartwell struck the lighter and a yellow flame bloomed.

Whoosh! The scatter of soft toys ignited in flame.

At the side of the bed, Price wrestled the lighter from Hartwell's grasp, but it was too late. The soft toys had caught quickly. So had the sheets. And, I saw with mounting horror, so had the ruffled white dresses worn by the corpses of his little girls.

'I'm not leaving, Mr Price,' Hartwell coughed, sliding down the wall, his knees drawn up to his chest.

I glanced at the flickering image on the wall: the younger Hartwell, nine or ten, and the girl, slightly older. I bolted to the shattered desk, suddenly sure of what I would find.

'What the hell are you doing, Sarah? We have to get out!'

A blinding rush, and the bed, along with its tragic occupants, went up in flames.

Tongues of fire darted up the moth-eaten curtains and licked at the carpet. Price jumped to his feet as I yanked open the desk drawer.

There they were, as somehow I had known they would be. Scrolls of drawing paper. Marie Hartwell's spirit drawings.

Price erupted into action, grabbing my wrist, but I kept good hold of the drawings. The room was seething with heat and smoke. I strained to look at the bed and those three little girls, at the floor, Sidewinder's body in a pool of blood, and at Hartwell, who was huddled on the floor against the wall.

Finally, I glanced at the flickering image thrown by the magic lantern. It had followed me to this moment, all the way from Brixton Picture Palace.

'Who is she?' I demanded. 'Who's the girl in the picture?'

Hartwell shook his head contemptuously, as the flames from the bed began licking at the sleeve of his jacket.

Price had my hand, was dragging me out of the room.

When I looked back, I saw, for the last time, the ghostly projection: the young Hartwell and the older girl with the blue eyes, flickering spectres in the black smoke.

Then came the scream, and I saw that Hartwell was alight, thrashing wildly.

The two of us tore headlong out of the nursery and down the corridor, stumbling in the dark. With flames raging behind us, we careened down the staircase, lurching across the pitch-black hallway to the main door, only to find it barred.

Hartwell must have locked it.

Shaking, I banged desperately on the door.

Price cast a panicked at the top of the stairs. 'We can't go back up there.' He nodded towards the nearest corridor – a stretching tunnel of darkness. 'We'll try the back of the house.'

It's not safe out there. The commander warned us . . .

With the torchlight bouncing off the walls, we tore to the back of the house, passing room after gloomy room, every window boarded up. Again, the noise of the protesters – drums, horns, whistles – carried through the rain to the mansion. *'Imber forever,'* I heard them chant. *'Imber will live.'*

Bursting into what had once been the kitchen, both of us began coughing harshly, the acrid smoke seeping down through the floorboards above us. We must have been right underneath the blazing nursery. It was harder to draw breath now – much harder.

Price started to the exit, another steel door.

'Sarah – help me!'

We pushed it, battered on it, but the door didn't give.

'It's bolted from the other side!' I realised.

'Have to get out,' Price croaked. More smoke was seething through the ceiling, thick and hot. I closed my eyes, weakening.

Please, don't let this be the end.

In desperation, I slammed on the door with all my strength and there was a *chink* as the bolt on the other side snapped. It must have been old, rusted. Price threw his body at the door. Once. Twice.

It swung open. Coughing and choking, we ran out into a hellish landscape of fog, rain and barbed wire.

'Who was the girl on the lantern slide?' I shouted at Price.

He let go of my hand, shaking his head in defiance, then nodded towards the centre of the village, beyond the stream and the belt of elm trees, to the crowd of men, women and children who were openly ignoring the soldiers' warnings of mines and the signs that were planted everywhere.

TO LEAVE THE ROADS IS DANGEROUS.
THERE ARE MISSILES THAT CAN KILL!

Whistles shrieking and banners raised high, hundreds of people swarmed towards the ancient cottages that we had never dared enter.

'Stop!' I yelled. 'For God's sake, it's NOT SAFE!'

Behind us, black smoke was pouring from Imber Court. The heat from the blaze was at our backs, the rough terrain glowing orange in the light of the flames. Price was beckoning me to follow him.

'Come on, Sarah, run!'

We bolted for the road, splashing through muddy craters, until Price skidded to a halt, one hand raised.

'Freeze!'

We became statues.

Price was staring down in horror.

Now, just a few centimetres from Price's muddied boot, I saw it, protruding from the mud – a dark-green land mine. One wrong move and we'd be blown to smithereens.

There was a long moment of hopeless silence, broken finally by Price. 'I'm sorry, Sarah,' he said in a defeated voice. 'I'm so, so sorry.'

'What for?' I asked. His maddening secretiveness, his refusal to tell me everything he knew about this village and my connection to it?

'I should never have brought you here,' was all he said.

'What do you mean?' I demanded. '*I* brought *you* here.'

He shook his head. 'I'm sorry, Sarah, I am. But I needed to know if it was true.'

'What? If what was true? Harry?'

'I needed to know they weren't delusions, Sarah. I needed to know if the memories were – '

Suddenly, a massive explosion detonated, reverberating through the ground, through my every bone. I screamed, looking wildly about me. Only Price's hand clamped on my sleeve kept me from moving. He tilted his face, squinting into the sky.

Another explosion; a flash of white lightning.

Relief surged through me. It wasn't mines we could hear exploding around us, but thunder. I stood rooted to the spot. Then an awful cracking made me glance back at Imber Court, just as its roof collapsed, devoured by the leaping flames. I tried picturing the chaos inside – the floorboards, the great wooden staircase, surrendering to the raging blaze – but all I saw was the nursery, the children. *Oh God, those poor children.*

Quickly, tightly, Price clasped my arm. His face was pained, pleading with me. 'Swear to me, Sarah, never to tell. Of what has happened here. Of my fleeting belief in the spirit child. Promise me you will say nothing of my foolish mistake, not to anyone. Not ever.'

I nodded my answer: I promise.

Then, urgently, I said: 'We have to get back to the road.'

He nodded but he was looking down at our feet, at the land mine almost touching his boot. 'We can't move,' he said hopelessly. 'There's bound to be more.'

That was when I felt it, with shocking suddenness – a hand closed around my wrist.

A hand?

I looked all around, but I saw no one.

But there *was* someone, wasn't there? I could feel that hand tugging my wrist, firm yet freezing cold. I knew instinctively it was the hand of someone dead.

'Sarah, what's wrong?'

Another sharp tug. This felt like a man's hand. It seemed to be signalling, *Come now, follow me.*

The Devil's Snare again? Another hallucination?

Price looked terror-stricken. Was I really going to allow this invisible hand, which he couldn't feel, to lead us to the road?

Then, beyond the stream, the bells of St Giles' Church started tolling.

I drew a breath, so scared. The dead man's hand tugged urgently.

A flash of memory:

'Sarah, my angel, if ever we are parted, if you should find yourself

alone, then close your eyes and remember this place. I'll always be here.'

I held Price's gaze a moment longer. Then, swallowing a gulp, I stepped into no man's land.

'Sarah, what the hell are you –'

'It's all right, Harry,' I said, with a new and unexpected confidence. 'Trust *me* now.'

The sky flashed white again, and now more bells were tolling at their loudest, as if warning of the direst emergency.

I closed my eyes and focused, my head down. Still clutching Marie's drawings, I put one foot forward . . .

PART FOUR

OLD SOULS

For who can wonder that man should feel a vague belief in tales of disembodied spirits wandering through those places which they once dearly affected, when he himself, scarcely less separated from his old world than they, is for ever lingering upon past emotions and bygone times, and hovering, the ghost of his former self, about the places and people that warmed his heart of old?

CHARLES DICKENS, *Master Humphrey's Clock*

– 37 –

THE REVENANT (II)

October 1978

All that happened forty-six years ago.

Forty-six years . . .

It feels longer, and I don't think that's just because I'm slipping ever deeper into old age: seventy-four now. The village itself couldn't harm me, only the memories of what happened there. And those memories took their toll.

So, I pushed them down, held my silence as I had promised. I moved on, but what had happened behind those barbed-wire fences and Keep Out signs was almost impossible to leave behind.

And like I said, reality has a way of intruding. Recent events have forced me to look back. One week ago, I saw the spectre of Harry Price reflected in my kitchen window, whispering a name to me, and pleading with me never to tell what happened in Imber. And despite my almost crippling arthritis, I have not stopped writing since.

The words have come in a flood.

Now, as I wait for dawn, I look back through these memoirs, feeling pensive and drained. Consumed with sadness. There's a part of me that doesn't feel able to finish this story, but finish I must. Because of the story in the news.

The news I never wanted to hear again.

Perhaps you remember? It was reported on the radio and in all the newspapers. The army had made a gruesome discovery in Imber: skeletal remains.

The remains of a child.

Nothing could have prepared me for the sadness, the sheer disbelief and anger that rose in me when I heard that on the radio. Scant information was given – no cause of death, no estimation of how long the remains had been in the earth. But a policewoman interviewed by the BBC did say the discovery was being treated as suspicious.

Hearing that made me remember my promise to Price never to tell about his fleeting belief in the spirit child. And it taught me an all too painful lesson: some promises should not be honoured.

The military conducted their own internal investigation, but so much was suppressed that Hartwell's deeds remained secret from the public.

Now I *have* to tell the police what I know. There was foul play in Imber. I know that as surely as I know it was the spirit of my father who had piloted Price and me through the land mines to the road.

Can I prove it? No. But a secret, strange knowledge tells me I don't need to; and the same knowledge tells me the skeletal remains unearthed in Imber belong to a member of the Hartwell family: a little girl, just twelve years old.

And yes, I think I also know how precisely that little girl met her demise.

Because some stories are never finished, are they? Some voices insist on being heard, even after death, and who are we to ignore them? Now, as I prepare to put down my pen with shaking hands that are spotted with age, I feel afraid and old and alone; but I know what I must do.

I need closure. Never more so than now. The police need information, and I can help with that. But I would like something in return. There is someone I would like to meet. And I'm hopeful the police can help make that happen.

Still curious, Sarah . . .

Before returning to Imber, I have Vernon drive me to West Sussex, to a place I've managed to spend my whole life avoiding.

St Mary's graveyard, Pulborough.

I want to pay my respects to the man I am about to betray.

Looming before me, in the black shadow of an elm tree, is a cross-shaped headstone, choked by ivy.

'Hello, old friend.'

I kneel beside it and put my hand gently on the rough weathered stone. Just visible through the spotted moss is the inscription.

IN LOVING MEMORY OF
HARRY PRICE
PASSED AWAY 29 MARCH 1948
AGED 67

I have to swallow before I speak, and when I do, the words come in a dry whisper. 'The military suppressed so much of what happened but I'm going to tell the police everything about Imber, Harry. It's right that they know. It's the right thing for Pierre. I'm setting him free.' I take a breath. 'And it's right that you know something, too.'

My mind drifts back to my youth. To the dark days, the quiet desperation of an expectant single mother. In a flash I see myself, alone and terrified at the convent. Concealing the birth of my son from his father.

'Our son – the boy you never knew – lived. He *lived*, Harry, and if you can hear me now, there's something I'd like you to know. I am so, so sorry. I am sorry I lied. Sorry you never knew him. But there hasn't been a day I haven't struggled with the guilt. I thought he would have a better chance in life with parents who were ready for him. It was the right thing to do. I hope.'

The gravestone stares back at me, silent and cold. Just like the man himself, it is holding on to its secrets.

'I'm not proud of what I did. I hope that you can – ' My voice cracks. 'I hope that you can forgive me.'

I kiss my fingertips and gently touch the headstone again, as if caressing the face of a child. I think of our ill-fated affair and another wave of regret envelops me. Moments that might have been, drifting through my mind like snowflakes.

'So long, my old friend. Rest in peace.'

Slowly, I stand and turn. And just as I begin walking away, the wind stirs. I hear it lift and scatter some dead leaves. I feel its breath sigh on the nape of my neck.

And without looking back, I wipe away a tear.

It is as if Harry Price is saying goodbye.

*

We're about a mile away from the military range. Very little about Salisbury Plain has changed. It is still barren, rugged. Destitute of life.

We drive west over this vast expanse, passing the crossroads and a battered sign that points the way like a crooked finger to a low stone bridge, and as we crest the hill, I see it: the spire of St Giles' Church, jutting defiantly into the open sky.

Vernon is clenching his jaw as he steers our car along the bumpy track, past the red flags, the warning signs, the abandoned tanks rusting ever further into decay.

'How many were there, Sarah?' Vernon asks me in a flat voice. 'How many cases did you and Harry investigate? I mean, cases you never told me about?'

A stretch of awkward silence.

'Sarah?'

Old memories swarm back in. I think of our many confrontations with objects that floated, with people who levitated. Kuda Bux's jaw-dropping demonstration of fire-walking. The Battersea Poltergeist, which drove a Stockwell family to despair. The incredible haunting of Cashen's Gap, an isolated farmstead on the Isle of Man.

So many cases I could tell Vernon about – but I don't. I simply shake my head.

At the present moment, I think he would prefer not to know.

The fog has become low and thick, rolling down off the plain. At the military checkpoint, a guard appears, checks our identification. We are waved past the Keep Out and Danger signs, into the village of lonely dwellings whose windows and entranceways are mangled with barbed wire.

The years have not been kind to Imber. Some of the

original grey cottages I remember have disappeared altogether, replaced by modern concrete buildings that look
as though they're designed to replicate conflict zones in
Northern Ireland.

The village may have changed, but one thing is still clear:
army training here continues.

We get out of the car and events from long ago loom in
my memory like monstrous silhouettes. Behind me, beyond
the muddy stream, is the burned-out ruin of Imber Court. I
know it's there, daring me to look, but I can't. Not yet. I see
movement ahead. A male figure stepping out of the shadow
thrown down by the church tower.

Harry Price?

He is standing there in a black coat, the brim of his hat
tipped against the sky, looking down at a grave. Shakily, I start
towards him, towards the church gate, but then I realise I am
alone. I turn back to Vernon, who hovers anxiously by the car.

'I can't come with you, Sarah. I'm sorry.'

He's come this far and that's good enough. I give him a
reassuring smile and ask him to wait.

Then I turn towards the churchyard. The hallowed building
looms ahead of me, imposing against the sombre sky.

I stand for a moment next to the church gate, watching him:
the solitary figure, standing in the shadow of the bell tower.
Not Harry Price, but the man I have requested to meet. Pierre.

Breathing a deep sigh, I walk slowly to him.

He looks up, and his eyes widen. 'Miss Grey? *Sarah?*'

I smile. He has the same sensitive and intelligent expression
I remember so well.

'I never dreamt this would happen, that I would be so fortunate to see you again. I owe you my life,' he says, in a rush

of words and emotion. 'I never heard from you, after . . . what happened. I thought you must have died.'

The boy I rescued has become a man in his early fifties, his greying hair swept in a side parting.

For a few minutes, we skirt around the maltreatment and the tragedy that has reunited us in this hellish place. I notice that Pierre is also unable to look in the direction of Imber Court. Seeing the sallow hollows under his eyes, it occurs to me that the guilt of his own involvement has weighed heavily upon him; he too has been haunted by the ghosts of Imber, by himself.

'It was a hard time,' he tells me, 'recovering from the trauma, the starvation . . . It was so long before I could trust anyone. After they dragged Albert's body from the river, I realised he must have killed himself. And I wondered what had happened to you.'

'I kept a low profile,' I say. 'But I often thought about you.'

'I spent the rest of my childhood in Wiltshire. Of course there was a military investigation, most of the details were suppressed from the public. I said as little as possible, certainly nothing about the séances. I didn't need a story like that following me through life.'

'Who raised you?'

'My real father. Gregory Edwards.'

I try to disguise my surprise, remembering the horribly scarred sergeant, his volatility. 'They granted him custody?'

He nods, smiling. 'Eventually, after his rehabilitation. He was very good to me.'

'I can't tell you how that pleases me,' I tell him. And truly, it eases this old woman's regrets to know that from events so heinous came something good. 'Where is Gregory now?'

'He passed away, ten years ago.'

The tenderness in his voice brings tears to my eyes.

Then Pierre raises a question I've anticipated.

'Perhaps you can help me understand something, Miss Grey. Why did Hartwell concoct this whole illusion with Sidewinder – use me in his deception, fake my death?'

The idea that he would do such a thing, orchestrate hauntings in the area, just to persuade the army to leave, had always struck me as unlikely. Perhaps that had been part of Hartwell's motive, but it wasn't all. Now I believe there had indeed been a deeper, more emotional reason for the perpetration of this hoax.

'I think it was a number of things, but the main reason, I'd say, was Gregory Edwards' affair with Marie, your mother. When Hartwell began to suspect it, his mission to have Imber returned to the community became so much more. It became revenge against the army, against the establishment, against your mother for her affair. Pierre,' I say softly, taking his hands, 'I think a part of Hartwell knew you didn't belong to him. And I believe he faked your death partly out of fear that your true father might attempt to take you away from him.'

Pierre nods at me with soul-tortured understanding.

'Hartwell wanted Sergeant Edwards – your real father – to suffer.'

'And he did suffer,' Pierre says with a sigh. 'The burns covered most of his body. My father would often cry himself to sleep. He had to contend with a lifetime of that pain – and of course the mental trauma. But he was always grateful that you listened to him with an open mind.' Pierre gives a raw smile. 'I'd never have found him, Sarah, if it weren't for you and Mr Price.' A pause. 'Is Harry . . .'

'Dead, yes.' I say nothing about the spectre that appeared to me one week ago. Or the name he whispered to me.

The sound of laughter rings across the churchyard. Some young policemen stride confidently past the church gate, heading towards the top of Carrion Pit Lane. The sight of them draws Pierre back to the task at hand.

'The police brokered this meeting, Miss Grey. But I'm not sure why. I don't like this place. This village is full of old memories.'

Yes, I thought. *And old souls.*

'These human remains they unearthed . . .'

His expression darkens.

'A little girl, isn't it?' I whisper.

Pierre pales. 'Yes, but how do you –'

'Strangled,' I tell him.

He straightens. Startled, and a little afraid. 'Did Hartwell tell you that?'

'No.'

'The how can you –'

'Oscar Hartwell, the man you thought was your father, killed one more person.'

'Who?'

I lay my hand softly on his arm. 'I'll tell you everything, but first I'd like to – I have to – see the remains. Please, Pierre. I mean . . . if that's all right with you. The police said I could.'

He nods, and I link my arm with his. As we reach the top of Carrion Pit Lane, the edge of the woods, that fearful wilderness, I turn to look out over the valley, the long-neglected meadows and the shell-shattered cottages. And there it is, the army's kill house.

Imber Court.

I see it now as it was on the day of the protest – engulfed in flames, the roof falling in. I can almost hear the protestors' drums and whistles. How distant they seem, and yet how near.

Yes, there we are, Harry and I, bursting from the back of the mansion, burning wood spitting and crackling behind us. Making our way so carefully through the minefield, stepping oddly, veering left, then right, almost as if someone is leading us on.

I realise Pierre is looking expectantly at me, as though he knows there is one final revelation to hear, and of course there is.

So I tell him.

– 38 –

PROVENANCE

Imber, 1932

We had navigated the land mines and just made it onto the road, to safety, when I saw Vernon running desperately towards us.

'Thank heavens you're safe.'

'Vernon, what are you –'

'I couldn't just leave you out here, Sarah!'

He shrugged off his coat and draped it over my shoulders, then pulled me close to him, so swiftly I hardly noticed him taking Marie's rolled-up drawings from me.

It was only later, when the protestors were dispersing and I was sitting in the back of Price's saloon, recovering, that I looked out of the window and noticed Vernon standing near the church gate, staring intently at the scrolls. I was suddenly worried that he still intended to write a news piece about these events, to impress his new employer.

I got out of the car, went to Vernon and said, 'Promise me you won't write about what happened here.' When he remained silent, I tried a different approach: 'Vernon, I can persuade Harry to do the same, to keep your name in connection with these events a secret, but you'll have to keep your end of the bargain. Our involvement here remains secret. Agreed?'

Only then did Vernon turn. His pallor made me instantly nervous. So did his eyes, which were wide and unblinking.

'Besides, it wouldn't be fair on Pierre to publish anything about this. We need to protect him now. Vernon?'

I angled my head to look at Marie's drawings in his hand. His *trembling* hand. He was already rolling them up.

'Whatever's the matter?'

'It's just that . . . I hadn't seen these drawings until now. I didn't know there were *more*.' I saw the agitation spreading over his angular face.

'More? What do you mean?'

'These drawings. There are others like them.'

'I don't understand,' I said dismissively. 'Pierre is safe now, yes? He can begin his life again. We can return to London. Take in a picture, perhaps? Vernon?'

'A picture.' The words came out slowly. Vernon walked away then, into the blur of rain. Then, suddenly, he turned and rushed back to me with a look of dread and pity. 'Sarah, I'm sorry. I'm so sorry. There's something I must tell you. Will you come with me?'

I nodded uncertainly, and he took my arm and led me towards the top of Carrion Pit Lane. Standing next to the commander's truck, Price was engrossed in conversation with Williams. Disconcerted soldiers were close by, encouraging

civilians to move on. They didn't see us as Vernon guided
me past the churchyard, towards the woods and, beyond, the
abandoned mill. As if to protest against the journey, the wind
gusted – and my heart thudded harder. It wasn't like Vernon to
behave so mysteriously; his nerves must have been unsettled
by the protest. At least, that's what I told myself.

'Vernon,' I said, 'what's this about?'

'You said you blanked out, somewhere near the old mill.
That you felt that spot was important to you.'

'Yes, but –'

'Show me *exactly* where that happened.'

I didn't feel I could refuse, even though I was apprehensive
and wanted to go back. It was quite a walk, but I led him to
the millpond. As my eyes locked on the rusty old wheel, I felt
a sudden tightness around my neck, a pain in my chest.

'You're sensing it again, aren't you?' Vernon asked, and I
felt the scrutiny of his eyes. 'I really am so dreadfully sorry,
Sarah, but I think this location – this exact spot, in fact –
might be crucial. For this whole investigation, but especially
for you.'

'I have absolutely no idea what you're talking about,' I said. I
began walking away, feeling that if I spent one moment longer
on that spot I might suffocate.

'Sarah, no, I'm afraid you've got to hear this.'

I wheeled on him. 'All right! What is it? WHAT?'

'These are spirit drawings, yes? Made by Hartwell's wife?
I've seen drawings very much like them before.'

'Before? When?'

'When I broke into Price's laboratory. Drawings of *you*,
Sarah.'

Albert's drawings.

Both Albert and Marie – individuals who claimed clairvoyant abilities – had made drawings of *me*. What were the chances? As I processed this thought I began to feel light-headed.

'I thought that perhaps Price had sketched them, that maybe he was obsessed with you or something. Maybe he missed you so much . . .' He stopped himself, embarrassed.

'I don't see –'

'Sarah, these drawings were tucked inside a file marked "Imber". Along with a detailed history of the village and papers, birth certificates, death certificates, referencing the Hartwell family name. And *your* name.'

I searched his face. 'Is that surprising? He knew my father trained here.'

But that was odd, now I thought about it, because I hadn't told Price about my father's connection to the village before we left London. In fact, I hadn't told him at all – he claimed to have figured it out after spotting the photograph on the wall of the commander's office.

The hypnosis session. Of course.

'Some time ago, Harry put me into a trance. He was trying to calm my nerves.' Dimly I recalled Price's gentle voice, coercing me into a state of deep relaxation.

'I told him lots of things. Too many things . . .'

'Sarah, you're referred to in those files – in a very strange way.'

'Strange how?'

'You're mentioned as an "old soul". Does that phrase mean anything to you?'

I was still. Silent.

He went on, 'Harry has been following this case for a long time, since long before I first heard of Imber.'

'No, Vernon, this began with you. The army confided in you. You came to me and I approached Harry.'

'But Harry already had an inkling of what was happening in Imber, don't you see?'

Of course, he's right. Albert sent him drawings. And letters.

'His has been a private, secret investigation, into a singularly unique phenomenon.'

'What sort of phenomenon?' I forced myself to ask.

'I believe experts call it past-life regression. Reincarnation.'

For several moments, I was completely incapable of speaking. Vernon was talking about me. He was talking about *me*! I started shaking my head in denial and, after swallowing, managed to say, 'I don't believe in reincarnation.'

Suddenly, Price was there, shouting: 'STOP, VERNON! NOT ANOTHER WORD!'

I whirled round. The ghost hunter stood before us, his face hardened, his voice like granite.

'Harry, what's he talking about?'

'Nothing, Sarah. Come on. We're leaving.'

'Harry, you have to tell her. It's right that you tell her!'

'Tell me what? What's he talking about? Harry?'

Price, breathing heavily now, turned to face me. He hesitated. Then he took both my hands and squeezed them gently, his eyes painfully apologetic.

'Harry, what is it?'

'I wanted to protect you, Sarah.'

I dropped his hands.

Vernon's expression was tense. He knew. Whatever it was, he knew.

Price averted his eyes; he was thinking furiously, I could tell. But Vernon wasn't prepared to give him thinking time.

'He's been lying to you, Sarah.'

Feeling afraid, so awfully afraid, I shot Price a worried look, searching his face for any vestige of honesty. 'Harry?'

His eyes remained riveted on the chalky grassland.

'He's been treating you like an experiment. Bringing you here to Imber. Observing your reactions. Studying you. Testing your memories. Memories he extracted from you under hypnosis. Memories he deliberately kept secret.'

But that couldn't be. I'd told Price I wasn't sure about the hypnosis; that I wasn't comfortable with the idea of dragging up old memories of my father, whom I missed so badly; that I was afraid of the idea of going into a trance, of not being in control. Hadn't I read somewhere that hypnosis could be used as a form of mind control? But Price assured me he was simply going to help me relax by inducing what he called 'an altered state of consciousness'. What could go wrong?

'Harry, this can't be right. Can it?'

With characteristic ambiguity, Price raised his head, put a hand to my cheek and said gravely, 'I should have you arrested.'

'*Arrested*?'

'I'm talking to that scoundrel journalist who broke into my office.'

He turned furiously on Wall, raising his fists.

'Harry, stop! It was me, all right? I asked Vernon to break into your laboratory!'

Price froze. Dropped his fists. Turned to face me, stunned. When he finally did speak, it was to Vernon.

'Stay away from me, understand? Stay the hell away from us both.'

I know now, of course, what I shared with Harry Price under hypnosis. Price kept a meticulous record of the memories, long buried, now uncovered. And, of course, I still have the papers. Looking back over them still makes me anxious, makes me sick with betrayal.

HP: What year is it?

SG: 1880.

HP: Tell me, what is your name?

SG: Alice.

HP: All right. How old are you, Alice?

SG: Twelve.

HP: Where do you live?

SG: I live here.

HP: Where is here?

SG: Imber. We live in the big house.

HP: Imber Court?

SG: Yes. But now I'm walking through Carrion Pit Lane.

HP: Where are you going?

SG: [Quietly, almost mumbling] I'm at the chalk pit. Walking around it. Hurrying.

HP: Yes, but what is your destination?

SG: I'm going to the mill.

HP: Why? What's there?

SG: That's where we agreed to meet.

But on that cold, wet afternoon in Imber, I knew nothing of this conversation. Thunder rumbled close by. The rain was coming down harder, the ground softening to thick, sucking mud.

'Harry?' I whispered. 'What's going on? Have you been lying to me?'

Price nodded, and his whole body sagged, as though that

admission had ripped out his heart. 'Sarah, there's a memory you've been carrying now for so long – since before you arrived in Imber, since that night at the picture house in Brixton, and even before that . . .'

'What memory?'

'Your memory of the warm place. The mill wheel turning. Waiting. You were here, Sarah, in 1880.'

'This is utterly absurd, even for you, Harry. I wasn't even born in 1880!'

He nodded weightily, as if he too were perturbed by this idea, and somehow that made me feel worse.

'I've heard many people speak of past lives, previous incarnations, but always in the vaguest, most unverifiable ways. But under hypnosis, your descriptions of this village, the life you led here as a little girl, were so precise, so vivid, I had to know the truth . . .

'Remember you said you felt as though you had been to this village before, that you were pulled here? That was because of these memories, long buried, surfacing. You even knew the layout of Imber Court. You knew about the secret room. Why? Because you lived there. In another time. In another life.'

Hearing this made me feel vulnerable. Scared and defence-less. And yet, it made sense.

I said, wonderingly, 'I remember the warm place. Waiting for someone.'

Nodding, Price held my eyes as the obvious question came to me.

'Who was I waiting for?'

Price turned and looked at Vernon with an expression of grim expectation, and in return Vernon handed him Marie Hartwell's drawings. Slowly, Price unrolled the papers and I forced myself to look. I saw a girl, maybe twelve years of age. She was wearing an expensive dress, her hair curling around her ears. The little girl whose image was timelessly preserved on the magic lantern slide I had found at the picture house in Brixton.

'Who is she?' I asked.

Price's face was tense with the weight of the revelation he was about to make. 'She's you.'

39

AN OLD SOUL

'This girl is you, Sarah, in a previous life. She's Hartwell's older sister. And Sarah, I'm sorry . . . she was murdered.'

The shock struck me like lightning, and I remembered his words to me inside Imber Court: '*There's one more, Sarah. One more little girl, who should have lived.*'

For a long moment, all I could do was stare at him. My whole body began to tremble with anger and fear. 'I don't believe it,' I said, in little more than a whisper. Although my logical brain was already calling me to doubt, why did this feel like a moment of cold understanding, disturbingly accurate?

'You kept this from me?' I asked Price, my voice cracking. 'Harry, you're a monster!'

'A monster? No. Can't you see I was trying to protect you?'

Without even thinking, I slapped him hard across the face. And then, when he didn't react, I felt an intense rage sweep through me.

'PROTECT ME? Is that what you were doing when I collapsed

when we arrived here? When I insisted there was a mystery here and you pretended not to see it? You knew everything.'

'That's not true. I didn't know whether the memories were real. I assumed you had subconsciously gleaned information about this village, its history.'

I jabbed a finger in his face. 'You deceived me.'

'Sarah, please, I only wanted to verify what was real and what was not. False memory syndrome is a common phenomenon – one even I don't understand.'

'So you thought you'd use me as your own little secret experiment?' I glared at him, remembering how, during our investigation, he had stared at me, scrutinised me.

He didn't answer; I didn't give him a chance to speak. I was incensed, ranting. 'What else have you lied about? The picture palace! You *did* follow me there! You knew there was something within that building drawing me in, some psychic bond between me and Albert and the projection slide with . . . with *me* on it?'

Price was shaking his head adamantly.

'What did I tell you under hypnosis? If Hartwell killed his sister – me – how did it happen?'

He was looking away from me, past the church, towards the burning house, and I saw then that my worst suspicions were true.

'You're a pathetic excuse for a man, Harry. My life would have been so much better without – '

Before I knew what was happening, he grabbed my wrist. 'You really want to see? Well, look. Look *there*!'

At his direction, I looked towards the rusty mill wheel. Something triggered.

A swirl of white light exploded in my head. Ripping me from the scene.

All around me, a warm breeze stirs the grass as, in the distance, the orange sun sinks over the chalky downs to the horizon. I see a boy with shaggy black hair.

It's him, of course: my brother, Oscar. He's smiling, pleased I've kept my promise to meet him here. He takes my hand, tells me not to be afraid – and why should I be? We're going to play in the mill, and perhaps later we will milk the cows together.

He snaps my wrist.

The pain rips up my arm as he grapples me to the floor. I'm crying. Screaming.

'Father says it has to be like this.' His voice is unfamiliar, cold. 'Father has shown me how.'

'Help me! Please, someone help me!'

My legs are kicking wildly, my whole body bucking against him as he climbs on top of me, using his legs to pin my arms to the ground. We used to play a game like this. His hands are around my throat. Squeezing.

Then one hand comes free and moves down, reaching for something. And suddenly, pain slides into me.

I open my mouth, but no words come. Just a ragged cough. And then hot blood.

He raises his arm. The blade glints in the last rays of the sun. Dripping red.

'Oscar, please, what are you doing?'

The blade slices into me again. As my insides spasm, I look down to see the spreading crimson stain, and then . . . nothing.

Just black.

40

IMBER FOREVER

October 1978

'Miss Grey?'

My eyes snap open. Pierre's voice has pulled me into the present, into the cold late afternoon in Imber's churchyard. From under the brim of his hat, he looks across the barren valley towards Imber Court, then searches my face. There's such a vulnerability to this man, an undercurrent of sadness from his childhood that is almost too painful to behold.

I apologise. 'I disappeared, didn't I? Blanked out.'

He nods, smiling softly, as if to say, *Don't worry about it.* But I do worry. I feel embarrassed and old. What must this man think of my incredible story?

Does he believe it? Would anyone?

'So,' he says, quietly. Warily. 'You're saying Price concealed evidence that suggested you were Hartwell's sister, in another existence . . . another time?'

I give a sorrowful nod.

Pierre looks doubtful – not exactly cynical, but I see the questions in his eyes. Did I acquire the memories from somewhere else? Was my past life, my death, more rationally understood as a narrative invented by my subconscious mind? It had to be possible. Not only had I visited Imber as a young girl, but I had also unwittingly witnessed Oscar and Marie Hartwell laying to rest one of their young. Had my own childhood memories become mixed up with fantasy?

Perhaps, but . . .

'You believe it, don't you, Sarah?'

I lean wearily against a tree, looking out over the expanse of Salisbury Plain. 'You know, the moment I set foot here, I hated it. It was as if I had been here before. Now, maybe, I know why. Perhaps I am exactly what your mother said – an old soul.'

It explains so much, like why I felt I knew this place, especially the patch of ground between the chalk pit and the abandoned mill. The patch of ground where the police tent is erected.

Now Pierre's eyes are sad and curious. 'Did you ever go back to work for Harry?'

I hesitate, unsure whether to tell him. Sometimes when we see our mistakes, it's easier to pretend they never happened. It is hard to say yes, even harder to look him in the eye. I'm afraid of the disapproval he might show me.

'Harry Price devoted his whole life to the study of alleged abnormal phenomena, to protecting the public from fraudulent mediums who preyed on innocents like my own mother. A maverick? Yes. An egomaniac? Yes. Manipulative? Of course. But in those days, you couldn't breathe the word supernatural without hearing his name. Pierre, he was famous! His masses of correspondence, the thousands of books he kept on a subject that most scientists scorned – all of this meant that after Imber, Harry represented the best chance I had of finding the answers I needed.'

'And did you?'

I consider the question carefully, remembering the horrors that followed the Imber case – horrors that eventually led to Price's death. I sigh deeply. 'What choice did I have? I was – '

'In love with him?'

I give a helpless, acquiescent shrug. Pierre nods. There are no words. He gives me a moment to wipe my eyes, then casts a glance towards the lane, which I know leads into the woods.

To the tent the police have erected over the human remains.

'The police said you insisted on seeing. You're sure you want to see?'

I'm not sure. The prospect of going anywhere near that tent is as upsetting as the thought of stepping up to your most cherished friend's grave. But I've come this far.

I introduce myself to the young policewoman standing guard outside the tent. The PC may not believe what I have come to tell her, but she is expecting me, which is why, after checking my identification, she unzips the tent door and escorts us inside.

The air is mouldy and damp. Laid out on the ground is the body bag. Without uttering a word, I kneel beside that black rubberised fabric and watch as the policewoman unzips the bag. Slowly. Respectfully.

Pierre turns his head sharply, averting his eyes, but I force myself to look at the skeleton. Blackened. Crumpled. I don't look at the skull, I look at the hands. No, where the hands should be – they have been severed at the wrist. And the world begins swirling.

'Miss?' asks the policewoman.

'Her hands were cut off and buried separately. Probably to make it harder to identify her.'

'You know who she is? Miss?'

Shakily, struck with anguish, I rise to my feet. It's an effort to voice my thoughts, but after a few long moments I'm relieved when the words come. 'She was his sister. He throttled her with his bare hands before putting a knife in her heart.'

'Who did?' I hear the confusion in the policewoman's voice.

'Oscar Hartwell. He murdered his three little girls. But this murder was his first. He was just a boy. Ten years old. That was during the summer of 1880.'

The policewoman looks dubiously at me. 'How do you know?'

'Because I was there.'

She frowns. She doesn't understand. And who can blame her?

I roll up my sleeves. Pierre stares at the distinct birthmarks on both of my wrists. 'Sarah? Oh my God . . .'

I give him a sad, knowing smile. The policewoman looks more confused than ever. Oh, she has her questions, but what I need most right now is fresh air, so I smile and apologise. And as I step out of the tent with Pierre, I deliberately neglect to mention my other birthmark.

The slightly curved birthmark on my chest, just above my heart.

Ever the gentleman, Pierre walks with me back towards the top of Carrion Pit Lane. The shadows are lengthening, and there is a moment of pure calm. The sky over Salisbury Plain stretches forever. From the top of the valley, Pierre and I gaze down upon Imber Court, a charred ruin.

'Her name was Alice.' The words puff from my lips in a white cloud. 'Alice Hartwell.' It is of course the name that Price's spectre whispered to me, just one week ago. 'She was Oscar's older sister, and, who knows, if she had lived, that hell house might have passed to her.'

Pierre presses his fingertips against the corners of his eyes. 'Now it belongs to the army. And like everything else in this village, it always will.'

I think about that in the dying light, surveying the shell-pitted cottages, the desolate roads, the barbed-wire fences and the churchyard with its slanting gravestones. I think of the manipulation, the entrapment and the black misery here, all emanating from two men – two depraved men – and I wonder whether Imber's spectres still return here.

Softly, I say, 'I think this village will forever belong to the people of Imber. Whether it's returned to them or not. I hope so.'

'What else do you hope for, Sarah?'

Remembering the leaning gravestone dressed in ivy in the churchyard in Pulborough, I revive my spirits by telling Pierre I hope I wasn't just an experiment to Price. It's easier to believe he was trying to protect me by not telling me the truth.

Somewhere out there, if he's listening and watching, I hope Harry Price has forgiven me, and understands why his old friend broke her promise.

On my saddest days, I think with sorrow of my son, and I hope he is happy and healthy. Not haunted, not driven like his parents to see beyond the veil.

I hope that if the dead are speaking, someone is listening.

Pierre smiles. And then we hear it. From the direction of the churchyard comes the slow and steady tolling of bells, and something else, a harsher sound, like a hammer striking metal.

Pierre's mouth falls open.

'Not everything dies,' I whisper, watching the words carry on my breath to disperse in the chill air.

'I have something for you,' I say to Pierre, as the church bells continue their mournful toll. 'Something I've written: your story and mine.'

The story of a lost boy and a lost village.

The story of the village where I died.

ACKNOWLEDGEMENTS

No book is written in isolation. I owe a debt of gratitude to my agents at Curtis Brown, Luke Speed and the wonderful Cathryn Summerhayes, and to the fantastic team at Quercus for their confidence and support. Special thanks to my editor, Kathryn Taussig; my copyeditor, Julie Fergusson; my publicist, Alainna Hadjigeorgiou; and Quercus's Managing Director, Jon Butler.

When my debut novel, *The Ghost Hunters*, was adapted into a one-off television film for ITV (*Harry Price: Ghost Hunter*), it was Quercus who suggested that readers and audiences alike would be excited to read more about the adventures of the enigmatic Harry Price and his intrepid assistant, Sarah Grey. It struck me, at once, as an irresistible proposition.

Harry Price was a real psychical investigator; a maverick who achieved infamy during the inter-war period for his other-worldly investigations, and although this story is entirely imaginary, some of it was inspired by Price's own writings and experiences. For example, there was a 'spirit child' that convinced Price, for a time, of the existence of an afterlife. Of all his investigations, 'Rosalie' is one of the most controversial, and anyone seeking information on the case should consult Paul Adams' book on this enduring mystery.

Likewise, anyone wishing to learn more about Imber's fascinating history should read Rex Sawyer's *Little Imber on the Down*.

My friends are a continual source of valued support. Thanks to Tobi Coventry, Tom Winchester, Howard Malin, Nick Hoile, Guy Black, Mark Bolland, Jurij Senyshyn, Jon Harrison, Lee Summers and Guy Chambers.

I would also like to thank Michael Wood for his encouragement. Every author needs a reliable sounding board and Michael is a trusted one, as well as being a talented writer.

For *The Lost Village*, we auctioned a character's name in aid of Stonewall. I'd like to thank Gregory Edwards for his generosity, and everyone who attended the charity dinner.

Finally, my thanks to my wonderful mum, Pamela, for her unfailing support, friendship and love; and to Owen Meredith, to whom this book is dedicated.

Finally, thank you to all my readers for coming with me on this journey. I hope – indeed, I know – we'll be venturing into the unknown again together, very soon.

Neil Spring
London
July 2017

ALSO BY NEIL SPRING:

THE WATCHERS

A chilling tale based on true events.

At the height of the Cold War, officials investigated
a series of unusual events that occurred along a strip of
rugged Pembrokeshire coastline nicknamed 'The Broad
Haven Triangle'. The events made national headlines:
lights and objects hovering in the sky, ghostly figures
peering into farmhouse windows...

Thirty years later, official files were finally released
for public scrutiny at the National Archives. The disclosure
prompted a new witness to come forward to speak
of what he knew.

His testimony rocked the very foundations
of the British Government.

This is his story.

Quercus

Stay in touch!

Get the latest news on upcoming books
and events from Neil Spring.

On twitter: @neilspring / @quercusbooks

On facebook: facebook.com/Neilspring.author